Collide
Hollows Bay Trilogy (Book one)

E. K Hunter

Copyright © E.K Hunter 2023

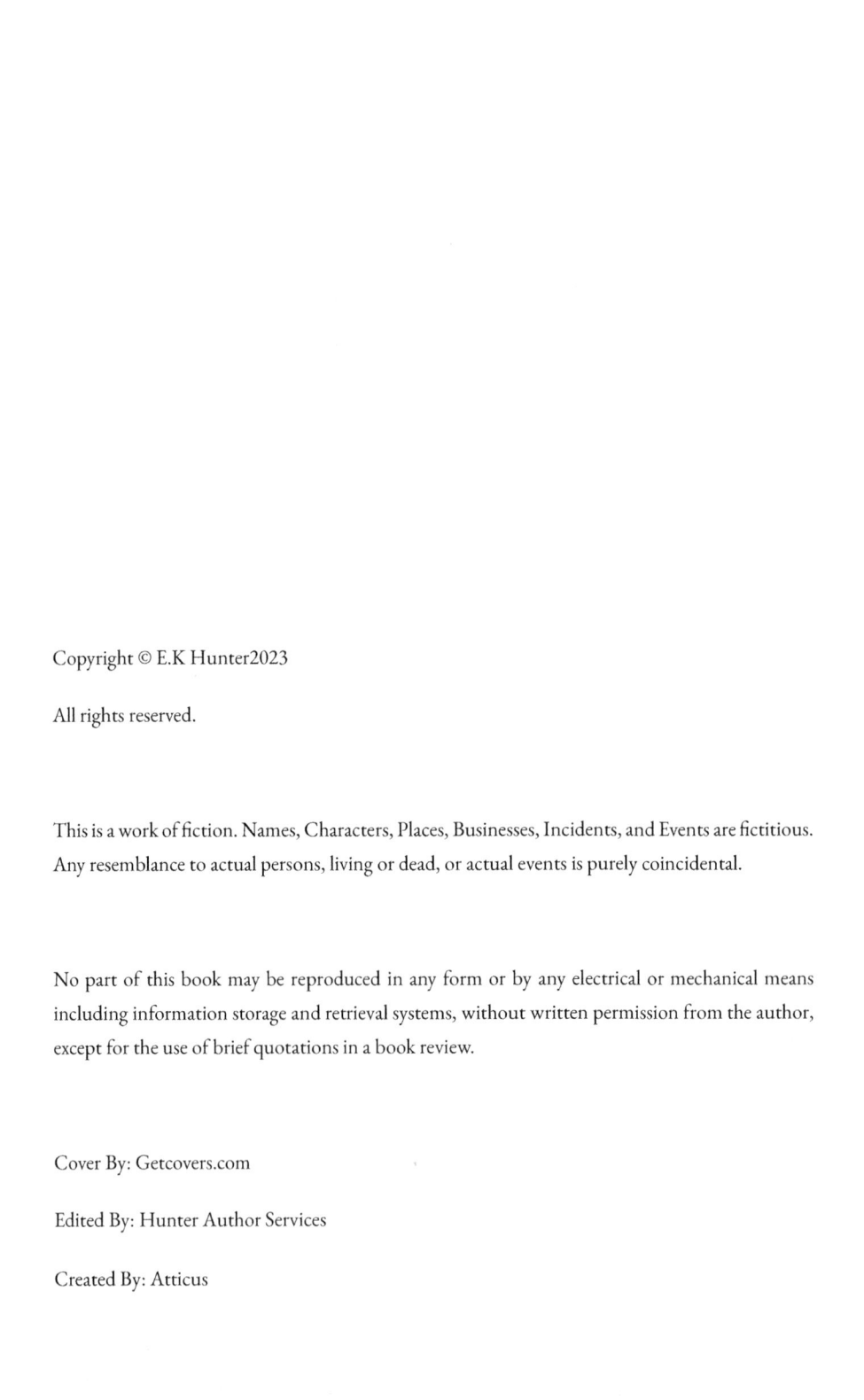

All rights reserved.

This is a work of fiction. Names, Characters, Places, Businesses, Incidents, and Events are fictitious. Any resemblance to actual persons, living or dead, or actual events is purely coincidental.

No part of this book may be reproduced in any form or by any electrical or mechanical means including information storage and retrieval systems, without written permission from the author, except for the use of brief quotations in a book review.

Cover By: Getcovers.com

Edited By: Hunter Author Services

Created By: Atticus

*To those who believed in me when I didn't believe in myself.
Thank you.*

Foreword

Readers should be aware that this book is a dark romance with morally gray characters and contains the following topics that may be triggering for some readers:

Drug Abuse

Familial death(s)

Torture

Murder

Rape (not of the main character)

Mentions of child abuse (not detailed on page)

This book ends on a cliffhanger.

Playlist

Queen Of The Night- Hey Violet
Poison- Alice Cooper
Love On The Brain- Rhianna
I'll Make You Love Me- Kat Leon
Never Let Me Go- Florence & The Machine
Running Up That Hill- Placebo
Daylight- Taylor Swift
Monster- Eminem & Rhianna
Numb Without You- The Maine
Psycho Killer- Rainne
Two Punks In Love- Bulow
Devil's Worst Nightmare- Fjora
I Can't Get Enough- Benny Blanco
Monsters- Camilyo
Adore- Amy Shark

Prologue

Remember in the Disney cartoon, *Aladdin,* where Aladdin steals the bread and gets chased by a bunch of fat fuckers, only to end up giving that loaf of bread to two homeless kids?

And that little shit, Abu, takes a chunk out of his half before he feels guilty and hands over his share. And then just after, Aladdin finds a genie, makes a wish, falls in love....yada yada yada.

Did you ever stop to wonder what happened to those two little kids?

You know the ones I mean, the little girl who is rifling through a bin trying to find food for her and her brother? Everyone feels sorry for Aladdin, the poor homeless boy who pretends to be a prince to get the girl to fall in love with him, but no one gave a fuck about what happened to those two little kids, so long as Aladdin got the princess.

Well, you know what?

It's total bullshit.

Disney has got a lot to answer for, they churn out stories about poor little boys and girls who go through some shitty event in their life only to come out at the end, head over heels in love with the prince or princess who saved them, and they live happily ever after in a beautiful castle without a care in the world.

I can safely say that life is no Disney film.

No, my life was very much like that little homeless girl in Aladdin who scavenged around looking for food to keep her and her brother alive. Only, in my story, I was doing what I had to do to keep my little *sister* alive.

Granted, it had been a few years since I'd had to raid bins to find food, but it had come close a few times.

There'd been more than one occasion where the crappy studio apartment we called home had been without electricity, hot water, and food in the fridge, but I tried my damn best to keep my little sister fed, watered, and warm.

Of course, it should *never* have been my responsibility to look after Angel, but at the tender age of fifteen, and when Angel was just six years old, my father was murdered, an innocent victim in a drive-by shooting, and instead of being a good mom and looking after her two fatherless children, my mother decided it was a brilliant idea to start injecting shit into her body.

Not actual shit, obviously, but you know, crack, heroin. Basically, anything she could get her greedy little mitts on.

I became Angel's mom overnight. It didn't matter about my schoolwork or the fact I was barely an adult myself, all of that went down the pan the second the selfish whore jabbed the needle into her veins in a bid to forget about the pain of losing my father like she was the only one affected by his untimely death.

Within eight months, the beautiful, carefree woman I once called my mom became nothing but a bag of skin and bones. Her face was sallow, her eyes sunken, not to mention the marks she constantly had all over her body, be that track marks from injecting or bruises from where her drug-addicted boyfriend would beat her.

Did I mention she got herself a new boyfriend within a month of us burying my dad?

Oh yeah, that was a real treat coming home from school one day to find a random guy in the living room, telling Angel and me he was our new daddy.

Then one day, the new life we were getting used to changed again.

It was the day after my not-so-sweet sixteenth birthday, and just before Angel was due to turn seven, I came home from school to find my mom dead on the sofa, needle still sticking out of her arm.

For as long as I live, I'll never forget what it felt like to walk in and find her lying there, white foam drying around her cracked blue lips, her eyes open but no longer seeing. Nor the instructions over the phone from the emergency responder who talked me through how to give CPR until the paramedics arrived.

But even as I pressed up and down on her rock-hard chest, I knew it was pointless. Her skin had started to turn gray, and she was completely still .....*lifeless*. The logical part of me knew I was going through the motions, even as I sobbed over her body, begging her to come back to me. When the paramedics arrived, they didn't bother getting their equipment out to resuscitate her, they took one look before deeming life was extinct. Their words, not mine.

Extinct.

And just like that, Angel and I were orphans, alone in the world. Both our parents were only children, and our grandparents on both sides had passed away when Angel and I were much younger.

We had no one.

What followed was a flurry of people invading our home and acting as if they knew what was right for my sister and me. The whole time I sat in the corner listening to conversations going on around me as if I wasn't there, social workers talking about how Angel needed complex care because of her needs, me needing counseling after I had found my mother.

Not one fucking person had the decency to stop and ask what *I* wanted, or what Angel might have needed. And complex care? Pfft, she was deaf, that's all. She was still an annoying little asshat who did everything any child her age could do, she just had the ability not to listen to all the bullshit that went on around her, the lucky little shit.

It was at the point when one of the social workers was on the phone with her boss, telling them Angel and I would need to go into different foster homes when I decided enough was enough, and over my dead body would we be split up.

Angel and I had always been close growing up, she'd been a surprise baby, and the minute my dad took me to the hospital to meet my little sister, I fell madly in love with her. We had only grown closer in the eight months my mom was using, I raised her as if she was my own kid, there was no way I would stand for her being taken away from me.

No one paid me any attention when I disappeared into my room to pack a bag, then into Angel's room to throw her crap in, and finally into my mom's room where I knew she had a couple of twenty dollar bills hidden in her underwear drawer.

I walked out the door with my head held high, not stopping to give my family home a second look. I collected Angel from school, and we hopped on the next bus out of that town. I didn't exactly have a plan for what our next steps would be, all I cared about was that Angel was with me.

I don't know if we were ever listed as missing children, but no one seemed bothered enough to try to find us. I mean, we only made it to a few cities away from where we grew up for fuck's sake, yet no one came looking. They were probably relieved it was two less children in an already overcrowded system to have to worry about.

The weeks that followed when Angel and I landed in the city of Hollows Bay were pretty fucking hard, and there were countless times when I questioned my stupid decision to run away. We really did raid bins, hiding at the back of café's and waiting for them to throw out their daily leftovers before finding a comfy park bench to spend the night, which normally resulted in me not getting any sleep because I was too worried a dirty scoundrel would do something to Angel while she slept.

I spent days exhausted and starving, and yet I couldn't bring myself to take Angel home for fear she would be taken away from me.

Selfish, I know.

It soon became apparent that Hollows Bay was a den of iniquity, or at least the parts where Angel and I frequented. Yeah, there was the rich side, known as West Bay, where skyscrapers towered over the city, cash exchanged hands in the casinos, and million-dollar deals were struck every day in the many businesses that were in operation.

Or so I heard, we never ventured to that side of the city, we didn't dare. Rumors on the street were that the rich folk wouldn't allow smelly, hungry, homeless kids to dirty up their neighborhoods, and so any street rat seen within a square mile radius of West Bay would wind up floating face down in the docks.

Even if they were just rumors, it was enough for me to keep Angel well away from the area, instead spending our time in the slums of East Bay.

East Bay was like any other dump in America, poverty on every corner, streets laced with graffiti, drug deals taking place on every corner in broad daylight, and girls, some younger than me but thankfully not younger than Angel, offering their bodies in exchange for pocket money to buy food.

Or drugs.

After a few weeks of sheer hell, Angel started to fall into a deep depression. One evening when the weather turned bad, we sought shelter in a derelict train station. Unbeknownst to us, the station had been overtaken by a bunch of homeless kids who had made it their sanctuary. I say kids, they were several years older than us and had lived on the street a lot longer than Angel and I had.

They took pity on us, and despite their own personal hell, they were mostly a good bunch. Almost overnight, they became family. They pulled Angel out of her slump, much to my relief, and everyone looked out for each other.

I instantly hit it off with a boy called Tobias, or Toby, as he liked to be called. He quickly became a close friend, and when I wasn't with Angel, I'd spend my days with him.

Toby taught me how to look after myself with some basic self-defense lessons, and then he taught me how to shoplift without getting caught. It wasn't something I was proud of but needs must, and I needed to look after my baby sister. Whatever happened, I refused to accept we would ever be split up.

Toby was the one who told me in detail all about the history of Hollows Bay. Apparently, it was controlled by the Wolfe family who had power over the city and city officials, and had done for generations. The guy in charge at that time was Christopher Wolfe, but Toby explained how his two sons were becoming more and more involved in the family business, and he'd heard rumors that Christopher was preparing to hand over the reins to his sons.

Toby told me all about the gangs who worked for the Wolfe family, how the junior ranks worked the streets in East Bay, dealing drugs and weapons and enforcing the Wolfe family's law to those who needed to be reminded of exactly who owned the city. Those in the junior ranks would aim to be promoted to the next level as it meant a ticket out of the dump. More importantly, it gave them better recognition which, according to Toby, the better recognized you were, the more respect you had.

It all sounded like a crock of shit if you asked me, but hey, what did I know?

It was evident in the awe in Toby's voice that he one day aspired to make his way up the ranks in the gang, and although he never admitted it, I suspected he was already heavily involved in the drug dealing side of things.

Although I had zero idea who the Wolfe family were or if they really existed, the rumors surrounding them scared me. Everyone knew they were neck deep in murder, torture, and only god knew what else, and with the Hollows Bay Police Department firmly in the pockets of the family, it seemed like they were untouchable.

But Toby assured me the Wolfes rarely stepped foot in the East Bay area, they didn't need to, the gangs did all their dirty work for them. So, as long as I didn't piss off the gangs, I had nothing to worry about.

And I had no intention of pissing anyone off.

I learned some good life lessons from Toby, we became closer and closer as the days went on, and life seemed to be on the up. Well, as much as it could be when you are homeless.

That was until one day, I made the mistake of trying to steal from Joe Mason, the owner of a small grocery store. On this particular day, Angel hadn't been feeling too well and I wanted to cheer her up with her favorite candy. There was only one cashier working and I timed it so she would be busy with the lunchtime rush, it should have been an easy win.

When her back was turned, I grabbed a stash of candy bars, shoved them in my pocket, and ran out as fast as my legs would take me. Only, I ran smack straight into the fat belly of Joe, who had seen exactly what I'd done. He grabbed my arm, demanded I emptied my pockets and threatened to take me down to the police station.

I'm not ashamed to admit all of my lessons from Toby went flying out the fucking window, and instead of fighting my way out of his grasp while accusing him of touching me, I cried like a little bitch, apologized profusely, and begged him not to shop me to the cops. And when Joe asked me to give him one good reason why he shouldn't hand my *thieving little ass* over to the police, I told him all I had wanted to do was feed my homeless, disabled sister.

OK, yeah I *may* have played on the sympathy card a little bit, you know, my sister is deaf, if I'm taken away, she'll be all alone with no one to look out for her, etcetera, etcetera.

I don't know what did it, but instead of rounding me and Angel up and taking us to the nearest cop shop, he drove us to a tower block, made us ride the elevator up to the fifteenth floor, and then led us to an empty apartment. Angel and I huddled together, all the while I was signing to her, telling her everything would be okay when really, I was shitting my pants.

But then Joe transformed from a mean-looking motherfucker to a friendly giant. He told us we could crash in the apartment for a few nights and he would bring us some food. I didn't know whether to laugh or cry or to get the hell out of there for fear Joe would want some kind of repayment for the gesture, namely my body.

Or worse, Angel's.

As it turned out, the old man was our savior. I guess you could say he was our Genie from the magic lamp.

You see, it transpired he had spent years on the street when he was younger, and no one had helped him. He'd had to claw his way out of homelessness, and was now the proud owner of a number of local mini-markets and some properties around the city.

Joe had a vision of making Hollows Bay a better place, and while he always knew he was fighting a losing battle, he would do what he could, donating food to shelters and hosting fundraising days. He was an angel disguised as a portly fifty-year-old man. It had been our lucky day when we met Joe and I thanked whatever deity was out there for him every day.

The apartment Joe let us crash in was a new purchase, and he hadn't got around to advertising it. It was empty with the exception of some old mattresses, but given Angel and I had spent the last few weeks crashing on concrete beds, we felt like we had landed in the fucking Ritz.

Days turned into weeks, weeks into months, but Joe never quite got around to advertizing the apartment. After Angel and I left the train station, Toby decided to leave Hollows Bay and make a life for himself somewhere else. I was sad to see him go but I understood his reasons for getting the hell out of the city.

After a while, Angel and I lost contact with the others from the station, but it was for the best, they were part of a life I didn't want Angel to remember.

Joe gave me a job in one of his shops, he even helped Angel enroll in a state school. He was fond of Angel, always showering her with affection that she was missing from our parents, and in return, she doted on him.

I didn't earn a huge amount of money in the shop but with Joe's help, I managed to turn the apartment from an empty building into something resembling a home for Angel and me.

Life was finally on the up.

We lived in that apartment for two years until I turned eighteen when completely out of the blue, Joe had a heart attack that claimed his life.

It's funny, in the weeks that followed, Angel and I mourned his loss more than we did for our own mom. We owed so much to that man and I never got the chance to repay him for the kindness he had shown us.

At his funeral, I made a promise to Joe that one day, I would pay his deed forward. I would show someone the same kindness and opportunity he had given to us.

But the world can be a cruel mistress and likes to fuck you in the ass when you are down.

Shortly after Joe's funeral, Angel and I were kicked out of the apartment by the city council who had taken ownership of Joe's shops and properties as he had no will in place nor legal next of kin. His legacy became the property of the city, who could do whatever the fuck they deemed appropriate to do, and they deemed it appropriate to sell everything and make as much money as they could.

Greedy fuckers.

Once again, Angel and I were on the brink of becoming homeless, and my already fragile heart was at risk of shattering into a million pieces at the thought of Angel having to live on the streets again.

That was until I saw an advert that piqued my interest. An advert I knew would solve a hell of a lot of problems.

I bet my last fucking dollar that the little girl from *Aladdin* didn't end up working in a strip club.

Chapter 1

Riley

"Babe, you're up in five," Kendra called as she walked into the dressing room, perky tits on full display and dollar bills shoved into her glittery G-string.

She was panting heavily, having just finished her routine on stage, and her gorgeous dark skin glistened with a delicate sheen of sweat.

Kendra was beautiful. If life had handed her a different path, she could have been a supermodel, but like most of the girls who worked in the club, she'd had a shitty upbringing, parents who didn't give a damn, and was doing what she could to get through life.

Tonight, she had pulled her black afro hair into a tight bun on top of her head, leaving curled tendrils to frame her face. The glittery hot pants were the only item of clothing she wore, showing off her *huge* boobs and toned figure. You never would have guessed she had given birth to her baby daughter, Zara, only four months ago.

"Thanks, K," I smiled at her in the reflection of the mirror where I applied the last flick of blusher to my cheeks. "What's the crowd like tonight?"

"It's a busy one out there, a couple of Bachelor parties that are well and truly here to party." Kendra winked at me as she finally pulled a top over her breasts.

I gave myself one last look in the mirror, feeling good about the way I looked tonight. I had curled my chestnut hair so it hung in soft waves down my back instead of hanging straight like it usually did. My dark brown eyes were framed with thick eyeliner and I had blended my eyeshadow to make it smokey and seductive.

To finish my image, I picked out a bright cherry-red lipstick which made my full lips look plumper than usual. The outfit I wore for my first dance of the night consisted of green and brown camouflage hot pants that were so tiny my ass cheeks hung out of the bottom, and an army green bra that tied into a halter neck and held my boobs firmly in place.

I'd opted to wear chunky black army boots on my feet. No, they weren't quite as flattering as high heels, but fuck did they make it easier to swing around the pole.

I had been working at Club Sin for nearly three years after finding the advert in the days after Joe died. I'd been hesitant at first, telling myself it would only be for a few months until something better came along.

Yet here I was, three years later, and if I was honest, I absolutely fucking *loved* it. Not only did I get to dance every single night, but I also made reasonably decent money. Money that helped keep a roof over mine and Angel's heads and helped to keep the little toerag in school.

So what if it was sleazebag central?

The best part was that I didn't have to strip completely naked. I had auditioned shortly after my eighteenth birthday fully prepared that I would have to bare all, so I was quietly relieved when Diana, the club's owner, said it was my choice whether I kept my clothes on, flashed the boobies, or went full-frontal.

She was confident that whatever option I went for, I would bring in the customers. It was a no-brainer really, even if taking every stitch of clothing off got me a thousand dollars a night, if I didn't *have* to do it, then I wouldn't.

Angel didn't know I worked at the club and if she ever found out, she'd be mortified. It would have been bad enough to know her sister danced around a pole, but could you imagine how embarrassing it would be for her if I stripped right down to my birthday suit? I couldn't do it to the kid, she had enough trouble with the brats at her school as it was, if they ever got wind her sister was a stripper, it would be hell for her.

It was risky enough just working at the club each night. I lived in fear that one of the pervy fathers of the kids she went to school with would come into the club and recognize me, but thankfully, it never happened, and Angel lived in ignorant bliss thinking I worked nights in the local supermarket.

Besides, my tits weren't anything fantastic, unlike some of the girls who worked in the club.

Don't get me wrong, they got me some good tips, even hidden underneath fancy bras and nipple tassels. But they were *au naturel*, not big and juicy and well, *fake*, like most of the men wanted.

I'm sure if I had bitten the bullet and paid extortionate amounts of money to get myself some fake titties, I would have got more tips but there was no way on God's green earth I would have gone under the knife.

Not that I could have afforded it even if I did want to expand the goods.

At that moment, Leandra burst into the dressing room looking flushed. Her bright red hair was a mess, black mascara streaking underneath her eyes, and her lipstick smeared around her mouth. It didn't take a genius to work out why Leandra looked disheveled.

On my first night of working at the club, Kendra had taken me under her wing and showed me the ropes, during which she informed me the girls could make extra money by giving the customers private dances.

Private dances usually ended up with the girls giving a little *extra,* if you know what I mean. There was money to be made by giving private dances, and there'd been times when the fridge at home had been bare and the electricity cut off that I seriously considered offering the odd extra, but I couldn't bring myself to do it.

Call it a moral compass or some bullshit like that.

Not that I had anything against any of the girls who did, in a way I almost envied that they didn't give a shit enough to go ahead and do whatever it was they needed to do to make ends meet. It just wasn't for me.

Leandra though was quite simply a whore. She would spend most evenings bouncing from one customer to the next, sucking them, fucking them, whatever it took to make as much money as she could in a night. All so she could blow it on whatever choice of drug was her favorite that night.

She and I had never particularly seen eye to eye, and we tended to keep out of each other's way. I don't know what I did to piss her off, but when I first started working in the club, she was an outright bitch to me, tripping me up on the club floor, setting clientele on me, and making snarky comments at every available opportunity.

It came to a head one night when I'd had enough of her nasty name-calling, and after she had purposely spilled a drink down my back, I snapped. In the changing room, I grabbed her by her throat, shoved her against the wall, and threatened that if she ever called me a name again or did anything else to piss me off, I'd rip out her silicone implants and shove them down her throat. She must have believed me because since then she tended to stay out of my way.

"Urgh, I just blew some guy whose come tasted like horseradish," Leandra said while making a face of disgust. Kendra laughed and even I couldn't help but smirk. "Seriously, I don't know why I put myself through this shit," she continued to moan, although the smugness on her face said she wasn't *really* all that put out by it.

"I don't know why you do it either," Kendra replied, and taking pity, handed over a stick of gum to her. Kendra was happy to take her clothes off but that was as far as she ever went these days now she had her little girl.

Leandra took the stick, gratitude shining in her eyes and quickly shoved the gum in her mouth.

"This is why I do it, bitches!" she sang as she pulled out a wad of cash from her ill-fitted bra.

There was easily a hundred bucks in her hands. Shame it wouldn't see the light of day outside of the club. Leandra's dealer was normally lurking somewhere in the audience, waiting to pounce.

"Rather you than me," I couldn't help but mutter under my breath as I got to my feet and found my aviator sunglasses to finish my look. I took one last glance in the mirror, making sure I looked sexy for my audience.

Over the years of pole dancing, my figure had become toned, and I had firm muscles in my arms and legs that gave my body definition. I had always enjoyed dancing as a kid but had to stop when my mom became a junkie and spent my dance class fees on crack. It was another reason why I loved this job, I was making money out of a hobby I enjoyed, and one I was good at.

Leandra rolled her eyes, which with the smeared makeup, made her look like she had momentarily been possessed by a demon.

"Heaven forbid you should get down on your precious knees, *Star,*" she sneered as she said my stage name.

Yeah, Star was my stage name. It wasn't very original but when Diana hired me, she told me every girl had a stage name and most girls used the name of their first pet or something equally ridiculous. Given my first pet was a hamster called Harry, I decided to opt for something else.

When life had been better and both my parents had been alive, they used to call me their little star, so it seemed only fitting to use their nickname for me as a stage name for my pole dancing act. I liked to think of it as a big, *'Fuck You'* to them.

Okay, so it wasn't exactly my dad's fault he got murdered. Sue me for being a tad bitter at him being taken away from us.

Deciding not to respond to Leandra, or Blaze as she was known as to the punters, I left the dressing room and made my way down the dimly lit corridor toward the stage where I would be performing in less than two minutes.

Diana allowed for a five-minute interval between each of the dancers. It allowed our guests time to get their drinks refilled or the opportunity to find one of the willing ladies to perform a private dance. The closer I got to the stage, the louder the hubbub got from within the club and the usual feelings of excited nerves fluttered in my belly.

The club was a popular place on a Saturday night and tonight was no different. The chatter and catcalls from the audience echoed all around me, and I could picture the place filled to the brim as it had been on nights gone by. It seemed like no matter how poverty-stricken residents of East Bay were, they always had cash to throw at naked girls, even if it meant their kids at home went without. Some people had their priorities all wrong in life, I knew that more than anyone.

Club Sin was one of the biggest venues in East Bay. The stage took up the entire length of the back wall, large enough so more than one girl could be on the stage at any one time. Every so often, we would put on shows where there'd be a few of us dancing provocatively together. Nights like that drew in a huge audience and I had on occasion walked away with a month's rent in just one night.

There were three poles positioned on the stage, and the ceiling was mirrored for optimum viewing, especially when those girls who went the whole hog and stripped right off were upside down on the pole with their legs spread eagle, which usually got the crowd going.

Beyond the stage and in the pit of the club were a number of circular tables to accommodate different party sizes. The bar ran the length of the club along the right-hand side, and it was always manned by five girls who wore the clubs uniform- a black push-up bra, black pin-striped hot pants complete with braces, and a white necktie which wasn't allowed to hang lower than their breasts. They spent the night walking around in white boots with killer heels.

I had done the occasional shift behind the bar, and *fuck me*, did my feet kill at the end of the night. I had a lot of respect for those girls, I wouldn't have wanted to do their job night after night.

At the front of the pit and on each side of the stage were VIP booths. They were situated so that the VIP had the best view of the stage, but also the entirety of the club. They were expensive to hire but each booth received its own personal waitress who spent the night being felt up by their customers.

The best thing about waiting on the VIP booths was the waitress always received a *very* generous tip which more than made up for the groping.

To the left of the stage was a door which led to a small corridor. Off that corridor, that's where you would find four small individual rooms, each one available at the right price for private dances, or you know, whatever else the customer was willing to pay for.

The club was kept in dim lighting in an attempt to create a seductive ambiance, but honestly? It was a sleazy place located in a shitty part of the city, and most of the men that came here were sleazeballs who couldn't keep their hands to themselves.

But hey, they paid my bills so who was I to complain?

I paused when I reached the stage, just out of view from the main club but I could see some of the VIP booths were filled, I guessed by the bachelor party. Kendra, or should I say *Foxy Brown* was right, it sounded busy out there which went in my favor, it would mean I'd likely get decent tips as long as I performed well.

I smiled at the thought. I'd wanted to buy Angel a new video game for her crappy, beat-up games console as she'd been feeling a bit down, and that girl was *obsessed* with her fucking games console, a new game was guaranteed to make her smile.

But it hadn't been the best month. I had paid out for an appointment with the hearing specialist for Angel which had eaten into a huge chunk of my monthly budget.

She'd got it into her head she could get a cochlear implant so she could hear and had presented me with tons of research she'd done at the library before begging me to book an appointment with a specialist.

The kid never asked for anything, and I didn't have the heart to tell her we'd never be able to afford the surgery even if she were eligible for it, but she was just so damn excited.

And so we went, only to be told that we'd be looking at a minimum of thirty thousand dollars for Angel to get the implant. My heart broke when I saw the disappointment on the kid's face and I wanted to do something nice to cheer her up.

A new game for her console might not have been a cochlear implant, but it would go some way to make her smile.

I'd been dreaming of the tips I'd hopefully be making after tonight's performances, I almost missed my introduction.

"Gentlemen, it's my great pleasure to announce tonight's next lovely lady," Dion, the club's Emcee, and Kendra's boyfriend announced. He was greeted with whoops and hollers from the waiting crowd and credit where credit was due, Dion had a way of getting the crowd going. "This girl is something special, I'll bet any of you chaps out here tonight would give your bottom dollar to feel her gorgeous legs wrapped around your head while you taste her."

I rolled my eyes. Dion might have been a good emcee, but he could be so damn crude at times, it was almost cringey.

"Please give it up for our beautiful.....Shining.....Star!"

He motioned for me to come on stage before walking off in the opposite direction. The crowd clapped wildly, encouraging me to step onto the stage. As I did, the lights dimmed so low I almost couldn't see the faces of the men waiting to see what I had to offer.

The audience fell quiet, aside from the odd muttering echoing around the club. I quickly made my way to the pole in the center of the stage and stood with it behind my back, the cool metal pressed against my spine. I raised one arm above my head, the other down by my side and I took a deep breath, preparing myself for the moves I was about to put my body through.

The routine I was doing tonight was a regular one in my bag of dancing tricks and I knew it better than I knew the back of my own hand.

I brought one knee up and placed the sole of my foot against the pole so my knee was bent, and then I waited for the music to begin.

Chapter 2

Kai

Club Sin was *not* the sort of shithole I usually spent my Saturday night's in, but it was the first lead I'd had in months and I personally wanted to follow it up. One of the sluts working in this joint knew something about my brother's murder and I fully intended on finding out what she knew.

The chick dancing on the stage was average at best. Yeah, she knew how to shake her hips, and her juicy ass wasn't at all bad to watch, but she was nowhere near the caliber of my girls in Sapphire, the club I owned in West Bay.

My supposed bodyguard, Vince, however, was far too fucking interested in watching Ms. Foxy Brown shake her tits rather than paying attention to our surroundings like I fucking paid him to.

Not that I was concerned about being ambushed in East Bay. Aside from the fact I was more than capable of looking after myself, most people didn't know my face. In fact, I couldn't even remember the last time I stepped foot into this area of my city, I had no real need to after all. I had people who oversaw the goings on in every area of the city, leaving me to manage the more important parts of my organization.

I swallowed down the scotch, relishing the burn as it glided down my throat. It wasn't the usual quality scotch I was accustomed to but in a place like this, it was the best one I could get. Besides, I had no intention of staying long, if we could just find this fucking whore.

I waved my hand at the girl who was our personal waitress tonight and indicated to bring me another scotch. She smiled in acknowledgment but didn't dare speak.

The slut had practically poured herself into my lap as soon as my ass hit the seat, no doubt recognizing my designer suit and thinking all of her Christmases had come at once.

She had wrapped her arms around my neck and told me her name was Vicky or something like that, and she was there to see to my every need. She'd purred in my ear and all I had wanted to do was cut her tongue out with the knife I had stashed away in my jacket pocket.

Instead, I took my sweet time to unwrap her arms before I pulled her close against me, her fake tits brushing against my chest.

"You ever touch me again and I'll slit your throat," I had whispered in her ear. The bright smile on her face immediately dropped, and her eyes widened with fear. She jumped to her feet on a whimper and muttered her apology before I instructed her to get us two glasses of their most expensive scotch.

The slut scurried away and had since kept her distance which suited me perfectly.

"Enjoying the show, Vince?" I enquired sarcastically, glaring at my bodyguard.

Bodyguard.

Laughable really, seeing as I was carrying more weapons than him.

Vince looked at me with a soppy fucking grin on his face but my expression must have told him I was *not* impressed because he rapidly lost the smirk and looked anywhere but at the stage.

"Apologies, Sir," he grumbled, before taking a sip of his own drink.

Vicky returned to our table and plonked my fresh scotch down, the scowl still firmly set on her face. Before she had time to walk away, I grabbed her wrist and spun her to face me.

"I'm looking for a girl who works here, bright red hair, about twenty-five, and snorts her body weight in coke most nights," I asked Vicky who was staring at my grip on her wrist with pure fear etched on her face.

She was a cute girl, petite with a pixie-cut blonde bob and a turned up nose. I imagined she could have been stunning if it wasn't for the fake tits which were far too big for her tiny frame, and the tell-tale sign of being a drug user, like I suspected most girls in this place were.

Had it not been for the fact I could have my pick of any of the girls working in Sapphire, I could have come around to the idea of fucking this slut, a hole was still a hole at the end of the day.

But I wasn't here for that. Tonight was about getting the information on the cunt who murdered Theo.

"That sounds like Blaze," Vicky replied with a shaky voice.

I stared at her expectantly. I didn't know who the fuck Blaze was, I didn't make it a habit of coming to this dump, and the man who told me where he'd heard the titbit of information didn't give any more description of the girl who had told him.

Granted, he hadn't said much else after my knife found its way into his throat, but that was beside the point.

Vicky quickly cottoned on to my look, *smart girl*, and looked around the club.

"She...She must be out the back or with a customer in one of the private booths, I can't see her."

"I need you to find her," I instructed the girl, leaving no room for arguing. Not that she would, not if she wanted to live at least.

"Yes, of course, Sir."

"Thank you, Vicky," I said as I released her wrist.

"It's Vixen," she snapped back, causing me to narrow my eyes and glare at her. The girl squeaked before disappearing into the crowd.

I watched her go, trying to keep my eyes peeled for a redhead but failing miserably to see much in the darkness of this fucking place. How anyone could come here on a regular basis was beyond me.

Just as Vicky or Vixen, whatever the fuck her name was, disappeared through a door, the music came to an end and the girl on stage took her time to thank the audience as she bent over and collected all the dollars that had been thrown on the stage.

To my relief, the lights were turned up a fraction, allowing me to cast my eye over the crowd. I had one goal in mind.

Find the redheaded whore who couldn't keep her mouth shut.

I spent the next few minutes taking in the crowd, wondering who in their right fucking mind would willingly come to a dive like this. There was at least one bachelor party, and it was evident which one the groom was. The one who was fucking *wasted* and not looking the slightest bit guilty at the topless girl grinding on his lap while his buddies cheered him on and tucked dollar bills into the girl's glittery thong.

In one of the other VIP booths near Vince and me, there was a group of young men celebrating a birthday, the birthday boy was passed out in the corner, oblivious to the evening carrying on around him.

In the main area of the club where the tables were, the place was packed full of customers. They ranged from groups of friends enjoying the evening's entertainment, to dirty old bastards sitting on their own, on the verge of masturbating at the near naked waitresses walking amongst them, serving drinks, and sticking their tits and asses into the faces of their customers at any given opportunity.

The club was a fucking slum and one I wouldn't be coming back to in a hurry.

I was beginning to lose my patience, both at the non-existent red-head and at Vicky for not finding her quicker, and it was never a good thing when my patience ran out.

People tended to die when that happened.

This whole damn place was quite frankly beginning to piss me off, from the whores walking around with their fake titties and pouty collagen lips, right through to the darkness of the club and the pounding music which was far too fucking loud for my liking.

I was about to order Vince to get off his ass and to go look for this elusive Blaze himself, but at the moment I turned to talk to him, the fucking emcee decided it was time to announce the next slut to strut her stuff. I decided to wait until the girl was on stage before ordering Vince to go look, at least that way every man in this club would be looking at the stage and it would have been easier to spot the whore I was looking for. In theory, at least.

I snorted into my scotch when the emcee made a comment about the men in this place wanting a taste of the next girl who was going to grace us with her presence. I dreaded to think what one could catch from going near any of the sluts in this dump.

The lights dropped, plunging the place into almost darkness before the opening bars of the next song started. The song, *Love on the Brain*, was not my type of music at all, but I'd heard it play in my club before and I had to admit it had a good beat, one that always got the ladies grinding.

The lights came back on but only low, casting a soft glow across the stage, and with it came catcalls and hooting from the men who were watching. I shifted in my seat to get a better look at the stage, wondering what all the fuss was about.

Instantly, my breath was taken away by the girl on stage. She was *stunning*, like no one else I had seen in this place, or *any* place for that matter.

The girls at Sapphire didn't have a patch on the beauty who was standing against the pole, waiting patiently for her cue to move.

I sat up straight in my seat to get a better view of her face, and at that very moment, she whipped her aviator glasses off and threw them to one side. She scanned the room and her dark chocolate eyes briefly found mine, only for a second, but I could have sworn her lip twitched into a coy smile.

As the lyrics started, the beauty suddenly twirled around and pulled herself up with strong, toned arms, twisting her tight little body until it was wrapped around the pole.

To say I was mesmerized would be a fucking understatement, and for the first time since seeing my brother's lifeless body, my cold heart started beating again.

There was something about this girl that meant I couldn't pull my gaze away from her. World War fucking three could have kicked off behind me and I wouldn't have noticed because I was so transfixed on her.

The way she moved around the pole was utterly intoxicating. I watched in awe as she spun herself around, flipped upside down, and held on to the pole using one strong thigh. Every movement was gentle, delicate....seductive, and I couldn't help but picture what it would feel like to have her wrapped around me.

There was nothing fake about her body. Her breasts were easily a good handful, not too big, not too small, but more importantly, completely real. Just how I liked them.

Her body moved in time with the music, she knew how to sway her hips and her ass to hold the attention of every man in this place. But despite how fucking gorgeous her body was, it was her face that held my attention. Her eyes were dark and sultry, and she had high cheekbones that gave her delicate face definition. She had soft, plump lips that I could imagine would feel fan-fucking-tastic wrapped around my cock as I fucked her mouth.

Her brows creased as she concentrated on the music like she couldn't see the crowd before her, it was just her and her pole. She had an air of vulnerability about her and the predator within me liked that, the vulnerable ones were always the easiest to break and I suddenly found myself wanting to see just how far I could push this girl.

She didn't remove any of her clothes, part of me wished she would so I could see what shade of pink her nipples were, or how beautiful her pussy was.

But the other part of me was glad she didn't remove a single item because I wasn't the only one enthralled by this girl. The whole audience was, and I was overcome with the thought that if any of them dared to look at her naked, I would slit each and every one of their throats and enjoy doing it as well.

This girl, this *fucking gorgeous girl*, was tempting as sin, and I knew right then I had to make her mine.

The wolf had just found his newest prey, and I would stop at nothing to make her mine.

She worked the pole like it was part of her, she knew exactly where to put her hands and her legs at the right moment, and by the time she was finished, the men in the pit were out of the seats, rushing forward to throw their dollars at her. She gave them a smile, looking almost surprised the audience had enjoyed her performance.

I silently begged her to look at me again, just so I could see those beautiful brown eyes once more, but she didn't. Instead, she thanked her audience as she collected the dollars, giving a wiggle of her pert little ass as she seductively bent over to retrieve the money.

And then she was gone, replaced by the emcee returning to the stage and asking the audience to give the girl, *Star*, another round of applause. I didn't clap. Instead, I sat back in my chair and looked at the crowd, the majority of them on their feet and calling out for an encore, completely oblivious to the fact I was sitting there, fighting back the urge to go backstage, find the girl and steal her away from this life.

It took a few minutes but eventually, the audience went back to their drinks, or to the conversations they were having before she came on stage, probably forgetting all about her and ready for the next act to appear. But I couldn't tear my eyes away from the now empty space, a strange feeling coursing through my body.

It was a feeling I had never felt before, at least not over a woman. A feeling of possessiveness, and a desperate need to make her mine, no matter the cost.

"Good evening, Sir, I believe you've been looking for me," a seductive voice pulled me from my thoughts and I turned to see a redhead leaning over the table with a sultry smile on her lips, her ass in Vince's face and her bra almost bursting at the seam from the size of her enormous tits.

She was an ugly cunt, evidently high on something if the tiny pupils in her eyes were anything to go by. My reason for coming to the club was standing in front of me, only now, she wasn't the reason why I wanted to stay.

I stood up abruptly and Vince did the same, the difference being I had to adjust my pants from where they had grown tight against my cock which had been hard from the minute *she* had climbed on the pole. I leaned into him, making sure the redhead couldn't hear me.

"Take Blaze to the warehouse and keep her there. I have some business to attend to before we deal with her."

I didn't give Vince the chance to respond before I was out of the booth and on the hunt for Diana, the old cunt who owned the place. I knew Vince wouldn't have been happy to leave me alone here but it wasn't like I didn't know how to look after myself.

Besides, Diana owed me a favor and I was going to cash it in.

She was going to get me a personal audience with the girl they called Star.

Chapter 3

Riley

I was feeling pretty good after my dance finished. The crowd had gone wild for my routine, and I'd earned a lot of tips, one hundred and twenty bucks to be exact, which was *way* more than what I earned during weeknight performances.

I had added a few extra moves to the routine tonight, an extra booty shake here, and a little caress of my boobs there, which must have impressed the crowd given the roar from them when I finished.

I made my way back to the dressing room, passing Kendra who was about to go back on stage for another routine. Never one to miss an opportunity to gossip, she quickly told me that Leandra had been bragging *very* loudly about some rich dude wanting to see her, and that she was aiming to make a shit ton of money from sucking him dry tonight.

Gross.

That was another thing with Leandra, the girl could not keep her mouth shut. She liked to brag about the guys she sucked and fucked, as if all the other girls were jealous of the amount of cocks she got each night.

Cue eye roll.

I briefly wondered if the rich guy Leandra had been summoned to meet was the mystery man who had been seated in one of the VIP booths. The usual customers who came to the club were definitely not wealthy, but the guy sat in the booth? Yeah, he *oozed* money.

And power.

I wasn't able to get a good look at him before the music started because of the crappy lighting in the club, but from what I could see, *holy hell*, was he freaking hot. All dark and brooding, and giving me such an intense look that I had felt it all the way to my core.

I hadn't seen him in the club before, and he certainly didn't look like one of the regular pervs we got in. There was just something about him sitting in that booth that made me keep glancing over, and every time I did, I was pleasantly surprised to find his eyes following my every move. It made me want to perfect my routine all the more.

It was most unlike me. I only really cared about dancing the perfect dance in order to get tips, but this guy? The way he was watching me made me want to dance perfectly just for him, tips be damned.

I collapsed into the chair in the changing room, surprised at the niggle of jealousy that maybe Blaze was going to be spending some alone time with Mr. Mysterious, which was ridiculous because I couldn't be sure she had been referring to Mr. Mysterious.

Anyway, it was beside the point. I didn't do extras. No matter how hot the guy was.

Putting the mystery man out of my mind, I started going over the routine for my next dance. The next dance wasn't quite as intense but it still contained a number of moves that could make me fall from the pole if I got it wrong. I changed my shorts into black sparkling hot pants and was in the process of changing my bra to match the shorts when Diana rushed into the changing room, looking harassed.

Diana was a large woman, not fat, but tall, easily over six foot. She had bleached blonde peroxide hair and had spent too much money on her appearance, she could barely move her facial muscles from the amount of Botox she'd had, and her eyebrows had been tattooed on in an over-the-top arch which made her look like she was permanently surprised.

She had huge boobs, *ridiculously* big compared to her skinny waist, and somehow she always squeezed herself into tight-fitting dresses. Tonight was no exception, and I briefly wondered if she could actually breathe in her leopard print dress that looked like it would rip at the seams at any given moment.

Despite Diana looking like trailer trash, she was one of the nicest women I'd ever met. She cared immensely about all of her girls, making sure we all texted her every night to tell her we were home safely, and that any troublesome patrons were dealt with by one of the club's many bouncers.

"Riley, hun, I need a huge favor," she rushed out with a distinct edge of panic to her voice which instantly worried me. Diana was practically unflappable having faced a number of adversities in her life, but something had rattled her.

"What's up?" I asked in reply, knowing that I would do pretty much anything for Diana. She had, after all, taken a chance on me when I showed up asking for a job with not even a pot to piss in. I owed her a lot, and she rarely asked anything of me in return.

"One of the customers has taken a shine to you and has requested a private audience."

I was about to tell her that I was very sorry but I couldn't do that when she held up a manicured finger and carried on talking.

"I know you don't do private dances, and you know I respect that, but this customer isn't someone who takes no for an answer."

"Well, I'm afraid this person-" I pointed to my chest, "Is going to be giving him no for an answer. I'm sorry, Diana, you know I don't do private dances."

I finished putting on my bra and reached for my shoes, this time they were black peep-toe stilettos with silver heels which were an absolute bitch to dance in but made me feel *very* sexy.

Diana dropped to her knees in front of me, totally out of character for her, the woman never begged for anything. She grabbed my hand and squeezed it, almost to the point of pain.

"Riley, please, baby," she pleaded desperately. "I *need* you to do this. I owe this customer, like *massively* owe him, and he's decided to cash it in by requesting an audience with you. He's not someone I want to piss off."

Despite the seriousness in her tone, I had to stifle a giggle. She almost looked comical on her knees, begging me for help, yet not a single muscle in her face moved an inch thanks to all the Botox. She really ought to lay off the cosmetic shit for a bit.

Instead, I hid my smirk and focused on the problem at hand.

"You're not really selling this to me, Diana. Why would I want to be alone in a room with a man who can't take no for an answer, and isn't someone you should piss off?" I mean, I had a point, right? He didn't sound like he was someone I would want to be alone with for ten seconds, let alone the duration of a song.

"He's willing to pay you whatever you want. And I'll get one of the door staff to stand outside the room in case you need any assistance, but I promise you, he won't hurt you." She gave me a look similar to when a puppy is begging for someone to pick them from the crate at the pound.

I had never seen her like this before. She was normally such a feisty ball-breaker, no one dared to cross her. To see her on her knees and begging the way she was, I couldn't help but pity her.

She must have sensed my resolve weakening because she abruptly stood, grabbed my hand again, and yanked me out of the seat.

"At least come and meet him," she said, before pulling me out of the dressing room and back into the corridor that led to the stage.

I could have stopped her, could have pulled my arm free from her grasp, and told her to get fucked. But I didn't, curiosity got the better of me. Whether it was the fact that Diana had said this customer was willing to pay me whatever I wanted, or because I was so intrigued as to who had ruffled Diana's feathers, I wasn't sure.

Either way, I let Diana pull me along the corridor, onto the club floor, and passed the VIP booths, where I noted that Mr. Mysterious was nowhere to be seen. I guessed that he was busy by now, probably with Leandra's mouth around his cock.

It wasn't often that I thought she was a lucky bitch.

I pushed the thought out of my head as Diana led me into one of the private rooms, the one furthest away from the exit which I wasn't exactly happy about but knew there was little I could do to change it.

Stepping inside, I was greeted with the back of a tall, broad man who was staring at a framed photo of an elegant woman wrapped around a pole, which happened to be one of my favorite pictures. My heart almost jumped out of my chest when I recognized the tailored suit he was wearing.

It was him.

Mr. Mysterious.

My observation was only confirmed when Diana cleared her throat and the man turned around to face us.

Being this close to him and in a better light, I drank in every single inch of him. He didn't smile, just stared at me with an intense look burning in his dark eyes. Eyes that were so dark, they were almost black. If I had to guess his age, I would have said he was mid-thirties. He was clean-shaven and had a sharp jawline, his jet back hair was shaved around the sides but slightly longer on top, which had been swept back with the exception of a strand that flopped against his forehead.

I couldn't resist eyeing up his body hidden underneath that expensive suit, it was clear that he was nothing but solid muscle underneath the tight white shirt that stretched across his broad chest. His long legs were powerful and strong, and he had an air about him that screamed that this man was dangerous and not to be messed with. I couldn't quite put my finger on what it was about him that gave me that impression, there was just....something.

Butterflies danced wildly in my belly, and there was part of me that wanted to run as far away from him as possible, while the other part of me wanted to move closer, drawn to him like a month to a dangerously hot flame.

"Sir, may I introduce you to one of our best dancers here at Club Sin. This is Star," Diana announced with a quiver of nerves in her voice.

Still, he didn't smile nor did he say anything. Instead, his eyes roamed up and down my body, and I was suddenly overcome with an eerie feeling that the man wanted to eat me alive. The worrying part was that I might have just let him.

"Bring me a bottle of scotch and two glasses," he ordered Diana without taking his eyes from me. They burned fiercely into mine and I couldn't stop the shudder that rolled through my body, but whether it was from fear or something entirely different, I didn't know.

Diana muttered something quietly before she scurried away, leaving me alone with Mr. Mysterious. Still staring, he slowly unbuttoned his suit jacket, revealing just how tight his shirt was against his firm chest. He placed it delicately over the arm of the sofa in the corner of the room.

"Is Star your real name?" he eventually asked after he finished gawking at my semi-naked body, still looking like he wanted to eat me alive, and that only made my heart race faster.

"No, Sir," I replied nervously. A ghost of a smile touched his lips, but it was gone almost as quickly as it had appeared.

"What's your real name?" His deep, gruff tone left no room to deny him the answer.

I was used to patrons asking me personal questions and sometimes getting a bit handsy, but I always held my ground with them and refused to give them even the tiniest snippet about my life. That didn't seem to be happening now though, my lady balls were nowhere to be seen.

"Riley...Riley Bennett." The words tumbled from my mouth, leaving a bitter taste. It felt like I was betraying myself by telling him my name.

He didn't offer his name in return, instead, he started to fiddle with the cuffs on his shirt and a thought flashed through my mind that he was about to start taking his clothes off.

A fleeting moment of panic rolled through me, but to my relief, he started rolling his sleeves up, revealing muscular forearms. Both arms were covered in black tattoos which started at his wrists and disappeared underneath the shirt that had now been pushed up to his elbows.

"Riley. Please, sit." He nodded to the sofa, before sitting down at the other end of it, gracefully crossing one long leg over the other.

I didn't dare argue. Diana had been one hundred percent correct: you didn't say no to this man. I perched on the edge of the seat, angling myself so that I could see him clearly. Whether it was accidental or intentional, he had offered me the end of the sofa closest to the door, something I was grateful for.

I was just about to open my mouth and ask him what his name was when Diana knocked on the door and walked in with a bottle and two glasses.

She placed them down on the table, still looking nervous and refusing to meet my eye. Her nervousness did absolutely nothing to quell my own. Once she placed the glasses on the table, she stood up and straightened down her knee-length dress.

"That will be all, Diana," the man growled without so much as casting a glance in her direction. In fact, he hadn't taken his eyes off me at all since I had first walked into the room. When Diana didn't immediately leave, he finally took his eyes from mine and glared up at her. "I give you my word. Riley will be safe in my company."

A brief look of confusion flashed over Diana's face when the man said my real name, but she gave him a small nod and then promptly turned on her heel, still without looking at me. Once again, I was left alone with the brooding man. I intended to have stern words with Diana before this night was finished.

"Do you know who I am?" he asked as he poured the amber liquid into the two glass tumblers, pulling my attention away from the door Diana had left through.

"No." It came out as a whisper and I internally cursed myself for sounding so unsure. Confidence was key when dealing with patrons who couldn't take no for an answer, but this man had the ability to zap every ounce of confidence I possessed. He again smirked but didn't elaborate on who he was.

"I watched you dance. You were magnificent." There was an air of pride in his voice which sent warmth flooding through my body. It was such a bizarre reaction to have from the words of a stranger.

"T....Thank you," I replied, and then finally, *finally,* finding my lady balls, I added, "I'm not sure if Diana told you, but I don't offer private dances or anything else you might be here for. I could get one of the other girls for you if you like....."

The words dried up in my throat when I saw anger flash across his face, making me recoil in my chair. It was as though I had personally offended him by telling him I wouldn't dance for him.

"Diana did mention it. But I believe that anything is available for the right price," he said with a *ton* of arrogance in his tone. I resisted the urge to roll my eyes.

Fucking rich people.

When I didn't reply, he reached out and took a glass before taking a mouthful of the drink. I couldn't tear my eyes away from his throat as he swallowed the liquid down. His throat was thick and muscular, just like the rest of him. He didn't return the glass to the table, instead, he kept it in his hand and swirled the liquid around.

"Consider this. I'm not your usual clientele that comes to this place. In fact, I'm pretty sure that after tonight, I won't be stepping foot back in here again," he sneered in disgust. "I would guess the going rate for a private dance is what, a hundred dollars?"

I nodded when he raised a questioning eyebrow, but the truth was, I didn't know what the going rate was, and quite frankly, his arrogance was starting to get on my nerves. I wasn't sure what more I could say to make him realize that I wouldn't dance for him.

"What would you charge, Riley? For one dance, any fee you could charge, what would it be?"

I couldn't help but snort.

This was utterly ridiculous. Evidently, the man had money, but if he was not our usual clientele, as he put it, then why the hell was he here wasting both of our time? He could obviously afford to go to one of the more upmarket establishments, he probably could have even afforded the ridiculously expensive places in West Bay. I figured if I gave him a stupid amount, he'd realize I wasn't being serious.

"Five thousand dollars. But not a single stitch of clothing would come off."

I waited for him to finish his drink, thank me for my time, and hotfoot it out of there, because let's be honest, who in their right mind would pay that sort of money for a girl to swing around a pole for them?

But instead, he smirked again and downed the rest of his drink before putting the glass down on the table. He uncrossed his legs and sat forward where he rested his elbows on his knees.

"I tell you what, Riley. Have one drink with me and dance for me, just once, just as you are. Do that and I'll give you ten thousand dollars, right here, right now."

Ten thousand fucking dollars?!

My eyes widened and my jaw dropped open at his offer. The smug bastard poured himself another whiskey before he sat back on the sofa, re-crossing his long legs, and stared back at me.

Ten thousand dollars?

Was he for real?

Thoughts whizzed through my head at just what I could do with that kind of money. I would have been able to buy Angel that stupid video game. Hell, I would have been able to buy her a laptop and pay for the internet so she didn't have to spend hours in the library trying to use their crappy computers to do her homework.

Ten thousand dollars would have solved a whole heap of problems, and all I'd have to do was have a drink with this man and dance just one song for him.

I could not believe I was considering it, but there I was, arguing with myself as to why I should or should not agree to it. This man was right when he said that anything was available at the right price, and from the look on his face as he stared at me, he knew he had me where he wanted me. Right in the palm of his big hands. As much as I didn't like that, I knew I'd be damn stupid not to take him up on his offer.

I tried to keep myself composed and not let on that I was genuinely considering it. This seemed too good to be true, nothing like this *ever* happened to girls like me in places like Club Sin.

"What's the catch?" I said, cynicism dripping from my tone. "You surely can't expect me to believe that you'll give me ten thousand dollars for having a drink and then dancing for you. I don't care how much you offer, I don't take my clothes off, and I certainly don't do what some of the other girls here do." I held firm, even sounding a bit angry at his audacity.

Okay, so even if there was a teeny-tiny part of me that said if I had to get down and dirty with this man, it wouldn't be the worst thing in the world, even if a ten thousand dollar offer wasn't on the table.

But if I didn't have my morals, then what else did I have?

The man reached over to where his suit jacket lay abandoned and pulled out his phone. I watched silently as he tapped away at the screen before holding it up for me to see. The screen displayed an online banking page, a bank transfer set up for ten thousand dollars, payable to me.

"I don't want you to take your clothes off, and I certainly won't pay you to do anything else. One drink, once dance, that's it. You have my word that I won't touch you. All you need to do is give me your account number and the money will be transferred into your account within minutes. Of course, that's only if you agree to the terms."

I gaped at the screen, an array of thoughts flying through my mind of what I could do with that money.

For some, it wouldn't have made a huge amount of difference. For Angel and me, it would be life changing.

Only an idiot would have walked away from the deal.

And I was no idiot.

Chapter 4

Kai

My time with Riley was over far too fucking quickly for my liking. But short of threatening the girl to spend more time with me, which I did not want to do, not yet at least, there wasn't much I could do other than watch her walk back through the atrium of the club.

I watched her go, right to the point where she reached the door that would lead her backstage, and when she finally reached the door, she turned and looked back to where I had been standing on the other side of the club. She gave me a small smile, and fuck, if I didn't want to storm across the shithole of a club, grab her and take her far, far away from here.

There was something about this girl that stirred something buried deep within me and it was unsettling, I didn't do feelings or emotional bullshit.

And yet there I was.

Fucking infatuated.

It didn't matter that Riley had disappeared from my sight though, I'd be seeing her again soon, not that she knew it yet.

She had no idea she'd become my prey, and I *never* let my prey get away from me. If there was one thing I had learned from my father, it was that patience was a virtue.

My phone had vibrated during Riley's dance, indicating a text had come through but I hadn't read it, I couldn't give two fucks as to who it was, they could wait. The whole world could have been burning for all I cared, there was no way I was going to miss one second of the enigma that was Riley.

Being in such close proximity to her was sheer torture. Countless times I wanted to reach out and touch her, feel how soft her skin was, and pull her close enough to inhale her scent. But I had given her my word that I wouldn't lay a finger on her, and I was always a man of my word.

Besides, when the time came, I wouldn't need to pay Riley for a taste of her sweet cunt, she'd be begging for me to fuck her.

Pulling out my phone, I found a message from Vince. He had secured Blaze at the warehouse, ready for her to be interrogated. It was followed by a second text telling me he had sent Frank, one of my drivers, to wait outside the club for me.

Despite his distraction earlier in the club, Vince was a good bodyguard, and I knew he wouldn't have been happy to leave me alone. I never normally went anywhere without at least two or three of my security team but I had wanted this visit to be low-key. I hadn't expected for one second I'd be staying put in the club while my one and only security detail took our target away.

Pocketing my phone, I made my way out of the club, glad to be leaving the dump but not at all glad to be leaving Riley. My black Mercedes AMG S65 was parked directly outside the club and my driver, Frank, was engrossed in a heated conversation with one of the door staff. As I approached, I realized instantly what they were arguing about.

It seemed Frank was not supposed to park where he had and was now being told to move on. I rolled my eyes, I didn't have time for this shit. I had things to do, a woman to torture for information, and another one to learn all about. I walked over to Frank just in time to hear him tell the doorman to get the fuck away, or he'd find himself unemployed. That was Frank for you, always trying to play peacekeeper.

What he should have been saying was, *'Get the fuck away or my boss will cut your throat out.'*

"Problem?" I asked as I reached the quarreling men. The doorman, who was a unit of a man, turned to face me, most likely about to tell me to mind my own business until he realized who I was.

This was the part I loved, the part where recognition dawned on people's foolish faces, and they realized they had about ten seconds left to live.

But no blood would be shed tonight, at least not with this man.

"Mr. Wolfe, my apologies. I didn't realize this was your driver. Please, Sir, accept my apologies," the doorman groveled pathetically. I stared at him, giving him one of my notorious looks, the look that said, *'any last words before I blow your fucking brains out.'*

When I saw his Adam's apple bob in his throat, I knew he had received the message loud and clear. Frank knew it too, he opened the rear door to my waiting car, a satisfied smirk playing on his lips.

I settled into the back seat, and as Frank pulled away from the club, I instructed him to head towards my warehouses down by the docks. It was a drive that would take around thirty minutes, which suited me fine as the drive would give me time to think about what information I wanted to extract from the red-headed whore.

Except, I couldn't get Riley out of my mind.

The conversation we had while sipping our drinks replayed in my head. She told me she was a student, working in the club to pay her way through college, and that her family lived in another state where she would rejoin them once she graduated.

It was all bullshit, of course. I was good at reading people, it was a skill that had helped me get to where I was now. Being able to spot liars easily meant I could catch traitorous cunts.

Riley probably didn't even know that when she told a lie, she would push a strand of hair behind her ear, even when there was no strand to be pushed behind her ear. I didn't blame her for lying to me, she was merely trying to protect herself, but it only added more to my curiosity as to who the fuck this girl was, and what had happened in her life to lead her to work at Club Sin of all fucking places.

She was something else. A vision of beauty who should be on a stage, dripping in diamonds and expensive lingerie, lit up for the world to see but only for me to touch. Not working in some seedy, dingy club where the peasants of this city hang out, drooling over her. Although, the more I thought about it, the more I realized I didn't like the idea of people seeing her dancing in her skimpy outfits.

It was something I would put a stop to, and soon.

My thoughts turned from our conversation to my private dance. I closed my eyes and tilted my head back against the headrest, my mind's eye conjuring up the image of Riley working her way up and down the pole that was in the corner of our private room, her petite figure twirling and twisting with ease, her pert ass gyrating against the metal. I couldn't even tell you what song she was dancing to, the only thing that held my attention was her, nothing else mattered.

My cock had hardened the second she started moving, much like it had when she danced on the main stage. And now, with the pictures playing in my head of her toned legs wrapping around the pole, my cock was once again hard as a steel rod.

I knew I should have been focusing on the interrogation of Blaze, but I also knew I wouldn't be able to concentrate on anything until I had done something to take care of the ache in my cock.

"Frank, I need a moment to myself." I didn't need to say anything more. Frank acknowledged my statement by closing the privacy glass between us, leaving me alone to my thoughts in the back seat.

I couldn't wait any longer. I undid my belt buckle, unzipped my pants, and took out my cock, pre-cum already glistened on the head and my balls aching in need of a release.

I stroked my shaft lightly and once again allowed my eyes to close and the pictures of Riley to take over my mind. I couldn't wait to make her mine.

Gripping my cock with just the right amount of pressure to feel fucking good, I thought about how it would feel to have Riley's cunt wrapped around my length instead of my hand. I jerked my hand up and down, moving faster and faster as the pressure in my balls increased.

I imagined Riley sitting on my lap, riding me hard as her juices trickled down my shaft. I pictured throwing her onto the back seat and feasting on her wet pussy before slamming back inside her and pounding her into oblivion until she came again and again on my cock, screaming my name. And then I imagined what it would be like to pull out of her and shove my cock into her mouth and down her throat, silencing her and forcing her to swallow my seed.

The images raced through my mind as the ache in my balls became unbearable, my hand moved faster until it was impossible to hold back. I couldn't stop the groan from escaping my lips as I came hard, all over my hand.

When I opened my eyes, disappointment swam through me that I was alone in the back of the car, and at that moment, I knew at some point in my near future, my fantasy would become reality. It really was only a matter of time.

Irrational jealousy washed over me when a thought popped into my mind that Riley may well be going home to a boyfriend after finishing work. The thought alone sobered me as jealousy turned to anger. I cleaned myself up with the handkerchief I kept in my jacket pocket, unashamed at the mess I had made and feeling like I could finally concentrate again.

Anger was good, it helped me to focus.

A short while later, Frank pulled up at the docks and opened my door for me. If he knew I had pleasured myself, he didn't show it. My staff knew the importance of discretion, especially if they valued their life.

I made my way into the warehouse, one of many I owned throughout the city. Whereas some of my warehouses were used for my illegal operations, this one was empty. The reason being that underneath the warehouse floor was a basement with reinforced steel all around the walls and a door that would only open with my or one of my trusted employee's fingerprints. A safety measure I used in every property I owned.

The basement had no windows, meaning the only way someone was getting out of the basement was on my say so. I crossed the empty warehouse floor, the smell of dirt and grease hitting my nose.

Years before, the warehouse had been used as a car manufacturing company but it was shut down after the company went bust, courtesy of the CEO not paying his debts to my father. The CEO lost his life and the Wolfe family gained another warehouse to take care of our businesses.

Stepping down the concrete stairs, my footsteps echoing, I made my way to the basement, pressing my finger on the scanner once I reached the steel door and stepped inside where I found Blaze tied to the chair in the middle of the room. Along the back wall was a long table where tools and instruments designed to inflict torture were laid out.

Blood trickled down the whore's face from a gash above her eyebrow, and from the scratch on Vince's cheek, I figured the stupid bitch had tried to flee. A cloth had been shoved into her mouth, held in place by a rope tied around the back of her head, her hands were bound behind her back and her legs tied together. Black smears of mascara trailed down her puffy red cheeks, evidence of her tears.

Although her tears were nowhere to be seen now, instead the bitch scowled at me causing a chuckle to fall from my lips.

"Was she a bit too much for you to handle on your own, Vince?" I asked my loyal bodyguard, humor evident in my voice. Vince was a big motherfucker, he wouldn't like being mocked at a tiny woman getting the better of him.

"She slipped out of my grip, Boss," he mumbled and glared daggers at Blaze.

I took a step closer to the woman and a hint of fear flashed through her eyes, but only briefly before she continued scowling at me.

"I don't believe we have been acquainted as yet, Blaze. My name is Kai Wolfe."

Recognition dawned and the scowl instantly dropped from her face. She suddenly started thrashing in her chair, attempting to break free as muffled screams emitted from behind her gag, which was annoying as fuck and wouldn't get her anywhere.

She knew who I was.

She knew she was fucked.

I let her shout, let her twist in her chair, and attempt to break free of her restraints until she realized there was no way out of this shit, and when she quietened down, I nodded to Vince to undo her gag.

"What do you want from me?" she rasped when she could finally talk.

"I want you to tell me all about the cunt who murdered my brother."

She didn't reply immediately and that was a sign enough for me to know that she did indeed know *exactly* what I was talking about.

"I....I don't know anything," she stuttered over her lie and my lips curled into a lopsided smile.

She wanted to play games?

Fine by me.

I walked over to the table at the back of the room and selected a pair of pliers. I thought we'd start small, I didn't want the whore to pass out straight away from the pain.

Not that I thought I'd actually have to torture her too much, I had a feeling Blaze was full of false bravado, and I was about to put my theory to the test.

Chapter 5

Riley

Did I feel like a traitorous bitch for forgoing my morals?

Yes.

But did I regret it?

Not in the slightest.

Especially not when Angel's face lit up like a goddamn Christmas tree when I gave her not only the stupid computer game but also a new games console to play it on.

I bought us both new beds so we didn't have to sleep on the crappy mattresses we'd been sleeping on for the last few years, and for once, our fridge was fully stocked with delicious treats.

Angel was suspicious as to where the money had come from. The smart ass was far too intuitive for her age, but I assured her the money had been as a result of a bonus at work, and not selling my body as she suggested. It was a teeny tiny lie, I hadn't actually sold my body, at least not in the way she thought I had.

It had been exactly one week since I had danced for the man I now knew to be Kai Wolfe, the motherfucking kingpin of Hollows Bay. The man who was rumored to control the police, the justice system, and the criminals of the city.

From what I had learned about him over the past week, it seemed everyone thought he was the man who owned this city and a man to be feared.

All of that should have been enough to keep him from my mind, but could I forget him?

Could I fuck.

Diana had a lot to answer for. Funnily enough, when my time with Kai was over, Diana was nowhere to be seen. Conveniently, she had developed a migraine and had taken the rest of the evening off.

Bullshit.

The following night, I went to work an hour early with the sole purpose of confronting Diana. I found her lurking in the club's basement, doing a last minute stock take on the bottles of beer stored down there, and I demanded to know who the fuck he was. Her face paled as she told me his name, and as the penny dropped, I didn't know whether to laugh or smack her in the face.

I didn't know much about the Wolfe brothers other than the rumors that had echoed around the streets of Hollows Bay since the day Angel and I had landed five years ago. Rumors that they were dangerous, violent murderers, and people not to be messed with, so I couldn't understand how Diana would put me in such a position.

That was until she told me she owed Kai a shit ton of money.

Two years earlier, she'd gotten herself into a bit of trouble when an ex-boyfriend had conned her out of her entire savings. He'd also taken out loan after loan, and credit card after credit card in Diana's name, so when the bailiffs came knocking and threatened to repossess Club Sin in order to pay off the debts, and despite Diana having proof she didn't take out the loans and cards, with no savings to fall back on, Diana had two choices, give up the club or find someone to bankroll the debt.

There was no way the banks would give her any more money, her ex had been very clever with his scam and the banks and the police had not believed her when she claimed she was innocent. The only way Diana stood a chance was to turn to a loan shark who gave her the cash upfront.

Diana was many things, but a genius she was not.

On the plus side of her decision, she paid off the debt and we all kept our jobs.

The downside was Diana's repayment plan was *astronomical* thanks to the interest rate charged by the loan shark, and although she had tried her hardest to meet the repayments, Diana had started to fall behind within a few months of taking out the loan.

It was a stroke of luck that Diana had been pouring her heart out to a friend who suggested he could help. One thing led to another and her so-called *friend* introduced her to Kai who agreed to buy her debt, and she could pay him back in smaller monthly installments. The catch was he would charge double the interest but she could pay it off over a longer term, meaning she was bound to him for the rest of her life unless she came up with a way of repaying the money back sooner.

I still felt like Diana had thrown me under a bus, but when she claimed the loan shark had threatened to break her legs so badly that she would never walk again, she had no choice but to agree to Kai's terms. She'd been paying off her debt without any issues until last night when Kai offered to wipe her debt completely clear in exchange for a private meeting with me.

Needless to say, Diana didn't hesitate to throw me to the wolf.

Literally.

My jaw nearly hit the floor when she told me exactly how much her debt to Kai was, and it made me all the more curious about him given the fact he had agreed to write the debt off in exchange for an introduction with me.

If I was honest, I couldn't blame Diana, it made sense and I couldn't help but think that I would have made the *exact* same choice if I had been in her shoes. And ultimately, it resulted in me earning a small fortune, so I guess it was a win-win situation for us both.

But knowing who he was, I was nervous that I was suddenly on the man's radar, and a feeling deep down in my belly said to me I hadn't seen the last of him.

As the week had gone on and he hadn't made a reappearance, I tried my best to put the man out of my head but I couldn't help constantly replaying my encounter with him over and over. It was like during the twenty minutes I had spent with him, he had somehow managed to burrow his way under my skin, and every night since meeting him, I had looked out into the audience longingly, hoping I would find him watching me from a dark corner.

It was stupid really, I should have been relieved he hadn't come back, he was not a man whose attention I wanted. Or needed for that matter.

And yet, every night, I found myself a tiny bit disappointed when he didn't show up.

Okay, maybe *a lot* disappointed.

It was a busy night in the club this evening, Diana had organized one of her special event nights which she did every few months. Nights like this were always sure to bring in the clientele and therefore the cash, and tonight was no exception.

And the theme?

Slutty school girls, of course.

All the waitresses were dressed up in matching tight-fitted white shirts which barely contained their breasts, knotted at the front to reveal as much of their slender tummies as possible. Black and red ties sat loosely around their necks, and they wore the tiniest black pleated skirts accompanied by white knee-high socks and platform shoes.

We dancers wore even less, if that were at all possible.

My evening had gone from bad to worse as the minutes ticked by. Diana had begged me to pick up two extra dances on top of my own two, as well as the group routine, all because fucking Leandra had disappeared.

Like, *poof!*

Vanished into thin air.

The last time anyone saw her was about a week ago when she was seen heading out the back with a customer, and then it was like she fell off the face of the earth. No one had seen or heard from her, and when Diana went to her apartment, her roommates said they had no clue as to where she was, nor did they care. Apparently, she was a lousy roommate, and they'd wanted rid of her anyway.

The girls and I speculated that she was probably passed out in a cocaine haze somewhere, completely clueless as to what day of the week it was, but Diana wasn't convinced so visited the local police station to report her missing.

Of course, the police gave zero fucks about a missing stripper, especially with one who had a rap sheet as checkered as Leandra's. Diana was sent on her merry way with a, *'We'll look into it'*, and Diana hadn't heard anything from them since.

But thanks to Leandra's disappearing act, we were having to pick up her extra slots. I didn't mind too much because it meant extra tips, but the additional practice and routines were beginning to take their toll, exhaustion was setting in, and my body ached all over. I think I would have given *anything* for a soak in a nice warm bath to ease my aches and pains.

Shame I had to settle for the crappy shower in my apartment that was no more than a trickle of tepid water.

My evening started off shitty when I'd been dancing in one of Leandra's slots, and a customer decided he wanted a piece of my ass before hauling himself on stage and making an attempt to grope me. Jamie, the security guard charged with keeping the over enthusiastic customers away from the stage had been trying to restrain two other customers from beating the shit out of each other, so it was a good few seconds before anyone was able to come to my rescue.

Clive, another security guard, flew through the club when he realized what was going on on stage, but his presence was practically pointless. My knee found its way into the groin of the customer who was writhing on the floor in pain by the time Clive reached us.

Still, Clive did manage to get in on some of the action. He promptly folded the customer up like a pretzel and not so gently tossed him out.

My second dance was just as disastrous, although at least I wasn't groped this time.

Nope. Instead, my heel decided to snap on my stilettos causing me to face plant in front of everyone. I kinda styled it out and ditched my shoes so I could carry on with the routine but my pride was dented, my knees were sore, and I was so damn tired.

Thankfully, the group dance with Kendra, Charlotte, and Harriet went well, and the audience went crazy for us, especially when it looked like Kendra and I were about to make out.

Men really were one-track minded sometimes.

To top my night, there was yet another fight between brawling drunks, resulting in one of the waitresses being pushed into me and spilling beer all down me. I was soaked through, sticky and stinking like a brewery, and quite frankly, I'd had enough.

Home time couldn't come soon enough.

Finally, the last customer was escorted out of the club at closing time and I said my goodbyes to Diana and the other girls, ready to walk the twenty minutes back to the apartment Angel and I called home.

I couldn't wait to get under the pathetic excuse we called a shower and wash the sticky beer from my skin. Diana didn't like me walking home in the early hours, but she also accepted it was just as dangerous getting a taxi in this part of the city so neither option was ideal. At least by walking, I wasn't wasting money.

I headed out the door, thanking Clive one last time for coming to my rescue, and started in the direction of home.

We were just coming to the end of summer and the nights were getting cooler, it wouldn't be long until my walks home would turn bitterly cold, and it wasn't something I particularly looked forward to. It also meant extra heating would be needed in the apartment to keep Angel warm, which meant an increase in my monthly heating budget. I internally cursed at the weather and the changes in the season which I knew was irrational, but it's not like I had much else to think about on my walks home.

I pulled my jumper tighter to protect myself from the chill in the air as I walked along the empty streets. I always put leggings and a jumper on along with my comfy sneakers before I left the club, no freaking way was I going to walk home in my dance wear, that was asking for trouble.

A shiver passed through me and I realized it wasn't necessarily from the cold. I had an eerie feeling I was being watched. I couldn't say what it was that made me feel that way, but there was *something*. I upped my pace despite protests from my achy muscles, and I quickly looked behind me to make sure I wasn't being followed.

I wasn't, but I wouldn't be the first girl to have some weirdo trail her from the club.

I took my usual route which included cutting through the park. It was my least favorite part of the walk home but it was the most direct and saved an additional ten minutes to my journey. There were always drunks and druggies lurking in the park, sometimes they'd ignore me, other times, depending on how off their faces they were, they'd try to engage me in some form of conversation.

One time, a guy was hallucinating so badly that he thought the park bench was a spaceship that had just landed and I was the alien who had come to take him away. Aside from witnessing firsthand the damage drugs did to someone, the smackheads in the park would be a good enough warning for me to steer clear of any illicit substances.

I always kept my head down and ignored them regardless. I wasn't being rude, I just didn't want to become the next victim of a robbery or a rape.

Or something worse.

As I entered the park, the feeling of being watched intensified, and nerves tingled in my entire body. I didn't know if I was being paranoid or if someone was actually watching me, but I sure as hell wasn't going to find out.

Once again, I quickened my pace and headed through the park, avoiding looking left and right and keeping my gaze focused on the other side of the park where I knew the gate was. My calves burned from the speed I was walking, and my mind started to play tricks on me, fear taking over.

Leaves rustled as the wind blew, the trees lurked ominously in the dark, and the blasted street lights flickered on and off causing shadows all around me to look like they were moving. At one point I thought I heard footsteps behind me. I tentatively peeked behind, but still, no one was there. I should have carried a weapon or something but if a time came that I needed to use it, I wasn't sure I'd actually have the balls.

When the gate finally came into view, I damn near sprinted to it, and when I burst back out onto the main street where the odd car was still driving around, relief like I'd never felt before flooded through me and I let myself relax a little. I even giggled at what a silly, paranoid idiot I'd been.

That was until a hand clamped down around my mouth as another hand wrapped around my waist, and I was dragged backward into a nearby alley.

The need to fight kicked in and I fought like a motherfucker, trying to scream behind the heavy hand. I didn't go willingly, but I weighed next to nothing so it wasn't hard for my attacker to pull me into the alley as I continued to kick behind and bite down on the hand clasped against my mouth.

I hit the jackpot when my teeth sunk into the palm of my attacker who winced in pain, momentarily loosening his grip. It was enough to allow me to escape the strong embrace. I turned around and anger rolled through me when I saw my attacker was none other than the douchebag from the club who had tried to grope me on stage earlier in the night.

He was an older man, maybe in his early fifties, bald and overweight. His brown corduroy trousers and yellow shirt had stains down the front, if I had to guess, I'd say he'd puked all down himself at some point since being thrown out of the club.

Nice.

"You're a fucking little cock tease," he slurred, his eyes fixed on his hand. From the faint streetlight, I could see I had drawn blood.

Good.

"Get the fuck away from me." I tried to keep the fear out of my voice but even I heard the nerves.

He was a big man both in height and build, and he could easily overpower me. It took all of a second to realize that the asshole had me at a disadvantage, he was standing at the entrance to the alley blocking it, behind me were trash cans and trash bags, and beyond that was a solid brick wall that must have been at least ten feet tall.

The only way out was passed the douche who had clearly come to the same conclusion as me if the cruel smile twisting on his lips was anything to go by.

I had two options. Fight or become a victim of whatever he intended to do to me.

Well, fuck that.

Huh, maybe I would use a weapon if I had carried one.

He took a step towards me and I took a step back but raised my fists, ready to go into battle. If I was going down, I'd be going down fighting.

"Oh, sweetheart, I like it when my girls fight," he chuckled and took another step toward me.

I didn't want to let him back me any further into the alley, even if I couldn't overpower him, I just had to do enough to get past him and then run like hell. I summoned the last bit of bravery I had, which granted, wasn't much, and then lunged at him.

He wasn't expecting my sudden attack which was fortunate, it meant I got a swift punch to his ugly face. But he was stronger than me, and within seconds he had my wrists pinned to my sides as he pulled me flush against his body. The overwhelming stench of whiskey, vomit, and body odor assaulted my nostrils and made me gag.

"I'm going to enjoy fucking you, you little whore," he whispered menacingly against my cheek.

Preparing myself to go into battle again, I managed to raise my leg enough to kick him square in the shin but all that rewarded me with was a hard shove to the chest, causing me to fly back and land in the pile of garbage bags.

"Cunt!" the man squealed, spittle flying out of his mouth and rage flashing in his piggy eyes.

True terror flooded my body. I was exhausted, and I knew there was no way I'd be able to fight this man off. Still, I wouldn't lie down and take whatever it was he wanted to do to me.

I was about to hoist myself up and try again to get away from the dickhead when a dark figure grabbed my attacker from behind.

I gaped in astonishment as I saw a pair of hands grab my attacker's head and twist in such an inhumane way that I instantly knew the move was intended to end a life.

The sickening sound of bones snapping echoed down the alley, confirming what I had just thought.

My attacker was dead.

Chapter 6

Kai

Riley Alyssa Bennett, born on 15th May 1999, in Richmond City Hospital, making her fourteen years younger than me.

Not that I gave a fuck about that.

Her father was Eric Bennett, Mother was Janine Bennett, nee Smith. Both were deceased, father killed in a drive-by shooting by a stray bullet, mother died from a drug overdose. Riley and her younger sister Angel, reported missing, although, when Riley turned eighteen, her file was closed and she was noted as being the legal next of kin for Angel. It seemed the authorities didn't give two fucks about where the girls had been the last two years, all that mattered was they no longer had two missing children on their books.

I had read and re-read the documents given to me by Isaac, my private detective, who had spent the last week finding out every little detail about my beautiful Star. I had called him as soon as I finished with Blaze at the warehouse and told him that obtaining information on Riley was to be his priority. Isaac had grumbled, he was in the middle of other cases, but as I said to Riley back at the club, anything is available for the right price. It cost me a pretty penny, but it was worth every cent.

Having read the documents time and time again, I was even more obsessed and determined to make her mine.

I should have been focusing on finding the cunt who killed my brother, but I couldn't focus on anything but her.

She'd gone missing from the city of Richmond at the age of sixteen with no sign of her or her sister for a few months, they were probably living rough on the streets. That was until some old bastard gave her a job and let her work for him. He'd even been good enough to put a roof over her and her sister's heads, although until I had more information on this alleged good samaritan, I decided to keep an open mind. Most people didn't do things just to be kind, there was usually more to it. I had recognized the name, Joe Mason, but I couldn't quite place it, so I asked Isaac to do some more digging on him.

I also hadn't been able to stop staring at the photos Isaac had taken of her every day he had been following her. I hadn't seen her in the flesh since the night at the club, much to my frustration I'd been too occupied dealing with that druggie Blaze, as well as securing some deals that were going to bring in a shitload of money, and making sure my other lines of business were running well.

Without Theo to help, I was running the show alone and it was taking up far too fucking much of my time. Instead, I'd asked Isaac and his team to trail her. I wanted to know what she was doing every single minute of the day.

She didn't do a huge amount, it was pathetic really.

A young, gorgeous girl like Riley should have been living life to the full, and yet, she didn't seem to have any friends outside of Club Sin. That's if you could call her co-workers friends, and the only person she spent any time with was her sister.

I had Isaac pull both Riley and Angel's medical records from the day they were born, I wanted to know everything about Riley, and I needed to find something in her past that I could exploit to get her to come *willingly* into my life.

My other option was kidnapping the girl, which wasn't off the table, and I certainly wasn't averse to going down that route. But that wasn't the best way to start a relationship.

Because that's what I wanted with her, I wanted her by my side, I wanted to make her mine.

To my surprise, the medical records showed that Angel was born Deaf, and I'd watched in sheer fascination video footage of Riley having a full-blown conversation with the younger girl in sign language.

It was impressive.

The medical records also showed Riley had recently taken Angel to an appointment at a private medical clinic to be assessed for a cochlear implant which would cost close to forty thousand dollars.

Based on the intel Isaac had gathered, and from what I had seen from photos of the dump the girls called home, there was no way on God's green earth that either Riley or Angel had that kind of money.

Of course, I saw this as a good fucking opportunity to get her into my life. Just how far would she go for her family?

I would have stopped at nothing to protect mine.

Only, I wasn't there when Theo did actually need protecting.

The photos Isaac managed to obtain of Riley gave an insight into her daily routine. She would finish at the club around 4 am when she walked home alone.

That pissed me off to no end. She should *not* be walking home alone in a city where monsters lurked everywhere.

I should know, I was the biggest fucking one of them all.

She'd practically run home, as though the devil himself was on her ass, and as soon as she stepped inside the communal area of her apartment, even in photos you could tell she was relieved to be somewhere safe.

She'd resurface around 7.30 am with Angel in tow, dressed in school uniform, and they'd take two buses to get Angel to school as it was too far for them to walk.

Riley always had dark bags under her eyes, and I'd wondered if she'd gotten any sleep from the time she got home until the time she took Angel to school. After dropping her sister off at school, Riley would take the two buses back to their apartment.

Twice during the week, she stopped in the supermarket and emerged carrying bulky shopping bags which she lugged back to the apartment. After that, she'd disappear inside and not resurface again until the early afternoon when she would then get back on the buses to meet Angel from school. Sometimes they would go to the library for an hour or so, other times they would go straight home. She then wouldn't make an appearance again until 9 pm when she'd leave the apartment and head to work.

It was evident from Isaac's observations that no one went to look after Angel when Riley went to work, and of course, I saw this as another opportunity to use to my advantage.

Aside from the photos being the only opportunity I had to see her face, they were very telling. In photos with Angel, Riley would smile for her sister and give the impression that all was fine in the world. She was clearly the protector, always holding Angel's hand, helping her on and off the bus, and kissing her cheek when Angel went inside the school.

When she was alone, however, it was a different story. She would walk with her shoulders hunched, not daring to look at anyone. Her brows were constantly furrowed as if she was trying to solve the world's hardest mathematical equation.

Alone, Riley looked like she was hauling the weight of the world around on her shoulders, and I wanted nothing more than to take that weight from her. And I would, I just had to make sure all the pieces of the jigsaw were in place before I made my move.

It had taken a week to get all of those pieces sorted but the time had finally come.

Whether she knew it or not, Riley Alyssa Bennett, *Star*, was mine.

Maybe once I had her by my side, I'd be able to refocus on finding out who murdered my brother.

Before I could execute my plans to get Riley into my life though, I had to deal with a small *issue* standing right in front of me at this very moment. Although technically not standing, *hanging* from ceiling hooks would be more appropriate. I mentally locked away the information I had on Riley and re-focused my attention on what was going on in the room.

Hendrix Becker and Danny Jones, two of my most trusted advisors and closest friends, along with my cousin, Miles Wolfe, were currently kicking the shit out of little Nicky Williams who was my current issue, and hanging naked from the ceiling by chains wrapped around his wrists.

He was known as Little Nicky out on the streets because he apparently resembled Adam Sandler from the film *Little Nicky*. I wasn't one to sit and watch films so I couldn't say who the fuck he looked like, but right now, he looked like most people did when they were hauled in front of me.

Petrified.

Nicky was stretched so taut that he could barely touch the floor with the tips of his toes, and every time one of my men hit him, he let out a painful grunt.

Yet he continued to deny his crime.

It seemed that Nicky, one of the newer recruits in The Shadows, my street gang who were responsible for drug supply, both at a local and national level, had taken a liking to my product and thought he was entitled to help himself.

I didn't tolerate thieves in my organization, a rule that nearly everybody followed but every so often, there was one arrogant cunt who thought they wouldn't get caught.

Spoiler alert. They did.

Nicky was only a young boy, eighteen, nineteen at a push, and like many of my employees had grown up in care. He'd been recruited with the promise of being looked after like the rest of my employees, but the temptation of the product had gotten the better of him.

Shame really, my employees were well looked after, no matter what rank they held in my organization. It kept them loyal to me.

Nicky could have had a comfortable life, a roof above his head, and food on his table, but now he was facing living in hell for the rest of his pitiful existence.

My phone pinged and I pulled it out of my jacket pocket to see a message from Isaac who had been keeping an eye on Riley.

'One hour until closing time.'

Time to wrap this shit up.

I stood from the chair I had been perched in and strode towards Nicky as I closed Isaac's message.

Flicking through the apps on my phone until I got to my video gallery, I selected the video that was undeniable proof Nicky was the one who had been stealing from me.

"Let's stop fucking around now shall we, Nicky?" It was the first thing I had said since coming down to the basement at my apartment block over an hour ago. I owned the entire block and had transformed it into my own castle, overlooking my city. And it came complete with my very own personal torture chamber in the basement.

My playground.

I had let Hendrix, Miles, and Danny take the lead in extracting the truth from Nicky.

Theo and I had grown up with Hendrix and Miles our entire lives, and Danny had joined our crew when I was in my early teens. Through loyalty, he had proved his dedication to my family, and the five of us became inseparable. Theo had been my second in command, and now that he was gone, I ought to have promoted one of them. I just couldn't bring myself to replace my brother.

"Boss, I swear, I never touched the product," Nicky wheezed, blood from the lashes inflicted by the chain Miles had used ran down his naked torso. He'd cried out like a little bitch at every lashing which had only made Miles hit him all the harder.

If I was honest, I was a little impressed he was still conscious.

"I don't like thieves in my organization, Nicky. I hate liars even less." My tone was cool, calm......*unemotional*. I held the phone out in front of him and pressed play on the video.

The screen flickered to life, a black and white film played from the secret camera I had installed in the drug packing warehouse when I was alerted to Conroy's suspicion that someone was stealing from me.

Conroy was the leader of The Shadows and was responsible for recruiting new candidates. He'd dropped the ball with Nicky, that was for sure. No one had known about the camera, not Conroy, not even Hendrix, Danny, or Miles so the look of amusement on their faces when they realized what they were watching was priceless.

Nicky however, well, his face dropped in sheer horror as he watched the video of himself sneaking into the warehouse in the early hours of the morning, and grabbing a packet of cocaine worth around $1000. He shoved it underneath his jacket before heading out. The camera had been positioned to get a clear shot of his face as he left the warehouse, a cocky smirk playing on his lips as he looked straight up at the invisible lens.

Funny, his smirk was nowhere to be seen right now.

"Boss, let me explain-" Nicky started. But Miles brought the chain down across his back once again to silence him. He screamed in agony as his body lurched forward, and his hands pulled on the ceiling restraints holding him in place.

"You had your opportunity. And now you're making me late for my next appointment, one of which is of great importance to me. Release him." I nodded to Danny and Hendrix who made quick work of untying Nicky's hands.

His legs gave out as he collapsed to the floor in a heap. He didn't have time to stay there before they pulled him to his feet. Meanwhile, Miles fucked around in the corner of the room, preparing the items we would need to teach this *boy* a lesson.

Nicky whined as my men made him stand upright, the hours he'd been hanging from the ceiling had clearly affected his ability to stand unaided.

"Had you just stolen from me and admitted it, I would have granted you a quick, fairly pain-free death, but you continued to lie." I grabbed his chin and held his face so that he had no choice but to look me in the eye. One eye was swollen shut, and his lip was split from the beating he had received.

"Please don't kill me," he begged, rather pathetically if you asked me.

It made me laugh, so much that I threw my head back and let out a hearty chuckle.

"I'm not going to kill you, Little Nicky," I stopped my chuckling to return to a look of seriousness. "I am, however, going to teach you a lesson about how it's rude to steal. One you won't forget for the rest of your life."

Miles had returned to the middle of the room, and at my nod, got to work on Nicky's arm. The boy was unable to pull out of Danny's iron-clad grasp, allowing Miles to tie a tourniquet around Nicky's upper arm. Nicky pleaded for us to stop as Miles found a raised vein and inserted a needle, before fixing a cannula into the crook of his elbow. He then pumped adrenaline directly into Nicky's veins.

The boy's eyes widened as the liquid surged through his body, his pleading becoming louder, but slurred. It wouldn't be long until he felt his heart rate start racing from the adrenaline.

Kicking and screaming, he tried to pull away from Danny and Hendrix as they dragged him over to the table that contained our tools, forced him to his knees, and yanked his hands down onto the table.

"It's ready," Miles informed me, referring to the poker that had been heating in the fire pit in the corner of the room. The end of the poker was a flat piece of square metal burning white-hot, and I couldn't help but enjoy the sadistic feeling that washed over me.

This was going to hurt.

Poor Little Nicky.

Hearing Miles' words, Nicky burst into louder sobs which only served to piss me off. Don't do the crime if you can't do the fucking time.

I picked up the meat cleaver that had been sitting on the table. Not my favorite tool for jobs like this, but it would certainly get the job done and really, I didn't have time to spare.

Miles brought the poker over to us. When he was close enough, I raised the cleaver, and with as much force as I could muster, brought it down onto Nicky's right wrist. Blood spattered my face and shirt as the limb came easily away from the body it was supposed to be attached to.

Nicky howled in writhing agony as blood spurted from the stump that had been left behind. Miles moved in quickly, and with the flat part of the poker, held it against the stump in a bid to cauterize it before Nicky could bleed out.

The boy screamed and screamed, and I knew it wouldn't be long until the little punk passed out despite the adrenaline pumping through his system.

Skin sizzled as the heat from the poker seared the gaping wound, and the smell of burning flesh hit my nostrils.

It was a smell I relished.

As predicted, Nicky's body sagged as he fell unconscious. Fortunately, he was still being held up by Hendrix and Danny. I didn't have the patience to wait for Miles to finish his job, he'd need to reheat the poker, and I was itching to get out of my bloody clothes and go to my girl.

I handed the cleaver to Hendrix who took it with a sadistic smile on his face, one that matched my own.

"Give him some more adrenaline, wait until he's regained consciousness, and then do the other one," I instructed as I wiped my bloody hands on a rag. "Make sure you get the word out to the troops what will happen if anyone dares betray me again."

The collective sounds of 'Yes, Boss' echoed around the room. Knowing that I could trust my men to finish the job, I left them to it.

Twenty minutes later, I was showered and dressed in a clean suit as Frank drove me to East Bay. Anticipation rushed through me at the thought of seeing her again.

I couldn't fucking wait.

My phone dinged, alerting me to a message from Isaac.

'She's left.'

My plan had been to meet Riley as she left the club. I didn't want her walking through town again on her own, but things had taken a little longer dealing with Nicky, so I was now running behind schedule.

'Follow her. Approx 8 minutes away.'

"Put your foot down, Frank, there's somewhere I need to be," I instructed my driver, who obliged by accelerating harder. I stared out the window as the affluent part of the city ebbed away, replaced with derelict buildings, graffiti, and whores on the street corner.

East Bay was an absolute shithole, but it needed to be. The city needed to have its rich and poor factions to work, there could be no Yin without Yang. And without the poverty and the need for drugs and crime, my organization simply wouldn't work.

Maybe that made me sound callous, but honestly?

I didn't give a fuck.

Isaac kept me updated on Riley's journey home as we edged closer. I was re-evaluating my plan to collect her, thinking I would just intercept her before she got to the dive she lived in when a worrying text came through.

'Someone's following her.'

I sat up straight in my seat and dialed Isaac.

"Who the fuck is following her?" I demanded angrily as if it was Isaac's fault.

"Dude from the club. He tried to dance with her and got kicked out for his efforts. Not before she got a knee to his nuts," Isaac replied casually.

Fury spiked my blood. Whoever this fuck head was better think twice about touching her.

"I'm only a minute away, if he touches her, put a bullet in his head."

"Ah, slight problem. She's gone into the park and I can't follow otherwise my cover will be blown," Isaac replied.

I couldn't stop the growl from leaving my throat. "Fuck your cover, Isaac, I'm paying you to keep her safe," I hissed.

Fucking Nicky, if he'd just admitted to stealing earlier then I wouldn't have been late to pick her up from the club.

"I know, Mr. Wolfe, but I work undercover!" he protested.

I hung up on the prick, vowing to wring his neck when I next saw him.

Frank turned the corner, and the park up ahead of us came into view. There were barely any street lights, but the glow of an oncoming car's headlamps lit up the exit, and a petite figure came flying out of the gate. Even from this distance, I knew it was her, and I breathed a sigh of relief.

That was until I saw the figure exit the park, grab her from behind, and drag her into an alley.

Frank saw it too. The car accelerated, and we shot down the last part of the road before screeching to a halt near the mouth of the alley. I opened the door and launched myself out, reaching the alley in time to see the dead man walking push Riley backward.

She stumbled and fell into a pile of garbage bags, panic etched all over her face. She was so focused on her attacker that she hadn't seen or heard my arrival.

"Cunt!" The man shouted.

It would be the last thing he ever said.

I didn't think twice about grabbing his head from behind. One hand on his shoulder, one on his forehead, and I twisted his head to the left as hard as I fucking could. I was so fucking angry that had I yanked any harder, his head would have come right off his shoulders.

The crack of the bones in his neck signaled that I had successfully broken his neck, and I let the piece of shit drop to the floor.

It took me a full minute to calm the rage sweeping through my body before I could look at her. Her tiny body flying backward kept repeating in my mind, and killing the fucker once wasn't enough. If I could have brought him back to life and killed him again, I would have. Only this time I would have taken my sweet time with the prick.

"Is...is he dead?"

The fear in her soft voice broke me out of the murderous thoughts swirling inside my head, and I was overcome with the need to bundle her into my arms and protect her from the dangers of the world.

It was an alien concept to me, I was usually the one people needed protection from, not the protector.

Fucking hell, I needed to man the fuck up.

"Yes," I finally replied as I ran a hand down my suit jacket, ironing out imaginary creases.

I turned to the tiny form still lying prone on the garbage bags, the look of pure terror etched across her gorgeous face. Her hair was piled up on top of her head in a messy bun but some strands had come free following her tussle with the cunt who had attacked her, and my breath hitched in my throat at seeing her again in real life rather than just from a photo.

The photos did not do her justice.

I took a step forward and offered my hand out to her, wanting to help her up, but she just stared up at me with her mouth gaping open and her beautiful brown eyes wide. Anyone would have thought I had three heads based on the way she was staring at me. I guess I couldn't blame her, she had just witnessed me kill a man with these hands and probably thought she was next.

"I won't hurt you, Riley."

She peered up at me with those chocolate brown eyes which widened further at my mention of her name, and a look crossed her face that said she was surprised I'd remembered it.

If only she knew.

Slowly, she reached her hand up and placed it in mine. It was small in my large palm, and her skin was soft, as soft as silk. I pulled her gently to her feet, and to my surprise, when she was standing again, she didn't immediately remove her hand from mine.

"Should we call the police?" she asked nervously, staring down at her would-be attacker.

I smirked. I supposed I could call the police, I owned them after all, and with the right payment to the right person, there would be no record of this. But I preferred to take care of body disposal myself, and the dead prick did not deserve to be recorded as a John Doe and given a funeral, no doubt paid for by the city.

No, he would rot in the deepest part of the waters that surrounded Hollows Bay, wrapped in a body bag, and weighed down with a ton of heavy rocks.

"No, I'll take care of it," I replied.

Shock must have been setting in because she didn't flinch, or even blink at not getting the police involved. She stared from me to the body, and then back at me again, her face growing whiter by the second. Once again, I wanted nothing more than to pull her into my arms and keep her safe.

"Did he hurt you?"

She finally removed her warm hand from mine and I instantly missed her contact.

"No, I'm fine. Thank you for-" she paused, struggling to find the next words to say, *'saving me, stopping him from raping me.'* Instead, she waved a hand toward the dead man. I nodded my response, finding myself in a rare moment of being at a loss for words, and in the seconds that followed, we just stared at each other.

I wondered if she finally knew who I was. Had Diana told her that I was the man who owned and ran this city, a man not to be messed with? Or was she thinking that I was just another customer who happened to be in the right place at the right time?

For some reason, I found myself desperately wanting her to know who I was, and for me to have been on her mind as much as she had been on mine this past week.

"Mr. Wolfe, I should probably go," she said as if to answer my unspoken question, and I had to resist the tug of a relieved smile on my lips.

Her eyes darted toward the mouth of the alley where her freedom waited. She gave me a small smile and then took a step away from me.

I immediately blocked her path.

There was no way she was going anywhere that wasn't with me, and while I had planned to coax her into my car one way or another before the night was over, this situation had presented itself, and it was an opportunity I was going to cash in on.

"I'm afraid you are going to have to come with me, Riley."

Grown men had pissed their pants standing before me, but my brave Star didn't show an ounce of fear. She didn't look like the downtrodden girl I had seen in the photos, she looked how she did when she was usually in the company of Angel. Feisty and ready to take on the world.

She crossed her arms over her chest, inadvertently pushing her tits up, and I couldn't stop my eyes from glancing at them. I couldn't wait to nestle my face between her luscious tits.

"I'm not going anywhere with you," she huffed and scowled at me. Begrudgingly, I dragged my eyes away from her chest.

She stood firm, arms crossed, and hip cocked to one side. I was so used to people falling over their feet to do as I said, to please me. And yet here was this little girl with the audacity to stand up to me.

It did things to me, stirred parts inside of me that I thought were dead.

She stared back, offering a silent challenge.

Well, if my Star wanted to play, then who was I to deny her?

"Riley, baby. We can do this the easy way or the hard way. Either way, you *will* be leaving here with me."

I took a step closer to her, and her scent invaded my nostrils. A mix of strawberries and sunscreen, unfortunately, mingled with the smell of garbage and stale beer. She tipped her head back to look up at me, her chin jutting out in defiance.

"I'll say it again, *Kai*. I'm not going with you," she hissed.

This time, I couldn't stop the smirk from gracing my lips. I was so used to people addressing me as 'Boss' or 'Mr. Wolfe' that it took me by surprise when she called me by my name. I was not one to back away from a challenge, and if Riley wanted to take the hard way, then so be it.

I moved quickly, not giving her a chance to react.

Lunging forward and bending down, I grabbed her around her slender thighs, lifted her up, and threw her whole body over one shoulder. "The hard way it is then."

The girl weighed next to nothing. Her shock at being manhandled quickly turned to anger as she pounded on my back and screeched her demands to be put down.

She didn't have much strength in her punches, I barely acknowledged her fists thumping against my back, and all her efforts did was make me chuckle.

Frank, who had stayed by the entrance of the alley this whole time dutifully popped the trunk of the car. Hell, I'd intended on putting her in the back with me so we could have a civilized conversation, but this would certainly show her that I wasn't taking any shit.

The sound of the trunk popping attracted Riley's attention.

"Put me down, you bastard!" she squealed and pounded harder on my back.

I accepted that putting her in the trunk was going to get us off on the wrong foot, but I had to show her who was in charge here.

It wasn't her.

Lowering her gently into the trunk, I had a brief glimpse of her beautiful face which was now contorted to a look of pure rage. Even so, she was still possibly the most stunning woman I had ever laid eyes on.

"Don't you dare shut me in here!" she cried, somewhat pointlessly.

I gave her a wicked smile before closing the lid on her, her curses aimed at me faded away as the lid locked back into place.

Chapter 7

Riley

How the fuck had this happened?

I mean, seriously!

How the fuck had my night gone from being covered in beer, to being locked in the trunk of the car of the man who owned the goddamn city?

How can a man even own the city anyway?

Urgh.

I tried to move in the confined space of the trunk, but there was hardly any room. At least he hadn't tied my hands and legs together, I guess that was some small relief.

The trunk was pitch black so I could barely make out my hands in front of my face. I managed to turn on my side and feel around, trying to find a release button or something.

Weren't cars supposed to be equipped with releases so it wasn't possible for someone to be kept in the trunk?

I couldn't find anything of the sort but that was no surprise. This wasn't an ordinary man we were talking about here, of course his car was going to be well prepared to keep a prisoner in the trunk.

Prisoner.

Fuck.

Panic began to bubble in my belly. I had been shit scared during our face off in the alley but I thought I had done my best to not let it show. Here now, in the darkness of this small enclosure, panic hit me full force.

I took a couple of calming breaths, trying to reassure myself that I would be okay. I had to be okay, for Angel's sake.

What the fuck did Kai want with me?

If he wanted to kill me for witnessing him murder a man he could have done it on the spot.

But he hadn't.

Was he worried I would go to the police? I'd have to convince him one way or another that I wouldn't tell another soul what I had witnessed.

Bile churned in my belly as rumors of the Wolfe brothers' violent tendencies circled my brain. Kendra had told me about how the Wolfe brothers had warehouses all over the city where they took people to torture them and then dispose of bodies in the most heinous of ways.

Was that my fate?

I couldn't let that happen, what would happen to my sister?

Angel's face kept appearing in my head, what would she think when she woke up in the morning and I wasn't in my bed? She'd be terrified, and then she wouldn't be able to communicate with anyone to tell them I was missing.

Fuck, I needed to get back home before she woke up. Before she realized anything was wrong.

The car rumbled along, heading to fuck knows where. I had no clue as to how long I'd been in the trunk, ten minutes, thirty minutes? Time seemed to move differently when you were shit scared and locked up.

Why the hell had I given him back chat and not gone willingly?

Maybe because I wasn't some servant willing to be ordered around.

I thought back to the moment when I realized it was Kai who was my savior from the man who was undoubtedly going to rape me. I had been relieved, but it had been a stronger feeling than just relief.

Excitement maybe, lust even?

I'd forgotten how fucking hot he was. I'd thought about him a dozen times in the last week but seeing him in the flesh again, *Holy hell*.

Whatever the feeling at seeing him again was, I wasn't sure. What I was sure of now though, was whatever I had felt, it was long fucking gone, replaced by anger at the man who had thrown me callously into the trunk of the car like some kind of fucking animal.

How dare he.

I needed to have a plan for when we eventually came to a stop. It was pointless trying to fight my way out of the trunk, and kicking and screaming would only tire me out. I had a feeling I would need all my energy for whatever I was going to face when we got to wherever the fuck we were going.

I needed to be smart, smarter than the man who ran the city.

There were no two ways about it.

I was fucked.

Okay, plan A. When he opens the trunk, I jump out, kick him as hard as I can in the balls and run.

There were several problems with this ridiculous plan, the main one being that I had no idea where I was being taken to. I knew the Wolfe brothers lived somewhere in West Bay but that part of Hollows Bay was *huge*.

It also meant I was at least half an hour away from home. There was no way I'd be able to make it back to East Bay without him stopping me, I only had a small amount of change and my crappy phone which had no credit in my bag.

Speaking of which, where the fuck was my bag?

I felt around in the boot but didn't find it. I must have dropped it when that asshole sent me flying into the garbage bags, meaning I really did have no way of getting back home.

Besides, Kai knew where I worked. I'd have to literally get home, gather Angel and whatever shit we could carry, and get the fuck out of Hollows Bay, but where would we go? What would we do to survive?

The other problem with plan A was that Kai Wolfe was one heck of a scary motherfucker, and a swift kick to the nuts was never going to bring him down.

Plan B. Don't fight. Let him take me to wherever we are going and see what happens.

That seemed like a pretty fucking pointless plan, let the man take me wherever, and do whatever he wants to me without putting up a fight?

Nope, not happening.

But what other choice did I have? Maybe he didn't want to kill me, he'd been very generous when I had danced for him, maybe he wanted another dance and to give me another ten thousand dollars. Maybe the rumors of him being a murdering son-of-a-bitch were just rumors, and really, he was a very good businessman and was going to offer me a job in a high-end strip club where I could finally earn a decent wage, and give Angel the life she deserved.

Maybe I was living in cloud fucking cuckoo land.

Plan C.

Fuck.

I didn't have a plan C.

And it didn't seem like I was going to have time to form one because the car had come to a stop and the engine switched off.

I held my breath as the car doors opened and then slammed shut causing vibrations to reverberate all around me. Footsteps came closer to the trunk and a noise indicated the lid had just been released.

Quick Riley, plan A or plan B.

The trunk opened, and Kai loomed above me, looking a mixture of menacing and amused.

If I wasn't so fucking angry, or in this situation, maybe I could have taken a moment to appreciate how gorgeous the man was, but right then, he could go fuck himself.

Behind him stood three other men, all looking as mean as Kai. One of them had dirty blonde messy hair and piercing blue eyes which were dancing with amusement at my predicament. He was slightly shorter than Kai but just as muscular.

The male standing next to him was the same height as Kai but was definitely the least muscular out of all the men standing before me. He had olive skin and gorgeous brown eyes that matched the same color as his hair which was tied back into a small ponytail. Aside from a quick glance at me, he kept his eyes focused on the phone in his hand, tapping away on the screen as if this whole situation was boring him.

The third male was huge and had a shaved head, tattoos crept up his neck and on both sides of his skull. He had dark eyes, a hook nose, and a prominent scar on his cheek that curved into the shape of a C. Out of the three of them, he scared me the most.

Not as much as Kai mind you, but he looked pretty damn intimidating.

One thing became crystal clear as soon as the trunk popped open, I was outnumbered.

"I apologize for putting you in the trunk, Ms. Bennett, I appreciate that it's not the most comfortable, but I couldn't risk you trying to throw yourself out of the car. I'm sure you can understand." Kai addressed me formally but almost sounded jovial, like he was making a joke at my expense. It made me want to leap out and punch him on the nose.

Or maybe the junk.

Perhaps I should have gone with plan A.

The gorgeous bastard had undone the top button on his white shirt and had taken his suit jacket off which he now held draped over his arm. I was pleased to see someone had been comfortable during our journey here.

Fucker.

I pulled myself up into a sitting position, my body aching from where I had been cramped into the small space. It became apparent we were in an underground car park, with flashy-looking cars parked along one wall. At the other end was an exit ramp with a closed gate, meaning I wouldn't have gotten very far had I tried to run.

"What do you want with me?" I asked, holding my nerve and trying my hardest not to let this asshole intimidate me.

"Perhaps you'd like to be a bit more comfortable while we discuss our situation?" Kai replied politely as if we were about to discuss the sale of a fucking car or something.

There were times in my life when I had a brain to mouth malfunction. My brain wanted to say one thing, my mouth went off on its own accord.

Growing up, it sometimes got me in trouble at school, both with teachers and other kids. You would have thought I'd learned to curtail it by now, but nope.

It was precisely this moment when my brain and mouth decided not to work together. My brain was telling me to go willingly, comply with the hot psychopath, and whatever was about to happen may not be as bad.

But my mouth had other ideas.

"Get fucked, Wolfe, I'm not going anywhere with you."

If looks could kill, the gorgeous man in front of me would be dead from the venomous look I was shooting his way. But clearly, looks didn't kill, and all I achieved was smirks and chuckles from the men standing in front of me.

Patronizing assholes.

"Oh, Riley, sweetheart. We are going to have a lot of fun together," Kai said with a wink.

A motherfucking wink!

Before I could respond, he nodded to the man with the dirty blond hair.

"Hendrix, do the honors, will you? Take Ms. Bennett to the guest room."

The man with the blond hair, Hendrix, shot me an evil grin before lunging toward me. A piercing scream left me, even though it was damn well pointless, and the second he laid his hands on me, I fought as hard as I could. But he was too strong, and within seconds he overpowered me.

For the second time in what I assumed was an hour, I found myself slung over the shoulder of a dickhead who thought it was perfectly okay to manhandle women. He trapped my legs with a powerful arm, turned, and started walking away.

My immediate reaction was to pound his back, the same way I had pounded Kai when he first threw me over his shoulder, but what was the point? He was hardly going to put me down and say I had hurt him and I was free to go on my way.

I was helpless, and it was a feeling I did not fucking like.

From the moment I made the decision to run away with Angel when I was sixteen, I had been in control of every aspect of my life, until this point. But in a blink of an eye, it had been stripped away.

I raised my head to look at Kai as Hendrix carried me through the car park. I met his eye and held his gaze, refusing to look away and glaring daggers at him right until the point where Hendrix walked through a door.

Just as the door started to close, and before I lost sight of Kai, I raised my middle finger and flipped him off.

His laugh echoed through the car park, reaching my ears and adding fuel to the rage burning through me.

Kai Wolfe could go to hell.

With blood pumping in my ears, I took calming breaths to clear the chaos racing through my head. I would need a clear head if I was going to go up against Kai Wolfe and walk away in one piece with my sanity intact.

Chapter 8

Riley

Panic like I had never known before hit me the second Hendrix stepped into an elevator, the doors closing and leaving me trapped in the metal box with him, and him alone.

Call me crazy, but as much as Kai had taken me against my will, thrown me in the trunk of a car, and then ordered his man to take me to the guest bedroom, I hadn't actually felt unsafe with Kai.

Yep, crazy, I know.

But in the elevator with Hendrix, I *did* feel unsafe.

Maybe it was the way one of his hands was gripping my thighs, hovering just below my ass. Or maybe it was the creepy way he'd smiled at me before throwing me over his shoulder, but there was something unsettling about him, and I did not like it one bit.

He didn't talk as the elevator rose to wherever the fuck we were going, which suited me fine.

Funnily enough, I wasn't in the mood to make small chit-chat.

The elevator took *forever* to get to where we were going, giving me an opportunity to come up with a game plan.

Which, right now, was pretty nonexistent.

I mean, what exactly could I do?

Firstly, I was in an elevator with no way out, and before I could even consider getting out of the elevator, I'd have to find a way of getting free from the hold the oaf had on me. Then I'd have to find a way to incapacitate him before breaking out, scaling down the elevator shaft, finding my way out of the building I was in, and then somehow making it back to East Bay, all without getting caught by Kai fucking Wolfe or one of his merry men.

That plan seemed like one even John McClane would struggle with and this was my actual life, not fucking *Die Hard*.

Finally, the elevator came to a stop and the doors slid open. Hendrix took long strides and I bounced on his shoulder from how fast he walked, which only added to the nausea swimming in my belly.

Not being able to see where we were going, I tried to make a mental note of the path he took, just in case an opportunity arose where I could escape, but trying to do that upside down was almost impossible, not to mention the place was like a fucking maze.

I managed to catch glimpses of rooms as we passed through. It seemed every room was surrounded by floor-to-ceiling windows, and the entire floor was made of black and silver marble floors that sparkled from the rows of spotlights up on the ceiling.

As Hendrix took me through one room, the living room I presumed from the *huge* sofa in the middle of it, I caught a peep out of the window. Wherever we were, we were high up, like *really* high up. Hollows Bay stretched out for miles, lit up by a million lights. Even in my predicament, I could appreciate the beauty of the scenery.

The living room opened up into a grand foyer, but Hendrix didn't stop. He took the stairs that were also made of the same black and silver marble, and marched up them with ease, not at all fazed by the weight of a human draped over his shoulder.

When we reached the top, Hendrix continued along a hallway until he stopped outside a door, and a nervous anticipation coursed through me as a horrible thought popped into my mind.

What if I was being taken to Kai Wolfe's sex dungeon?

From the difficult angle I was at, I managed to turn my head enough to watch him use the pad of his thumb on a scanner to open the door. He strolled inside, tossed me on a bed, and sped out before I had a chance to get my ass up off the bed, still without saying a word.

Fucking coward.

The door closed, and instantly, a click echoed around the room indicating the lock had been engaged. I ran to the door and tried the handle, frustrated when it didn't budge an inch.

"Let me out of here, you asshole!" I shrieked as I pounded on the door.

I'm not sure what I expected by making a racket, it wasn't as if Kai was going to stroll in here and tell me this had been a prank and I was free to go. Still, I thumped and kicked the door for a good few minutes. When I eventually stopped, I put my ear to the door to listen but all I was met with was the sound of silence.

It was at that moment I noticed another fingerprint scanner next to the door, just like the one on the other side Hendrix had used to open the door.

I knew full well putting my thumb against the scanner wouldn't miraculously open the door, but I tried anyway. Unsurprisingly, the blasted thing beeped angrily at me, but that was the only sound, no clicks of the lock disengaging.

Resigned to my fate, I sank to the floor and leaned back against the solid barrier stopping me from leaving this room.

There were no two ways about it, I wasn't going anywhere until Kai decided I could.

Unease swam through me as I wondered just what the hell he wanted from me. Hot tears welled in my eyes but I refused to let them fall. I was exhausted, both physically and emotionally. Dancing all night always took its toll on my body, not to mention the extra shifts I'd been picking up thanks to that slacker Blaze. Add to that the shit I'd experienced after leaving work, I felt like I could sleep for a week.

Taking a deep, calming breath, I let my eyes roam around the room that was now my prison cell, relief flooding me when I realized it was a bedroom and *not* a sex dungeon.

As cells went, I couldn't complain. Not that I'd ever been in a real prison cell, but you know, compared to what they show on tv.

For starters, it was a huge room, easily twice, if not three times the size of my entire apartment. The walls were a crisp white, but on the far side of the room opposite the door I was slumped against, a thick black curtain ran from one end of the room to the other. It didn't make the room dark though thanks to the dazzling spotlights in the ceiling.

An enormous bed dominated the middle of the room which was covered in black silk bedding, and a mammoth flatscreen television hung on the wall in a prime position to lay in bed and watch it.

Fucking rich people.

At the foot of the bed was a beautiful ornate chaise lounge. Before I knew it, I was off the floor and reaching out to stroke the silver velvet, the material softer than anything I had touched in my life. I stood for a minute stroking the arm of the chair, completely hypnotized by the feel of the material against my palm.

Near the door stood a sleek, shiny black dressing table, with a large oval mirror sitting in the middle. Around the frame of the mirror were small lights adding to the brightness of the room. The table was next to a small alcove that stood empty as if something was missing, like a pot plant or another small table. But I didn't give it much thought as curiosity got the better of me and I whipped open the black curtain.

I gasped at the sight.

This room also had floor-to-ceiling windows and looked out over the city. It was easy to see from here that I was at least twenty floors up, if not higher. I wasn't particularly scared of heights, yet fear crept up my spine at the realization there really was no way out of this room unless I wanted to plummet to my death.

I had yet to decide if death was preferable over facing the king of Hollows Bay.

Another door grabbed my attention and I marched across the room before yanking it open in hopes it might be another way out.

Of course, it wasn't.

The room opened into a large dressing room which was surrounded by empty wardrobes and shelves. A long mirror was in the corner of the room, next to which stood another door that was slightly ajar.

Seriously, this place never seemed to end.

Once again, I pushed open the door to see what was behind it and was relieved to find a bathroom.

Like the bedroom, this room was gorgeous too, completely covered in tiles of different shades of gold, browns, and creams which shimmered from the gold chandelier hanging from the ceiling.

There was a double sink with a large mirror hanging above it, and the toilet was next to the sink. At the end of the room stood a double walk-in shower, complete with a huge waterfall showerhead hanging from the center.

If I was going to be here for a while, at least I'd be comfortable.

I made the most of the bathroom, doing my business and washing my hands before splashing some water on my face. Exhausted, I made my way back into the main bedroom and collapsed on the bed, not bothering to take my shoes off because I had zero intention of laying there for long, and I certainly wasn't going to go to sleep.

The bed was *unbelievably* soft, almost like I was lying on a bed of feathers. Even though I had just bought new beds for Angel and me, they were nowhere near as comfortable as this bed.

The thought of Angel sleeping home alone sent a pang of guilt through my chest. She was going to wake up in a few hours and be all alone. I knew she'd panic and worry about where I was and there wasn't a damn thing I could do about it. Guilt turned to anger at Kai fucking Wolfe and the audacity of the man who thought he could take whatever he wanted, consequences be damned.

A string of curses escaped from my mouth as thoughts of what I'd like to do to that man churned in my head, mainly involving castration without anesthetic.

Those thoughts circled around and around until exhaustion took over, and as much as I tried to fight it, I drifted off to sleep.

I don't know what woke me, but I must have been sleeping for a few hours because when I next opened my eyes, the sun was beginning to rise outside and shining into the room. It took a minute to remember where I was, my bedroom didn't have any windows so I was never woken by the sun, and then everything from the night before poured into my head.

I sat up on the bed and rubbed a hand over my face, trying to wipe the sleep from my eyes, before letting out the biggest scream when I saw the figure sitting at the end of the bed.

"Holy hell, you scared the shit out of me," I said to Kai when I realized who it was. My hand shook as I clutched my chest, my heart pounding hard against my rib cage. I was sure the bastard could hear it beating.

"My apologies, Riley, I didn't mean to scare you," he replied with a chuckle.

"If you didn't mean to scare me, why the fuck were you watching me sleep?" I bit back angrily because that's what he'd been doing.

The weirdo was relaxed back on the chaise lounge as if he'd been there for *hours*. His smart shirt was crinkled and untucked, he'd undone another button, the start of a black tattoo creeping up his neck on display, and he had crossed one long leg over the other, much like he had done on the night I had danced for him.

He had a tumbler in his hand which had a small drop of clear liquid in it. Kai drained the glass, and I couldn't help but stare when his tongue popped out of his mouth and he licked his lips.

I may have hated him, but there was no denying just how fucking hot he was.

Dammit.

"I was merely waiting for you to wake up," he replied after a pause.

My eyes snapped back to his, guilt flashing through me at being caught staring at his mouth.

I glared at him, waiting for him to tell me what he wanted but he didn't speak again, just stared at me as if he was examining every inch of my face and committing it to memory.

Nerves fluttered low down in my belly under his intense stare until I couldn't take it any longer. I cleared my throat in preparation to ask the million-dollar question.

"What do you want with me, Kai? You can't keep me here. I have a life." I tried to keep my voice steady, to show bravery that I was not feeling.

"It's not much of a life from what I've observed." His tone wasn't unkind, yet he still managed to rile me up the wrong way.

"What the hell is that supposed to mean?" I snapped, glaring daggers at him.

"Only that you work your cute ass off for pittance when you deserve so much more," he replied, raising a brow.

It was said without a hint of pity or patronization, knocking some of the wind from my sails.

I certainly didn't dwell on the fact he said I had a cute ass. Definitely not. Fine. Maybe a little.

But this conversation wasn't getting me anywhere. I needed to get the hell out of here, there was still time to get home before Angel woke up. I briefly closed my eyes and let out a long sigh, trying not to let frustration get the better of me.

"Kai, please, I need to get back to-" I stopped myself before I mentioned my sister. I did *not* want this man to know anything about her. "I need to get back to home and work."

"You want to get back to Angel?" His lip twitched into a smirk as my mouth dropped open.

Fuck.

"How do you know about my sister?" It came out as a whisper, shock clearly stopping me from flipping my lid.

"I know everything there is to know about you, Riley Alyssa Bennett."

I don't know what possessed me, perhaps it was the anger that oozed through my veins at the mention of my sister's name, but before I had time to comprehend what I was doing, I was off the bed, and launching myself at Kai.

"You motherfucker!" I cursed as I aimed my nails toward his face.

I didn't get a chance to land a single finger on the man. He moved quickly, launching himself off the chaise lounge, grabbing me, and throwing me back on the bed before pinning me down with his body. Which, by the way, was rock-fucking-solid.

He held my wrists together above my head in one of his large hands, while he used the other arm to hold himself up so that he was hovering above me. His face was mere inches away from mine, and from being this close to him I saw tiny flecks of gold in his black eyes.

Kai managed to maneuver himself between my legs, and despite being furious with the asshole, I noted a definite hardness pressed against my core.

It should not have made me clench with need, it really should not have. But it did.

"Riley, calm the fuck down. I don't want to hurt you or your sister," he said soothingly, his breath warm against my skin, along with the faint smell of vodka.

"Then what do you want with me?" Tears pricked at the back of my eyes, but I'd be damned if I was going to cry in front of the bastard.

He held me for a few seconds, gazing straight into my eyes, my heart pounding even harder than it was when I first woke up.

For a brief second, fear started to course through me. Fear he would force himself on me.

What was more worrying was, I wasn't totally against the idea of it.

Abruptly, he released my hands and sat back up. I scrambled away from him, pulling myself up against the headboard and bringing my knees up to my chest as if they could offer me some kind of protection against the deranged man.

"I have a proposition for you," he said, ignoring my little outburst and suddenly growing serious.

"What kind of proposition?" I asked before I could stop myself, certain it wouldn't be anything good.

"I want you to be my personal assistant, and in return, I'll provide Angel with a private tutor and pay for her cochlear implant."

Well, knock me down with a fucking feather.

Chapter 9

Kai

Her gorgeous mouth dropped open to form a round 'O,' and I couldn't help the image flashing through my mind of what it would be like to shove my dick in those fucking plump lips.

I tore my eyes away from her mouth to try and stop my throbbing cock from getting harder than it already was. It would have been so easy to take her when I had her pinned down underneath me, but I'd never had to force myself on a woman, and I didn't intend on starting now, especially with the one woman I actually wanted for more than just a quick fuck.

Riley gaped at me, a million questions running through her head. I'd shocked her, whether it was with my job offer or the fact I knew so much about her and her sister's life, I didn't know.

I gave her a minute to compose herself, using the opportunity to take in her gorgeous features.

She had a cute heart-shaped face, with gorgeous big brown eyes, the color of melted chocolate, framed by perfectly sculpted eyebrows. Being this close to her, I could see the light spattering of freckles across her button nose.

I'd stared at her photos over and over again but they did not compare to the real deal.

I was fucking *obsessed* with the girl sitting in front of me.

Her long chestnut hair was messy from where she'd been sleeping, when I first came into her room, her hair was fanned out across the pillow. I'd watched her sleep for two hours, nursing my glass of neat vodka so I didn't have to leave her for a moment to get a refill.

Was I a creep for watching her?

Maybe, but I didn't give a fuck.

My Star was a vision of beauty.

"H-how do you know all of that?" she finally responded and stretched her legs out in front of her, her chest hidden under a gray jumper that swamped her. Her clothes had seen better days, the sleeves were frayed, and the color faded. If she agreed to my offer then one of the first things I'd be doing is getting her some new clothes.

"I told you, I know everything about you."

She glared at me then before opening her mouth to reply but I held out a hand stopping her from speaking.

"Look, Riley, let's not fuck around. You know who I am and what I'm capable of." It wasn't a question, yet she nodded her response, confirming she knew exactly who I was. "Good, then you'll know if I want to find information about someone, I have the means to."

"Why me?" she whispered, all her vulnerability shining through.

She acted tough, and she gave as good as she got, but the reality of it was that underneath the façade, she was an insecure young woman, probably still trying to process the abandonment of her parents, desperately trying to keep things together for the sake of her sister, and completely unaware as to how damn stunning she was.

"From the moment I laid eyes on you, Riley, you intrigued me."

That was all she was getting for now. I'd eventually let on just how fucking obsessed with her I was, but not now. I didn't want to scare her off even though kidnapping her had probably done exactly that.

She didn't reply, merely gazed at me intently, waiting for more.

"I want to show you something which might help you to make up your mind."

I stood from the bed and held my hand out to her. She hesitated, indecision marring her features, but slowly, she reached up and took my hand. I helped her off the bed and then dropped her hand as I walked across the room.

Grabbing the bag I had brought with me, I turned back to Riley and held it out to her. "Here."

"What is it?" she asked cautiously, eyeing the bag as if I was handing her a bomb that could go off at any minute.

"It's a change of clothes. Unless you want to carry on stinking like rotten food?" I replied with a raised brow.

She looked as though she was going to tell me where to go, but then her eyes dropped to her body, and on realizing she had dirty stains all down her, she sighed and took the bag.

"Thank you," she muttered, before disappearing into the walk-in wardrobe to change.

When she appeared moments later in a clean shirt and jeans, I used my thumb on the scanner to unlock it and the locks quickly disengaged. I pulled it open but turned when I realized Riley wasn't behind me, but standing with her hands on her hips, glowering at me.

She really was cute when she was pissed, and it took all of my control not to chuckle at her.

"Was it necessary to lock me in?" she grumbled.

"I didn't want you going anywhere until we had a chance to talk."

She glared back at me, looking as though all she wanted to do was fly across the room and bury her tiny foot into my balls.

After a few tense seconds passed between us, she sighed loudly and dropped her hands from her hips, waving one of them across her body to indicate she was ready to go.

I opened the door and stepped out into the hallway with her close behind me, the scent of her wrapping around me. It was a smell I could get used to, strawberries and sunscreen, and I wanted to both eat her up and rub her all over my body.

The penthouse apartment I called home was spread out over three floors, and I had designed it myself. It was in the perfect location, right in the middle of the city, and the floor-to-ceiling windows around the entire apartment allowed me to look over my city from every angle.

I really was the King of Hollows Bay.

Riley was silent as we made our way down the hall to our destination. I stole glances at her from the corner of my eye, her eyes were wide and curious as she took in my apartment.

Aside from my father, I had never felt the need to impress anyone, but right now, I found myself hoping Riley was impressed with where I called home. It was worlds away from where she had lived these last few years, and if my plan worked, she wouldn't be going back to that world.

And if my plan didn't work, I would find another way to make her mine.

We reached the room I was aiming for, and again, using my thumb on the scanner I unlocked the door. Pulling it open, I stepped aside to allow her to enter first. She raised a brow, giving me a quizzical look, but when I didn't say anything, she went inside, immediately gasping at the sight of her sister fast asleep in bed.

And then she did something I knew was coming, but allowed to happen anyway because quite frankly, I did deserve it.

She drew her hand back before reaching up to slap me with all of her strength across my face.

It barely stung.

"You fucking bastard!" she hissed, tears welling in her eyes. I knew it would upset her, that she'd fear the worst, but I had to get her to see what possibilities were open to her if she took me up on my offer, and the only way of doing that was getting Angel here. Otherwise, Riley would have scurried back home and not given my proposal a second thought.

She raised her hand again as if to hit me a second time, but I would only ever allow one free shot at me, and she was lucky I had allowed that.

No one *ever* hit me and lived to tell the tale.

I grabbed her hands and pulled her to me, holding her tight against my body so she couldn't move. She was so tiny against my broad body.

"She's safer here than she ever was at the dump you call home. Do you have any idea how easy it was for my men to go in there, drug her, and bring her back here without anyone noticing?" I whispered calmly in her ear.

She let out a sob, and it pained me right through my motherfucking cold heart, but I wouldn't let it show.

"I hate you, Kai Wolfe, why are you doing this to us?" she sobbed, fat tears rolling down her cheeks, thick and fast.

I dropped her hands and instead took her chin between my thumb and forefinger, tilting her head up so she had no choice but to look at me. Her beautiful brown eyes were filled with tears, and I wanted to do nothing but kiss them away.

"Listen to me, Riley, if you don't want to take me up on my offer, I'll let you and Angel go now and I won't ever see you again." I was lying of course, but she didn't need to know that.

She opened her mouth to reply but I quickly silenced her, needing to get the next part out so she wouldn't have time to take me up on the offer of leaving.

"But consider this. Your sister could have a good education, I'll get her the best damn teacher money can buy, and I'll pay for her to go to the finest college and university if that's what you want for her. I have the contact details for the best audiologist in the States, and I'll pay for her treatment. Angel could have the life you've only ever dreamed about giving her."

Her brows pulled up in surprise, and yet again her jaw hit the floor.

She blinked several times, seemingly trying to process what I had just said. I stared down at her, letting her see the truth in my face. Letting her know that despite being a callous bastard, everything I had offered to her would be delivered.

So long as she accepted.

"Why?" she whispered.

I couldn't stop myself, I reached up and swiped away a tear that had been rolling down her cheek.

I should have said something like, *'Because I can,'* or, *'Because money really can buy anything,'* but staring into those big brown eyes, I couldn't be anything but honest.

"Because you deserve the world, Star."

Her eyes widened at my candor before drifting to my mouth and I wondered if she was waiting for me to kiss her.

And fuck, did I want to.

But now was not the time.

Coming to her senses, she stepped back and out of my embrace. It took all of my willpower to let her move out of my touch, I wasn't used to playing this kind of game.

If I wanted something, I took it.

And I never had to bribe a woman to fuck me, they usually threw themselves at me. Not that I was bribing Riley to fuck me, I wanted so much more from her than just her cunt, but being patient and waiting for her to grow to want me was going to test my resolve.

She turned to look at the still form of her sister who was sleeping soundly, oblivious to the turmoil going on around her.

"What did you give her?" Riley asked as she turned back to face me. The tears had stopped, for now at least.

"A sleeping sedative. It was a small dose and will wear off in an hour or so, she'll be fine. She was asleep when my men broke in, and she stayed asleep when they administered it. She has no idea what happened to her."

She raised her hand again and for a second I thought she was going to try and slap me again but instead, she sighed and scrubbed her hand down her face.

"Riley-" I started, but she held up a hand, silencing me.

I didn't allow many people to do that, or rather most people knew better than to try and silence me. If she agreed to my offer, she'd learn.

But for now, I kept quiet.

Riley walked over to Angel and leaned over her sister who was snuggled under the covers, and smoothed a hand down her face. Angel didn't stir, her breathing didn't change, she just slumbered on.

After a minute or two of gazing lovingly at her sister, Riley stood back up with a determined look on her face, and I knew I had her.

She folded her arms, gone was the weepy girl who had stood before me moments ago. Now stood Riley the protector, fiercely courageous when it came to doing *whatever* she had to for the sake of her sister.

"What exactly would I have to do as your *personal assistant* if I was to accept?"

She sneered the words describing the job title I had offered her as if disbelieving it was a real job. She was perceptive, I'd give her that. Of course the job was made up, I didn't need some fucking secretary to manage my appointments, it was nothing more than a way of getting Riley to be by my side every day.

"Whatever I ask you to do," I stated simply, shrugging my shoulders.

"That's a bit ambiguous, don't you think?" she challenged with a raised eyebrow.

God, I loved how she didn't give a fuck about questioning me. It made me want to take her over my knee and spank the shit out of her, and drop to my knees and worship at her feet in equal measures.

No one ever challenged me, even Theo when he had been alive, and I found myself enjoying it.

"Not really, it's simple." I cleared my throat and tried to focus on the matter at hand, not the image of Riley over my knee with her juicy ass exposed and red from my palm. "I ask you to do something, you do it."

"And what if I don't want to do it?"

"Riley, if you agree to my terms, that's it. There is no gray area, you will do what I ask, when I ask." I used the tone of voice I used in most business meetings, my no-room-for-arguments tone. "But if you refuse, there will be consequences, I'll make that very clear now."

Slowly, she moved away from the side of the bed and came to stand in front of me, the cogs turning in her head, weighing up the risks of my proposal versus the life her sister could have.

I won't lie, I felt like a royal prick for making her choose. I could have easily paid for all the things I had promised for Angel. I could have taken my time to get to know Riley the right way, dated her, and made her fall for me the way people do in normal relationships, but that wasn't me. I didn't date and do all that romance bullshit.

I was Kai Wolfe, and I did things *my* way.

"Before you make a decision, you need to know the full terms of the deal," I said.

She raised an eyebrow in question. "Go on."

"If you agree, you and Angel will live here with me. She will be cared for by my staff and you will get to see her only when I permit." I didn't want to stop Riley from spending time with her sister, but I was a selfish cunt and I wanted her attention on me as often as possible.

Her nostrils flared in anger, and once again, before she had the opportunity to speak, I silenced her with a raised hand.

"As I've already said, you will do whatever it is I ask of you, whenever I ask of you without any question or hesitation. You will give up your job in that godforsaken club, and you will not leave this place without my permission or without one of my men assigned to you. If you agree, you and Angel will have everything taken care of. You will never need to worry about money or where your next meal is coming from again."

She didn't blink once during my speech, but I caught the tick in her jaw that told me she was struggling to keep her anger in check. Anger, I suspected at the fact she wanted to accept the deal but was not happy with the terms.

"And how long will I have to work for you?" she gritted out through clenched teeth. I wanted to say indefinitely, but if my plan worked, by the time her 'contract' with me was up, she'd be firmly by my side, and in my bed, and she wouldn't be going anywhere.

"Six months."

Six measly months to make her mine. I was certain I would need less than a month before I had her falling for my charms.

Did that make me a cocky prick?

Absolutely.

Did I give a shit?

Not in the slightest.

The cogs continued turning in her mind, weighing up the pros and cons of my offer. She knew it was a life-changing opportunity but something was holding her back, something stopping her from jumping in head first like I'd hoped she would.

"What's stopping you, Riley? What's stopping you from giving your sister the world?" It was a cheap shot, and we both knew it.

Her gaze hardened as she stared at me. "I don't trust you. You want me to do whatever you ask of me, whenever you ask of me? I can't agree with that. For all I know, you could order me to put a bullet through some unsuspecting person's head. I'm not like you, Kai, I'm not a murderer."

It would have been foolish of me to expect her trust straight away, trust always took time to build, and if I was honest, I had only ever trusted Theo implicitly.

The rest of my men, nope.

Don't get me wrong, I trusted Danny, Miles, and Hendrix but even with them, I didn't keep them in the knowledge of every element of my business.

Could I learn to trust Riley to the same degree I had trusted Theo? Only time would tell.

"Riley, you will come to learn I am a man of my word. No matter the consequences. I give you my word, I won't order you to kill anyone," I said reassuringly because if that was all it took for her to agree to the deal, it was an easy win for me.

Her eyes narrowed at me, and silence encased us for several seconds while I waited for her to tell me the next thing she wouldn't do.

But it never came.

"Can you promise me Angel will be safe here?" she asked quietly.

"You have my word."

She looked over her shoulder once more at the sleeping form of her sister, and as she stared, she let out a resigned sigh, her shoulders slumping in defeat.

Turning back to face me, she bravely held my eyes as she softly spoke her next words, resignation heavy in her tone.

"In that case, I agree to your terms."

It occurred to me then that Riley had ample opportunity to tell me I couldn't put my hands on her if I demanded to. That I couldn't order her to her knees in the middle of Hollows Bay and tell her to suck my dick until I came down her throat.

But she hadn't.

A mistake on her part?

Or did the thought of me touching her, tasting her, *fucking her,* excite her as much as it excited me?

My lips curled into a sly smile as the thought of all the ways I'd fuck her sprung to my mind.

Silly, silly Star.

Chapter 10

Riley

I must have had a brain to mouth malfunction again because my head wanted to tell Kai to go fuck himself but my mouth had other ideas.

"In that case, I agree to your terms."

I think he was as surprised as I was, but how could I turn down the offer to give Angel the best possible life?

And it was for six months.

One hundred and eighty-two days.

That was all I had to get through to make this happen. I'd never be able to forgive myself if I walked away from a once in a lifetime opportunity like this. I tried not to dwell on all the things I'd be required to do during that time, there was no point fretting about it now.

Kai's lips turned up into the most wicked smile I had ever seen on a man, sending a shiver of fear down my spine and made me want to rewind the clock and take back my words of agreement.

Terrifying did not sum up just how scary this man was.

"Seal the deal, Riley," he said smugly as he offered his hand to me.

This was it, there would be no going back after this. I peeked over at my sleeping sister once more, just to remind myself of what was at stake.

Seeing her fast asleep and remembering Kai's words about how easy it was for his men to take her, I knew without a shadow of a doubt I was doing the right thing. Angel needed to get as far as fucking possible from Hollows Bay, and this was going to be a step in that direction. He was offering her a life I'd never be able to give her, no matter how hard I tried.

Summoning up as much bravery as I could muster, I reached out and took Kai's hand. His large, cold hand wrapped around my tiny one and he gave it a firm but quick shake. Butterflies stirred deep in my belly as a strange feeling washed over me, one of fear mixed with morbid curiosity.

"I'll let you spend some time with Angel to explain things while I get everything organized. Her tutor will start tomorrow." His tone was all business, his face void of any emotion.

As he turned to walk towards the door, my fists clenched. His comment of *'letting me spend some time with her'* sent waves of anger through me and I almost told him to shove his deal where the sun doesn't shine.

But it was too late, the deal had been struck. He said he was a man of his word, and until he proved otherwise, I would be a woman of *my* word.

Best get fucking used to this.

Besides, I'd been through some shit over the years. Surviving six months with Kai Wolfe was going to be hard, but I'd get through it one way or another.

Whether I'd walk away unscathed was yet to be seen.

"One of my staff will bring you both some food, I imagine you're starving," Kai said.

I hadn't really thought about food until then, I was used to going days without much sustenance, but now he had mentioned it, I was suddenly ravenous.

I didn't reply, just watched as he used his thumbprint to unlock the door and walk out without giving me so much as a backward glance.

The second the door shut and the tension evaporated from the room, I let out an enormous sigh. My whole body had been tense throughout our conversation, but now he was gone, I unclenched, leaving behind a dull ache in my muscles.

I made my way over to Angel's sleeping form and lay down beside her so I was facing her. I don't know how much time passed as I lay staring at my sister, just looking at her face.

She was the spitting image of me, with the same straight chestnut brown hair, long lashes that fanned under high cheekbones as she slept, and pouty lips, all traits we'd inherited from our mom. The only difference between us was our noses. Mine was small, round, and slightly flat, the same as my father's, whereas hers was longer but upturned, a trait she didn't get from either parent.

I barely blinked as I lay there watching her breathing in and out, all manner of thoughts about what the fuck had happened running through my head.

A soft knock on the door caught my attention, and I dragged my eyes away from Angel to the door and sat up, just in time to see it open and a woman walk into the room carrying a tray of delicious smelling food.

The woman appeared to be in her mid-50s, she was a small lady, her mousey-brown hair tied into a tight bun on her head, and she wore a black shirt and pants. I felt like a bitch for thinking it but there was nothing remarkable about her, a face that would disappear into the background.

"Excuse the intrusion, Ms. Bennett, My name is Jacqueline, and I'm going to be your maid. Mr. Wolfe wanted me to bring you some food."

She placed the tray on a table and then scurried off with her head down before I even had a chance to thank her or object to her being my maid. I didn't need someone to look after me, I was more than capable of doing that myself.

I swear my sister had a sixth sense when it came to food, that girl could smell a cake baking from ten miles away and sniff out the exact oven it was baking in.

Minutes before the woman dropped the food off, Angel showed no signs of waking up for another few hours, yet the second the aroma of crispy bacon and eggs filled the air, her eyes flew open and she sat bolt upright in bed, looking around manically for the source.

It must have only taken her a few seconds to realize she was not home in bed where she had gone to sleep, and panic filled her face. I gently placed my hand on her arm to capture her attention, and relief flooded her eyes when she saw I was next to her.

'*Don't panic, you are safe,*' I signed to her.

'*What's going on? Where are we?*' she signed back, eyes still roaming around the room and taking in her surroundings.

Her room was pretty damn nice, slightly smaller than mine but the décor was the same. The only difference with her room was that there were two doors leading off the main room as opposed to one. I figured she had a separate bathroom and walk-in wardrobe.

'*We are going to be staying with a friend of mine for a bit. He's going to take care of us, there is nothing to worry about.*'

It was an outright lie but I hadn't quite figured out what I was going to tell her. There was no way I'd be telling her the truth of the matter. Kid was only eleven for fuck sake, she shouldn't have to worry about bullshit like this.

Angel shrugged, not fazed by what I had told her, and why should she? I hadn't done her wrong in her whole life, she trusted me without question. I only hoped this wouldn't come back to bite me on the ass.

'*Is that bacon?*' she signed before pointing to the tray on the side.

Fucking typical. While I was doing my best to not spiral into a world of panic, she was thinking about bacon. I couldn't help but smile though, this girl was my world, and I would have done *anything* to keep her safe and give her the life I wanted her to have.

I hopped off the bed and strode over to the tray where a number of plates under dish covers sat, Angel following closely behind me. The pair of us whipped off the lids and then shared a delighted grin at all the mouth-watering food that had been brought to us. For once in our lives, we weren't going to go hungry.

The next couple of hours passed in bliss. Angel and I devoured our breakfast, eating every last scrap on the plates, and then spent some time exploring her room.

It transpired she did have a walk-in wardrobe that led into the bathroom, behind the second door was her own personal lounge area, equipped with the biggest plasma television we'd ever seen. Angel begged me to get her game console from our apartment, and I promised her I would, all the while worrying what I'd have to do for Kai in order to get it. I was beginning to learn that nothing came for free with him.

She'd been unhappy about the personal tutor and didn't understand why she couldn't carry on going to her usual school, but I told her if she did well and paid attention, then the nice man who was looking after us would pay for her cochlear implant.

Seems I'd already learned a lesson in blackmail from Kai.

A knock on the door interrupted us from our hysterical laughter. We'd been jumping on the bed to see who could bounce the highest, not giving a shit if it caused any damage to the furniture.

I didn't pay for it, so fuck it.

"Come in," I called through laughter, even as my stomach plummeted.

Angel and I stopped jumping on the bed and stared in unison as the door opened. I was expecting Kai to walk in so was surprised when the woman who had brought us breakfast, Jacqueline, entered the room.

I stepped down from the bed, but Angel stayed where she was, no doubt hoping our game would continue the moment the woman left again.

The poor woman barely looked at me as she spoke, instead keeping her eyes on the marble floor. "Pardon the interruption, Ms. Bennett, but Mr. Wolfe has asked for you to join him. He asks that you say goodbye to your sister as you will be required elsewhere for the coming days."

The good mood I had been enjoying only moments ago fucked right off, and a feeling of trepidation and regret crept over me.

I looked at Angel who was still standing on the bed, her smile too was nowhere to be seen, and it didn't take a genius to know that she had lip-read what Jacqueline said.

'*Where are you going?*' she signed, and my heart split down the middle.

I didn't know when I'd be allowed to see Angel again, and I didn't know how either of us would cope with that. Not a day had passed since leaving home nearly five years ago where we hadn't seen each other. I had a feeling our separation was going to be harder than any damn thing Kai was going to make me do, and suddenly six months felt like an eternity.

I stepped back and took Angel's hand, gently pulling her down and sitting her on the bed. Letting go of her hand, I tried my hardest to keep my emotions in check so the perceptive little bugger wouldn't be able to see how much my heart was cracking.

'*I've got to go and do some work for the man who is looking after us, but you'll be safe here, and anything you need, I'll make sure you get it.*'

Fear flicked across Angel's face, and so I pulled her into a hug, wrapping my arms around her and holding her tight, not knowing when I would get to do this again.

'I have a bad feeling,' Angel signed, pulling out of my grasp. Her eyes darted over to where Jacqueline stood awkwardly by the door, and when they came back to me, my heart broke even more as they filled with water.

Angel rarely cried, in fact, I couldn't remember the last time I had seen her cry. Not even when she came home from school covered in cuts and bruises where nasty little bullies had pushed her around.

'Sweetheart, there is nothing to worry about. I promise you, no one will hurt you.' I tried to allay her concerns, but I knew I was doing a bad job of it.

'No, I have a bad feeling for you. I'm scared for you.'

I gave her a small smile, not wanting to lie to her because if I was totally honest, I was more than a little scared something bad *was* going to happen to me. But no matter how scared I was, I wouldn't let Angel know.

'You have nothing to worry about, I'll be fine. I'll see you again in a few days, and I want to hear all about how well you are doing with your new tutor.'

A lump formed in my throat, and I was glad for once that Angel was deaf. She wouldn't have been able to hear the choked emotions in my voice if I said the words aloud. I forced my lips into a reassuring smile and Angel returned a fake smile of her own.

"Ms. Bennett, apologies but we really need to go now, Mr. Wolfe is waiting," Jacqueline said with an ounce of fear in her voice.

I wanted to tell her to fuck off and not be so impatient, but I knew it wasn't her fault.

Damn Kai Wolfe. Damn him to hell.

I leaned down and kissed Angel on the forehead. *'I'll see you soon sweetheart,'* I signed and gave her one last smile. I turned away as the first tear slid down her cheek, and at that very moment, I felt like the worst sister in the world.

I knew what I was doing was going to give her a life I could never give her ordinarily, but that made it no easier to walk away from her.

Jacqueline used her thumb on the electronic pad to open the door. It was a little reminder that even if I decided to flee in the dead of the night, there was no way I was getting out of this apartment without help. She pulled the door open and held it for me to step out into the hallway.

I took one last look at Angel, whose cheeks were now streaked with tears, and it took all of my strength to not run back into her room, grab her, and take her as far away from here as possible.

I was well aware I had agreed to this deal with Kai, and that I wouldn't walk away from it.

But right now, I hated the man with everything I had.

Chapter 11

Kai

The camera in Angel's new room gave me a front row seat of Riley interacting with her sister. It was clear just how much she doted on the little girl, and being the cunt I was, new ideas sprung to mind as to how I could manipulate Riley to do *whatever* I wanted her to do by using Angel as a bartering tool.

I couldn't believe how quickly and how much food the two girls ate. Both of their faces lit up like a Christmas tree at the food that was placed in front of them, and they scoffed the lot.

I knew what Riley earned from working in Club Sin as Isaac had also provided me with her bank accounts. There were some months when she barely covered her bills. Knowing how much Riley put her sister first, I imagined that in those months when money was tight, her priority was to keep Angel fed over herself.

At least now they were living under my roof, they wouldn't go without, and if Riley did want to leave after our six month agreement, I would just remind her of what Angel's life was like when they lived in that shithole apartment they called home.

A knock on the door drew my attention away from the video feed, and I called for whoever was outside to come in, but I didn't take my eyes off the screen.

"Boss," Danny said as he came into my office and sat down in the chair in front of my glass desk.

Danny was one hell of a crazy son-of-a-bitch, the scar on his cheek was proof of that. He'd given himself it years ago, back when he first came to work for the organization, and had decided he wanted to make himself look even scarier than he already did. I'll never forget the day I found him in a bathroom, staring into a mirror as he cut his cheek, blood trickling down his face as he stood there laughing like a hyena.

Reluctantly, I looked away from the screen as Riley and Angel started exploring the room.

"So she's staying then?" Danny asked as he looked at the screen, a knowing grin on his face. Fucker had been taking the piss out of my infatuation with Riley for the last week, he was lucky he was one of my closest associates and could get away with it.

Otherwise, he would have had a bullet in his brain by now.

"What do you know?" I ignored his question and glared at him expectantly, hoping he had a damn good reason for taking my attention away from my girl. He sighed and leaned forward.

"There's no cop in Hollows Bay by the name of Anderson. Either Blaze gave you shit intel or the cunt she claims told her gave her a fake name," he explained, his voice gruff. Danny sounded like he smoked 40 cigarettes a day, which was ironic because the man was vehemently against smoking.

"She wasn't lying," I told him confidently as Blaze's bloody body popped into my mind.

Surprisingly, it had taken longer than I thought it would to extract the information from Blaze. She had screamed like a banshee as I used the pliers to rip her fingernails out, followed by her toenails, but it hadn't been enough to make her squeal. She was probably able to tolerate it because of the amount of drugs she had swimming through her veins.

It was when bones started breaking she eventually caved and gave me the information I needed. I was one hundred percent certain she had been truthful.

"Maybe he wasn't even a cop after all," Danny added unhelpfully.

The truth was, we had no idea who the man was that Blaze had got her information from, he was like a goddamn ghost. She claimed she'd been entertaining a man who had been going to the club for a few weeks and had taken a shine to her.

On one occasion when she'd been sucking his dick, he'd taken a phone call, answering it as 'Detective Anderson' and Blaze had overheard him discussing the murder of someone whose throat had been slit and their body left at the docks. Blaze said she could only hear bits of the conversation but had distinctly heard the man on the end of the phone claim responsibility for the kill. The conversation ended with the Detective saying their plan was moving in the right direction.

Blaze said she didn't give the conversation much thought until several days later when news of Theo's murder broke. It hadn't taken her long to realize the cop she was blowing had been talking about Theo Wolfe, and in her drug-addled state, she and her dealer concocted a half-witted plan to try to blackmail me.

Fucking laughable.

They thought they were being smart, telling me they had information on Theo's murder which they would share in exchange for $100,000, which undoubtedly, they'd blow on crack. The morons didn't consider for one second that as soon as I heard they had information, I'd extract it from them without paying a single cent for it.

They had learned the hard way.

"Did you speak to Griffin and get a list of all cops in the state?" I asked.

Victor Griffin was the Chief of Police in Hollows Bay. He was also one hell of a corrupt motherfucker. Fortunately for me, that meant he was well and truly in *my* pocket.

I mean, he had little choice in the matter after I discovered his secret interest in male escorts, young ones at that, and I didn't think Mrs. Griffin would have been too thrilled about it.

"He gave me a list of cops in the city but said it would take him longer to get the list for everyone in the state. I dunno, Boss, something was off about him, he was acting all kinds of shady."

Danny was right, Griffin had been avoiding my calls this past week.

I'd been trying to track him down all week since Blaze had given me the nugget of information about Detective Anderson, but he hadn't answered my calls and hadn't returned them either. In the end, I'd instructed Danny and Hendrix to pay him a personal visit.

The Chief was playing a dangerous game.

"I think it's about time I paid Chief Griffin a little visit. Remind him who pays his second wage," I said out loud, more to myself than to Danny. He hummed his agreement.

"What about the whore? You think she could give any more intel now she's had a few days off the gear?" Danny asked.

As much as I'd wanted to end Blaze, I decided it would be prudent to keep her alive until I could confirm her information. As much as I believed what she had said, I also wasn't going to rely completely on the word of a crackhead.

She'd been locked in the warehouse for the last week going cold turkey which I'm sure had *not* been fun for her. I was also hoping that once she sobered up, she could shed some more information on the mysterious detective.

A little part of me hadn't wanted to kill her either because of her association with Riley. The two worked together, and from everything Isaac told me about Riley, her only friends were the girls she worked with. If using Angel as bait hadn't lured Riley in, Blaze was a backup plan. But now I had my girl right where I wanted her, if Blaze had nothing left to give me, there was only one thing left to do with the bitch.

"Leave her to me." Time had run out for Blaze.

Danny smirked but he didn't make to leave, and I realized he seemed tense.

"What else?" I growled, a feeling growing in my gut that whatever he was about to say was going to piss me off. Sure enough, a flash of concern washed over his face. I waited as he let out a frustrated sigh.

"There's been some rumblings on the street. Some of the workers are restless about Theo's killer not being found, and Little Nicky being able to pilfer from the warehouse for as long as he did yet still managed to walk away with his life. There's murmurings that you are starting to lose focus," he replied almost like it pained him to tell me.

I understood why. My mood could be unpredictable, and news like this was bound to turn my mood sour. I stared at Danny as my brain repeated the words he'd just said.

I knew I had been distracted since meeting Riley, but that was only a week ago, Theo had been dead for nearly three months. Of course I'd been fucking distracted from focusing my *full* attention on running the organization. Theo wasn't just my brother, he was my best friend, and the only person I trusted with my life. I lost a part of myself the night he died.

I hadn't grieved for my brother, nor would I. Death was inevitable in our lives, especially with as many enemies as we had. Instead, I focused my attention on trying to find the cunt who killed Theo, and I had vowed to leave no stone unturned to do so, but every trail I had followed so far had led to a dead end.

It was fucking infuriating.

Despite hunting the murdering fucker, I had still been overseeing my businesses. Drugs were still being shipped in from my contacts in South America and being pumped out onto the streets quicker than ever. My weapons factory was running smoothly, and the legitimate businesses I had a hand in were consistently turning over a profit. To me, that didn't look like I had lost focus on the organization.

My employees, whether criminal or legit, were loyal to me, and I rewarded them well for their continued loyalty and service. I made sure they had roofs above their heads, food in their bellies, and weapons to protect themselves. They got a fair wage for their services but more importantly, they were under my protection and no one dared fuck with them.

Except me.

They knew the consequences if they tried to fuck me over, or at least I thought they did. Perhaps keeping Nicky alive and sending him back out on the streets with both hands missing wasn't a message enough.

I ground my teeth together and felt the tension in my jaw. My crew had it good, for fuck sake, but if they wanted to tip the apple cart, then so fucking be it. Maybe a timely reminder to show who was in charge wasn't necessarily a bad thing.

"Well then, I guess we need to show them that my focus is exactly where the fuck it needs to be," I said to Danny and watched as a malicious grin spread over his face.

Danny was just as brutal as me when it came to dealing with cunts who didn't play by my rules. In fact, sometimes he was more savage. That's why he was my head enforcer. He had a whole team who worked directly for him but everyone knew if Danny paid you a personal visit, you wouldn't live to tell the tale. Nor would your family.

"Conroy fucked up letting Nicky into the gang and not watching him properly. He knows he is responsible for every member of the crew he hires, and this is the second time he has fucked up," I said to Danny, reminding him of the time several years ago when Conroy allowed a younger member of the gang to be robbed for the stash of cocaine he'd been carrying.

He had only managed to redeem himself by finding the prick who had done the robbery, getting the stash back, and blowing both the robber and his gang member's brains out before I had been made aware. He'd been on warning ever since, and although years had passed and Conroy hadn't fucked up since, I had a long memory, and I only ever allowed one mistake to be made.

Sometimes not even one.

"I've heard rumors that his second is making a name for himself. A chap called Ernie," Danny replied and finally relaxed back into his chair, the tension no longer plaguing him. "I've seen him at a couple of meetings. He's got a good head on his shoulders and is an avid supporter of yours even though he has never met you. Apparently, his dad used to work for your dad so there is family loyalty."

I nodded my head, considering the next move. I liked having people work for me where there was a family history. They would have been brought up knowing that the Wolfe family ran Hollows Bay, and if you wanted to get anywhere in life, working for my organization was the way to go.

"Bring Conroy in, and tell Ernie he has earned himself a promotion," I said to Danny as I stood from my chair. I didn't need to say what needed to be done with Conroy, Danny would know what to do with the man, and

I trusted him to make it as painful as possible. "I want the word out that if anyone dares question my focus, they will find themselves in my basement dealing with me."

Danny's face contorted into a wicked grin, and I knew he'd be taking great pleasure in bringing Conroy to meet his fate. He'd never been a fan of the man.

"I also need someone to bring Jane Timpson in." I scribbled an address down on a post-it note and handed it to Danny.

He raised an eyebrow, giving me a confused look. "Who the fuck is she?"

"She's going to be the kids' new tutor," I told him as we both stood, ready to go about our business for the day.

Jane was the only teacher in the city who could fluently sign American sign language. She also had a shit load of debt which she was incurring on a daily basis, trying to pay for a top end care home for her mother who had been diagnosed with dementia. A debt that would be paid when she started working for me.

"And does this chick know she's coming in?" Danny asked, the amusement back in his voice.

"What do you think?" I replied, returning his smirk. His laughter followed him out of the door, and I couldn't help but let out my own chuckle.

Sometimes it was fucking awesome being the King of this city.

Chapter 12

Riley

"We have something to attend to," Kai said after the maid disappeared back down the hallway we had come from. I didn't reply, just stared blankly at him, trying my damned hardest to keep my emotions in check.

My heart was hurting like nothing I had ever felt before at having to say goodbye to Angel, not knowing when I would see her again, and I kept trying to remind myself of why I had agreed to this preposterous agreement.

To give Angel a better life.

But walking away from her, I wasn't so sure about my decision now.

The elevator dinged behind Kai, and he motioned for me to get inside. I kept my head down and walked past him, refusing to acknowledge how fucking handsome he looked. He was the devil dressed in a designer suit, and he knew it.

When he left me in Angel's room earlier, he had ditched the suit jacket and tie, and the top buttons of his shirt had been undone, he almost looked casual. Now though, he was back to his intense business look. His shirt was immaculate, his dark blue tie was perfectly straight and tucked underneath his matching blue waistcoat. Over the top, he had his tailored suit jacket back on. His whole outfit clung to every part of his sculpted body, and it was easy to imagine women throwing themselves at him.

For some inexplicable reason, a twinge of jealousy rolled through me at the thought of him being with other women, but I quickly shut that down. That was not a road I was willing to travel down.

As soon as the doors to the elevator closed behind us, his masculine scent wrapped around me. It was *intoxicating*. Not that I'd ever admit it to him.

"Did you explain everything to Angel?" he said as the elevator started gliding down smoothly.

"Yes." I avoided his heated stare which was burning into the side of my face, my cheeks heating, but I still refused to look at him.

"Good. If you behave yourself, you can see her again in a few days."

Rage swirled deep in the pit of my gut as I finally swung my gaze to meet his.

"If I behave myself? I'm not a fucking child, Kai," I sneered and instantly regretted the words leaving my mouth when his eyes hardened and a menacing look crossed his face, one that scared the absolute shit out of me. He took a step toward me, and I took one step back, my back hitting the wall of the elevator. Kai placed both hands on the wall behind me, caging me in. His nostrils flared in anger and his eyes narrowed on me. Never in my life had I felt like a little mouse caught in a trap, until now.

"I will say this once and once only, Riley," he snarled. "You knew the terms of the deal when you agreed to them. You work for me now, and I expect my employees to speak to me with respect. I will not have you acting like a stroppy child now reality is sinking in."

I glared back at him, not letting him see just how frightened I was. I hadn't decided if I thought Kai was going to hurt me, I believed every single one of the rumors I'd heard of Kai and his brother's hobbies of torture and murder, but something deep down inside of me said Kai wasn't going to hurt me.

Not intentionally anyway. Why would he make the deal we had if he was just going to hurt me?

But there was something about this asshole that made me want to press every single one of his buttons just to see how he would react. Someone needed to show him not everyone would bow down and kiss his ass when he demanded it, and I was only too happy to be that person.

What can I say? I was a dumbass at times.

"Respect isn't just given, Kai, you have to earn it." In my defense, he never said anything about respecting him when he made the terms of his deal.

I didn't have time to react to the movement of his hand which swiftly wrapped around my throat as he pinned me against the wall. He didn't grip me hard, certainly not enough to leave a mark or cut off my breath, but enough of a grip to let me know he was in charge.

Like this was going to earn my respect.

Prick.

"Do not test me, Riley. I am not someone you want to push," he hissed in my ear. "You will show me respect or you are going to find yourself over my knee with my hand tanning your fine ass before you even realize what's going on."

I should have been scared of his threat, should have apologized for my outburst and begged for his forgiveness. But I didn't.

Like I said, dumbass at times.

What was a surprise though, was the fact I *wasn't* scared, but turned the fuck on at the thought of him bending me over his knee and spanking me. Clearly, it'd had the same effect on him given how his eyes filled with unadulterated lust.

For once in my life, I managed to stop the snide remark from leaving my mouth before it did. I wanted to tell him to go fuck himself, instead, I kept my lips sealed.

We glared at each other for a moment, and it was only the ding of the elevator and the doors sliding open that drew our attention away. He let go of my throat and instead grabbed my hand, dragging me out of the elevator, and through the basement car park where the man who had driven me here earlier waited with the back door of a sleek black SUV standing open.

"The docks, Frank," Kai growled as he roughly shoved me into the back of the car.

I climbed in and scrambled to the other side, wanting to get as far away from the asshole as possible. To my horror, he got in next to me and slammed the door shut, locking us both in the back of the vehicle. Rage rolled off him, his knuckles clenched in a fist. I'll admit to feeling slightly smug that I'd successfully pissed him off as much as he'd done to me.

The car pulled out of the underground basement and started weaving through traffic. I stared out of the window, watching as the city passed by.

Now that it was daylight, and I wasn't locked in the trunk, for which I was grateful for, I took the opportunity to soak in the sights of West Bay.

It was a world away from the shithole where I had spent the last five years. The streets were lined with little boutique café's, designer shops, posh hotels, and even a casino. There wasn't a smidgen of graffiti or litter to be seen anywhere, and the people walking the streets looked smart, the men in tailored suits and carrying briefcases, and the women tottering around in high heels and designer dresses. There was absolutely no sign of any homeless kids begging for money on street corners.

The roads were full of traffic, commuters no doubt making their way to the office buildings that towered over the city. Every single car on the road must have cost a fortune, *Ferraris, Porsches, Jaguars*, cars I'd only ever heard about. From the brief glimpse I'd seen as I was dragged through the basement car park, I bet Kai owned at least one model of each of the brands.

We must have been driving for about ten minutes, or rather, sitting in traffic, before boredom kicked in. I was getting fed up with watching the rich and privileged going about their lives when I knew that just a few miles down the road, good people were struggling to make ends meet and having to resort to all kinds of shit to put food on the table.

Every so often, I could feel Kai's intense stare on me, and it seemed the longer I ignored him, the more annoyed he became.

"Where are we going?" I asked, eventually allowing curiosity to get the better of me. I looked over my shoulder to see him give me a smug look like he was pleased I was the one who had conceded to our little game of who could stay silent the longest.

He shifted in his seat so he could face me but I kept my body turned towards the door, not wanting to get drawn into him.

I didn't expect the next words that came out of his mouth.

"Did you know my brother was murdered a few months ago?"

I hadn't known Kai long but it was the first time I had heard him speak with a tinge of emotion in his voice as opposed to his usual arrogance.

"No," I replied honestly, now turning in my seat and blinking up at him. "No, I didn't. I'm sorry."

I don't know why people say sorry when they find out someone's loved one had died. It wasn't as if it was my fault his brother had been killed, and yet it felt like the right thing to say.

Kai stared at me for a beat, and for a split second, he almost looked *vulnerable*, almost as if it was taking him a whole load of effort to not let a tear fall for his dead brother. It was the first time he was showing real, raw emotion, and despite my current hatred towards him, I couldn't help but soften.

Losing someone was hard, and from the rumors I'd heard about the Wolfe brothers, it sounded like they were close. I couldn't bear to think of what it would be like to lose Angel.

Anguish was written all over his handsome face, if only for a brief moment, but it was enough for me to see that under all his bullshit and bravado, he was grieving for his brother.

The monster was human after all.

"How did it happen?" I asked tentatively.

He inhaled deeply and his eyes hardened once more, the moment of real emotion hidden under the walls Kai had built around himself.

"He went out one night without his usual entourage of security. He didn't come home and I made the mistake of assuming he'd hooked up with some whore. But he was found the next day down at the docks with his throat slit." Kai looked down at his hands briefly and I followed his gaze. His hands had curled into fists, his knuckles turning white.

I had the sudden urge to reach out and take one of his hands but I resisted. I hated this bastard, no matter what grief he was feeling, I had to remember that I hated him.

"Do you know who did it?" I asked and immediately regretted the words that had left my mouth when Kai's head snapped back up, a look of pure fury etched on his face. I flinched in my seat. "Sorry, I didn't mean to pry," I whispered.

He unclenched his fists and took another deep breath, attempting to calm himself down.

I'd just hit a nerve.

"No. It's almost like a ghost appeared one night, did the deed, and disappeared again. I've tried every fucking avenue to find the cunt who killed him but the trail is stone cold dead, just like Theo," he growled, his eyes darkening with raw need to avenge his brother's death.

I could sympathize with Kai. If the shoe was on the other foot, I would do whatever it took to find Angel's killer, and I would take great pleasure in ending their life. I guess the difference between Kai and I is that I would happily spend my life behind bars knowing her murderer was rotting in hell. Kai though, he'd never spend a day behind bars, he'd make it all go away and carry on ruling this city like the king he believed he was.

I stayed quiet for a minute, processing what Kai had said. I genuinely hadn't known Theo Wolfe had been murdered, I didn't exactly make it my business to know the ins and outs of the Wolfe brother's lives, and I didn't go out of my way to find out the gossip on people I had no intention of ever meeting.

Sure, in the club the girls always gossiped about what they were told or what they'd overheard, but I paid little attention. I didn't go to work to gossip, I worked to support Angel.

"You never said where we were going," I said, realizing Kai hadn't answered my initial question.

"You'll see," he replied cryptically as he pulled his phone out of his jacket pocket and started tapping away at the screen, dismissing me from the conversation.

Eventually, we made it out of the city, and it took another twenty minutes to arrive at the dock. Kai and I didn't speak again, which suited me fine. I had nothing to say to the man, and I certainly had no intention of making idle chit-chat with him so he could get to know me.

The docks were located on the outskirts of West Bay, almost bordering East Bay. They didn't appear to be in use, there were no boats docked, no persons around, and derelict buildings stood empty with smashed windows and broken doors.

When the car came to a stop outside one of the buildings, Kai got out and offered me his hand. His anger which had been evident during the car journey had started waning, and not wanting to rile him up again, I took his hand, ignoring the jolt of electricity that shot up my arm the second our palms touched.

He led me to a door that was opened by the douchebag who had carried me up to my room back at the apartment, Hendrix I think.

"Boss. Ms. Bennett." He nodded his greeting as we walked past him and into the empty warehouse.

I didn't have time to take in my surroundings, Kai walked us through the warehouse floor and over to another door that led down a set of stairs. As we descended, our footsteps echoed in the corridor, and an ominous feeling grew in my belly about where we were going and what in the world was going to happen next.

I didn't have to wait long. Kai stopped at a door that had a fingerprint pad on the outside, much like he had in his apartment. As soon as he placed his thumb on the pad, the locks disengaged.

"After you," Kai said and motioned for me to enter. I hesitated for a moment, not knowing what fresh hell I was about to face, after all the last time he let me into a room first, my sister was fast asleep on the bed.

Kai moved his hand to my lower back and gave me a gentle push. Reluctantly, I stepped into the room.

"Leandra!" My eyes widened in surprise at the sight of my colleague tied to a chair in the middle of the room. To say she looked fucking *awful* would be putting it mildly.

She was wearing the same clothes I'd last seen her in, a crop top and tiny shorts, and her pale skin was covered in dark, angry bruises all over her body. Her head lolled to one side, but upon hearing me, she managed to look up.

It was evident her nose was broken from the crooked angle it sat at and the black bruises around her eyes. Her hands were tied behind her back and my stomach churned when I took in her bare feet and the blood that caked them from where she was missing toenails. From the blood pooling underneath her hands, I guessed she was missing her fingernails as well.

To top it off, her collarbone was at a funny angle, and it didn't take a genius to figure out it was dislocated.

"Riley?" she croaked as recognition dawned on her face.

"What the fuck did you do to her?" I spun around to face Kai who was glaring at Leandra, looking like he was seconds away from finishing her off.

"Don't have any sympathy for her, Riley, your friend Blaze here knows who killed my brother," Kai said, his voice filled with pure and utter hatred.

What the actual fuck was happening right now?

Why did he think she knew anything about Theo's murder?

Questions kept circling in my brain as I tried to take in the scene in front of me. This at least explained where she'd been this past week.

"I've told you everything I know!" Leandra choked out in despair. Her voice was scratchy, and her lips were cracked from dryness. I wondered when the last time she had something to drink was.

"Fuck, Kai, can she at least have some water?" I asked as I took several steps towards her. I was not Leandra's biggest fan, far from it, but she did not deserve to be treated like this.

No one deserved to be treated like this.

Kai considered my request for a few seconds before nodding his head to Hendrix who had followed us into the room. Hendrix disappeared back into the corridor but returned quickly with a bottle of water in hand. He unscrewed the lid and then stood over Leandra as he poured some of the liquid into her mouth.

She gulped it down, or at least as much as she could. Hendrix poured the water too fast, practically waterboarding her. The water spilled out of her mouth, onto her chin, and down her chest. I never thought I'd feel sorry for Leandra, yet here I was, feeling sympathy for the woman who had been a complete bitch to me.

"What the hell are you doing here, Riley?" she asked, her throat seemingly less croaky, but still sounding as if she could do with a gallon of water before her voice would be anywhere near normal again. Drops of water trickled down her chin and I reached out and wiped her mouth with the palm of my hand. I don't know why, it seemed like a decent thing to do.

"I made a deal with the devil," I whispered to her, not loud enough for Kai to hear.

For a second she looked horrified, and then she burst into laughter. Wicked laughter aimed at my expense. Funnily enough, the sympathy I had for her somewhat waned.

"You stupid bitch, you're so fucked," she gasped through laughter. "You always were a stupid cunt."

Before I had a chance to say anything, Kai strode into the middle of the room and smacked Leandra square across the face with the back of his hand. The slap echoed around the room as her head fell to one side, and her laughter immediately stopped.

"Do not fucking talk to her like that," he roared.

Okay, so I don't condone violence against women, but did the fact Kai standing up for me do all sorts of funny things to my insides?

Yes, yes it fucking did.

"Kai, don't," I warned, somewhat half-heartedly. Warned him against what though, I'm not sure.

Of course, he ignored me.

"You fed me a load of bullshit, Blaze," he sneered and then launched at her, wrapping his big hand around her throat. His hand squeezed her delicate neck and her eyes widened in fear. Within seconds, her lips started turning blue, and her whole body shook in the chair she was tied to.

I froze in the spot I was standing in, this was the real Kai. The one I'd heard rumors about, and I understood in an instant why people were scared of him. I would have to remember this moment the next time I sassed him, remind myself what he was truly capable of.

"I told you the truth," Leandra wheezed when Kai let up on his grip a little.

I was sure if her hands weren't tied behind the chair she was sitting in, she'd be doing her best to pry his big hands off her. Her panicked eyes found mine, and it was enough to snap me back into the here and now.

"Kai, what in the ever-loving fuck is going on right now?" I practically screamed in order to draw his attention away from the woman he seemed intent on killing.

His head turned in my direction and thankfully, he released his grip. Leandra sucked in huge gulps of air in between sobs.

"This bitch and her smack dealer thought they could blackmail me with bullshit information about who killed Theo," he growled.

If I thought he had seemed mad when we were in the car earlier, it was nothing to how he was now. So terrifying, I was pretty sure my knees would start knocking together any minute.

"What are you talking about?" I choked out past the terror gripping me. Kai straightened himself, and marched over to me, getting right up into my face. I couldn't help but flinch at his anger now being directed at me.

"Her crack dealer showed up at my nightclub one night claiming he knew who killed Theo. Claimed he would tell me everything I needed to know for the right sum of money," Kai spat.

I looked back at Leandra, tears sliding down her puffy cheeks. She at least had the good graces to look remorseful, although I suspected that was because she was currently fearing for her life.

"How does she fit into all of this?" I wasn't sure I wanted to hear the answer but my brain was struggling to comprehend what the hell was happening.

"Her crack dealer knew fuck all. She on the other hand-" he pointed to Leandra, "She knew. Or at least her dealer said she did. He told me Blaze had the information, and the pair of them concocted a plan to blackmail me into getting the information from them."

Fuck me.

Leandra was an idiot and her brain was drugged up half the time, but seriously? She thought it was a good idea to try to blackmail the craziest motherfucker in the city.

She really was the biggest dumbass I'd had the misfortune of knowing.

"I told you what I knew," she sobbed loudly as tears and snot streaked down her face. Kai turned back to face her, and I hated myself for admitting it, but I was glad his anger was focused back on her instead of me.

"Bullshit. There's no cop by the name of Anderson in Hollows Bay. You fed me shit, Blaze, and I don't tolerate being lied to."

"It's true!" She howled before turning her tear stained face to me. "Riley, you remember him. He was the one that showed up every day for like three weeks and insisted on only me dancing for him."

Oh, shit.

I knew exactly who Leandra was talking about. There was a dude who showed up in the club one night looking like he had the weight of the world on his shoulders. There was nothing distinctive about him, he was just like any other dirty Bertie the club attracted.

Leandra had pounced on him the moment he had sat his ass down and had pawed at him for the entire night, she had a way of sniffing out those who were at their lowest. It was a total cringe-fest to watch, but he ate her attention up like a starved man, and then after that, he came back every single night for three weeks.

She harped on and on about how much money he was paying her, and he had zero interest in any of the other girls. He'd come in every single night and request Blaze dance for him. And then one night, he just stopped coming to the club, vanished into thin air.

Kai turned his beady eyes on me and a malicious smile grew on his face.

"You know who she's talking about?" he asked.

I slowly nodded, wondering what this meant for Leandra. This couldn't be good for her, surely she would realize this meant Kai no longer had a need for her.

"I don't know who he is as such, I mean I couldn't tell you his name or anything," I clarified, hoping to throw Leandra a lifeline. "Who is he?" I asked her, but it was Kai who answered.

"She said he was a detective in Hollows Bay. She was being a good little whore and sucking his dick when she overheard him on the phone talking to the cunt who killed Theo. Apparently, he gave his name as Anderson. But there is no cop with that name."

"He must have lied about his name, but I swear to you, he said he was a cop. He even showed me his badge. Please believe me!" Leandra cried.

"Oh, I do believe you, Blaze. But you see, if my girl over there-" Kai pointed to me before continuing, and the blood drained from my face. "If she knows who you are talking about, then I don't have a need for your drug-addled ass anymore."

It was as I had feared. The next second, Kai pulled out a gun from the back of his waistband and aimed it at Leandra's head. She gasped and her eyes widened in alarm.

I didn't think before acting. I couldn't stand Leandra, that much was true, but did I want to see her brains splattered everywhere?

Absolutely not.

Before Kai had a chance to cock the weapon, I jumped in front of Leandra, putting myself in the way of her and Kai's bullet.

Yep, dumbass. I know.

"Wait, you can't kill her," I squeaked and held my hands up as if trying to placate the madman holding the gun.

Kai narrowed his eyes at me, and I had a horrible feeling that before the end of this long-ass day, there was every chance I may just end up being put over his knee.

"And why the fuck not? She tried to blackmail me, Riley. No one does that and lives to tell the tale."

Had I wondered what Kai had done to Leandra's dealer, I would have just had my answer.

"She's told you everything she knows. Please, Kai, let her go," I said as boldly as I could muster.

He stared at me like I was a mouse and he was a snake, ready to enjoy his next meal. My heart was beating so damn hard I'm sure everyone in the room could hear it. But I held my ground, and his gaze.

After what seemed like an eternity, Kai lowered his gun, and I felt a moment of relief.

I should have known it would be short lived.

"What's it worth, Riley? What does her life mean to you?" Smugness crept across his face, and I knew then I had played right into his manipulative hands.

The absolute fucking bastard.

"Wh-what do you mean?" I stuttered.

"You know how this works, nothing in life comes for free. You want to save this bitch's life, you tell me what you are willing to offer in exchange."

For about the twentieth time in less than twelve hours, I wanted to ram my knee into Kai Wolfe's junk.

"You're kidding, right? Is it not enough that you've got me at your beck and call for six damn months?" My shrill voice echoed around the room.

"It'll never be enough when it comes to you, Riley," he replied softly, almost *romantically*. I glared back at him, a million and one insults on the tip of my tongue ready to throw at him.

"What more could you possibly want from me, Kai?" I whispered, the feeling of dread growing to epic proportions in my belly.

From the corner of my eye, I could see Leandra hanging on to every word that was being said, after all, her life depended on what would happen next, it was in her interest to hear what was going on.

"I want a night with you, Riley. One night whenever I choose, to do all the things I've been dreaming of to that tight little body." His heated eyes roamed the length of my body and I felt it all the way to my core.

Ho-ly. Fuck.

"Oh jeez, I'm fucked then. No way is Riley the prude going to open her legs for you," Leandra snorted.

I rounded on the bitch.

"If I were you I'd be groveling at my goddamn feet. Your life depends on my answer, Blaze, and let's not pretend for one second that I actually like you," I sneered at her, an overwhelming desire to wrap *my* hands around her throat for her stupidity.

Seriously, you'd think she'd be offering to follow me around for all eternity, licking the shit off my shoe in exchange for saving her life. I turned my furious glare back to Kai.

"You. You're an absolute bastard, and you are going straight to the pits of hell," I spat, needing him to feel my wrath. He took a step forward so that his chest brushed against mine, but I held my stance, refusing to be intimidated by him.

"Oh, sweetheart, I've had a one-way ticket to hell booked since the day I was born. I may as well enjoy the trip," he said with a wink.

He lifted his hand again, aiming the gun directly at Leandra's forehead but keeping his eyes on me.

"What's it to be, Star?" he said, and this time, he cocked the trigger.

I looked from him to Leandra, realization *finally* dawning on her at just how much trouble she was in. Her eyes were wide, pleading for me to save her life.

She wasn't my friend, in fact, she'd gone out of her way to be a pain in my ass from the minute I'd met her. But did I hate her enough to see her life snuffed out?

The alternative was spending a night with Kai fucking Wolfe, letting him do whatever he wanted to my body.

Fucking hell.

Chapter 13

Kai

Riley was silent the entire way home. I didn't bother to talk to her, I knew I wouldn't get anywhere with her. She was fuming, which was putting it mildly.

I hadn't planned to offer the deal, and if I was honest, I don't really know what possessed me. I'd never needed to bribe a girl into having sex with me before, I had a number of whores on my phone who would drop everything they were doing to come over and let me do whatever the fuck I wanted to them.

But Riley, she was the only one I *actually* wanted, and right now, she hated me.

The only conclusion I could come to as to why I made the offer was out of sheer desperation. Desperation from her being in my head for a week and not being any closer to getting my dick inside her.

One thing was for sure though, I wasn't going to force myself on her. I fucking *despised* rapists. Call me a criminal with a moral compass or whatever, but if I had my way, I'd castrate every fucker who ever forced themselves on a woman.

That said, I wasn't convinced Riley *didn't* want me. I'd seen the lust reflected on her face when I told her I would put her over my knee and spank her. I'd seen how her pulse sped up when I was near her, and I'd caught her eyes roaming over my body several times since she'd been in my company.

Perhaps this deal was a good thing. Riley's head told her she needed to hate me, but her body behaved in the opposite way. Perhaps she just needed a little shove in the right direction to get her head and her body on the same page. She didn't need to know I wouldn't actually go as far as forcing myself on her.

Traffic back to my penthouse was lighter, and it wasn't long until we pulled into the underground car park. Once we were parked and Frank opened my door, I stepped out and offered my hand to Riley, but the stubborn little thing slid out of the car and stomped past me without my assistance. She marched her *very* cute ass over to the elevator, and I followed with thoughts of all the things I'd like to do to her ass when I finally got the chance.

"She must have been a good friend," I said when the doors slid closed and the elevator started taking us up to the penthouse.

I didn't think for one second that was true. From watching Riley and Blaze interact in the warehouse, it was clear neither woman liked the other.

So why then had Riley agreed to the deal?

"That woman has never, nor will ever be my friend," Riley huffed, folding her arms across her chest but refusing to meet my gaze.

"Why did you agree to the deal then? Why not let me kill her?"

Now she turned to face me, piercing me with a venomous look. "Because I'm not like you, Kai. I can't just stand back and let someone be murdered for the sake of it."

"So you'd rather let me fuck you and violate you in ways you can only imagine, just to save the whore's life?"

I allowed myself to bathe in the smugness that washed through me when I noted Riley's reaction to my words. Her pupils dilated, her pulse point in her delicate neck thumped harder, and her breath caught.

Riley wanted me, she was just in denial.

It was her reaction that made my hand smash the emergency stop button, bringing the elevator to a halt. I had Riley pinned against the wall, her wrists gathered together and held in my hands between us, and my hips pressed against her. A small breathless whisper left her lips when I lowered my mouth to her ear.

"Or did you agree 'cos you liked the idea of all the things I could do to you? Did the thought of me fucking your cunt so hard you see stars make you agree?"

My tongue darted out and licked the curve of her jawline, trailing it down to the sensitive area of her neck, and causing a shudder to pass through her. The taste of her skin instantly went to my dick, which had already started to harden at her proximity. I thrust against her, my erection rubbing against her core, making her gasp.

Pulling back slightly so I could see her face, I knew she was at war with herself. She hated that she wanted me so much, but she did. It was written all over her.

I chuckled, satisfied I'd proven a point to myself, but my chuckle only earned me a scowl from my beautiful Star.

But I still had one more point to prove.

"Tell me, Riley. If I were to shove my fingers into your tight cunt right now, would I find you dripping wet for me?"

The question seemed to snap her out of her lust filled haze, and her eyes narrowed in anger. Finding strength from somewhere, she yanked her arms out of my grasp and shoved me away. Her attempt was pathetic, but I took a step back anyway. I was sure I had proved my point, she had realized how wet she was for me.

"Fuck you, Kai, you're deluded if you think I want you. I hate you, you are a fucking parasite, and I bet your brother is glad he is dead so he doesn't have to deal with your shit anymore."

She pushed past me, striding to the emergency button where she hit it with her fist, and the elevator started to rise again. My smugness at winning our little game immediately evaporated at her words.

How dare she bring Theo into this. She was fucking lucky I didn't drag her back by her hair, spin her around, and fuck both her cunt and ass in this elevator while she screamed my name and begged me to stop.

As soon as the doors slid open, Jacqueline was waiting.

"Take Riley to her room. She is to stay there for the rest of the night," I growled, struggling to keep my temper in check. Without a word, Riley followed the maid, disappearing down the hallway that would take her to her room and out of my sight.

Later that evening, I found myself in the VIP section of Sapphire. My mood had gone from bad to worse as the day progressed. Riley's words echoed in my head, and I had to get out of the apartment before I took my anger out on her. It wasn't just what she said about Theo, but it was her denial.

She fucking wanted me, she was just too damn stubborn to admit it to herself.

What was so fucking spectacular about Riley that made me obsess about every inch of her? Maybe I needed to fuck another girl to get it out of my system. I hadn't been near or by a pussy since I saw Riley dance a week ago. Perhaps that was foolish of me. Perhaps I should have gone straight to Sapphire, picked one of the whores there and spent the night balls deep in her to help me get over my Riley fascination. I convinced myself that all I needed to get over my obsession was blowing my load in another woman.

Thankfully, the majority of people could tell I was in a foul mood and gave me a wide berth. I was scanning the girls who were walking around in tiny bikinis, trying to pick out the one I wanted to hate fuck. I had the most beautiful girls working for me at the club, all of them could have easily passed for models.

Yet none of them compared to the girl who was back at my apartment, and not one of the girls in the club stirred my blood the way she did.

I downed my shot of vodka before nodding to the waitress, letting her know I wanted my glass refilled. She didn't hesitate, promptly coming to my side with the bottle of Grey Goose vodka and refilling my shot glass.

"Will that be all, Mr. Wolfe," she purred seductively in my ear as she bent over, flashing her pert tits. It did nothing but add to my already pissed off mood. I glared at her and that was enough for her to let out a little yelp before scuttling off to the other side of the bar where she turned her attention to Miles and Danny, who were shooting some pool.

The lounge was busy tonight, not only were Miles, Danny, and Hendrix all here enjoying themselves, there were a number of CEOs from my legitimate businesses mixing with the waitresses and getting steadily drunk. Only my most valued employees had access to this area, and the girls who worked this section made a killing each night by being the best hostesses money could buy. It was a privilege to work in this area, and I only employed the best of the best.

The VIP lounge was sectioned off from the main part of the club, it had its own private entrance and bar, and was on the second floor, overlooking the main stage and dance floor. Sapphire was for the elite of Hollows Bay, thousands of dollars were spent here on a nightly basis, and only the best brands of booze were served. Not to mention the best quality of cocaine that was sold by the bucket load.

I had owned the club for two years now, having transformed it from a run down bar to a buzzing, trendy nightclub. To even get access to the club, you had to be a member which meant paying a small fortune in membership fees. To gain access to the VIP area, you had to be recommended by an existing member. I was proud of the place, a project I had developed without Theo's help which now meant it was one of the few places I could go and not be haunted by memories of my brother.

But tonight, *nothing* was calming the burning rage coursing through my body. I threw the vodka down my throat again, relishing the burn it left behind, and I pulled out my phone from my jacket pocket. I tapped in my pin and loaded up the security app that would show me what Riley was doing. I was bordering on stalker, but I couldn't help myself.

The camera was hidden in Riley's bedroom, it was so tiny I knew she would never find it. The feed showed Riley standing in the walk-in closet, a look of awe on her beautiful face as she admired all the clothes and accessories that had been brought in while we were out. I'd spent an absolute fortune in practically every designer store in the city to make sure she would have everything she could have ever wanted and deserved.

I zoomed in on the camera but my heart sank when the look of awe turned into a scowl and she stomped out of the wardrobe, slamming the door behind her. It seemed I wouldn't be able to do anything right when it came to her.

I nodded for another shot and the waitress tottered back over, her hips swaying. She barely made eye contact as she bent over to fill my glass again. As she straightened up and went to walk away, I reached out and wrapped my hand around the bottle.

"Leave it," I growled, not looking at her.

She relinquished the bottle and went back to the other side of the bar where Danny and Miles were clearly playing much nicer with her than I was.

Putting the bottle down on the table, I closed the app that showed Riley now sitting cross-legged on her bed, deep in thought. I was about to put my phone away when I noticed the symbol indicating I had an email. Opening up the app, I found a new email from Isaac.

I'd completely forgotten I'd asked him to delve into why the name Joe Mason rang a bell with me, but the attachment to the email reminded me I'd asked him to look into the man who had helped Riley and Angel several months after arriving in Hollows Bay five years ago. I pulled up the attachment and scanned it, the dots joining in my head as to why I recognized the name.

Joe Mason was a fucking pedophile.

He'd been accused of using a number of his properties for the purposes of allowing dirty old bastards to fuck young girls. He'd been busted by the cops but around a week later, the fucker had a heart attack and died. The city officials had quickly brushed the allegations under the carpet because it meant they could claim ownership of his assets and sell them for a small fortune.

I remembered the bust because I had not long taken over the reins from my father, and when Theo and I had found out what had been going on under our noses, we both wanted to make examples of the dirty cunts who had been abusing the girls.

With the assistance of some police files, we found a handful of men and publicly executed them, it had not only shown that we wouldn't tolerate rapists in my city, it had gone a long way to show just how ruthless Theo and I were. The remaining monsters fled the city and truth be told, Theo and I became so caught up in establishing ourselves, we never gave the situation another thought.

Until now, that was.

I hoped to god that Riley hadn't been one of his victims. If I found out she had been, I was likely to dig up Mason's body and murder him all over again. I'd have to speak to her at some point about it, but it could wait. It wasn't like Mason would be able to hurt her now.

The email only added to my worsening mood, if that was even at all possible. So when Monica, one of the waitresses I had fucked several times swung herself onto my lap, it took all of my effort not to pull my gun out of the back of my waistband and shoot her in the head.

Monica was a pretty girl, pale skin, platinum blonde hair, and a figure to die for, but compared to my Star, she was nothing. She always wore bright red lipstick which usually turned me the fuck on, especially when her luscious red lips were wrapped around my cock, and I fucked her mouth so hard the bright lipstick would smear across her cheeks.

She was up for anything, and I mean *anything*. I'd had many good nights with Monica, maybe she was what I needed tonight. Maybe if I pounded her pussy, I wouldn't be so fucking hung up on Riley.

"Mr. Wolfe, I haven't seen you for a while," she said in a husky voice as she rubbed her hips against my groin, trying to elicit some sort of reaction from me.

I wrapped my arm around her, giving her bare thigh a squeeze. She beamed back at me as if I had hung the moon for her.

"I've been busy," I replied, moving my hand higher up her thigh until the tips of my fingers grazed the lace of her thong.

"You work too hard, Mr. Wolfe. You need to relax and let me take care of you," Monica whispered in my ear as her hand slid up my tie and started to loosen it. Her fingers pulled at the knot, and as she did, her tongue crept out of her mouth and licked her lips.

It did absolutely fuck all to get me going. My cock didn't stir like it would have done by now. In weeks gone by, I'd be hauling Monica down the corridor to my office and sinking my cock into her pretty pussy. Or her ass. But now, it felt like I was going through the motions, and there was not one single twitch of my cock for the woman on my lap.

For the first time since knowing Monica, I looked into her eyes. I mean, really looked, not just saw her. She had bright blue eyes and her pupils were blown. She was clearly on some shit, and while I didn't usually give a fuck, these were not the eyes that I wanted to be looking into.

Once she had managed to undo my tie and had unbuttoned the top two buttons of my shirt, she ran her finger gently along my collarbone. The touch of her fingers felt like my skin was being assaulted by a thousand needles, and I found myself hating her touch. Before I could stop myself, I grabbed her hand to stop her from touching me and her eyes widened in surprise. But then she smiled even wider.

"Oh, are we going to play rough tonight?" she leaned in and ran her tongue down my cheek. "I love it when you are rough."

I reacted quickly, shoving her off my lap and standing up out of my seat. She winced as she landed in a heap on the floor, her tits almost spilling out of the red lace bra they were stuffed into.

"What the fuck?" she sneered, forgetting who the fuck she was speaking to. I reached down and grabbed her arm before yanking her back to her feet. She instantly looked terrified, and rightly so.

"Get the fuck away from me," I hissed and pushed her away.

She wobbled on her heels and looked as though she was going to say something but remembered that she valued her job, and her life. Her bottom lip wobbled, but she quickly pulled herself together and stomped away, heading out the door to the VIP section, and down into the main club.

"Kai. You good?" Miles appeared at my shoulder, his brows furrowed in concern.

"I'm good." I brushed my hand down my shirt and pulled the tie off seeing as it was already undone, and threw it down onto the table. Glancing around the club, people were staring at me but the second they met my eyes, they got back to whatever it was they were doing.

People never saw me lose my cool. But Riley, *fuck,* she had gotten under my skin, and now I was losing all control of my emotions. I sat back in my seat and grabbed the vodka, pouring myself another shot and downing it before filling the glass again.

Miles cleared his throat before sitting down in the chair opposite me. He looked nervous, which wasn't an unusual trait for him.

Miles was a genius, he was my expert in all things tech, but he'd also been trained to the same level of combat that Theo and I had. He was smaller in build than me or what Theo had been, but it didn't stop him being just as lethal in a fight. In fact, he had an advantage by being a bit smaller, it meant he could move quicker. But even though he could kill a man with his bare hands, he always looked nervous.

"What's going on, Kai?" he asked tentatively.

It was on the tip of my tongue to tell him to fuck off and mind his own business, but looking at him across the table, it was almost as though Theo was sitting there.

Miles was mine and Theo's cousin but they had also been the best of friends, and had been born just a few weeks apart. Miles' father was my uncle, brother to my father. Uncle Brian had worked for my father, although the two of them didn't have a good relationship, and Brian hated that my father had stepped up to take the place of my grandfather after he was killed by a rival gang.

Brian was a complete bastard, bullying Miles for being into computers and geeky shit, he hadn't appreciated just what Miles could do with the right kit. But I watched him bloom over the years, watched his skills develop, and I always knew that when I took over from my father, he would have a place by my side.

Brian met his untimely death when he pushed Miles too far and Miles put a bullet in old Brian's brain. I'll never forget the look of relief that had been on Miles' face when his father's body hit the ground and his lifeless eyes had stared back up at us.

But since losing Theo, Miles had barely smiled. The two of them were thicker than thieves, and he'd taken Theo's death harder than what I did. He was so similar to Theo, not just in looks but in personality, it was often like Theo was still around, and on bad days, I actively went out of my way to avoid Miles because looking at him was too fucking hard.

I sighed and scrubbed a hand down my face. "Riley," I said, not needing to say anymore.

I hadn't told my boys about Riley until a couple of days after I first met her. Hendrix and Danny had ripped the piss out of me, calling me a pussy for being whipped by a girl. I wouldn't have expected anything less from them. But Miles, he'd clapped me on the back and said it was about time I'd met someone, and that was all he had said on the matter. Even when I was concocting my plan to get her to live with me, he remained silent.

"What happened?" he asked, settling back into the chair and helping himself to a shot of my vodka. He grimaced as he downed it, he never was one for spirits.

I relayed everything that happened in the warehouse, including the deal I had struck with her. I didn't intend on telling him what had happened in the elevator, but once the words started flowing, I couldn't stop them.

Credit to Miles, he didn't say a word as I regaled my story, and when I finished, he poured himself another shot but this time, he didn't drink it.

"That was a dick move in the elevator, Kai, it's no wonder she retaliated," Miles finally said. I glared at him. I didn't need him to add to my sour mood.

"Miles, I have got no problem with popping a round in your kneecaps," I threw him a murderous look. I was deadly serious, I loved him like he was my own brother, but right now, he was pissing me off.

My words earned a chuckle from him and it felt foreign to my ears. Miles hadn't really laughed since Theo died.

"Keep your bullet in the chamber for now, Kai. All I'm saying is you might have gone about this the wrong way, but it's not too late to fix it. You've got her here, for at least six months, and every day is going to count," he said casually. He picked up his shot and downed it, once again grimacing as he did.

I rolled my eyes. Why the fuck did he insist on drinking vodka if he damn well didn't like it?

"What the fuck do you suggest I do then, Miles? Come on, you know me. I don't fucking date, I don't do flowers and shit. I've never had to work to get a woman into bed. Tell me what the fuck I need to do."

Anger and frustration mixed together, not helped by the amount of vodka now swimming in my system. Popping a cap in someone's knee was beginning to sound more and more like a good idea. If I couldn't fuck to get the anger out of me, maybe inflicting pain on someone would.

"Just treat her with respect, Kai, that would be a good starting point. You've spent the last week learning everything there is to know about her, but she knows nothing about you. Show her who you are. You know, despite the murdering and torturing, and being a controlling motherfucker, you're a decent guy." He gave me a smirk, knowing full well I wouldn't appreciate being called a motherfucker, but also knowing I wouldn't do anything about it.

As much as I hated to admit it, he had a point. Not about being a decent guy, fuck no, I was a cunt. But about treating Riley with respect and letting her get to know me. I'd never allowed a woman to get to know me, why would they need to know me when it was just a quick fuck I was after. And I certainly didn't respect the whores.

But Riley was different, and to win her over, I needed to show her she meant more to me.

As if he had decided the conversation was over, Miles abruptly stood up, taking me by surprise.

"Look, I'm not exactly prince charming with the ladies myself, but I do know they want to be treated with respect, and they want to be listened to. Do that for her as a starting point and I guarantee she'll be eating out of the palm of your hand in no time."

With that, he clapped me on the back and walked back towards the pool table, wrapping his arm around the waist of a redheaded waitress, and leaving me alone with my thoughts.

Chapter 14

Riley

For the second morning in a row, I was awoken by sunlight beaming into my bedroom windows. Despite my predicament, I couldn't grumble at the view. The sun rising over the city in all its gorgeous orange, pink, and red hues was a sight I wouldn't tire of.

What I could grumble about though was the lack of sleep I'd had last night. I had barely slept a wink.

The events of the past 24 hours churned over and over in my mind, starting from when Kai killed the man in the alley, right to the elevator ride where Kai had pinned me against the wall. I shouldn't have said that about Theo, but in my defense, I was scared, and we all say and do stupid things when we are backed into a corner. I wasn't scared of him hurting me, but scared because he was right.

My panties *were* soaking, and all sorts of images of him fucking me had been running through my head from the minute I agreed to his stupid deal.

I didn't want Kai touching me because the thing that scared me the most was I might just like it.

I *never* should have agreed to his deal, Lord knows Leandra didn't deserve to live. The truth was, I *could* have stomached seeing Kai blow her brains out, and I for one would not have missed the stain on the world that was Leandra. I could only blame it on another brain to mouth malfunction which seemed to be happening a lot around the jackass.

The worst part was, as soon as Kai untied Leandra and instructed Hendrix to drive her to the edge of the city, she hobbled out without even a thank you, telling me to, *'have fun'* as she disappeared out of my life for good. I mean, I wasn't expecting her to actually follow me around and lick the shit off my shoe for saving her life, but a little, *'thank you for saving my life, Riley,'* wouldn't have been difficult.

I didn't think I'd have to see Leandra ever again, Kai had told her to get on the first bus out of Hollows Bay, and if she ever came back then he would put a bullet in her brain.

She was free to start again, while I was left to clear up her fucking mess.

I dragged my sorry ass out of bed, stretching and yawning as I headed to the bathroom to take care of business. As I passed through the walk-in closet, I was reminded that the shelves and rails had been filled to the brim with clothes, shoes, handbags, purses, sunglasses, and god knows what else while I had been out yesterday.

I hadn't immediately noticed someone had been in and stocked the wardrobe with designer gear, my thoughts had been totally consumed with what had happened in the elevator. It was only later in the evening when I'd got bored of laying on my bed, staring at the ceiling when I'd had another nose around the room, only to find the once empty wardrobe was no longer empty.

I shouldn't have been surprised, obviously Kai would want his *personal assistant* to look the part but, holy hell, he'd gone way over the top. Seriously, why did he feel I needed so many items of clothing? I would have quite happily made do with the few pairs of jeans and tops I owned which were back in my apartment.

I'd spent the next couple of hours going through all the items, daring not to think about how much they cost. After a while, I'd found myself feeling dejected. It was abundantly clear Kai had spent a ridiculous amount of money on filling my wardrobe when really, the money could have been better spent elsewhere.

I know that sounded a little ungrateful, but I swear, the contents of my closet could have funded a new school for young kids or a drug rehabilitation center in East Bay. Instead, it was being wasted in my closet. I'd never feel comfortable in those sorts of clothes, they just weren't me. I figured I'd speak to Kai and thank him for the gesture but ask him if I could please go to the apartment and get my old clothes, thank you very much.

The thought of my old apartment reminded me that I needed to ask him for Angel's computer console, and a dreaded feeling had consumed me, fear of what the fuck I'd have to offer Kai in exchange to get something I wanted. I'd gone to bed with the hump, and quite frankly, I wasn't feeling much better now that a new day had dawned.

I had just finished in the bathroom when someone knocked lightly on the door. Quickly grabbing the new robe that had been hanging in the wardrobe and wrapping it around me, I prayed it wasn't Kai at the door, I wasn't ready to face him yet. I quietly told the person to come in, and was very relieved when Jacqueline walked in holding a tray full of deliciousness. She'd tried to get me to eat something last night, but I hadn't been hungry, but now, I was starving.

"Good Morning, Ms. Bennett," Jacqueline said softly as she put the tray on my dresser. She avoided my eyes, instead opting to look at the floor which made me feel all kinds of uncomfortable.

I thanked her anyway and crossed the room to find pancakes smothered in maple syrup on my plate, the smell hit my nose and I instantly salivated. They looked and smelt so good I didn't wait another second before tucking in. I only paused when I looked over to see Jacqueline making my bed. I dropped my knife and fork in horror, and stared at her as she busily went about shaking my bed covers.

"What are you doing?" I asked and then immediately felt stupid. Duh, it was obvious she was making my bed. "I mean, I can do that myself."

"There's no need, Ms. Bennett, that's what I am here for," she replied and carried on her chore.

I opened my mouth to protest but stopped myself. There was no point arguing with her, she was no doubt acting under orders. I hated that Kai deemed I wasn't capable of simple chores, and I hated having a maid to pick up after me. I stared back at my pancakes, but suddenly they didn't look as appetizing, and I wasn't all that hungry anymore. I sighed and pushed the plate away.

"Mr. Wolfe wanted you to know he has some business to attend to today. He said you are free to roam the penthouse as you wish, but your sister will be starting her education with her new tutor and he would rather you didn't interrupt," Jacqueline said as she finished tucking my sheets in.

Credit where it is due, the bed did look much neater than how I would have made it.

The anger I felt yesterday had been lying dormant underneath my skin, but at the reminder of the stupid deal I had made, and Kai's orders that I would only be able to see Angel when he deemed I could, it suddenly reared to life again.

I cursed under my breath, low enough so Jacqueline wouldn't hear, and glared at the abandoned pancakes as if they had personally offended me. I hated every single thing about this stupid agreement. I tried to remember the bigger picture, the life Angel would have if I could just get through the next one hundred and eighty one days.

It was by far going to be the most challenging thing I had ever faced in my twenty one years on earth.

Once the bed was made, Jacqueline asked me if there was anything I needed. Aside from my sister and getting the hell out of here, I thanked her but told her I was all good, and off she scurried to do god knows what.

I spent the next couple of hours taking a leisurely shower, followed by lying on the bed to dry off. I was so used to rushing around and working to a schedule around Angel's school and my work, it was nice to just lay down and do nothing but let my body relax. But after a while, boredom set in.

Dragging myself over to the wardrobe, I once again looked over all the clothes Kai had bought me, but feeling somewhat rebellious, I decided to put on the leggings and sweater I had been wearing when Kai brought me here. It had been laundered at some point while we were dealing with the Blaze situation and returned back to me. So what if it was old and frayed, it was the only thing here I owned.

It felt surreal that it had only been a little over 24 hours since the encounter with Kai in the alleyway, yet so much had happened that it felt like weeks had passed, not just a day.

It took me a few minutes to pluck up the courage to try the door, not really believing Jacqueline when she said Kai had given me freedom to roam. From what I knew of Kai, he was one controlling asshole so I didn't quite believe he would let me explore on my own.

Placing my thumb on the scanner like I had seen Kai do, my brows shot up in surprise when the locks clicked, indicating the door had indeed opened. Before I could second guess myself, I was out in the hallway, retracing the steps Kai had taken the day before when he led me to Angel's room.

The apartment was huge, and I wasn't entirely sure I was going the right way. I was also pretty sure that even if I did find Angel's room, I was never going to get in. But the overwhelming need to see her was guiding me, and that was all I could think about.

I had to admit, the apartment was impressive, and now I was seeing without being slung over a shoulder, I could really take in the decor. It was clear Kai had spent an absolute fortune on his palace in the sky. The entire place seemed to stretch on for eternity. The coloring was simplistic with white walls and the black sparkly marble floor, but it was the accessories that gave the entire place personality.

Each of the hallways were lined with impressive artwork, the odd bit of modern furniture dotted randomly were sleek and shined under the spotlights, and it appeared there wasn't a speck of dust anywhere. Everything had its place, tidy and organized, just as he was, and I knew confidently that Kai would have had a hand in every inch of the design of this place.

Controlling bastard.

Eventually, I reached a room I was sure was Angel's and nervous butterflies fluttered to life in my belly. Not necessarily at the thought of seeing my sister but more from anticipation of what might happen if Kai caught me trying to get into her room when he had specifically said I couldn't see her. Still, I was so close and I wasn't yet prepared to let Kai rule over me completely.

I reached my thumb out to the scanner, almost making contact with it when a deep rumbling voice scared the absolute bejesus out of me.

"I wouldn't do that if I were you."

Gawking up at the mountain of a man who was leaning against the wall, I realized he was one of the men who had been in the garage when I'd been released from the trunk of the car.

And he was one scary motherfucker.

He was the one who had a shaved head, was covered in tattoos, and had an angry looking scar down the side of his face. Where the hell he had appeared from I had no idea, it wasn't like you could miss him.

"You scared the hell out of me," I said, clutching my hand to my chest where my heart was pounding against my rib cage and looking guilty at being caught in the act.

The giant chuckled at my expense and then surprised me by holding his hand out for me to shake.

"The name's Danny. And it's a pleasure to finally meet you, Riley," he said, seemingly sincere.

Despite my better judgment, I found myself reaching out and taking his huge hand which engulfed my tiny one. He gave me a firm but gentle shake, but I had a feeling that if he wanted to crush every single bone in my hand, he would be able to, no problem whatsoever. I quickly pulled my hand away before he had the opportunity.

"Kai said you'd probably try to get in to see your sister. He knows you well," Danny said, still chuckling.

"He's only known me a day, he can't know me that well," I snapped back, irritated that Kai had indeed known the first place I would go was to Angel's room. The giant frowned back at me and then sighed.

"Come on, your sister has just met her new tutor so best not to disturb them." He turned and nodded his head, indicating for me to follow.

I gave one last look at the closed door but felt a little better knowing that I at least knew where Angel's room was if I ever needed to make a quick escape.

"Where are we going?" I asked tentatively to the back of Danny's head where there were even more tattoos. He had already started walking away but he paused and turned back to face me.

"I'm going to show you around, unless you'd rather not know where you are living for the next six months?" He shrugged as if to say he wasn't bothered either way.

I deliberated for all of ten seconds and then came to the conclusion that yes, I did want to know where I was living. Knowledge was power after all, and I wanted as much knowledge as possible when it came to handling Kai Wolfe.

I had been wrong about the apartment. It wasn't just amazing, it was *fucking spectacular*.

Danny showed me around the three floors that Kai had made home. The place was beyond insane. It had a rooftop terrace complete with a garden and pool which had a retractable roof cover in case it rained. There were seven bedrooms, five bathrooms, a cinema room, snooker room, library, wine cellar, although technically not a cellar, and a state of the art gym which we didn't go in to, but Danny said I could use any time I liked, and he would happily show me how to use the equipment. He laughed when I told him I was in no hurry to get my ass into the gym.

I learned Kai owned the entire apartment block, and that Danny, Hendrix, and Miles had their own apartments within the block, as did the maids who kept Kai's apartment spotless, and the chef who prepared all of Kai's meals.

Danny, Hendrix, and Miles were the only ones who could come and go as they pleased. Oh, and Jacqueline too. Apparently, she had worked for the Wolfe family from a young age and was in charge of all the other staff. When the maids and chef came on duty, they had to be let into the apartment by Jacqueline.

I still hadn't met Miles properly other than seeing him in the garage, and I supposed the same could be said about Hendrix. Being carried over his shoulder was hardly an introduction.

I noticed Danny never showed me which room Kai slept in, and for some reason that kept creeping into my mind, but I was too scared to ask. I didn't want to give off the wrong impression after all. It's not like I *needed* to know where he slept as I had no intention of ever going in his room.

The place was like nothing I'd ever seen before, nor probably would again once Angel and I left in six months. The staff worked their asses off to keep the place in pristine condition. When I told Danny that I had only seen Jacqueline in my short time here, he told me it was unlikely I would see any other staff members, apparently Kai insisted they went about their work unnoticed, they were to act like ghosts, and if Kai walked into a room they were working in, then they were to leave and not disturb him.

I snorted when Danny told me that, thinking it was pretty darn rude Kai didn't talk to his own household staff, but Danny shrugged and said it had been that way with Kai's father and grandfather, and that the staff didn't mind so much given how much they were paid by Kai.

The place didn't seem so much of a maze once I started learning which hallway led to where. Once Danny had shown me around the entire three floors, he led me down a hallway which I now knew led to the kitchen. He was telling me he had worked for the Wolfe family for around twenty years, and that his role was as an enforcer. I could see why, not only was he huge, but there was just something about him that screamed he was one heck of a dangerous man.

That said, the longer I spent with him, I came to think maybe he wasn't *all* bad, he had made me feel nothing but welcome as he had given me the tour, and dare I say it, I even felt safe with him.

As I followed the giant into the kitchen, I couldn't stop the little 'oh' from escaping when I realized there was someone sitting at the island. The man had been staring at an Ipad that was propped up in front of him, but when he discovered he was no longer alone, his eyes found mine before roaming my body, not in a creepy way, more like he was assessing me, and for the first time, I felt damn stupid for wearing my crappy clothes.

"Riles, this asshole here is Miles. Asshole, this is Riles," Danny said by way of an introduction. I'll admit, Danny's new nickname for me had sent a wave of warmth through me, one I wanted to ignore but couldn't.

It made me feel like I belonged.

Dammit.

"Nice to meet you, Riley. Has this fuckface been looking after you?" Miles retorted with a slight tug of a smile on his lips.

There was something different about Miles when compared to the others. He wasn't as broad for starters, and although there were some similarities between his and Kai's features, Miles had an air of nervousness to him like he couldn't quite hold my eye.

His brown hair was longer than the others, which right then was tied back into a small ponytail. He was dressed casually too, from where he was sitting at the island, I could see he was wearing a t-shirt, whereas Danny was wearing a shirt, tie, and pants despite being at home. Or well, you know, Kai's home.

"Course I've been looking after her, she's our most important guest," Danny joked or at least, I hoped he was joking.

He pulled open the fridge and pulled out a can of lemonade and a can of coke and offered them both to me. I thanked him as I took the lemonade and quickly opened it. I was parched.

"Pleased to hear it, the boss will have your balls if you treat her as anything less," Miles replied and then turned his attention back to the screen, thankfully missing the blush creeping on my cheeks at the way they were talking about me.

Danny pulled out a stool on the opposite side of the island and indicated for me to sit, which I did, before he pulled out his own stool and sat next to me.

"How's it going?" Danny asked. It took me a second to realize he was asking Miles.

Miles tapped at the Ipad before answering, not taking his eyes off the screen. "Fine. The meeting with Ernie is going well, I think he'll be a good asset. Look."

Miles turned the Ipad to show Danny the screen and curiosity got the better of me, so I peeked across.

The screen showed video footage of a group of men sitting around a table clearly in deep conversation. My eyes were immediately drawn to Kai who was sitting at the head of the table, looking incredibly powerful, not to mention dangerous, with two guns strapped to a holster he wore on his body. I fidgeted on my stool and looked away when butterflies fluttered low in my belly at the sight of the man I was supposed to hate.

Danny and Miles started talking about Ernie and someone called Conroy. I didn't have a clue what they were on about, and in all honesty, I wasn't sure I wanted to know. It didn't sound quite legit. Instead, I gazed around the kitchen.

Even this room was grand, with its sleek marble surfaces, shiny silver appliances, and an impressive view over the city. I sipped on my soda while the two of them talked.

When the two men fell silent, I braved a question that had been running around my mind while I had been watching Miles tap away at the screen.

"So, Kai's the boss, you're the enforcer," I pointed at Danny, "What do you do in this little gangbang?" I directed to Miles while Danny let out a chortle.

"I'm the tech guy," Miles replied casually as if that was obvious. I supposed it should have been based on how he refused to let the tablet leave his hands.

"What exactly does that entail?"

"It means I'm the brains of the organization," Miles said, a smug smirk gracing his face.

"Don't let Kai hear you say that, fuckface," Danny chimed in and clipped Miles around the back of the head with one of his giant hands, it was a playful slap which made me laugh.

"Yeah, yeah. Kai knows he wouldn't get half his shit done without me." Miles carried on tapping away at the screen as if whatever he was doing was far more important than this conversation.

"To be fair, he's got a point," Danny said, turning to look back at me. "There isn't a database in the world Miles can't hack, or a phone conversation he can't intercept."

My mouth dropped open and I stared in awe at the man sitting opposite me.

That was pretty impressive. Scary, yes. But definitely impressive. I literally knew nothing about technology, I had a basic phone that allowed me to text Angel. It would have made calls if I had anyone to phone, but that was all it could do. I'd heard all about social media of course, the girls at work were always bragging about how many followers they had on *Instagram* or how many likes they'd gotten on a *Facebook* post, but it meant nothing to me, so I really had no experience when it came to computers.

"Wow." That was all I could say as my brain raced through a hundred different government databases that Miles could allegedly hack. Eventually, I settled on believing that Danny was bragging and there was no way Miles could really hack into all the databases. "What about Hendrix then, what does he do?"

"He's in charge of logistics. You know, setting up deals, finding new importers, making sure people pay. And if they don't, he gives me their names and I deal with them," Danny explained as Miles let out a big sigh.

Danny glared at him then, and a silent exchange passed between them. My eyes darted between the two of them before Miles looked away and returned to his screen. I raised a questioning eyebrow at Danny.

"Miles gets nervous about outsiders knowing our business, but you're part of us now, Riley," Danny said with a wink and humor in his voice.

I wanted to protest and tell them I was not part of them, nor would I ever be, but when I opened my mouth, the words just didn't come out. I'd never been a part of anything, and while I didn't want to be part of a criminal organization, I didn't quite have it in me to ruin the feeling of what it felt like to hear someone say I belonged.

Call me fucked up, but there you have it.

I closed my mouth and decided to ignore Danny's comment.

"What about Theo, what did he do before-" At the mention of Theo's name, Miles and Danny both glared daggers at me, cutting off my words. Silence filled the room and I swallowed nervously, realizing I'd clearly said the wrong thing.

"If you'll excuse me," Miles said abruptly before practically launching himself out of his stool, grabbing his tablet from the side and storming out of the kitchen as though his ass was on fire.

"I'm...sorry. I didn't mean to upset anyone," I said quietly to the table, not able to make eye contact with Danny. Damn me and my nosiness.

"Don't worry about it. Miles, he has a hard time talking about Theo. They were cousins, but they were closer than brothers, did everything together. When Theo died, he took it hard." Danny's tone was gentle as if coaxing down someone who was standing on a ledge about to jump.

His words registered that Miles was Theo's cousin, meaning he was Kai's too.

"Oh," I replied, still avoiding his gaze.

"The thing with Miles is, he wears his heart on his sleeve. He was never very good at hiding his emotions so it seems like he is hurting more than anyone, Kai included. The truth is, losing Theo almost killed Kai, he just doesn't show it as much. He knows the life we live could end up with any of us getting a bullet to the brain, we just never thought it would be Theo."

There was a tinge of emotion in Danny's voice, and I thought back to how Kai had reacted in the car when he had told me of Theo's death. He'd become so angry that it had scared me. It was evident losing Theo had affected them all in different ways.

Learning all of this about Theo made me feel even worse for what I had said to Kai, and a little voice in the back of my head kept saying I needed to apologize. But the stubborn part of me, the part I tended to listen to said, *'fuck Kai Wolfe.'*

I didn't know what to say back to Danny so I offered him a sympathetic smile and remained silent.

"These past few months, Kai has been so consumed with finding Theo's murderer, I thought we would lose him in the process. But this last week, there has been a change in him, Riles. Since he met you, he's had a new lease of life, he's had something else to focus on."

"Don't, Danny." I held up my hand and tried to keep my voice firm. "Please don't put that on me. Kai is nothing but a controlling, self-centered asshole who doesn't care about anything but getting what he wants."

"That's not true, Riley. Yeah, he may be controlling and self-centered but he does care about more than just getting his own way. He cares deeply about his family, he'd do anything to keep them safe and protected. And he'd do the same for you," Danny replied softly.

I opened my mouth to refute everything he had said, but this time he held his hand up to stop me from speaking.

"Just give him a chance, you'll see he isn't the monster you think he is. He wears his bravado like a shield of armor but underneath it, he is a scared man who has already lost the one person he loved more than anything in this world. He sometimes doesn't know how to handle his feelings, and yeah, he acts out because of that. But in the end, he just wants to make sure that those he loves are safe."

Huh.

What the heck could I say back to that?

Danny had stumped me, he had been nothing but jovial the entire time he had been showing me around, but now, sitting here talking about his boss, there was no joking, no inoffensive insults, just cold, raw truth.

And didn't that leave me feeling all confused.

Silence once again filled the room as Danny and I stared at each other.

After several awkward beats passed, Danny rose from his stool. "I best get back to it, I've got work to do if I don't want to get my ass fired."

I nodded my head to acknowledge him but all I could do was stare back as his words echoed around my head.

"Enjoy the rest of your day, Riles. It's been good to get to know you." With that Danny took several large strides out of the kitchen, hollering when he was halfway down the hallway, "And stay away from Angel's room!"

It took me a few more minutes to gather myself and head back to my room where I spent the rest of the afternoon churning over Danny's words.

Was Kai really the monster I had come to believe? Or was he just living a life he had no choice in being part of and was doing what it took to survive and protect his loved ones?

Hell, I knew what it meant to make difficult choices to look after someone I loved. Maybe Kai and I weren't too dissimilar after all, and didn't that just scare the ever living shit out of me.

The questions kept circling my head as night fell outside my bedroom window. I eventually fell asleep but it was anything but peaceful.

Instead, my dreams were haunted by a faceless man who had dark eyes with flecks of gold in them.

Chapter 15

Riley

I woke the following day feeling a little different.

Lighter.

Danny's words had plagued me for the entire night but I couldn't help but resonate with them, and it led me to making a decision.

To give Kai a chance.

I had, after all, agreed to the deal to live with Kai for six months, and wouldn't it be a heck of a lot easier if Kai and I were on the same page?

Don't get me wrong, I still thought Kai was a controlling bastard, and yes, I was still pretty pissed off about his demand to have a night with me, but I couldn't help but feel a little different towards him.

The man had lost his brother for Christ's sake, maybe he just wasn't thinking like a rational man. I hadn't exactly been thinking rationally when I decided to run away with Angel after our mom's death.

I ignored the part of my brain that reminded me of all the rumors I had heard about the Wolfe family over the years. Rumors would do me no good, surely I was better off listening to someone who knew Kai personally rather than gossip I'd hear out on the street, right?

Besides, hadn't Danny said Kai would want to protect me, to keep me safe? He'd already proven that when he broke the neck of my would-be attacker in the alleyway, something of which I should have been concerned about. But the truth was, it didn't really bother me Kai had killed him. If he hadn't been there to stop it from happening, without a shadow of a doubt, I would have been raped, and probably left for dead.

Despite Kai being a truly terrifying man, something in the pit of my stomach said he wouldn't want to hurt me. The way he looked at me sometimes made me think that maybe, *just maybe*, he genuinely cared for me.

That was the lifeline I had decided to cling to and I hoped and prayed that I was right.

Only time would tell.

The morning started the same as the day before. Jacqueline came to my room with a tray of goodies, this time granola, honey and yogurt, and a glass of orange juice. I had avoided dinner the night before, too consumed by my thoughts to eat, so this morning, I was famished.

Jacqueline put the tray on my side, and as per yesterday, as soon as I started eating, she went about making my bed. I still wasn't happy about it, but wasn't life about picking your battles? And this seemed like a pointless battle to pick.

Once she had made the bed, Jacqueline turned to face me but kept her eyes on the floor, but at least I understood why this morning.

"Mr. Wolfe has asked that you are dressed and ready to leave in one hour." Her voice was soft, barely audible over the crunching of my granola. I nodded in acknowledgment and with that, she left.

Nervousness swept through me but I wasn't sure if it was not knowing what Kai had planned or anticipation of seeing him again. Either way, with my decision made to give him a chance, I finished my breakfast and started to get myself ready.

Bang on the hour, I was dressed in the most casual clothes I could find in the closet. It had taken me a little while to rifle through the insane amount of clothes Kai had bought, eventually settling on a pair of black skinny jeans, a plain white vest top, and a black leather jacket, which I had to admit was pretty darn nice, and fit me like a dream.

There wasn't a flat pair of shoes in sight though, and while I wore high heeled shoes when I was dancing, I never wore them outside of Club Sin, and I wasn't about to start now. High heels hurt.

I laced my old sneakers up, not giving a shit if they were starting to fall apart and didn't match the quality of my new outfit. I'm sure Kai would have something to say about it, but the fact was, I was wearing *some* of the clothes he had bought, so he may not have objected.

Also, pigs might fly.

Just as I'd finished tying my lace, the door lock disengaged letting me know someone was coming in, not even bothering to knock. Good fucking job I was dressed and not standing butt naked.

The door opened, and in strolled Hendrix who walked into the room like he owned the place. I did not like this man one little bit, there was something *off* about him. In fact, I think I might have hated him more than I hated Kai, which was saying a lot.

A smirk was planted firmly on his face but upon seeing me dressed and ready to go, he quickly wiped it.

"Good, you're ready," he said as he raked his piercing blue eyes up and down my body, lingering on my boobs for *far* too long, and giving me the same creepy feeling I had when I first met him.

I wanted to say, *'Good morning to you too, asshole,'* but instead, I smiled sweetly and kept my mouth shut.

Hendrix was a good looking man, but he was one of those douchebags who knew it. Today he had styled his dirty blonde hair to one side and was clean shaven, showing off his sharp jawline. He wore a suit, much like Kai always did, but Hendrix looked more casual in his, he didn't wear a tie, and the sleeves to his jacket and shirt were pushed up to his elbows.

"Right. Come on then," he grunted, narrowing his eyes at my fake smile.

Turning to walk back out of my room, I followed behind him like a little dog, grateful Danny had taken the time to show me around, otherwise I could have quite easily gotten lost given how fast the asshole was walking.

My heart panged as we walked past Angel's room. I was so desperate to see her. But I didn't have time to dwell on the matter, Hendrix carried on stomping down the hall, clearly not giving a fuck about my inner turmoil.

We eventually reached the foyer where the doors to the elevator stood open and waiting, but to my surprise, Kai was nowhere to be seen.

"Where's Kai?" I asked, stopping in the foyer.

Hendrix reached the elevator and had taken a step inside before spinning back to face me.

"He's busy. You're with me today," he replied with disdain in his voice, even though his eyes once again scanned over my body.

Yeah, so not happening.

"I'm not going anywhere with you." I folded my arms across my chest, almost as a way to protect myself from Hendrix and his wandering eyes.

I don't know what it was about him but something gave me the heebie jeebies, and the only way I'd be going anywhere with him was if he put me over his shoulder and carried me.

Again.

The asshole smirked and folded his arms too, mirroring my image.

"Too bad for you, sweetheart, boss's orders. You either come with me willingly or you'll be going back in the trunk of the car. Your choice."

Fuck my life.

"I want to see Kai," I said, hoping I wasn't sounding like a petulant child, but also hoping Kai would take pity on me and not force me to go with this goon.

Hendrix dropped his arms and walked towards me, narrowing his eyes. Despite almost shitting my pants, I stood my ground and refused to be intimidated by him.

"I told you, the boss is busy. He won't want to be disturbed." He stopped mere inches away from me, his chest almost brushing against my folded arms, but still, I refused to step back.

"And I said, I want to see him."

We glared at each other for a minute, an intense face off with neither of us backing down.

What in the hell was his problem?

Hendrix suddenly grinned maliciously, then casually shrugged. "Your funeral," he sneered before marching back the way we had come.

I followed him through the apartment and up the stairs to the floor where Kai's office was. I'd assumed that's where we were going, but Hendrix walked straight on passed it towards a door at the end of the hallway.

I hadn't been in this room on the grand tour yesterday, but I knew it was where the gym was. Loud bangs echoed from whatever was going on behind the door, and my confidence in demanding to see Kai began to fade. Maybe I should have just gone with Hendrix and not caused a fuss.

As we reached the closed door, Hendrix stopped and turned to face me.

"Sure you want to disturb him?" He was amused, and as much as I was now majorly doubting myself about disturbing Kai when he was busy, I didn't want to give Hendrix the satisfaction of backing down.

Raising an eyebrow at the buffoon standing before me, I waited for him to open the door. He shook his head before placing his finger on the pad which was fixed next to the door of the room Kai was inevitably in.

"After you," he said smugly as he opened the door. Swallowing down my fear, I stepped inside.

Unsurprisingly, the room was huge, and housed practically every piece of gym kit imaginable. One side of the room was lined with machines; treadmills, bikes, cross trainers, rowing machines, and some I didn't know. They were all lined up to look out the ginormous windows, allowing the user to take in the view of the city while working out.

On the other side of the room was a variety of weights, weight machines, and benches. And at the far end of the room was a boxing ring, and in that ring beating the living shit out of a punchbag was Kai Wolfe.

The noises I'd heard from outside became apparent every time Kai smashed his powerful fists into the bag, they were from the thud of his punches followed by a loud grunt which echoed around the room.

It was a sight to behold.

"Holy shit," I whispered as my eyes fixed on Kai and my throat went dry.

His back was to me, the only thing he was wearing was a pair of tight black shorts. My jaw dropped open at the sight of the man pounding the bag, and I couldn't tear my eyes away from him.

He was *breathtaking*.

His broad shoulders were *huge,* and the muscles in his neck, shoulders, and back were solid and defined, so much so I swear I could see every single one from where I was standing on the other side of the room. Every time he threw a punch, his impressive muscles rippled throughout his entire body.

He was standing with one foot in front of the other, ducked slightly down in order to hit the bag with as much power as he could muster, and given how the bag was swaying, I imagined he was hitting it with some force. His legs were like solid tree trunks, and it was only now that I really appreciated just how dangerous Kai was.

But the thing that held my attention more than his defined body was the enormous tattoo on his back. The black wolf tattoo started at the tip of Kai's shoulders and covered his entire back, right down to his narrow waist. It was the head, chest, and front paws of a snarling wolf which had been designed to give the effect that it had ripped straight out of Kai's body.

The entire tattoo was made up of different shades of black and gray, and the only color was the piercing emerald green of the wolf's eyes, making it look like the wolf was watching you no matter where you stood.

I'd never seen anything like it, it was simply stunning.

Hendrix slammed the door behind us, making me jump out of my damn skin. Kai spun on his heel to face us, and boy, did he look *fucking mad* at the interruption.

Now he was facing me, his naked chest was exposed in all its glory, and holy hell, was he spectacular. I couldn't stop my tongue from peeking out and licking my bottom lip as I watched sweat roll down his solid pecs, which rose up and down as he tried to regain his breath. I cast my eyes down to his rock hard abs. Tattoos covered his strong arms, from shoulders to wrist and across his chest, all designs in black ink.

As my eyes roamed his firm body, I wondered what it would be like to run my hands all over it, or even my tongue.....

"Boss, sorry for the interruption but Riley here wanted a word," Hendrix said, breaking me out of my inappropriate thoughts and throwing me straight under the bus. The fucker still had a tinge of humor in his voice making me want to jab my elbow into his ribs.

It was evident he thought I was going to get into trouble for disturbing Kai, and that made me hate Hendrix just that little bit more.

Kai's snarling face softened before he used his teeth to undo the strap on one of his boxing gloves. Once he pulled it off, he undid the other one and threw the gloves down into the ring, the bag behind him forgotten about. He climbed out of the ring and stormed towards us, making butterflies in my stomach spring to life.

My jaw was on the floor at the sight of the God marching towards me. I should have been hot footing it back to my room and apologizing profusely for disturbing him, but I couldn't move. My feet were glued to the spot, and my eyes were practically bugging out of my head, all logical thought gone from my brain.

Never in my life had I had such a visceral reaction to a man. He was something out of this world, and I knew I'd be fantasizing about this moment for weeks, scratch that, *months,* to come.

Not that I'd tell him, of course.

"Is everything okay?" he asked when he reached us, his voice surprisingly soft and at odds with the way he had stormed over to us.

His question was aimed at me, barely acknowledging Hendrix, and he did look like he was genuinely concerned.

"Uh...I...erm."

Fucking hell.

I think I had a stroke or something because I'd lost the power to speak. I couldn't think of anything but the sexy-as-fuck man standing next to me, heat radiating off his sweaty body.

Kai's concerned gaze turned from one of concern to one of amusement, and he gave a jerk of his head to Hendrix, dismissing him from the room. From the corner of my eye, I saw Hendrix's eyes widen at being dismissed, but like the good little lamb he was, he turned and walked out, slamming the door behind him.

I couldn't help but be a little bit smug. Guess it wasn't going to be my funeral after all.

Once the door was closed, Kai brought his hand up to my chin and gently closed my mouth.

"You good there, Star?" he said, his dark eyes alight with mirth. The touch of his damp hand against my heated skin sent little tingles of pleasure straight to my core.

I wasn't sure if it was his touch or the mention of my stage name which snapped me out of the spell that had temporarily been placed on my sanity. Either way, I cleared my throat and took a tiny step back, causing his hand to drop.

"Er, yeah. I'm sorry for disturbing you, I just..." Why the fuck had I wanted to speak to him again? Jeez, I needed to get my shit together.

"You don't need to apologize, Riley, you can disturb me any time," he replied warmly.

It was like I was speaking to an entirely different Kai, completely different from the one who had been in the room with Blaze and me, the cold, callous bastard who'd not only bartered for Blaze's release in exchange for a night with me, but had also pinned me against a wall and whispered wicked things in my ear.

That guy was nowhere to be seen.

"I didn't want to go with Hendrix," I blurted, immediately feeling stupid.

Kai looked towards the door Hendrix had not long departed through before meeting my eyes again.

"Hendrix is one of my best men, he won't hurt you."

"He scares me. He walked into my room earlier without even knocking. I could have been naked, Kai." I was being honest, but I felt like a bitch for dobbing Hendrix in. In my defense, I *really* didn't like the fact he'd waltzed into my room. If he could do it then, he could do it when he damn well pleased, and that left me feeling uneasy.

Not to mention the creepy way he looked at me all the time.

A frown appeared on Kai's face as he took in my words, and relief that he seemed to be taking me seriously swept through me.

"I'll speak to him," he said coldly as his eyes found the door again before drifting back to me. "But I assure you that won't happen again. I've got things to take care of today, that's why I need you to go with Hendrix, but I give you my word, he won't hurt you."

He took my hand in his and gave it a reassuring squeeze. It was so out of character from the man I had come to know.

What in the world was going on?

It was on the tip of my tongue to argue, but hadn't I promised myself that I was going to give him a chance? That started with learning to trust him.

"Okay."

He stared at me for a beat, as if waiting for the argument. Instead, I gave him a tentative smile. I realized then he was still holding my hand. Not that I had pulled away either.

"Was there anything else?" he eventually said, breaking our stare.

"Actually, yeah there was." *Here we go.* "I said to Angel I would get her games console from our apartment. She's obsessed with the damn thing and I think it'll make her time here a bit easier," I rushed out, and then held my breath, waiting for whatever bullshit demand Kai would make in order to get the blasted games console.

"I'll ask one of my men to collect it today."

Wait.

What?

"Just like that?" I asked in surprise. "Isn't there something you want in return?"

Kai let out a deep sigh and frowned. "Riley, I-" he paused, trying to find the right words. "No, I don't want anything in return. I'll make sure she has it before the end of the day. Is there anything else you need from your apartment?"

I wondered for a moment if Kai had had a personality transplant overnight because this *definitely* wasn't the man I had dealt with so far. Or maybe Danny had spoken to him in the same way he had spoken to me, and this was Kai offering me an olive branch.

Either way, if Kai being amenable made my life a bit easier then I was going to grab it with both hands.

"No, that was all. Thank you."

I should have left, should have walked away, and not given the man a second thought. But my feet were having a hard time listening to my brain, and instead, I just stood there, still with my hand in his sweaty palm and his eyes holding mine, an array of different emotions running through me.

"I should go," I said, removing my hand from his.

"I hope you enjoy your day, Riley," he replied cryptically, and in response, I gave him a small smile.

As I walked away, I couldn't help but turn back, only to find him watching me intently. The way a wolf would watch its prey.

"Erm, thanks for the clothes as well. That was kind of you," I said, nervously picking at the skin around my fingernails, a habit I had when I was anxious.

"You're welcome." His eyes roamed my body, landing on my feet. I waited for the complaint to come but then he shocked the shit out of me once again. "I'll make sure you have some more sneakers delivered if that's what you'd prefer to wear?"

"Oh, yeah, I don't really like wearing heels unless I have to. Thank you."

He gave me a soft smile and nodded his head. Leaving him to his workout, I opened the door to find a rather pissed off looking Hendrix waiting for me. Without saying a word, he started walking back down the hallway.

I reluctantly followed, trying my hardest not to think of the strange feelings that had stirred deep in my belly following my latest interaction with Kai Wolfe.

Chapter 16

Riley

"How was your day?" Kai asked in his deep voice from across the table.

We were in some posh as fuck restaurant called *The Orchid,* and were seated in a room that was separated from the main restaurant, giving us privacy from the eyes that followed Kai as we walked through. Not that I could say much, I was one of those who couldn't keep my eyes off him.

"It was amazing. Thank you for arranging it."

My cheeks warmed from his heated gaze, and I started to pick the skin around my newly manicured nails discreetly under the table. I didn't want to ruin my new perfect nails, but it was the only way I could deal with the nerves rampaging through me as I sat opposite the man.

I had spent the day in a spa. Not just *any* spa either, but the best one in the city. It was incredible.

I'd been totally spoiled, enjoying a full body Swedish massage, exfoliated, and moisturized to within an inch of my life, followed by a manicure, pedicure, and facial. I'd walked away glowing and feeling like a total princess, something I'd never experienced before, and it was all thanks to Kai.

I really was beginning to think he had undergone a personality transplant overnight.

"You're welcome," he replied, as he raked his gaze over my new hairstyle.

It was the first haircut I'd had in years. The stylist had wanted to cut it short but I had been adamant that wasn't going to happen, so we met in the middle. I kept the length, but she added lots of layers to it to get rid of all the split ends I'd accumulated over the years from not taking better care of my hair.

I struggled to meet Kai's eye across the table, mainly because he was looking more and more edible every time I peeked at him, and the tingly feeling that had started in my core when I first saw him had only grown. Especially as my mind kept conjuring up images of him from this morning wearing just those blasted gym shorts.

Tonight, he was wearing a very smart dark gray three-piece suit, complete with a crisp white shirt. For once, he'd left off the tie, leaving the top buttons open enough to see some of his impressive artwork creeping up his neck. His hair was swept back neatly instead of the messy look he usually wore.

I knew I was supposed to hate this man, but I couldn't deny the attraction that was there, simmering underneath the surface, and didn't that just leave me all sorts of confused.

After being pampered in the spa all day, I was whisked to a beauty parlor where I'd had my hair washed, cut and styled, and makeup done. I always thought I did my makeup well at Club Sin, but it was *nothing* compared to the classy but sultry look the makeup artist had given me. I was then given a gorgeous strapless red dress to wear that flaunted my curves and flashed way too much thigh, along with matching *Christian Louboutin* shoes to wear. I hadn't questioned why I was being instructed to get all dolled up, I figured I'd find out soon enough.

Sure enough, I was brought to the restaurant where Kai was waiting for me. He asked, yes, *asked,* if I would join him for dinner at the restaurant, all the while looking at me like I was the main course. While I couldn't exactly say no seeing as I was dressed for the occasion, it meant something to me that he had asked, not just demanded.

And the way he had looked at me? Yeah, that made me feel all sorts of crazy feelings deep in my belly.

"How was your day?" I asked in return, genuinely curious as to how the most powerful man in the city spent his day. You know, when he wasn't torturing people for information on his brother's murder or peddling drugs to kids.

Kai momentarily looked surprised but gave me a small smile.

"It was fine, Riley," he said with a hint of humor in his voice and a smirk on his lips.

I narrowed my eyes at him, irrational anger spiking at why he thought me asking how his day had been was funny.

"Why is that funny?" I huffed.

"Because I don't think anyone has *ever* asked me how my day was," he replied, stroking his hand down over his shirt and offering me a rare glimpse of vulnerability.

"Oh."

I wasn't sure what else to say. It was pretty sad no one in his entire life had bothered to ask how he spent his days. Thankfully, the waiter chose that moment to enter the room before awkwardness could descend.

"Allow me to top up your drinks before dinner is served," the young waiter said. He must have been a similar age to me, probably paying his way through college, and I'd bet my last dollar he knew he was going to be getting a big tip tonight so long as he did his job properly.

Neither of us said anything as the waiter made a show of taking the champagne bottle out of the ice bucket and refilling our glasses.

I'd only drunk about half of my original glass, it was damn good stuff, but the girls at the spa had been giving me flutes of champagne all day, and I had a nice buzz of alcohol flowing through my veins. I knew I shouldn't drink too much more otherwise I'd end up either puking all down myself, or worse, giving in to the lust I was feeling for Kai and throwing myself at him, and I could *not* let that happen.

Kai never took his eyes off me as the waiter filled our glasses and then left the room, leaving us alone again. Nervously, I sipped my drink, appreciating the smooth taste of the champagne. I was by no means a wine or champagne connoisseur, but I knew a good bubbly when I tasted one.

"Tell me about your time growing up, Riley," Kai said.

The question caught me off guard, and I wondered why he'd want to talk about something as boring as my life.

"I thought you knew everything there was to know about me?" I sassed, giving him a flirty smile. The warm buzz of alcohol was making me brave, and I already had a problem keeping words from falling out of my mouth around Kai. I wondered what it would take to get Kai to threaten to put me over his knee again.

What the heck was wrong with me?

Champagne, that was what was wrong with me. Definitely not the insane attraction I felt toward the man sitting opposite me.

"I do," he replied with his usual air of arrogance. "But I want to hear about it from you."

I sighed. It wasn't an exciting topic, but seeing as Kai knew it all anyway, what was the point in refusing him?

"There's not much to tell. I had a good life until my dad was murdered and my mom turned into a junkie and OD'd. After that, the only thing that mattered was keeping Angel safe, and trying to give her the best life I possibly can."

There wasn't much more to it. I didn't think too much about the life I had before dad was killed, what was the point? I could never go back to that time, and dwelling on it wouldn't help provide food and shelter for Angel.

"Did the cops ever find the people responsible for shooting your dad?" he asked, confirming he did indeed know how my father was killed.

"No."

Despite telling myself to stop drinking, I took another swig of my drink, desperately wanting to change the topic and refusing to let memories of my mom and dad seep in.

Thankfully, Kai took pity on me. "How did you end up in Hollows Bay?"

"It wasn't planned or anything. I put Angel and myself on a bus and rode it to the end of the line. By the time we got to Hollows Bay, we were both exhausted and there were no more buses until the morning." I shrugged and stared at the bubbles fizzing in my glass. "We found a bench to crash on for the night, and then after that, well, I guess it didn't make a difference where we went. We were going to be homeless for a while, and it didn't matter whether that was in Hollows Bay or any other city in the country."

The memories flooded back to the day we arrived in Hollows Bay. I had been terrified to the point of wanting to walk straight into the nearest police station and admit what I'd done. But the fear of losing Angel was greater than the fear of living on the streets, so no matter how scared I was of being alone in a big city, I put it to one side and got on with it.

I peeked up at Kai when he didn't say anything and found him once again watching me closely, a look of curiosity mixed with sympathy on his handsome face.

It was a look I'd never seen from him before, and I'd be lying if I said it didn't warm me.

"What happened next?"

I sucked in a deep breath before replying, knowing the weeks that followed were the hardest both Angel and I had ever struggled through.

"Truthfully, it was hell on earth," I told him honestly. I blamed the alcohol for my loose tongue, but surprisingly when Kai wasn't being a scary bastard, he was quite easy to talk to. "We spent the following weeks sleeping on benches and doing what we could to find food. It was horrible, and people would look at us like we were nothing but dirt on their shoes. After a few weeks, we found other kids who took us to a derelict train station where pretty much all the homeless kids were living, and we stayed there for a while."

Kai listened with rapt interest, and I had a feeling this was part of my life he didn't know anything about. He may have known some of the facts, but not the personal details, and it seemed I was only too happy to share with him.

I drank some more of my champagne. I hadn't appreciated that talking about this part of my life was going to be as emotional as I was finding it, but the drink was helping.

Kai followed suit and took a large gulp of his drink. I couldn't tear my eyes away from the way his throat moved as he swallowed the drink down. Fucking hell, how did everything he did get me so goddamn hot. I was rapidly forgetting the hell this man had put me through over the last few days.

Damn him.

Before Kai could ask me any more questions, the waiter knocked and entered the room with trays of yummy smelling food. My mouth watered the second he put my dinner down in front of me, and I had to remind myself that this was a classy establishment, and it would *not* be ladylike to gobble down my dinner like I wanted to.

Kai and I ate in silence, enjoying the delicious meal. The first bite of the tender steak I popped into my mouth tasted like nothing I had ever experienced before, it was simply exquisite. I couldn't help but close my eyes and let out a little moan. When I opened them, Kai's dark eyes had turned even darker and burned fiercely into mine. For a brief second, he looked like he was about to swipe everything off the table and devour me instead.

Holy fucking hell.

Once we had finished, and I wasn't ashamed to admit that I demolished every tiny morsel on my plate, the waiter came back and swiftly cleared the table. He moved quickly, and before I knew it, he was gone again.

"That was delicious. Thank you," I said to Kai.

He smiled softly at me, sending warm fuzzies straight to my belly. The worrying thing was, the food had soaked up some of the alcohol and my head wasn't as fogged, which meant whatever I was feeling was not a result of champagne.

I wasn't the sort of girl who wanted to rip the clothes off a man and have her wicked way with him, don't get me wrong, I was no virgin, but I'd never really had time for men. But Kai, well he made my imagination run wild with all the naughty things I wanted him to do to me, and me to do to him.

For the millionth time, my cheeks heated.

"Would you like to step outside for some fresh air?" he asked, noticing my flushed cheeks.

Fresh air, yeah, that was what I needed. Maybe that would cool the burning lust zapping through me right now.

"Sure," I replied, trying to sound casual but Kai gave me a knowing look, the bastard knew the effect he was having on me.

He stood and offered me his hand which I accepted without giving it much thought. I shouldn't have though, the touch of his hand on mine did absolutely *nothing* to calm my erratic thoughts. In fact, all I could think about was what it would be like to have his hands roaming everywhere over my body....

Fuck! I needed out of this room, and right now.

Kai led me to a door at the back of the room, he opened it and let me pass through onto the private balcony. The cool air immediately hit my overheated skin, thankfully cooling me down. I stepped up to the glass barrier and gasped at the view.

The restaurant was in one of the city skyscrapers, and was on the thirtieth floor so the view overlooked the city. I'd seen the view from Kai's apartment of course, but I'd never been outside to *feel* it.

It was incredible. The city was full of life, cars honking their horns in the busy streets, bars and clubs playing loud, pounding music, and people down below shouting in enjoyment. The whole city was lit up brightly and full of life, a stark contrast to the opposite end of the city which I could just make out in the distance. It was almost like East Bay had its own personal storm cloud constantly floating over it.

Kai stood next to me, and I breathed in his luscious scent. I wasn't sure what cologne he was wearing tonight but it smelled *incredible*. He was so close his arm brushed against mine as he came to stand next to me, sending a shiver down my spine.

We stood silently for a minute taking in the view. I watched him from the corner of my eye, watching how he stood tall peering over the city that he believed he owned.

I wondered what it would be like to have that kind of power, it wasn't something I'd want. I also had to wonder how people *allowed* the city to be ruled by one man. I mean we had a police force, we had city officials, all for the purposes of running a city, how on earth could they allow one family to dominate it?

I was about to ask Kai those very questions when he turned to ask me one of his own.

"How did you come to meet Joe Mason?"

Oh good, we were back to this. Seriously, how could he be this interested in my past?

"I stole from him," I said with a grimace. I wasn't proud of stealing but I had a mouth to feed and I would have done what I could to keep Angel fed, and I'd do it again tomorrow if I had to. Kai's eyebrows rose in surprise. "It's not something I've done in a very long time," I quickly added, suddenly worried I'd just confessed my crime to the king of the city. To my relief, he smiled and took my hand.

"I'm not judging you, Riley. You did what you had to do." He gently ran his thumb over the back of my hand, sending tingles through my body and into my core.

So much for cooling down.

"Joe took us in. He gave us a place to stay and let me work in some of his shops. He was a good man, he didn't charge me a penny for letting us stay in his apartment. He died of a heart attack about two years later, and even now it still guts me I won't ever be able to thank him for his help." I swallowed the lump in my throat that had formed while talking about Joe, I missed that man so much.

My brows furrowed when Kai's eyes darkened and a murderous look appeared on his face, one I had seen before. I didn't know what the hell I'd said to make him react like that, but his reaction had me instantly running scared. He was still holding my hand and he gave it a tight squeeze.

"Riley, Joe was a pedophile," he said, void of any emotion.

"What?" I replied, confused.

What the actual fuck was he talking about? Joe was no pedo, Kai was talking shit and I wouldn't stand for him bad-mouthing someone who had been my savior. I yanked my hand out of his as anger consumed me.

"What the hell are you talking about?" I snapped.

He didn't take his eyes off me. Didn't let any emotion show on his face, he just glared at me.

"I'm sorry, Riley, but Joe was responsible for running a sex ring. He had a number of apartments across the city in which he arranged for men to abuse little girls." His face twisted in revulsion, a look that reflected my own at the sheer nonsense Kai was spouting.

"You're lying. Joe would never have done anything like that. Seriously, Kai, what the hell is wrong with you?" I was getting angrier the more he spoke, and my hands balled into fists.

He was lying, he had to be. Joe was a good man, a *kind* man. He had helped Angel and me when we needed help, and he'd never given me any cause for concern.

Instead of replying, Kai fished in his pocket and pulled out his phone. He tapped at the screen several times before shoving the phone under my nose. I skimmed the words on the report that was in front of me and felt my world start to crumble.

Sex ring.

Girls as young as ten.

Raped.

Trafficked by Joe Mason.

Kai was telling the truth.

Tears welled in my eyes as I snatched the phone and read the police report. Joe had been accused of countless offenses against young girls aged between ten and fourteen. Not just accused, the evidence gathered against him was there in black and white in the police report Kai had accessed.

It didn't take a genius to work out that when we met Joe, Angel would have been too young for his preferences, and I would have been too old. But had he survived to see another year, Angel would have been the perfect age. The thought sickened me to my stomach.

All this time I had been thinking Joe was a hero, taking two young girls off the street to give them a better life, all the while ruining the lives of other young girls. Fuck, what if he had hurt Angel? I never would have been able to forgive myself.

My stomach churned, the nice steak I'd not long devoured looked like it was going to make a reappearance. I turned to look at Kai who was watching me intently.

"I....I can't believe this," I whispered. Kai took his phone out of my hand and repocketed it.

"I'm sorry, Riley. But I thought you ought to know. He wasn't the man you thought he was, and he certainly didn't deserve to have your affection." There was some emotion back in Kai's voice, a mix between anger and regret.

"I didn't know. There was nothing that made me think he was anything but a kind man helping us. How did I not see it?" The shock was beginning to wear off, but instead of feeling anger or betrayal, I felt numb.

"He was a clever man. It took the authorities years to find out what was going on. He moved his victims around to different places, he was never caught with them, that's why it took so long to gather the evidence against him. There's no way you could have known."

The tears that had been threatening finally slid down my cheek. Kai took my hand again and pulled me against his firm body. I went willingly, needing to feel something other than this numbness. He dropped my hand, and instead cupped my face with both of his large palms, tilting my face up to his. With a thumb, he tenderly brushed away my tears.

"I wish I had the opportunity to kill that man with my bare hands, Riley, his death was too easy." He sounded murderous again, but this time, I couldn't blame him.

It surprised me when the thought that *I* wanted to kill Joe popped into my head.

"I remember when the case broke. Theo and I took care of some of the other dirty cunts in the ring, but I'd love nothing more than to bring Joe Mason back from the grave and inflict the sort of pain he inflicted on innocent girls," Kai whispered.

He was so close to me, all I could focus on was the touch of his thumb on my cheek and his words that shouldn't have been comforting, but they were. They really were.

We stared at each other for a minute, neither saying anything. He was so close that I could smell the champagne on his breath, and I was suddenly overwhelmed with wanting a taste. My eyes drifted to his lips, and I found myself silently begging him to move closer, wanting to feel them pressed against mine, *needing* to know how he tasted.

He swallowed, and ever so slowly, he inched forward.

My eyes drifted closed when his mouth was mere millimeters away from mine.

And then his blasted phone rang.

Chapter 17

Kai

"This had better be fucking good," I snapped at the cunt who had just interrupted my moment with Riley. I was *this* close to finally getting a taste of that perfect mouth.

I'd answered in such a hurry I didn't even take the time to acknowledge who was calling.

"Boss, we have a problem down at warehouse 4. You need to get over here now," Miles rushed down the phone.

Warehouse 4 was my weapons warehouse, and I knew Miles would never disturb me unless it was something serious. Talk about the worst fucking timing. I looked at Riley before stepping away, her beautiful face etched in disappointment.

I knew the fucking feeling.

She looked absolutely breathtaking tonight. The spa had done wonders for her, and she was glowing when she stepped out of the car.

And that dress, *fuck me,* it clung to her like a second skin, showing off every single curve and flashing her luscious toned leg. It had taken every bit of willpower not to storm over to her, bend her over the car, and fuck her into oblivion.

I'd made a promise to myself after Miles' little pep talk that I was going to do whatever it took to win Riley over and recover from the fuck up of the ultimatum I'd given her over Blaze. I couldn't tell her I would never force myself on her, I needed to have something to hold over her, I was a manipulative bastard after all, but I was determined more than ever to win her over, and if that meant playing nice and making her think I was a decent guy, then so be it. Hence why I'd arranged for her to be treated like a fucking princess today.

The way she looked at me when she got out of the car, I knew I'd done something right.

"What the fuck is the problem?" I growled, still fucking furious my night was being interrupted, and not at all understanding why I paid Miles to do a job when he clearly couldn't fucking do it.

"It's bad, Boss. Luis attacked one of the workers, one of the women. Apparently, it's not the first time, but the girl is threatening to go to the authorities."

Fuck.

"I'm on my way," I said to Miles and hung up the phone.

I was nowhere near ready for the night to end but the shit at the warehouse needed to get sorted immediately, my hand had been forced.

I was beginning to get tired of my employees taking liberties and forgetting who the fuck they worked for, it was time to put a stop to it.

"Riley, I'm sorry but something has come up and I need to go," I said as I walked back to her, trying to keep some of the anger out of my voice.

Someone was going to die tonight for fucking this up for me.

My radiant Star was looking back out at the city but when I stopped next to her, she turned to face me. Her eyes were filled with sadness and I hated seeing it there.

"Is everything okay?" she asked softly. Unable to resist touching her, I reached up and tucked a strand of her hair behind her ear.

"There's a problem at one of my warehouses, it can't wait. I'll get one of my drivers to take you back home." I couldn't break my stare away from her mesmerizing eyes, and I silently cursed Miles for phoning when he did, wondering what would have happened if he'd waited one minute more.

"Can I come with you?" she almost begged, and as much as I wanted to give in to her and have her by my side every minute of the day, after what she'd just learned about Joe, taking her to the warehouse was a bad idea. I didn't know the extent of what had happened, but a bad feeling had taken root in my gut, whatever had gone on at the warehouse was not going to be pleasant.

I was about to tell her no, when she put her delicate hand on my chest, igniting a fire in my body.

"Please, Kai, I don't want to be on my own," she whispered, her eyes wide and pleading.

How the fuck did I say no to that? It was like she had reached inside my chest and squeezed my black heart.

"It won't be pretty."

"I don't care."

And so, against my better judgment, I found myself in the back of my car heading towards my warehouse with Riley sitting beside me. She didn't say anything for the entire journey, but she did let me hold her hand, finding comfort in the way my thumb brushed over her knuckles.

Or maybe it was me who found comfort.

Before I knew it, we had reached the warehouse. It was situated on the outskirts of the city, surrounded by forest in an area where no one had cause to go. And anyone who thought they did have cause to go there, found themselves staring down the barrel of heavily armed guards before they got anywhere near the goods within the confines of the warehouse.

I made a shit load of money through importing and exporting weapons of various kinds, I wasn't going to be taking any chances by not protecting the heart of my organization.

The guards opened the gates when the car got close enough, not bothering to check if it was me, they knew my car. Frank drove us down the rough track, and I noticed Riley's interest peaked. She was looking around, taking everything in but still not asking any questions, even though I was sure they were on the tip of her tongue. If anything, her being present when this shit was about to go down was going to be a testament as to whether Riley could really hack the life I led.

I really hoped she fucking could.

When we reached the main entrance, the car came to a stop and Frank opened my door. I stepped out first and held my hand out for Riley. She gracefully got out of the car which was no easy thing to do in her tight dress, and gaped at the enormous warehouse standing behind us.

"What is this place?"

Curiosity got the better of her, she couldn't tear her wandering eyes away from the building as she asked.

Not letting go of her hand, I started walking us toward the side door which would take us to the staff quarters, the area where I had an office, where security sat and watched the cameras installed throughout the place, and where there was an empty room used only on rare occasions when an employee failed to follow my rules.

I had a feeling the room would be utilized in the coming hour.

"This is where all my weapons are imported to," I told her casually, as if arms dealing was an everyday occurrence.

I guess for me, it was.

"This is where my staff check the weapons, assemble them, and then prepare them for exporting onwards."

"Oh."

She was so focused on staring at the building that she wasn't watching where she was going and tripped in her ridiculously high heels. She grabbed hold of my arm with the hand that wasn't already in mine, and I quickly wrapped my arms around her waist to stop her from falling.

"You okay?" I asked when she was solidly standing on two feet.

Under the bright light from the warehouse lights, I could see her cheeks flush red.

She was so fucking cute.

"Yeah. Sorry. This place is huge," she said, her gaze landing back on mine and looking……impressed?

"This branch of my business accounts for 40% of my income, Riley. I have a reputation for being able to source any weapon available on the black market. People from all over the world contact me to do business, I supply to some of the largest gangs across the globe. I needed somewhere big enough to store the goods and house the employees who work here."

It didn't phase me sharing this level of detailed information with her, it's not like I was ever going to let her go so she could go off and squeal. I wasn't sure if she realized it yet, but Riley was mine and I was keeping her.

"Doesn't that bother you?" she asked, narrowing her eyes at me. Fuck, when she gave me that look, I felt like I was a naughty kid being scolded.

"Why would it?" I retorted. "People use weapons every day, if it isn't me supplying them, it'd be someone else."

She stared at me, considering this. I didn't think she'd understand it, but I'd grown up with the philosophy that human nature meant people would always do dumb shit. There would never be a way to stop murders, people taking drugs, or whatever other bullshit people got up to, and there would always be someone to cash in on it. You could stand back and watch some other schmuck gain from people's stupidity, or you could be the schmuck that reaped the rewards.

I knew which schmuck I'd rather be.

"Come on." I held her hand again and led her to the door.

Miles was walking up and down, pacing the floor with his hand tugging roughly at his hair. Behind him, six or seven of the security officers loitered, all equally looking concerned, and rightly so. The fact I was here meant they hadn't done their jobs properly.

Miles' shoulders slumped in relief the second I walked through the door.

"Thank fuck," he said, walking towards me. His eyes darted to Riley, surprised to see her here.

Him and me both.

"What the hell is going on, Miles?"

"Boss, Luis," he said by way of an explanation and a wave of his hand. When I didn't reply, he continued. "He managed to sneak off to the living quarters. The shipment had just arrived and I was dealing with that. The fucker took the opportunity."

That at least explained why Miles was shitting his pants. He and the other guards knew to keep watch on Luis, and he'd fucked up.

Epically.

I don't think I had ever despised someone as much as I despised Luis Rodez, and if I'd had it my way, he wouldn't be within a thousand feet of my warehouse. But he played an important role.

His father, Jose Rodez, was a valuable contact in Argentina for dealing in weapons, both importing and exporting, and I got a hell of a lot of business from him. His son, Luis, was a fucking prick though, and acted like *he* was the one in charge of my weapons business. Jose had insisted Luis worked in the warehouse to ensure smooth transactions and it was, frustratingly, one of his terms of conditions to agree to the deal we had.

I'd since come to realize that Jose wanted rid of Luis, he was nothing but a pain in the ass. The man was an untrustworthy, smarmy cunt, and I wouldn't have pissed on him if he was on fire. A sentiment I was sure his father echoed. I had agreed to the deal but I'd warned both Jose and Luis that if he did anything to piss me off, I wouldn't hesitate to end his existence, something Jose had quickly accepted. However, in the eight months he had worked for me, he hadn't put a toe out of line and I'd never had a reason to put a bullet through his head.

Looked like that would change tonight.

"Why wasn't anyone watching him?" I growled at Miles who cowered under my glare.

"I thought one of the others had him on camera, Boss. We've got a quick turnaround on the latest shipment, I was trying to get it sorted. Kai, I'm sorry, I didn't mean for it to happen."

"What did he do?" I questioned, ignoring Miles' pleading. I'd deal with his stupidity later and he damn well knew it.

Miles swallowed before he spoke, and once again, his eyes darted to Riley before coming back to mine, an unspoken question passed between us. He was making sure it was ok to talk freely in front of my girl.

I nodded my head once.

"He…uh…he broke into a room where one of the girls was. She was sleeping and he attacked her." Miles looked to the floor, he didn't need to say the words out loud for me to know what he meant when he referred to the girl being attacked.

"Did he rape her?" Riley had been quiet up to that point throughout the exchange between Miles and me, but now she spoke up, sounding a heck of a lot more confident than she looked.

Miles looked back up and met her eyes, giving her an apologetic look. His mouth tightened into a thin line and he nodded. She let out a small gasp which echoed around the room and every fucker in the room stopped what they were doing to look at her.

I did *not* like them looking at my girl.

"How old is she?" she asked quietly, her eyes filled with horror.

"Sixteen, I think," Miles replied.

Her whole body tensed. I dropped her hand and instead put my arm around her shoulders and pulled her close against my chest. She'd already had to deal with enough shock for one night, and I cursed internally at bringing her here, but with Riley, I couldn't always think straight with her around.

"Where's the girl now?" I asked Miles.

"She's in her room. She kept saying she is going to go to the ATF."

This was going from bad to worse.

The fucking Alcohol, Tobacco, Firearms, and Explosives Department had been snooping around these past few months, I'd managed to hold them off for the time being thanks to my hold over Hollows Bay Police Department, but all they needed was the tip-off they'd been waiting for.

It was rapidly looking like I was going to have no choice but to end two lives tonight, not that the girl deserved to die but I had to protect my business.

"And Luis?"

"He's in there." Miles tilted his head to the side and indicated the room that had two armed guards standing outside. The fucker wouldn't be going anywhere.

Unless it was in a body bag.

"Fuck, Miles, you really fucking screwed up with this," I huffed. He ducked his head, having the good sense not to answer back.

Options swam around in my head. But every option came back to the one that would have to happen.

The girl would have to die.

As if reading my mind, Riley pulled out of my grasp.

"Let me talk to her," she said with pure determination. She didn't ask, and if shit wasn't happening right now, I'd find it amusing she thought she could demand anything from me.

"No," I told her firmly.

She knew, she *fucking knew* where my mind was going, and if I went down that route, it would undo the progress I'd made with her today. But I couldn't let Riley be my weakness, and I couldn't let my attraction to her dictate how I dealt with my issues.

"Kai, please. Let me talk to her, I can talk her out of wanting to go to the authorities. She doesn't deserve this."

Her eyes filled with tears and her voice shook, losing the burst of confidence she had just had. Once again, I kicked myself for bringing her here.

I'd have to deal with her undermining my decisions, especially in front of my staff, I couldn't let it happen.

I was about to tell Frank, who had been waiting by the door we'd come in, to take her back to the car when Miles opened his stupid fucking mouth.

"Boss, for what it's worth, the girl wants out of here. For the right price, I think she could be paid to keep her mouth shut."

I gave him my death glare for daring to fucking interfere, and he muttered an apology under his breath before looking down again.

"Riley, she could ruin everything if she goes to the ATF."

I glanced down at my Star who was wearing that look on her face, the look she had worn a few nights ago when she was refusing to come willingly with me. Despite the tears shining in her eyes, she wasn't going to back down.

Stubborn little minx.

"Let me try. What harm can it do?"

I let out a sigh and threw my head back to stare at the ceiling, counting to ten before I exploded.

But she did have a point, what harm could it do to see if the girl's silence could be bought? As long as I had reassurances she wouldn't go to the authorities, then it was something I could consider. I didn't relish the idea of killing an innocent girl, I wasn't a *total* monster.

"If you can't convince her, Riley, then I have no choice, you have to understand that. That's just the way it is."

Anger flashed across her face for a split second but then her features softened. "I understand."

I stared at her for a moment, realization dawning that this was a turning point in our relationship, if you could call it that, I wasn't sure what the fuck it was. But if I wanted her around, she had to understand how I worked, and she had to accept it. Her eyebrow arched as though she had come to the same realization.

"Take her to the girl," I ordered Miles, breaking our stand-off.

I watched her go, her heels echoing around the room attracting the attention of every man in the room whose heads turned to watch her luscious ass sway in that damn dress. My already boiling blood was about to bubble over at the thought of them ogling her.

"Back to fucking work," I growled at the remaining men in the room. The guards at the door straightened, as others darted off in different directions. I walked over to the room where Luis was currently being held. The two men stepped aside and I tapped in the code to the lock and pushed the door open.

A wave of wicked glee rolled through me at the sight of Luis hanging by his wrists from ceiling hooks. His face was bruised and broken, swollen so badly his eyes were forced to shut. Blood trickled from various wounds, and his leg was broken, evident from the unnatural angle it hung at. Miles may have fucked up, but he'd gone some way to redeem himself with the damage he'd caused to Luis.

I stared at the man who was swaying slightly from where his feet couldn't touch the ground, and I couldn't help but let my mouth curl up into a smile.

I fucking *loved* this.

"Kai, this is a misunderstanding," Luis said when he managed to open an eye to see I was in the room with him. His South American accent was thick with pain which pleased me no end. "Let me down and I can explain."

"You have no idea how long I've waited for this day, Luis." I moved closer to him, eyeing my prey like the predator I was.

His eye, because he could only open the one, followed my movements as I circled him, removing my suit jacket as I went, and rolling my shirt sleeves up to my elbows. Luis winced in agony when he tensed his body up as I came to stand in front of him, his eyes widening when he saw the guns and knife in the holster I had been wearing underneath my jacket the entire time. I never went out unarmed.

"You can't do this. My father-"

"I warned your father what I would do if you put a foot wrong, and you were there when he shook my hand and agreed to the terms."

I didn't give him a chance to reply, with all my strength I punched Luis straight in the gut. The wind flew out of him, and for a few seconds after, he struggled to breathe. I'd probably caused some internal damage but I had no fucks to give, he wouldn't be seeing another day. But I would make his final hours on earth as painful as possible.

It took almost a minute before he managed to suck air back into his lungs, and as he took deep, gulping breaths, I thought of all the ways I was going to destroy this piece of shit.

"Let me tell you something, Luis, I'm a man of many things. I kill people, I torture people, and I fucking enjoy every minute of it. But I don't rape people, especially little girls. There's a special place in hell reserved for people like you."

"She wanted it!" he suddenly burst out, spittle and blood flying everywhere and unfortunately landing on my arm.

The anger I was struggling to contain erupted out of me like a volcano. Grabbing the knife out of the belt holster, and without giving it a second thought, I aimed at his shoulder and threw. With precise accuracy, the knife embedded into its target and Luis' screams of agony echoed around the room. It wouldn't kill him, I knew where to strike to avoid any major arteries, but it would hurt like a motherfucker.

"You...are...going to....pay for this," he gritted out, clenching his teeth so hard I was surprised they didn't pop from his mouth.

I threw my head back and let out a hearty laugh.

The man was a comedian.

Striding over to him, I ripped the knife out of his shoulder, blood spurting from the wound and ruining my white shirt. And then I let rip on his body.

See, I could have just put a few bullets in him and been done with it, but where was the fun in that?

Raining down punch after punch all over his body, his cries of pain spurred me on, and it didn't take long until his cries became mere whimpers. It felt fucking good to let loose on him, I wasn't just taking out his crime on him, but I was taking out Joe Mason's crimes as well. I'd never get the chance to cause that man pain, but this, this was good enough. With every punch I threw at Luis' body, I pictured the look of heartbreak on Riley's face, and as crazy as it sounded, with every hit against his body, it felt like I was helping to heal Riley's pain.

It was only the soft knock on the door that stopped my assault on Luis. Sweat rolled down my back, and my chest heaved after my sudden burst of energy, but I felt fucking incredible, I loved the surge of adrenaline rushing through my body.

Luis was barely clinging to consciousness. I knew the right amount of pain to inflict on someone without them falling unconscious, after all, I didn't want him to miss out on the fun.

Backing away from his limp body, I opened the door to find Riley standing there. She'd evidently been crying if the red tracks and mascara streaks down her cheeks were anything to go by, and as much as I wanted to take her in my arms and comfort her, I didn't want her getting covered in blood.

She gaped at me, taking in the splatters of blood on my white shirt and my bruised knuckles, and then her gaze darted over my shoulder to where Luis hung. For a minute she didn't say anything, just stared at him, a sneer taking over her face.

"Star," I barked, catching her attention. She pulled her gaze away from Luis and fixed it on me. "What did she say?"

"She'll be on a plane first thing in the morning back to Mexico. You're going to pay for her and her family to relocate to a safe part of the country, and you're going to pay for her to get an education. Do that, and you have her word you won't hear from her ever again."

She stood tall as she relayed the terms, she didn't stutter and she was full of confidence, and it made me fucking proud. She'd done this for me, despite me being an outright prick to her, she'd done this to help my business.

It made me all the more determined to make her mine.

"You believe her?" I raised a brow in question.

"Yes."

"Then it's done," I told her, and her body sagged with relief. She looked behind me again and the tears began to well in her eyes once more. I wanted to get this shit over and done with and get her the fuck out of here.

I started removing my gun from my holster, fully intending to turn around and put a bullet straight between Luis' eyes.

"Kai, wait," Riley said, stopping me in my tracks.

She looked at Luis again before looking back at me. I waited for it, waited for her to tell me not to kill him, but this was one job that had to be done. Surely she would fucking realize that after everything she knew about the cunt?

"Don't kill him," she said in a whisper.

"Fuck, Riley, you know I can't let him live." I hissed.

"I know, but death is too good for him. He deserves to live every day for the rest of his miserable life with the knowledge of what he did to that poor girl."

I put the safety back on my gun and reholstered it, intrigued with where she was going with this.

"What do you suggest, Riley?"

For the final time, she looked at Luis, only this time she kept her eyes fixed on him, filled with a look I had never seen from her before, and as a malicious smile curved her lips, she spoke.

"Hurt him, Kai. Take away his ability to ever hurt another woman again."

Well. Fuck.

I always knew she was perfect for me.

Chapter 18

Riley

It wasn't watching as Kai hacked off Luis' dick that kept me awake the following nights. Nor the echoes of his screams bouncing off the walls as Kai squished his eyeballs in their sockets with his bare hands.

And it wasn't from the guilt that I had been the one to condemn Luis to the life of hell that kept me tossing and turning each night.

Fuck no, I didn't feel the slightest bit bad for what happened.

Why should I?

The man was a dirty rapist, and the pain Kai had caused, well, Luis deserved to suffer through it every day for the rest of his life. If he even survived the night, which I wasn't sure he would have given how much blood he lost from his missing appendage, not to mention the beating Kai had given him beforehand.

No, the thing that kept me awake each night was the face of the girl who had been raped by that evil man. I'd been expecting her to be inconsolable, to beg for Luis to be arrested. But she wasn't *anything* like that. Her eyes were empty of any emotion, and when she looked at me, it was like she was looking straight *through* me.

It was chilling.

There was no hysteria, she was stoic as she made her demand. She wanted to return to Mexico, and she wanted Kai to pay for her and her family to move out of the village her family lived in otherwise she was at risk of being sent back to America to work. She held her nerve as she told me to make it happen or she would find a way to report the illegal activity in the factory. She was very brave for a young girl, and in a way, reminded me of, well, *me*.

Behind the bullshit bravado though, she was terrified. When I walked closer to her, she flinched as if half expecting me to pull out a gun from the stupid skin-tight dress I was wearing, and fire a bullet into her. I'd sat next to her and put my hand on her arm in what I'd hoped was a reassuring gesture, and sure enough, the dam broke. Tears streaked down her eyes as she begged for her mom and to go home. And fucking hell, didn't that break my heart.

Before I knew it, I'd wrapped my arms around her and held her as my own tears fell. She was someone's daughter, maybe even someone's sister.

I didn't know how anyone would be able to get over something as traumatic as what she'd experienced, and despite her pleas of just wanting to go home, she deserved more. So I told her not only would Kai agree to her returning to Mexico and moving her family to a different village, he'd pay for her to be educated in the best goddamn college in Mexico. She'd been stunned, and that's when she gave me her promise that she would never tell on Kai, managing a small smile when I said goodbye to her, but her eyes were still void of any emotion.

I was sure they would haunt me until my dying days.

It had been a week since the incident with Luis and the girl, and while relatively uneventful, *thankfully*, several things had happened.

The first being I'd got to spend not one, but two days with Angel. The day after I'd learned about Joe, Kai permitted me to spend the day with her. It still fucked me off he *gave* me permission to spend time with my sister, but a deal was a deal after all, and I was grateful for any time I had with her.

Angel looked like a different kid, the transformation was amazing in just a few short days. The time spent sleeping in a cozy bed, three meals a day, and brand new clothes gave me confidence I'd made the right decision by agreeing to this crazy deal. Gone were the heavy bags from under her eyes, her skin glowed, and for the first time in five years, she didn't look malnourished. She had given me a bright smile when I walked into her room, and it was the first genuine smile I had seen on her cute face in such a long time.

I met her tutor, Jane, who was not only kind and sincere, but had developed a strong bond with Angel. Admittedly, it did stir up some jealousy in me but I did my best to ignore it because Jane was just helping Angel when I couldn't.

Besides, it wasn't going to be forever.

Jane was pretty, in an understated way. She was in her mid-30's, and slightly taller than me. She wore baggy clothes that hid her figure, but at one point she'd taken off a jumper revealing she was hiding killer curves underneath. I'd commented that she should show her figure off a bit more and she blushed deeply at the compliment. She wore her mousy brown hair tied on top of her head in a tight bun, and her green eyes were hidden behind black thick-rimmed glasses. She was one of those women who, with a bit of makeup and styling would be drop dead gorgeous. Jane had a friendly feeling about her, and I instantly warmed to the woman, especially as I could see with my own eyes that she was taking good care of Angel.

I'd spent the day helping Angel with her school work and then we'd played some games on her console. Kai had fulfilled his promise to get it from our old apartment and Angel was over the moon with the three new games that had arrived with the damn thing. She took great delight in kicking my ass at every game we played and taking the piss out of my inability to coordinate my controller with the on-screen character. It was a rare moment, normally I was so focused on making sure money was coming in and making ends meet that somewhere along the line, I'd forgotten to have fun with her.

Kai let me spend some more time with her a few days later. I learned she'd been allowed out of the apartment with the escort of Danny and some other security guards, and she and Jane had spent a day at the city's history museum, followed by a picnic in the park, and while I had been pleased to know Angel wasn't being kept locked away with no fresh air, the pang of jealousy had only settled deeper into my bones. I wanted to be the one to experience those things with her.

The second thing to change was that I spent time getting to know both Danny and Miles, almost to the point I would have considered them friends.

Danny really was a gentle giant, and while I was sure he was nothing but brutal when doing his job, I never saw that side of him. He would spend time with me whenever he could, he taught me how to play snooker, and I taught him how to make cocktails in the bar that was in the snooker room. It was almost as though he had become an older brother figure to me, and spending time with him left a sense of contentment settled within me. It had been a long time since I had something that resembled a family.

He informed me Kai had given him the role of protecting Angel whenever they went out, and it became apparent he *absolutely* doted on her. If he wasn't working or spending time with me, he would be with Angel, thrashing her at her computer games or trying to teach her some self-defense moves, much to my annoyance. He was even trying to learn some basic sign language which she found hilarious.

It didn't escape my notice he was somewhat fond of Jane, and the shy tutor blushed whenever he walked into the room so I suspected the feeling was mutual.

As for Miles, once he came out of his shell, he wasn't so nervous. He was a complete geek though, always talking about new software he had designed, or about another hacking breach the government had only just discovered. Miles was a genius, and I could totally see why he had said *he* was the brains of the operation. Kai might have been the King of the court but the King never got far without his faithful servants, and it was clear to me as the sky was blue that Miles and Danny were loyal to Kai.

Hendrix was too, but he was a whole other story.

I tried to avoid that man as much as possible. No matter what I was wearing, his eyes would roam over my body every time like he was mentally undressing me, and it freaked me the hell out. But he was careful when Kai was around, he'd either ignore me completely or communicate by grunting at me. His attitude toward me didn't phase me, but the letchy looks he gave did.

Still, I didn't say anything to the others though, I was sure I was being paranoid. Besides, the four of them had a close relationship, and I didn't want to be the thing that ruined it.

The final thing to happen was that my feelings towards Kai changed.

Dramatically.

I tried my damned hardest to hold on to the hate I felt when he first kidnapped me off the street, because let's face it, that is *exactly* what he had done, kidnapped me. But over time, hate turned into something else. Something I tried hard not to think about, but it was damn impossible when he consumed my thoughts pretty much every single minute of every single day.

He'd been nothing but thoughtful and considerate, even if it was mixed in with him being a controlling asshole. For example, he insisted I ate every meal with him, there was no choice in the matter, and he maintained it was because he wanted to make sure I was eating enough. But then he'd spend the entire meal asking me questions about my life and making sure I was okay and had everything I needed.

There was a little part of me that told me to keep my guard up, that he was lulling me into a false sense of security, but I couldn't help but ignore it. Even when I replayed scenes in my mind of when he had scared the living shit out of me, like when I thought he was going to kill Blaze, I just couldn't stop the feelings of wanting him creeping in.

I was sure it'd come back to bite me on the ass one day, but I'd worry about that if and when it happened.

Kai spent some of the days showing me around Hollows Bay and taking me to meetings for his legitimate businesses. Aside from the weapons warehouse, he'd kept me away from any other shady shit, which I was glad for. I hadn't yet discovered how the Wolfe family came to believe they owned Hollows Bay, but it was evident from the way people reacted when Kai made an appearance at meetings that no one would ever challenge his authority.

I'd also learned bits about Kai's life. I figured if he got to know everything about me, then surely I got to know everything about him too, right?

Kai wasn't always willing to answer my questions, especially when it came to his father or Theo. From the information he had shared, it sounded like his father, Christopher Wolfe, was a complete asshole. He was manipulative, and a bully to Kai and Theo, not to mention a womanizer, and it sounded like not many people were sad when he eventually died and the control of Hollows Bay passed to Kai and Theo.

As for his mom, Kai was a little more open about her. She'd passed away from cancer when he was thirteen and Theo was eleven, and although they were devastated at her passing, they were relieved as it meant she would no longer have to put up with the way Chris treated her. Apparently, he regularly beat her, raped her, and cheated on her, and Kai was sure the only reason she stayed married to him was for the sake of her boys.

Every time Kai revealed a little piece of himself to me, I saw him less and less of the monster I once thought he was, and my feelings towards him grew stronger.

There hadn't been any more moments like the one we shared on the balcony the night we had dinner, the moment where, had his phone not rang, I have no doubt we would have kissed. But there were other signs Kai was feeling for me what I was feeling for him. He made excuses to touch me, be that a brush of my arm or a palm to the small of my back when escorting me somewhere, and every time I felt his touch on me, sparks zapped through my body, or shivers shot down my spine. And I always felt his gaze on me, even when he thought I wasn't looking, I knew he was watching me with that intense stare of his.

And you know what, I found myself liking it.

Craving it, even.

I'd clearly lost the plot.

As I turned over in my bed for the millionth time exactly a week to the day after the incident with Luis, I'd decided this was ridiculous, and if I didn't get a good night's sleep soon, I'd be walking around like a zombie.

In the hopes that maybe some warm milk would help me sleep, I hopped out of bed, wrapped my silk robe around me, and tip-toed out into the hallway on my quest for the kitchen.

The hallways were eerily silent, it was gone 3 am after all, anyone in their right mind would be sleeping. Alas, I was not in the right mind. I crept along, wondering for the umpteenth time where in this place Kai's room was. Not that I was planning on venturing into it or anything.

Honest.

As I silently walked along the hallway, my feet cold against the marbled floor, light filtered into the hallway from the kitchen, and from the hushed voice I could hear, I knew someone was in there. I figured it must have been Kai, why would one of the other three be in his apartment at 3 am, but hope quickly disappeared when, as I crept closer, I recognized the hushed tones to be Hendrix.

It was strange, the way he was keeping his voice down. I mean, yeah it was late, or early depending on which way you looked at it, but the kitchen was nowhere near any of the bedrooms, so there was no real reason for him to be keeping his voice down.

Also, why was he here?

It didn't feel right, and it was because of that I didn't immediately breeze into the kitchen. Instead, I hid in the shadows by the doorway. Hendrix was sitting at the island in the middle of the room holding a hand up to his ear. I didn't need to be a genius to know he was speaking to someone on the phone. Something had made him flustered, his cheeks were red, and his hair was mussed up like he'd been tugging at it.

"I told you, I'm working on it. It's not that easy," he said, almost like he was pleading with someone.

He was quiet for a minute then, listening to the response. If I strained my ears, I could just about hear the voice on the other end of the line, it was definitely a man. Kai maybe?

"Yeah, I'm aware," Hendrix snapped before pausing again. "Fine," he said, this time sounding more resigned.

He paused again to look up at the doorway as if he sensed my presence, despite me being as quiet as a mouse. I held my breath and tried to shrink into the shadows a little bit more, I doubt he would have been happy at my eavesdropping. When he didn't move and dropped his head down to look at the table, I breathed a sigh of relief.

"It'll be done, Boss," he said, and then hung up the phone. So, he was talking to Kai, but what needed to be done?

You know what they say, curiosity killed the cat, and I really wasn't ready to die so I figured it was none of my business.

Instead, I stepped out of the shadows and into the kitchen, intent on getting some milk and getting my ass back to bed. The second I stepped in, Hendrix looked up at me, and a look of guilt flashed across his face before it disappeared as quickly as it had arrived.

"What are you doing up?" he snapped.

What the hell was his problem?

His tone took me by surprise. I was so used to him either ignoring me or being creepy that I wasn't prepared for him to bite my head off.

"I couldn't sleep so I thought I'd get some milk," I answered, keeping my tone cool and not reacting to his snappiness.

He watched me like a hawk as I crossed the kitchen and took the milk out of the fridge. I was very much aware of his eyes burning into my ass as I reached up for a mug. Being here alone with him was setting my nerves on edge.

Something was *definitely* off about him, more so than usual.

Ignoring the creepy feelings he was setting off within me, I poured myself a mug of milk before heating it up in the microwave. For the minute it took to heat, neither Hendrix nor I said anything, there was an awkward tension in the air as he stared at me, shooting daggers in my direction while I pretended to look anywhere but at him. The second the microwave pinged, I grabbed my mug and was about to head off to bed, away from the weirdo as quickly as possible.

But the creepy bastard had other ideas.

Leaping from his seat, he blocked my path out of the kitchen and glared down at me with his bright blue eyes. My stomach churned with dread, I despised him being this close to me. Surely he wouldn't try something, would he?

"I bet you're loving this aren't you?"

"Loving what?" I snapped back at him, taking the bait and then internally cursing myself for doing so.

"Living here, freeloading off the boss," he sneered, he was close enough for me to smell the bourbon on his breath, and to see his eyes clearly, they didn't seem to be focused.

"Freeloading? Are you fucking serious right now?"

Seriously, what the hell was his problem?

I hadn't asked Kai for a single fucking thing. I tried to step around him, fed up with his bullshit, but he moved with me. He was twice the size of me, so I had little chance of actually getting past the prick.

I wondered how he'd react to a knee to the balls.

"I've seen the shithole of a place you called home, this is a palace compared to that. I bet you were laughing your ass off when Kai offered you the deal. Tell me, *Star*," he sneered the name only Kai used for me. "What does Kai get out of this little arrangement, 'cos he sure as hell isn't interested in fucking you," he hissed venomously.

Won't lie, that hurt.

Not the part about my old apartment being a shithole because he was spot on about that, but the part about Kai not being interested in me.

Yeah, that hurt.

"Firstly, what the fuck has it got to do with you what Kai gets? That's between me and him." I stood my ground, displaying bravado I did not feel in front of this man, but I'd be damned if I was going to show him any weakness. "And secondly, how the fuck do you know Kai isn't interested in fucking me? Given the way he's been with me the last few days, I'd say he was *very* fucking interested."

I let a smug smirk grace my lips when really, I was feeling anything but. Kai hadn't tried to kiss me or anything more than touch my hand, maybe Hendrix was right, maybe I had read it wrong and Kai wasn't interested in me, but I sure as hell wasn't going to give Hendrix the satisfaction of thinking he was right.

He took a step closer to me, towering intimidatingly over me. I tilted my head back to look up at him, and in his eyes was nothing but pure hatred aimed at me. It scared me right down to my bones.

"Where do you think he is right now, huh?" Now it was his turn to look smug, and when I didn't reply, he smirked. "I'll tell you where he is, he's at his nightclub where he can fuck any of the girls he wants. In fact, he has a different girl most nights, sometimes he even has two at the same time. I assure you, sweetheart, he ain't interested in your skanky cunt when he can have any elite pussy he wants, *whenever* he wants." He said the last part slowly, just to make sure I understood every word he had said.

Tears pricked my eyes as my face twisted into a snarl. But I couldn't say anything, I knew my voice would crack, and I couldn't let this asshat know he'd upset me. Instead, I bit my cheek to stop the tears from falling.

We stared at each other for what seemed like an eternity, before he chuckled.

"Night, Riley. Sleep well," he said as he walked away, his laugh echoing in the silent hallways.

I stood for a few more moments, making sure Hendrix was long gone before I slammed my now cold milk down on the side, and stomped off back to my bedroom knowing full damn well I had even less chance of sleep coming to me now.

Chapter 19

Riley

I'd been in a foul mood all day.

I wished I could say it was purely down to lack of sleep, but it wasn't. The constant images of Kai at a club with scantily clad women draping themselves all over him had lodged itself firmly in my brain, and jealousy like I'd never felt before was burning through my veins.

Kai fucking Wolfe had turned me into a maniac.

He'd given me a wide berth all day which of course only added to my theory that he was exhausted from being awake all night having a threesome, or a foursome, or a fucking orgy.

Gah!

I wanted to spend the day hiding under my bed sheets, and sulk like a toddler who couldn't get their own way, but of course, Kai had plans for me. Which is why I found myself staring at my reflection in the mirror, having had my hair and makeup done, and wearing the most stunning dress I had ever seen.

Yep, Kai had sprung on me that we were to attend a charity ball in the City Hall, and I was beside myself with excitement.

Not.

Earlier in the afternoon, Jacqueline had been brave enough to knock on my door to announce the arrival of a young girl called Hannah, who had come to do my hair and makeup, and to dress me, like I was incapable of dressing myself.

Poor Hannah had tried to make conversation with me but after only getting grunts and one-word answers, she gave up and focused on the task at hand. I hated to admit it, but she'd done an excellent job. If I were in her shoes, I would have made my face up to resemble that of a clown. But then, she probably valued her life.

Hannah had done something amazing with my hair which was now tied up in an elegant braid, with several curled strands hanging down around my shoulders, and a beautiful ornamental clip holding it all together. My makeup was classy and natural, but she'd used a vibrant shade of red lipstick which made my lips pop.

The black velvet mermaid dress was out of this world. It was strapless, and the bodice, which had a V shape dip between my breasts, fit snugly against my curves, accentuating my hourglass figure. It was tight against my hips and thighs, but flared out as it got lower to the floor. Up the left-hand side of the skirt was a split that went as high up as my thigh, allowing me to show off the five inch silver stiletto sandals I had on.

The dress resembled *Jessica Rabbit's* dress only in black, and obviously looked better on her, 'cos let's face it, she's a total babe.

It didn't matter how much Hannah harped on about how beautiful I looked, or how much I did indeed feel like a million dollars, I was still in a foul mood, only exacerbated by the thought of having to spend the evening with Kai.

The prick.

I met him in the foyer where he was dressed in a black tuxedo, complete with a bowtie. He looked fucking *divine* which only angered me more, it was no wonder he had a harem of women eating out of the palm of his hand.

Not reading my mood, he gave me a dazzling smile that faltered as soon as he was met with a scowl.

"Riley, you look beautiful," he said as I reached him and he leaned down to kiss my cheek. His lips brushed softly against my skin sending tingles all through me. I tried not to react to his touch, but my traitorous body was not in tune with my brain, and I shivered.

"Thanks," I replied glumly, not meeting his eyes. He frowned at me and opened his mouth to say something, but footsteps behind him stopped whatever he was about to say. My mood soured further when Hendrix, Miles, and Danny, all dressed in tuxes joined us, evidently coming with us tonight.

The men exchanged small talk about what weapons they had concealed on them. I tuned out of the conversation, not really giving a shit about who carried what. They made it sound like it was a competition as to who had the biggest balls, for fuck sake. My eyes found Hendrix who was smirking at me, and I was just about to fake a migraine and tell Kai I couldn't come when he grabbed my hand and pulled me towards the open elevator.

Hendrix, Miles, and Danny piled in behind us, and as the doors slid closed, I found myself wedged between Kai and Hendrix.

Just my fucking luck.

A heavy atmosphere filled the small space. I had no doubt it was from the tension vibrating from me, my whole body rigid with anger, and I refused to make eye contact with any of them in the mirrors surrounding the elevator. Kai glowered at me, quietly seething at me and my attitude. Like I gave a fuck.

When the elevator stopped at the parking level, Kai once again grabbed my hand and marched me to the waiting Rolls Royce. As I got in, Hendrix, Miles, and Danny got into a black SUV behind us. I breathed a sigh of relief knowing I would have at least a little bit of respite from Hendrix for the journey.

It was a shame the same couldn't be said about Kai.

"You okay, Riley?" Kai asked tersely after we started making our way through the city.

"Fine," I replied nonchalantly, not looking away from the window.

He'd taken to holding my hand any time we went out in the car, but tonight, I kept my hands folded neatly in my lap.

"Riley," Kai growled, like actually growled my name, and if it wasn't so intimidating, it would have been a complete turn on.

I turned my gaze away from the passing city to look at him. He was mad, in fact, that was putting it lightly. He looked murderous.

"What the fuck is going on with you?"

"Nothing, Kai. I told you, I'm fine," I snapped back.

Shit.

Brain to mouth malfunction. I needed to remember not to snap at a murdering bastard.

He stared at me intently for a minute, holding my gaze with his narrowed eyes. With anyone else, I would have held my nerve, but with Kai, I lost my lady balls and looked away, going back to staring aimlessly out the window. He didn't speak again, but spent the rest of the journey gawking at me like I was some sort of creature who had sprouted a third tit.

All too soon, we were pulling up outside City Hall where throngs of glamorous people gathered on the red carpet that led up the stairs into the old building.

Frank, who I'd come to learn was Kai's personal driver, opened the door, and Kai stepped out. He offered me his hand to help me, but being the stubborn bitch I was, I ignored him and pulled myself out of the car as gracefully as I could. Kai's features twisted with rage at my ignorance, steam practically bellowing from his ears.

Maybe one of the girls from his club could calm him down.

The other three got out of the SUV and started making their way towards the stairs. I turned to follow, but Kai grabbed my arm, pushed me back against the car, and stepped in, so close our chests were pressed together. His cologne hit me, he was wearing the one that sent my hormones into overdrive and tonight was no different, the scent was so alluring that heat flooded my core. He was downright intoxicating.

Fuck my life.

He raised an arm, putting his hand on the roof of the car, and with the door still open, I was caged in. With his other hand, he roughly grabbed my chin and tilted it upwards to look at him.

"I don't know what the fuck is going on with you tonight, Riley, but you better drop the fucking attitude." His tone was low and cool which made him sound all the more deadly.

Why the hell then did I find that so hot?

"Or what?" I challenged.

Seriously, I was going to get myself into so much trouble one of these days.

He moved closer, if that was possible, and looked me directly in the eyes, anger flaring in his dark ones. He was so mad that I couldn't see any of the normal flecks of gold.

"Don't push me, Riley, you won't like what happens."

Fear sliced its way through me at his menacing tone, and thankfully for once, my brain and mouth worked together to keep silent. The real Kai was making an appearance, Kai the monster. The man who tortured and killed for a living and didn't bat an eyelid when he sliced someone's dick off. He was not someone I wanted to piss off. Or at least, piss off any more than I already had, and that thought banged in my head loud enough for me to keep quiet and not antagonize him any further.

I nodded my head slightly, indicating I would indeed drop the attitude, for now at least. He stared at me, not quite believing me, before stepping back and once again taking my hand to lead me inside.

As evenings went, I could have been in worse places. In fact, I *had* spent many evenings in worse places. There were hundreds of people in the hall, every person dressed up to the nines. The men wore tuxes, and the women wore beautiful gowns, it really was a party for the elite. From the minute I walked in, a champagne flute had been shoved in my hand, and at no point in the evening had I been without a glass of bubbly. It wasn't cheap shit either, it was crisp and refreshing, and going down *way* too easily.

In fact, it eased my bad mood so much I actually started to enjoy myself.

Kai refused to let me go all night, he held my hand as he made his way around the hall speaking to different people. He knew everyone, and from the way he spoke with them, I noticed that he was selective about what information he shared with them. For instance, to some people, he introduced me by name and explained I was his new personal assistant, although I was still waiting to find out exactly what he wanted from his personal assistant, because at no point had I done anything that resembled work. To other people he introduced me only as his date, and to others, he didn't bother introducing me at all. I figured I'd ask him about it at some point, but he'd hardly spoken to me since gripping me up by the car, other than to ask if I needed my glass refilling.

Aside from one or two older women, Kai only spoke to men at the party, all of whom wanted some of his time, and the majority of the time was all business talk which meant I was excluded from conversations. It suited me fine, they were talking about stocks and shares, and shit like that, which I had no clue about and zero interest in trying to understand.

There were a few men who had the balls to talk to me, but for the most, they barely looked my way, and I couldn't help but wonder if they'd all had some kind of warning not to even look my way. I wouldn't have put it past Kai to make some kind of vague threat about what would happen if anyone dared talk to me without his permission.

There was one older guy though who did make the effort to talk to me. He'd been introduced as Mr. Johnson, and while his son was in deep conversation with Kai, the old guy asked if I was having a nice evening. He was a sweet old man, old enough to be my grandfather, but had a kind and warm face that had me instantly liking him. He told me that thanks to Kai investing in his international courier business, he was able to retire and hand the reins over to his son, and he and his wife were soon to be heading on an all-inclusive round the world cruise.

Mr. Johnson made me promise to dance with him later at which point Kai abruptly finished his conversation and dragged me away.

As the evening wore on and people were getting more and more merry from the endless champagne on tap, couples found their way to the dance floor and started swaying to the live orchestra that had been playing throughout the night. I finished my glass of champagne, and as I reached out to a passing waiter to grab another, not that I needed another, Kai took my hand and pulled me into his chest.

"Dance with me?" He asked it like a question, but he and I both knew I didn't have a choice in the matter.

It was on the tip of my tongue to tell him he should go and find one of his girls from his club to dance with, but I didn't want to make a scene in this posh place, it wouldn't have ended well for me. Instead, I responded with a simple, "Okay."

Taking my hand in his big one, he led me to the dance floor. As we did, women from all over the room subtly looked at Kai, looks of desire etched across their faces. I knew how they felt. All night I had been sneaking glances at him, taking in how the tux showed off his broad frame. He was pure sex in a suit, and so, despite my mixed feelings of lust and hate towards the man, I'll admit I was feeling quite smug that it was me he was leading to the dance floor.

We made our way to the center, pushing through couples who were engrossed in the music. Kai pulled me in close to his firm body, his alluring scent surrounding me. He placed one hand on my lower back, just above my ass, and took the other one in his, and I rested my other hand on his shoulder. The music changed into a slow tune, one I recognized but couldn't quite place. It wasn't exactly the music I'd pole danced to.

Kai's face was mere inches away from mine, and with every breath he took, his warm exhale brushed against my cheeks. Underneath the spotlights, I could see the gold flecks back in his black eyes, and with music going on around us, and his hand lingering above my ass, I was getting drawn into him, and beginning to forget why I was mad at him. That was until he ruined the moment.

"You want to tell me why you were so pissy earlier?" he said low enough that only I could hear, not that anyone could have heard over the music. But he wasn't angry now, in fact, there was a hint of amusement in his tone.

"Does it matter?" I replied, my tongue feeling loose after one too many champagnes.

"If something has upset you, Star, then yes. It does matter." He gave me a genuine look like he really wanted to know what had upset me.

I didn't want to tell him, I'd make myself look like a jealous fool, and that was not a look I was going for. Instead, I went on the defensive.

I blame the alcohol.

"Did you have fun at your club last night?" I said accusingly.

His brows creased in confusion momentarily before he composed himself. "I had some business to attend to at my club, Riley. How did you know I was there?"

I couldn't help the undignified snort that left my lips. "Business. Sure."

The burning jealousy that had been bubbling away all day spiked, and if he kept pushing, it wouldn't be long until it erupted.

I couldn't be bothered to deal with this shit, I wanted more champagne. I tried to pull my arm out of his grasp, but Kai's grip on my back and hand tightened. He leaned in closer to me so his mouth was next to my ear.

"You need to start talking. Right. Now." The threatening tone was back, but I was so done with his bullshit.

"Why are you bothering with me, Kai? I mean, what's in this deal for you? Especially when you can go to your club every night and fuck any woman you want?" I hissed.

The thread of dignity I had been holding on to snapped, the jealousy spilling out. The second the words left my mouth I wanted the ground to open up and swallow me whole which was only compounded when the gorgeous bastard smirked at me.

Fucking smirked.

At me.

"You're jealous," he accused, mockingly.

"You know what, Kai, fuck you. I want to go."

I tried to pull out of his arms again, but he was too strong. He gave a subtle look around to the crowd to make sure no one had witnessed my little outburst, which had been louder than what I'd intended. Thankfully, people were too engrossed in the music, or too drunk to notice our little spat.

"Riley," Kai said, and any hint of amusement that had been in his voice had disappeared. "I don't know where you got your information from, but it's wrong. I do regularly go to my club, and yeah, in the past I've fucked some of the girls there. But two weeks ago when I laid eyes on you, I haven't touched another woman. I haven't so much as *thought* about touching another woman." He paused, letting that sink in and holding my stare, letting me know that every word he'd just spoken was true.

"Oh."

"Yeah, *oh*. I obviously haven't made my feelings clear for you Riley, but you are the only woman who consumes my thoughts, the only woman I want to take to my bed, and the only woman I want to be inside of."

As if to prove that, he rubbed his hardening cock against my belly, and I swear, I had to clamp my thighs together to stop myself from gushing.

"I'm trying to do the right thing and not rush you, but if you need me to be more obvious about my fucking feelings for you, Star, I will."

I didn't have time to react before his lips were upon me.

Kai didn't seem to care that we were in the middle of a dance floor at the city ball with a whole heap of important people as he devoured my mouth. His tongue swept inside my mouth, which offered no resistance to him, finding my tongue and stroking it. His teeth nibbled against my bottom lip sending lightning bolts straight to my already wet core. I moaned against his soft lips, and he responded by thrusting his hard cock against my stomach again.

There was nothing sweet about the kiss, it was rough, raw, and typically Kai. He took what he wanted. The hand holding mine suddenly gripped my chin and pulled me in closer against him, and my now free hand grabbed his hip in an attempt to steady my weak knees.

Holy fuck, did Kai know how to kiss.

The kiss lasted no more than ten seconds but it felt like it went on for eternity. When we finally broke apart, my eyes darted around to see people staring at us, some with smiles on their faces, some of the women with scowls. But Kai only had eyes for me, and right now it looked like it was taking him a lot of strength not to hike my dress up and thrust inside of me, onlookers be damned.

We stared deeply at each other for a minute, my stomach doing all sorts of crazy acrobats. My head was a mess, and there was too much noise going on, too many people around for me to think clearly. I really wanted, no, *needed*, to get out of there.

"Kai, can we go?" I whispered.

Completely unintentionally, my eyes drifted to his mouth as his tongue darted out to lick his lips which were stained with my red lipstick.

Holy fucking hell, I wanted his tongue licking every part of me.

My pussy throbbed in desperate need of Kai's attention, and from how hard his cock was in his pants, he seemed only too happy to give it the attention it wanted.

Before he had the chance to respond though, we were interrupted by the old man from earlier.

"Pardon the interruption," Mr. Johnson beamed at me, "but this young lady promised me a dance, and I'm not getting any younger." He chuckled at his own joke which gave me a chance to look at Kai, who looked like he was doing his best not to pull his gun out and pop a cap into old Mr. Johnson's ass.

"Of course." I smiled as best as I could at the man, but my brain was not firing straight, not after that kiss.

Reluctantly, *very reluctantly*, both Kai and I let go of each other.

"Don't keep my girl for too long, Johnson," Kai said darkly. Mr. Johnson laughed, but there was nothing funny about the way Kai had said it. "I'll be waiting at the bar for you."

He gave me a kiss on the cheek, swiping a thumb across my smeared lipstick, and turning to walk away. I watched him go, desperately wanting to go with him and wishing for a time when we weren't interrupted by phones or people.

"Shall we?" Mr. Johnson asked, holding his hand out to me, and begrudgingly, I accepted.

One dance turned into a second. For an old man, Mr. Johnson sure knew how to move, and before I knew it, I'd been waltzed across the dancefloor, and had completely lost my bearings, and sight of Kai. One thing I was sure of though was that my bladder was at bursting point.

"I'm so sorry but I need to excuse myself and visit the ladies," I told Mr. Johnson when he was preparing himself for dance number three. He thanked me for the dances, and as I made my way across the room heading for the direction I knew the bathroom was, I tried to find Kai, but there was no sign of him. I figured I wouldn't be long, and surely he couldn't get mad at me for nature calling.

Making my way out of the room, I gave one last glance over my shoulder to see if I could see him, but there were just too many people.

I made my way down the deserted corridor and found the bathroom quickly. Once I had taken care of business, much to the relief of my bladder, I washed my hands and reapplied a layer of the lipstick I had carried in my little clutch bag. Looking back at myself in the mirror, my face was flushed. I wasn't sure if it was from the kiss that kept replaying in my mind, or from the unexpected energetic dances with Mr. Johnson.

Either way, I tried to cool my cheeks down with a splash of water. Taking one last look in the mirror and making sure I was presentable, I headed out of the bathroom.

Only, the second I stepped outside, a hand grabbed my arm and yanked me backward, almost causing me to topple off my heels. I was shoved up against the wall and my mouth hit the floor when I recognized the man who had grabbed me.

"What the-! You! You're Detective Anderson!" I gasped.

The man smiled at me.

"Hello, Riley."

A shudder of fear swept through my body, and my eyes darted left and right along the corridor hoping to get someone's attention, but there wasn't a soul in sight.

"I'm afraid you need to come with me, there is someone who is desperate to meet you," Anderson said before grabbing my arm again and yanking me away from the wall.

"Get your hands off me," I squealed, yanking my arm out of his grasp, but I wasn't quick enough to get away thanks to my stupid heels.

Anderson grabbed me again, harder this time, and once again shoved me against a wall, holding me in place with his forearm pressed hard against my throat, constricting my airways.

"I've got strict orders not to kill you, Riley, but if I have to hurt you, I will," he warned.

He looked different from how I remembered, more tired, and definitely more menacing from the customer who sat in the bar eyeing up Blaze as though she was the only woman to grace the planet.

He was a short man, only a few inches taller than me, and while he had some muscles under his tux, he was nowhere near as big as Kai or any of the men who worked for him.

Anderson grabbed my arm again and held me in a bruising grip as he started to drag me down the corridor toward an emergency exit. I didn't know what the hell to do, should I try to get out of his grasp and run? Not that I'd get far in my shoes. What if he was armed? He said he wasn't allowed to kill me, but what would he do to hurt me?

Panic bubbled up my throat as I let him drag me down the corridor, and as we were about to reach the exit, another door opened, and a young waiter stepped outside. Anderson released my arm and moved it to my waist, holding me as if I were his date, happy to be in his presence.

"Good evening," Anderson beamed at the waiter, acting as if all was right in the world. This was my chance but fear stopped me. I had a feeling that as much as Anderson was under strict instructions not to kill me, I suspected that didn't extend to anyone who stepped in his way, and I was not going to be responsible for the death of an innocent young man.

I gave him a small smile and desperately fucking hoped he'd seen me with Kai at some point in the evening, and would go and tell him what was happening.

The waiter muttered his greeting before scurrying away back down the corridor, and as soon as he was out of sight, Anderson once again grabbed my arm and dragged me towards the exit.

We burst through the door, and the chilly air hit me, goosebumps erupting all over my exposed skin. The exit led out to the back of City Hall where there were no vehicles other than an ominous dark van sitting in wait. Even the windows were blacked out, and fear churned in my belly. If I was forced into that vehicle, there was no way Kai would find me.

When Anderson started dragging me towards it, panic really kicked in and I went into fight or flight mode.

And backed into a corner, I would always come out fighting.

There was no way I was going with Detective Douchebag willingly. Pretending to stumble on my heel, I let myself fall to the floor with Anderson still gripping my arm.

"Get up you clumsy bitch!" he roared, and leaned down to pick me up.

This was my one opportunity and I couldn't mess it up. Using the arm he wasn't holding, I clenched my hand into a fist, and with all my strength, threw a punch directly in his junk. Anderson jerked back, letting out an *'Oomf,'* and let go of my arm as he folded over in pain. Not wasting a minute, I got to my feet and started running in the direction of the door.

But I wasn't quick enough.

He grabbed me again and twisted my arm painfully behind my back, before spinning me around to face him. His eyes were wide and crazed with rage.

Dropping my arm, and without any hesitation, Anderson smacked me hard across the face with the back of his hand. Pain shot through my cheek as my head whipped to the side, my brain rattling in my skull. Before I could think of what to do next, he pushed me against the brick wall before wrapping his hands around my throat and squeezing tightly.

"I warned you, you little whore!" he spat.

I tried to prise his hands off me, but I wasn't strong enough. Besides, the more he squeezed, the weaker I could feel myself getting.

"You could have come easily, Riley, my boss won't kill you just yet. You're going to be leverage. You'll regret the day you made that deal with Wolfe." His voice was full of wicked glee, and his eyes were bloodshot. Spittle flew as he spat his words, and a sense of doom flooded my body.

I vaguely acknowledged Anderson's words. Darkness was seeping in, and my vision was getting blurry as my brain started shutting down.

I couldn't fight it, it was too hard.

My chest burned with the lack of air, and I had no choice but to let the dark wash over me.

As my eyes closed, the last thing I heard was an almighty bang.

Chapter 20

Kai

Despite Joey Johnson Junior chewing my ear off about a business deal I had no interest in, I didn't lose sight of Riley as Johnson Senior twirled her around the dancefloor.

I'd fucking kissed her. Finally tasted those sweet lips, and knew what it felt like having her mouth pressed against mine. It had only been one kiss but already I was addicted.

I wanted more.

I shouldn't have done it in front of all these people though. I'd only been introducing her as a staff member or as a date, I didn't want people to see how much she meant to me. My enemies could exploit her if they thought she was my weakness. It was too little too late though, and if I was honest, I didn't fucking regret it. Claiming Riley had been inevitable, and it would have only been a matter of time before word got out that she was my girl, it just meant I would have to take her security even more seriously.

I watched her dance around the floor, smiling her dazzling smile for old man Johnson. She looked incredible.

From the second she had stepped out in that dress, I'd wanted to ravish her over and over, and my dick had been uncomfortably hard since then, but it was ten times worse now I knew how her lips felt against mine, and the little moans she made when I devoured her. I could not fucking wait to get her back to my apartment. I was going to spend the rest of the night with either my face, fingers, or cock deep in her cunt.

I was glad she finally told me what had been pissing her off, and at some point, I'd get more from her about who had fed her complete bullshit. Hendrix, Miles, and Danny knew I hadn't fucked anyone in recent weeks, and they were the only ones who knew about the girls I fucked. Either Riley had got the wrong end of the stick, or someone had tried to stir shit, and I didn't take too kindly to that.

The song Riley had been dancing to came to a close, and I made a move to go and get her back from Johnson Senior when it became apparent he intended to keep her for a second dance. It was a good job I liked the old fucker, and I regretted not going into business with him sooner but there was good reason for that. He was a law-abiding citizen, content with playing on the right side of the law and making his money legitimately.

His son, however, Joey Johnson Junior, was a whole different kettle of fish. He was a greedy fucker, and could be easily manipulated. All he had seen when I offered to buy into the business was dollar signs flashing in his piggy eyes when really, I was the one who was going to profit monumentally from the deal. I wasn't his biggest fan, but that was okay. I wouldn't need to have too much to do with him once I'd set my plans for the business in motion.

I finished my glass of champagne, only my second glass of the night. I never drank too much when at public events like this, there was always the possibility of an attack, and I'd never weaken my reactions by drinking too much. Especially with Riley being here. Every man in the building had eye fucked her tonight, and it had taken a lot of control to not put a bullet through their skulls. A simple threatening glare had done the job though, and with the exception of old man Johnson, no one seemingly paid her much attention.

Johnson Junior kept droning on and on, and other than the occasional nod of my head and the odd grunt, I paid him no attention. His old man spun Riley around, and she threw her head back laughing in sheer delight, and fuck did that make my heart rate spike. She was beautiful, but when she laughed like that, she lit up the whole damn room.

I was growing fed up with her being away from me, itching to taste her mouth again, but I also didn't want to ruin her evening, she looked like she was enjoying herself.

I took the opportunity to scan the room, checking that Hendrix, Miles, and Danny were where they should be.

Hendrix had been tasked to seek out Chief Griffin, who had still been avoiding my calls, to warn him I would be visiting his office tomorrow to personally get the list of cops for the entire state. To make sure the message was loud and clear that I was not happy about his lack of co-operation, Hendrix was to give him an envelope containing a picture of him in a rather compromising position with his latest fuck buddy, who happened to be a seventeen year old boy. It was a reminder to Griffin that I owned his ass, and I would have no hesitation in releasing the photos to the media if he lost the need to give me what I wanted.

Fucker had still avoided me all night though.

Danny was on enforcement duty. Several of my clients were in debt to me, bankers, stockbrokers, and high-flying lawyers, who had bought my product on tick, but were now falling behind on their payments.

Getting a visit from Danny was like receiving a visit from the grim-reaper himself, people usually stumped the cash up fairly quickly after a little word in their ear from Danny. And there was only one person worse than the grim-reaper.

Me.

If Danny failed to get the money we were owed and I had to pay a little visit to our clients, you could guarantee blood would be shed for days.

As for Miles, he was my eyes and ears. Miles had hacked the camera feed for the ballroom this fancy do was being held in, and he was monitoring all comings and goings from the app on his phone. I had other security stationed outside the building who would be able to get here in less than a few seconds if we ran into any trouble, not that I was expecting any at a charity ball raising funds for disadvantaged kids in third-world countries.

What can I say, I may have been a murderous bastard but I did my bit for charity.

From a scan of the room, all three of my men were where they needed to be, and I refrained from letting out a little laugh at the fear on Griffin's face when Hendrix handed him the envelope. I returned my gaze to the dancefloor only to find Riley wasn't where I had last seen her.

Panic washed through me. As much as I wasn't expecting trouble tonight, it didn't mean it wouldn't happen. I shouldn't have let Riley out of my fucking sight. My eyes darted around the room, and I let out a sigh of relief when I saw the back of her walking towards the door to the bathroom. Not wanting to seem like the obsessive stalker I actually was, I pulled up Miles' number on my phone and pressed the button to call him.

"Boss," he answered after the first ring.

"Riley's heading towards the door on the east, she's probably going to the bathroom but I want eyes on her," I instructed Miles. Johnson Junior had finally come to the realization that I wasn't listening and he gave me an exasperated look.

"Sure thing, Boss."

From across the room, Miles pulled his phone away from his ear, tapped the screen a few times, and then raised it back to his ear.

"Yep, got her. She's just headed into the bathroom. I'll keep the camera on the door."

I was being paranoid but when it came to Riley's safety, I would never take chances. I hung up the phone and turned back to Johnson Junior.

"Your ideas are interesting, I'd like to discuss them further so put them in an email to me and I'll review your proposition." It was bullshit of course, but until I had the courier business under my complete control, I would do what was needed to appease him.

His frown turned to delight, and he eagerly nodded. "Of course Mr. Wolfe, I'll get them to you first thing tomorrow." He beamed at me as though all of his Christmases had come at once.

"Good. Now, if you'll excuse me." I turned away from him, dismissing him before he had a chance to reply, and instead fixed my eyes on the door where Riley had exited minutes before.

A minute passed.

And then another.

Getting anxious, I pulled my phone out again and phoned Miles.

"Has she come back out yet?" I'm sure Miles could hear the frustration in my tone but I tried not to snap at him. I could have gone and waited outside the bathroom for Riley but I wanted to give her space, I wanted her to willingly come back to me.

"She's still in there, Boss. You know what women are like, they take forever touching up their makeup and shit," Miles said casually, and I couldn't help but let out a chuckle. He was right, what went on in women's restrooms was a mystery to every man on the planet.

I hung up on Miles feeling a little bit more relaxed that he was one hundred percent focused on keeping an eye on my girl.

Another minute passed and then a figure appeared in the doorway, a waiter. I let out a sigh of frustration at how long she was taking, desperate to get her back to my penthouse and out of that damn dress, but then I noticed the waiter scanning the crowd, a panicked look on his face. As his eyes roved over the crowd, they landed on me, and he then immediately started pushing his way through the throngs of people, trying to make his way over.

Fear pooled in my gut. It was an alien concept, I wasn't scared of anything, but at that moment I was. I was scared shitless something had happened to her.

I started making my way toward the waiter, catching the attention of Hendrix, Miles, and Danny who started making their way toward me from where they had been standing in the room.

"Mr. Wolfe," the waiter panted as we met in the middle of the room at the same time my boys joined us. He was panic-stricken. "I, uh, I think something might be wrong. The girl you were with tonight was in the hallway with another man and she looked scared."

Blood turned to ice in my veins, and before I heard the rest of what the waiter was saying, my feet were moving on their own accord to the door where I'd not long watched Riley go through. Out of habit, I pulled my pistol from the holster underneath my suit jacket, not giving a fuck if anyone from the ball saw I was armed. Hendrix, Miles, and Danny were following me, and the waiter was also keeping pace, but all I could think about was the murder I was about to commit.

"What did you see?" Danny asked the words I couldn't find, too intent on finding where the fuck she was.

"Erm, it looked like she was being dragged down the hallway but when they saw me, the man held her around the waist and pretended everything was fine. They were heading towards the emergency exit when I walked away. I thought something was wrong, that's why I came to tell Mr. Wolfe."

An involuntary growl left my chest that seemed to echo down the hallway we had all stumbled into. Whoever had put their hands on my property was going to die.

The emergency exit was at the far end of the hallway and I took off towards it, the others flanking behind me with their guns out. Hendrix grunted to the waiter to fuck off, and the kid did exactly what he was told, disappearing through a staff door. When we reached the exit, I kicked the door open so hard it practically flew off its hinges, and as it swung back, it ricocheted off the wall behind it, causing an almighty bang that echoed into the night.

The first thing I saw when I stepped into the rear car park was a dark van parked up.

The second thing I saw was a dead man walking holding Riley by the throat.

Time seemed to stand still as the man holding her snapped his attention to me, recognition dawning on his face.

And then the cunt ran.

Riley's limp body fell to the floor, and for a split second, I was torn between going after him or going to help her. But when she gasped for air, I knew I had to get to her.

"Get him!" I roared at the three men behind me as I started to run toward her. They too had been in some kind of stupor until I yelled, and then they burst into action. "Do not fucking let him get away!"

Hendrix and Danny took off after the retreating figure of the man who had made it to a fence and had started to climb it like he was fucking *Spiderman.* They didn't hesitate to follow, and the last I saw of them as I reached Riley, was them disappearing over the other side.

"Riley!" I fell to the floor next to her and pulled her into my arms, the delicate skin of her neck was mottled from where the bastard had throttled her. I could make out the outline of his fucking fingers, and I silently vowed that I would break every single bone in his hands for daring to lay a finger on her.

Her head lolled like she had no control of it and her eyes were only open just a fraction, but she was alive, and that was all that mattered.

"I've got you, baby, take deep breaths," I coaxed.

Her breath was shallow so I sat her up, leaning her back against my chest and opening up her lungs to get oxygen into her. She gasped for air in between panicked sobs, and I whispered in her ear trying to calm her down so she could control her breathing. Her perfect face was smeared with streaks of black where tears had spilled down her face, and all I wanted to do was kiss away her pain.

Miles hovered over us, gun in hand and phone in the other which he was intently staring at, but I couldn't look at him for long because I wanted to ring his neck. He was supposed to be keeping an eye on her.

"Kai...." she whimpered. Hearing the pain in her voice felt like I had just been stabbed through the heart.

"It's okay, Riley, you're safe now, I've got you," I reassured her.

As she took in more air, her tiny hands gripped my arms that were holding her to me.

"That...was....Anderson," she managed to get out between sobs.

I froze.

Motherfucker.

"Fuck!" Miles suddenly shouted, echoing my thoughts exactly.

He started tapping at his phone again before walking away from us, shouting down the phone to either Hendrix or Danny to make sure they had caught up with the bastard.

I turned my attention back to Riley, as much as I wanted to go after Anderson myself, I trusted my men to do their job. Besides, Riley needed me. She had managed to get her breath back and her sobs had calmed to barely a whimper. I moved her, just enough so I could look at her face. Her eyes were red and filled with tears, and that's when I saw the start of a bruise on her cheek, making me see red all over again.

I would kill the cunt for hurting her, and I would make sure it was an *extremely* slow and *very* painful death.

I held her against me, rocking her gently and stroking her back to console her. It was the first time I had been gentle with someone in my entire fucking life, but my Star needed it. Big fat tears rolled down her cheeks, and I wanted nothing more than to be able to erase the last ten minutes, to go back to when I kissed her on the dance floor. I should have told Johnson to fuck off and taken her home, I should have followed her to the fucking bathroom, I should have insisted she wasn't left alone.

It was a mistake I wouldn't be making again. Riley would have a permanent shadow attached to her ass from now on, *nothing* would ever happen to my girl again.

Time ticked passed as I sat there holding Riley, she clung to me like she was worried I was going to disappear despite my constant reassurance I wasn't going to leave her. Eventually, Miles walked back to us.

"Frank is bringing the car around and Doctor Harris is on his way to the apartment, he'll meet you there."

My only response was to give him a curd nod. I was grateful he had arranged that, but there would be consequences for Miles' ineptitude tonight.

"Did they catch him?" I finally asked, disdain heavy in my voice.

Miles shook his head, guilt flashing across his face before he answered. "He got into a car, Boss, they couldn't get to him in time."

It was only the fact Riley held on to me so tightly that I didn't launch myself at Miles and throttle him until *he* had no air left in his lungs.

Headlights lit up the car park and I saw my Rolls being driven in. I hoisted Riley into my arms as I stood, she weighed as much as a bag of feathers and still, she didn't let go of me. She was quiet in my arms, and I wasn't sure if that was worse than when she had been whimpering. Frank got out of the driver's side and opened the rear door, a somber look on his face. As I was about to get in with her, Hendrix and Danny reappeared.

They were both panting and disheveled, their shirts untucked, and Hendrix was missing his bowtie. Both men looked frustrated, and while the rational part of me knew they both would have given it their all to catch the man, I still wanted to tear them both a new asshole.

"Get back to the office, I want a full report on what the fuck happened here tonight. I want CCTV, I want that van torn apart, and I want a fucking explanation as to why that cunt isn't hanging by his balls in my basement." I nodded to the single vehicle parked in the corner. I didn't know for certain if the van was involved but given that it was the only other vehicle in the car park, it was a safe bet it was Anderson's getaway vehicle. But if that was the case, then whose vehicle did he get into?

Questions churned through my head the entire way home, and all the while, Riley didn't make a sound. I didn't let her out of my arms until we were back in her room at my apartment where Doc Harris was waiting with a worried looking Jacqueline. I laid Riley down on her bed but she quickly grabbed my hand, silently begging me not to leave her.

And so, I sat with her while Harris examined her, running my thumb over her knuckles in the only way I knew to comfort her. She winced several times as he moved her neck from one side to the other, and then looked down her throat with a little light. Throughout the examination, my hand that wasn't holding Riley's was clenched tightly into a fist, ready to fly at the first person who pissed me off.

"I don't believe there is any permanent damage, just bruising where he grabbed you," the doctor said to Riley without any emotion, like this was an everyday occurrence. Although, it kinda was.

He'd worked for my family for years so he was used to the late night phone calls to come and patch up one of my men who had been wounded one way or another. There were even a few times he'd had to patch me up.

"You'll probably be sore for a few days but I can give you some pain relief." When Riley didn't say anything, I stood up and shook his hand.

"She's not been sleeping well, is there anything you can give her to help?" I asked, looking back at Riley who didn't flinch at my confession that I knew she hadn't slept a full night in over a week.

I'd been checking in on her each night using the hidden cameras in her room. Since the shit with Luis, she'd been having trouble sleeping.

"I can give her a mild sedative," Harris said before rummaging in his bag. He pulled out a couple of pill pots and explained one was for pain relief and the other would help her sleep before saying his goodbyes and telling me to expect his bill.

Money grabbing asshole.

"You need to get some rest, Riley," I ordered her once the door closed behind Harris. She looked exhausted, and as I ran my thumb down her uninjured cheeks, her eyelids fluttered closed. "Jacqueline will help you get undressed and I'll come back to check on you shortly."

"I don't want to be alone, Kai." Her eyes flew open and were filled with fear. And fuck, I wanted nothing more than to forget this mess until the morning and stay with her all night, but I needed to find out what the fuck had happened to her, and we needed to locate Anderson before the trail went cold for a second time.

"I promise you, Riley, no one will have access to your room except me and Jacqueline and I trust her with my life. I won't let anyone hurt you ever again." I tried to be reassuring, and it must have worked because she didn't argue. Either that or she really was just *that* exhausted. I kissed her on the forehead and then stood to leave the room. "Look after her, Jacqueline."

I looked at the woman who had worked for my family for pretty much her entire life, hell she had even helped raise me as a child. She gave me a small smile, something she hadn't done since the day I took over from my father, but for her to do that now, she must have known what Riley meant to me.

"Of course, Mr. Wolfe," the maid replied curtly, and as I left the room, she carefully helped Riley into a sitting position to help her out of her dress.

I closed the door softly, taking a minute to calm the white-hot rage bubbling underneath the surface. I needed to keep a cool head if I wanted to get to the bottom of this shitshow.

The problem was, when it came to Riley, I was likely to shoot first, ask questions later.

Making my way to my office, I found Hendrix, Danny, and Miles already waiting, all three looking solemn.

Hendrix and Danny were seated in the chairs opposite my desk, Hendrix held a glass of whiskey while Danny had the deepest scowl set on his face. Miles stood, leaning against the wall with his head back, staring at the ceiling. None of them had changed from their tuxes but they'd all ditched their bowties. Their eyes fell on me as I walked in and made my way around to my side of the desk.

"How is she?" Miles asked timidly.

It was like holding a red rag to a bull.

"How the fuck do you think she is? That prick throttled her to the point where she was barely conscious and you-" I pointed at him so there was no mistaking that I was holding him personally responsible, "were supposed to be watching her! What the fuck happened?"

I was seething, so much that my hand shook. I grabbed the crystal whiskey decanter that sat on my desk and poured myself a glass to try and quell some of the fury thrumming in my veins. It took an awful lot of control to not launch the decanter at Miles' head.

"Someone hacked the feed, Boss. They set up a loop to play a clip of the empty corridor," Miles said sheepishly.

"Explain that to me again, Miles, because you are supposedly the best fucking hacker money can buy, and yet you're telling me someone what, out hacked you?"

"I had no way of knowing, Boss," he said quietly. "It was only when I hacked back into the system, I could see there had been an overwrite from an anonymous source. There was no way of knowing someone had done that."

I didn't understand all the tech shit he spoke about, I didn't need to know, that's why I employed him. And as much as I didn't want to admit it because it was far easier to blame Miles for this fuck up, but he really was damn good at his job and I believed him when he said there was no way he would have known.

Instead, I turned my glare to the other two.

"And how the fuck did he get away from you two?" My tone was deadly, they had both seen me this angry in the past and it usually resulted in blood being splattered.

Neither one spoke for a minute until Danny found his balls.

"We chased him down the back streets of City Hall, he had a good thirty seconds on us and it was enough of a head start for him to get into a waiting car."

I downed my drink and poured myself another one.

"Did you get anything about the car?"

"It was on false plates, just like the van was. Miles has already run the plates," Hendrix finally spoke up. "I managed to get a shot off and it shattered the rear window, but it was gone before I could get a decent aim."

"Fuck," I sighed and scrubbed my hands down my face. This was a fucking nightmare, I was no closer to finding this fucking *Anderson* now than what I was three months ago when Theo's body had been found, and now Riley had been targeted.

"I want the CCTV for the ball reviewed, I want to know when that cunt came in, who he was with, and I want a picture of him put out to everyone in our gangs. Put out a $50,000 reward for anyone who gives me information that leads to the cunt being caught alive. Is that understood?" The three of them murmured their acknowledgment. "Good, now get the fuck out of my sight."

Once I was alone, I stood and stared out the window to my city below, the image of Riley's petrified face when Anderson had hold of her haunted me. I had never been so fucking scared.

The tiny woman had only been in my life for a little over two weeks, and yet she had become my everything. I didn't know what I would do if I lost her now. She didn't know it but just being a constant presence was helping to put the shattered fragments of my heart back together after losing Theo, and if I lost that now, I wasn't sure I would survive.

I didn't regret anything in my life, but right now, yeah I was regretting my path ever colliding with my precious Star.

Chapter 21

Riley

I didn't take the pills the doctor left to help me sleep. I couldn't, I didn't want to be left alone.

Yeah, I was being a coward.

But as soon as Jacqueline turned the lights off and left, I didn't want to be on my own. I lay there for a few minutes under the covers, trying to tell myself to be brave, and that no one would be able to get to me, but when the events of the evening started playing on my mind and the fog in my head cleared, I was scared.

And then, as I replayed the events a second time around, I bolted up in bed, remembering what Anderson had said.

"You could have just come easily, Riley, my boss won't kill you just yet. You're going to be leverage. You'll regret the day you made that deal with Wolfe."

It wasn't sitting right in my head, Kai wasn't the sort of person to brag about things, or at least I didn't think he was. I supposed I didn't really know him all that well. But Anderson making reference to our deal, it bothered me.

Like *really* fucking bothered me.

Because if Kai had only told a handful of close associates, someone had betrayed his confidence.

And therefore, his trust.

There was only one way I was ever going to know and that was to speak to Kai, and I wasn't going to wait until morning.

Throwing my covers back and grabbing my robe to cover up my sleep shorts and vest, I opened my door and crept out of my room. I still didn't know where Kai's room was though so I figured I'd start with his office, he'd only left me an hour or so ago anyway, chances were, he was still going over the details of everything that happened with the three musketeers.

Sure enough, as I padded silently down the hallway, I found a sliver of light coming from where the door to his office stood ajar. As I got closer, I listened for voices, not wanting to interrupt any meetings he may be in the middle of, but I was met with a deathly silence.

Nerves suddenly got the better of me, I don't know why, maybe because I wasn't sure what mood I would find Kai in, or rather how *bad* a mood he would be in. Swallowing down the ball of fear lodged in my throat, I knocked gently on the door.

"Yeah," came the gruff reply, it sounded like he had the weight of the world on his shoulders.

I thought maybe this was a bad idea and I should have just gone back to my room but I couldn't ignore the feeling of something being wrong in my gut. Pulling up my big girl panties, I pushed open the door to find Kai with his back to me, staring out the window. He'd lost his suit jacket and bowtie, his shirt was taut across his broad shoulders, and he'd rolled his sleeves up to the elbows, his tattoos on his forearm on full display. Even from behind he was god damn fine.

Kai didn't turn to look at me, but he knew exactly who had come into his office.

"You should be getting some rest."

"I couldn't sleep," I countered.

His shoulders were bunched up, tension vibrating from his body. He was wound tighter than a coiled spring, and I had no doubt he would explode at any given moment.

"That's why the doctor gave you some pills," he snapped, pissing me off. I didn't come here for an argument but if he continued to be an asshat, he'd certainly get one.

Taking a deep breath, I opted for honesty, hoping it would defuse the bomb that was about to detonate. "I didn't want to sleep alone."

He finally turned to me, his face hard, the muscles in his jaw tense. I felt like a lamb about to be slaughtered under his heated gaze. His eyes started at my bare legs and traveled up my body to where the robe clung to my figure before they came to rest on the bruising on my neck. As he stared, a million different emotions passed through him, before fury settled deep in his eyes.

"It doesn't hurt, Kai," I said softly. He didn't reply, just continued to glare at me, his jaw twitching.

Before I could really comprehend what I was doing, my feet were moving across the room to where he stood. He watched me cautiously as I crossed the space, never once taking those dark eyes off me. When I stopped in front of him, it seemed like I completely forgot how to talk under his intense stare. After what seemed like an eternity, he slowly raised his hand, and gently, almost to the point where I didn't feel it, ran his thumb over the bruise forming thanks to Anderson's backhander.

"You could have died tonight, Riley, and it would have been my fault," Kai whispered, any trace of anger gone in an instant.

And holy fuck, did he seem different from the Kai I was used to. Real, genuine fear showed on his sharp features, and all I wanted to do was comfort him.

"It wasn't your fault, Kai, Anderson did this. Not you. And he wasn't going to kill me, he said as much." The reason for coming to find Kai popped back into my mind as he raised a questioning brow. "He said he was under instructions not to kill me but he would hurt me if he needed to. He said his boss was going to use me for leverage."

"Fuck," Kai growled, dropping his hand from my cheek and turning back to look out the window. "You should never have got mixed up in this shit, Riley. I never should have brought you into my life."

Ouch.

That comment hurt more than Anderson's smack to my face or his hands around my throat. Two weeks ago, if Kai had said that to me I would have agreed in a heartbeat, but now? Now he had treated me like a princess, showered me with affection, and made me feel something for him, that fucking hurt.

"You don't mean that," I said, holding back the lump in my throat that had formed. He looked down at me, his eyes glacial.

"Riley, you got hurt because of me. I'll never forgive myself for that. And all this means now is that you've got a target painted on your back because of me, because Anderson knows you're my weakness," he shouted and then punched the window. The glass didn't break but by the noise his fist made, it must have hurt.

For a minute I gawked at him, his admission that I was his weakness ringing in my ears.

And then, I did the only thing I could think of doing at that moment. I reached out and took his hand in mine and pulled him, so he had no choice but to face me. He turned but gave me a questioning look which was met with me reaching up on tiptoes and kissing him lightly on his beautiful mouth. I sighed at the feel of his lips against mine once again, feeling content. He didn't react at first, and so I wrapped my arms around his neck, pulled him closer, and pressed my mouth harder against his.

And then he was kissing me like he had on the dance floor, like I was his lifeline and the only thing he needed to survive. I opened my mouth when his tongue invaded it, and our tongues twirled together. Kai snaked one arm around my waist and pulled my body closer while the other hand knotted in my hair and tugged.

He was taking control and I gladly let him.

Kissing Kai was like nothing I had ever experienced before. Tingles shot through my entire body, but it wasn't enough, I wanted more. As if reading my thoughts, Kai's hands moved from where they were to the knot in the belt holding my robe together and started prising it apart. It didn't offer much resistance, and within seconds, he slipped the robe off my shoulders where it pooled at my feet, leaving me standing there in my skimpy sleep shorts and vest.

He grabbed my ass and hoisted me onto his desk, at no point breaking our kiss. My legs parted and he moved to stand between them, and as he did, his hard cock pressed against my core. It wouldn't have taken much to unzip his pants, pull his cock out and slide my shorts to one side so he could bury himself in me.

The thought alone made me groan into his mouth.

But suddenly, he pulled back, leaving me panting and desperate for more. I'd had sex before, twice to be exact, and on both occasions, I had never felt like this. If I was honest, I never really got the hype around it, but right now, yeah I understood it, and all I wanted was to feel Kai thrusting into my cunt.

"Riley, I can't," he said as he rested his forehead against mine, squeezing his eyes closed as if in pain.

Well, shit.

I hadn't expected him to say that. Talk about a bucket of cold water dousing the fire burning its way through my body.

"I can't be gentle with you, I've got too much fucking anger pumping through my body. I don't want to hurt you." His eyes were hooded as he stared down at me, before raking over my body and fixing on my hardened nipples.

I reached up to cup his face. "I don't need you to be gentle, Kai. I need *you*. All of you." It came out husky, not that I meant it to, I was just too hyped up from his kisses. Indecision washed over his handsome face, it was such an unlikely reaction for him, he always knew what he wanted and he always took it.

But his body's reaction was not lining up with the words spilling from his mouth, he was gripping my hips hard like he couldn't physically bring himself to let go, and he stared down at me like he wanted to eat me whole.

And you know what?

I was so down for that.

I wanted him, and for once in my life, I was going to take what *I* wanted.

I reached for the hem of my vest and yanked it over my head, exposing my bare breasts. A rumble formed in his chest, and any indecision he was feeling was long fucking gone.

His mouth slammed down on mine, giving me a bruising kiss, and my hands found their way into his hair, tugging hard and eliciting a groan from him. His hands gripped my hips tightly, pulling me into him, and my core grinded against the hardened bulge in his pants.

He tore his lips from mine, and just as I was about to complain, his mouth found one of my nipples. He sucked it into his mouth, and fuck, it was like waves of electricity flowed through my body. I had never been so turned on in my entire life, my pussy was throbbing, and all I wanted, *needed,* was to feel him moving inside of me. He roughly bit and sucked my nipples, leaving his mark as he alternated between the two. Come tomorrow, there would be bruises where he sucked my skin so hard, but I didn't give a single fuck, I wanted him to brand me as his.

He moved one hand frustratingly slowly to the inside of my thigh where he squeezed the tender flesh. It was on the tip of my tongue to beg him to move his hand higher and give me what I so desperately wanted, but I didn't need to. Kai moved the material of my shorts to one side, and I gasped as he swiped a finger down my slit before pushing three fingers into my aching pussy. It was just on *this* side of painful, but it also felt so fucking good.

"Fuck, you're soaked, Star," he growled as he pulled his fingers out, only to shove them back in again, stretching my opening wide.

I'd lost the ability to form any sort of coherent sentence, groaning my reply instead.

His mouth found mine again, and with my hands around the back of his neck, I arched my back, my sensitive nipples brushing against his shirt. He wasn't gentle, his fingers were rough as he pumped them into me several times, and my pussy clenched around them with every delicious thrust.

"So goddamn tight," he hissed in my ear as my hips bucked in time to meet his thrusts. I was so close to coming, I just needed a few more pumps. Without warning though, he abruptly withdrew his fingers, leaving me disappointed and achingly desperate for more.

"Kai," I breathed as I pulled my mouth away from his. He heard the plea in my voice because the smug bastard grinned down at me.

"Lay back, Riley, I want to taste you. I want to be eating your delicious cunt when you come."

Ho-ly hell.

I should have known Kai wouldn't have a problem expressing exactly what he wanted.

His tone was back to one of authority, making it clear he was in charge, and hey, who was I to argue with the boss?

I did as he said, lying back across his desk as he pulled my shorts down my legs and tossed them to the floor. He put his hands on either side of my thigh and pushed them wide open, exposing my glistening cunt to him. For a minute, he didn't do or say anything, just stared down at my exposed pussy like it was one of the wonders of the world. I should have felt embarrassed at how exposed I was, and that he hadn't taken off a stitch of clothing, but I wasn't.

He made me feel like I was the most precious thing on earth, and I simply didn't have it in me to be embarrassed.

"You have no fucking idea how many times I've imagined this," he croaked out.

Deciding he could wait no longer, he grabbed my ankles and pulled me hard toward him so my butt was almost hanging off the edge of the desk. Kai dropped to his knees and hooked both my legs over his shoulders, and then dived face first into my cunt. His tongue found my clit, which he licked a couple of times before he wrapped his lips around the sensitive bud, sucking it hard into his mouth. I almost came there and then, but then he eased off, toying with me.

When he did it again, I screamed his name, uncaring if the entire city heard me.

"Fuck, I could eat this pussy every day for the rest of my life and it would never be enough," Kai hissed before diving back in.

He feasted on me like I was his last meal. He licked, sucked, and nipped my clit, and when I thought I couldn't take anymore, he pushed two fingers inside, curling them and hitting my internal walls and the sweet spot I had only ever heard about from talk amongst the girls at Club Sin.

If anyone had asked me my name at that moment, I wouldn't have been able to tell them. My mind had turned to mush, and all I could focus on was the intense orgasm building inside of me, getting stronger and stronger every time he pumped his fingers in and sucked on my clit. I grabbed hold of Kai's hair and tugged hard, not able to decide whether I wanted to push him away because the pleasure was too much or to hold him where he was until he finished the job. He was also letting out little groans of his own, and hell, did that just turn me on all the more.

When Kai added a third finger to my pussy and then sucked on my clit, I went over the edge.

"Fuck, Kai!" I shouted, probably waking up the entire apartment block, as my orgasm crashed through me. My thighs tightened around his face, holding him against me and my back arched off the desk as I literally died and went to heaven. Kai lapped up every drop of my release, and I shuddered through the aftermath of my orgasm, desperately trying to regain control of my breathing.

He wiped his mouth on the inside of my thigh, and I don't know why, but fuck that was hot. As he stood, he dropped my legs from his shoulders, and I managed to sit myself up with shaky arms as I came down from my high. Kai stood in front of me, his eyes burning into mine with wicked intent as he licked his fingers of my release. Despite what he had just done to me, I couldn't help my cheeks from blushing.

"You taste like fucking heaven, Riley. I always knew once I got a taste of your sweet cunt, I would be more obsessed with you than I already was."

Oh, Lord.

He smashed his mouth against mine, and the instant I tasted myself on his lips, I couldn't stop myself from grabbing his shirt and pulling him towards me. Once again, Kai's hand wound into my hair and he tugged my head back so our kiss broke apart and I had no choice but to look at him.

"Tell me, Star. Do you want me to fuck you hard and fast over this desk? Does your needy little cunt want my cock to pound it into oblivion?" Kai hissed, and if it wasn't for the look of unadulterated lust in his eyes, I could have been mistaken in thinking he was angry with the way he said those words.

But for once, I wasn't afraid of the venom in his voice.

"Yes, Kai. Fuck me hard," I whispered back, never breaking eye contact with him, letting him know how sure I was that I could handle anything he gave me.

"Take my shirt off," he ordered, releasing my hair.

Ordinarily, I hated it when Kai ordered me around, but this time, I relished it. Reaching up, I slowly undid his buttons, purposely taking my time to drive him mad. His eyes darkened the longer I took, and when he couldn't take any more, he knocked my hands out of the way and ripped the shirt open, the remaining buttons popping off.

Kai grabbed my chin roughly. "Don't play games with me, little girl, you won't like it when you lose."

I smirked at him, which was a huge mistake. Kai yanked me off the desk, forcing me to my knees, and with one hand, he undid his belt and pants and pulled out his huge cock. Gasping at the length of it, he took the opportunity to shove his cock into my mouth. Wrapping a hand around the back of my head so I had no choice but to take him, he fucked my throat hard, hitting my gag reflex, and almost making me choke. Hollowing out my cheeks, I did my best to accommodate him, but he was so fucking big.

After several thrusts, Kai pulled out of my mouth, grabbed my arms and made me stand. Once I was on my feet, he spun me around so my back was to his chest.

"You have no idea how much I want to come down the back of your throat, Riley. But right now, I need to claim your pussy," he whispered in my ear as his fingers gripped my hips, leaving yet more marks.

I didn't reply. Instead, I bent forward so my tits and cheek were pressed against his desk. Kai dragged a hand down my spine, eliciting a delicious shudder to run through me, and when he reached my ass, he stroked a finger down to my forbidden hole and lightly pressed his finger against it.

"One day, I will fuck you here, Riley, and you will fucking love it. But right now, I need to hear you tell me that you belong to me."

He positioned his cock at my entrance but didn't enter me. Not yet, not until I told him what he wanted to hear.

Everything would change after this, and that's why Kai hadn't thrust inside me yet. He was giving me a final warning, letting me know that once I had allowed him into my body, he would own me. I should have heeded the warning, but honestly? He already owned me. He owned me from the minute he laid eyes on me, I just didn't know it at the time. And since then, I'd been trying to deny it from day one rather than embracing it. There was no denying it, Kai was a monster. But he was also fiercely loyal to those he loved, dangerously protective, and as much as he would deny it, he did have a kind streak in him somewhere. Two weeks ago, I wished I'd never had the misfortune of meeting Kai Wolfe, but now, I couldn't imagine not having him in my life.

I knew without a shadow of a doubt, I belonged to the man.

"I'm yours, Kai."

That was all it took before he slammed into my wet pussy. I screamed at the intrusion. It didn't hurt, but I was suddenly so full of him, it felt incredible.

"Fuck, Riley," he hissed before pulling out and thrusting in again. His fingers gripped my hips harder as he found his pace, slamming in and out of me, and grunting with each thrust. My pussy clenched around his length as he grabbed my hair and pulled me back, making my back arch as he drove deeper into me.

"Kai, please," I whined as a second orgasm started to build.

"So fucking tight, Star," he panted as his thrusts increased. "You feel so fucking good, I'm going to love every second of claiming this pussy as mine."

With my back almost pulled to his chest, Kai leaned down and bit my shoulder, before stroking the mark with his tongue and brushing his lips over it, instantly turning the pain into pleasure.

The office was filled with the sounds of thrusts and pants and moans from both of us, and with his relentless pounding into me, I was so close. But Kai was a mean bastard, and just as I was about to go over the edge for the second time, he pulled out, spun me around, and held me against him with a hand at the back of my neck.

"I want to see your pretty face when you come on my cock, Riley." His hands dropped to my thighs, and he lifted me effortlessly. I wrapped my legs around him and held on to his shoulders as he walked us over to the black leather sofa in the corner of his office. As he sank down, he repositioned me so his cock was inside me once again, and from this new angle, it felt like he was deeper in me.

Placing my hands on Kai's shoulders, I moved up and down his length, moving faster as the need to come built inside me. There was something primal about looking into his eyes as we both neared our climaxes.

"You're so fucking beautiful, Riley, the way you are milking my cock. I can't fucking wait to fill you up with my come," Kai said in my ear, giving me the encouragement to ride him harder.

He looked as though he was about to come undone, and a thrill shot through me that I was making this man, this powerful man, come apart. Kai wrapped his mouth around my nipple, his teeth and tongue grazing against the sensitive peak. I threw my head back, exposing my neck, and Kai's hand stroked down gently. It was the only tender touch that was happening right now, the way Kai and I fucked each other was hard and fast, and what we both needed.

One of his hands left my hip and he moved it between us, finding my clit, and rubbing it as relentlessly as I was riding him. I was so close, my orgasm was building, and I didn't think I would be able to go for much longer because everything felt so fucking incredible. Sure enough, with one more flick of my clit, and Kai's mouth wrapped around a nipple, I exploded.

I came hard on his thick cock, crying out his name. I lost the ability to move, to even think straight, so Kai took over.

He flipped me onto my back on the sofa and held his huge body above me, his hands gripping my hips as he thrust into me hard and fast several more times before he groaned with his release. His warm come shot deep inside my pussy as a feeling of satisfaction washed over me.

We stayed like that for a minute or two, neither of us wanting to move. To be honest, I wasn't sure I could move, my whole body was like jelly. Kai placed little kisses on my lips, my nose, and my forehead before he pulled out, and our release slipped out of me and onto the leather sofa. He didn't care, he pulled me up and into his lap, and I snuggled into his neck as my whole body was overcome with exhaustion.

Kai wrapped his strong arms around my back and held me tight against his broad chest.

"We didn't use a condom," I said after several minutes of silence, my voice thick with sleep. It had only occurred to me that we hadn't even considered protection as I was sitting on Kai's lap, leaking our combined juices all over him.

"You've got an IUD, and we're both clean," he replied as if it was obvious.

I should have been pissed that he knew I had an IUD, he would have only got that information from my medical records, but I wasn't in the least bit surprised. Instead, I smiled against his neck, secretly pleased I'd got to feel him inside of me without a barrier. I'd only agreed to have the IUD so my periods wouldn't interfere with dancing at the club but it had its advantages now.

When I yawned against his neck, he suddenly stood but lifted me into his arms as though I was as light as a feather. Like a balancing act, Kai kept me in his arms as he bent down to pick up my robe which he draped over me before he carried me out of his office. He obviously wasn't bothered by the fact he was naked as he made no attempt to put his clothes back on, but it was kind of sweet he made sure I was covered up.

I thought he was going to take me to my bedroom, but he strolled right past it to the room next to mine, which turned out to be his. A tired laugh escaped my lips, and he gave me a confused look.

"I should have known your bedroom would have been next to mine," I told him, and nuzzled further into his chest. I was so on board with spending the rest of the night in his arms. Despite who he was, it felt safe there like no one could get to me so long as I was wrapped in his embrace.

Kai pulled back the bed sheets with one hand, the other still holding me, and then he laid me down gently before getting in next to me. He pulled the covers over us, pulling me back into his arms. I went willingly, cuddling into his side.

I don't know what made me think of the reason why I went to see Kai, but the memory popped into my head.

"Kai, did you tell anyone about our deal?" I asked sleepily, my eyes were struggling to stay open.

"A few select people, why do you ask?" he replied before kissing me tenderly on the head.

"It was something Anderson said to me, he said I would regret the day I made the deal with you."

The way Kai's body tensed around me told me everything I needed to know.

I wasn't alone in thinking someone had betrayed him.

Chapter 22

Kai

I watched Riley sleep, her breathing steady, and her beautiful long lashes fanned out on her cheekbones.

Being inside her was better than I ever imagined, and the way she screamed my name when she came, *fucking hell*. I'd die a very happy man if I got to hear Riley scream like that every day.

But every time I looked at the bruise under her eye and on her neck, my tenuous grasp on my control slipped further.

I had to find Anderson, no matter the cost.

But who the fuck was he? And what business did he have with me? He seemed hellbent on destroying my family, and I refused to lose any more of them, and that now included Riley. She had always been mine, but after giving herself to me, the deal was sealed. No matter what, she belonged to me, and I was never letting her go.

Finding the man determined to ruin my life was easier said than done though, and now it looked like I had a fucking turncoat to contend with as well.

The obvious person was Hendrix based on what Riley had said. Before she fell asleep, she told me her concerns about him which was understandable given that he was the prick who lied to Riley, telling her I was fucking girls at my club, but I didn't want to believe it would be him. Hendrix was the closest thing I had to a best friend, I was a year older than him, but we'd grown up together, his father was my father's second in command, and if it hadn't been for Theo, Hendrix would have been my 2IC. In fact, recently I'd been thinking about promoting him, I just hadn't been able to bring myself around to do it, it would have felt like I was replacing Theo.

No, I didn't want to believe Hendrix would betray me, but it was just as unlikely that Miles or Danny would.

Miles was family, and had been Theo's best friend, he was as devoted to finding Theo's killer as I was. Danny was an anomaly, he wasn't family or born into this life. He started working for my father about twenty years ago after I found him fighting in an illegal underground fight, and he worked his way up the ranks with his loyalty and dedication. I trusted the three of them more than anything.

I ran through the names of other people who knew about the deal, Frank, Jacqueline, and a couple of other good employees I trusted to make sure Riley and Angel were safe. There was no one I believed would deceive me. But I couldn't ignore the obvious, and until I found out who had betrayed me, I'd keep a close eye on every one of my men. I'd told Riley we'd keep the information between ourselves, it would allow me to watch my men without them becoming suspicious.

She moved in her sleep, moving closer to me, and as I held her in my arms it occurred to me that she was the only one I could trust implicitly. Ironic really that I could trust someone I'd known for only a matter of weeks over people I had known my entire life.

The sun was beginning to rise, and even though I'd only had a few hours sleep, and as much as I didn't want to tear myself away from her naked body, I had business to take care of, and there was no time like the present. I gently rolled my sleeping Star to the other side of the bed, she barely stirred, she was that exhausted. Quietly, I got out of bed and dressed in my closet, fastening my holster around my shoulders, placing my two handguns in their holders, and hooking my sheathed knife onto my belt, making sure all my weapons were hidden under my suit jacket. I didn't relish the idea of breaking and entering in a suit, but it was part of my image, suits made me look and feel powerful.

Once I was dressed, I bent to kiss Riley's forehead. Still, she slept on, and as I took one last look at her before I left, I couldn't help but smile at the sight of her in my bed. She belonged there, and I'd be making damn sure that from now on, that's where she'd be sleeping.

Not bothering to get coffee or breakfast, I made a quick stop at my office, grabbing the envelope I needed from the drawer, before heading to the foyer and straight into my waiting elevator.

Aside from the household staff, no one was up. It was just after 6 am, not that it mattered, I didn't want anyone to know where I was going. The elevator dinged when it reached the parking level, and I grabbed the keys to my SUV from the key safe. I didn't often drive myself, mainly because I could conduct my business from the back seat of a car while someone drove me, but occasionally needs must, and today was one of those times.

The SUV, like most of my cars, was reinforced with bulletproof body work and shatter-resistant glass, they had cost me a small fortune but were worth every penny if one of my enemies decided to take a cheap shot.

I drove out of the basement, pulling onto the deserted street. It didn't take long to get to where I was going with no traffic on the road, and within fifteen minutes, I was stopping short of the house I'd soon be breaking into.

Chief Victor Griffin lived in a typical suburban house, it even had the fucking white picket fence and perfectly pruned flowers. It was a large house in one of the nicest areas of the city. It wasn't like Victor couldn't afford it though, not with his Chief of Police salary and the second income he earned from me by turning a blind eye to certain shit, and giving me information when I needed it.

Only, he'd failed to give me the information I needed, and I was about to find out why.

Helen Griffin, the wife of Victor would be heading out to church in thirty minutes which was what she did every Sunday. She was a good woman, always volunteering for some charity bullshit, and was very religious which was why Victor was absolutely terrified of her finding out about his little addiction to rent boys. Once she left, Victor would be home alone for a few hours before he would head off to work. Their only child, a daughter called Heather, was at university on the other side of the country, meaning Victor and I would have plenty of time to discuss his misdemeanors.

I fired off a few texts to Hendrix, Danny, and Miles to tell them I was out on an errand and I wanted updates from them later about their progression to fix their fuck ups from last night. I was being unreasonable by holding them responsible, but fuck it, it was easier to hold them accountable than accept the truth: Anderson had got the better of me.

After reading their replies, all acknowledgments of their tasks and Hendrix's offer of assistance, which I ignored, I sat back in my seat and watched the house. It wasn't long until my thoughts turned to Riley, something that seemed to be happening more and more.

My mind flashed back to the previous evening when I had eaten her delicious pussy over my desk. I wasn't lying when I told her I had imagined that scenario over and over again. My cock jumped awake at the memory which was a bad fucking idea if I wanted to concentrate on what I was about to do, but I couldn't stop thinking about how perfect her tits were as they bounced when she rode me, and how tight her cunt clamped down on my cock when she came.

Fuck, my dick was standing at full attention now, and I had to bite my knuckle to stop myself from pulling it out and nutting here in the car. The sooner I could get this shit over with Griffin, the sooner I could get back to my girl and fuck her seven ways to Sunday.

Like clockwork, at 7 am on the dot, the front door to the Griffin residence opened, and Helen appeared. She kissed Victor on the cheek and got in her car which was parked on their drive. At the sight of him, all thoughts of Riley disappeared from my mind.

Victor, the old fuck, waved his wife off as he stood there in a motherfucking stripey dressing gown, and as soon as she drove off, he shut the door, no doubt thinking he would have a couple of hours to enjoy some of the hardcore porn I knew he had on his computer thanks to Miles' hacking skills.

Helen drove past my parked car without so much as glancing at me, and as soon as she turned the corner, I made my move.

Leaving the car where it was parked, I grabbed the envelope and walked casually down the street. No one was up at this time of day, so I made it to Victor's without anyone seeing me. Not that it would have mattered if they did, I practically owned everyone living in this part of town. Victor's home office was at the back of his house, I'd never been in it before, but I had his floorplans memorized, it was amazing what information you could get at the right price.

I walked up the driveway, making a beeline to the side gate and kicking it open. The gate led to the backyard, and I walked through like I owned the place. The noise would have disturbed Victor but I'd been counting on that. I drew my gun, in case the old fucker thought he was being burgled and tried to get a shot off first, and then I crept around to the back of the house.

I rolled my eyes at the neatly mown grass, his whole house was such a fucking cliché.

Quickly locating the window to his office, I used my elbow to smash a small pane of glass before reaching in and pulling the handle down. If he hadn't heard the bang from me kicking the gate open, the smashing window certainly would have got his attention. Given that Victor was the Chief of Police, he didn't seem to take security seriously because the window opened easily. Using the frame to hoist myself up, I crawled through the open window which wasn't the fucking easiest thing to do in a suit, but I made quick work of it.

There was nothing spectacular about his office. Bookshelves covered three of the walls surrounding the room, and the closed door leading to the rest of the house stood in the middle of the other wall. His desk was polished oak, and his computer sat in the middle of the desk, a family picture of him, Helen, and Heather on holiday was on display.

How fucking lovely that he had their picture to look at while he was knocking one out to gay porn on his computer.

There was a leather seat on one side of the table facing the computer, and another chair on the opposite side of the desk. Throwing the envelope on the desk, I sat my ass down in the leather chair, trying not to think about the bodily fluids I may or may not have been sitting in, and aimed my gun at the door.

And then I waited.

I didn't have to wait long. The door leading to the rest of the house slowly opened before the nozzle of Victor's gun rounding the door frame appeared, followed by his shaky hand. He peered around, his eyes widening in surprise.

"Hello, Victor," I said, giving him a smile that was anything but friendly.

"K-Kai, you scared the shit out of me." His voice was shaky, and he lowered the gun, thinking I was no threat.

The fool.

"I think it's time we had a chat, don't you?" I nodded to the chair on the other side of his desk, inviting him to sit in it.

Of course, I wasn't giving him a choice, and he knew that. He frowned but did as he was told, sitting down and wrapping his pathetic stripey dressing gown around him as if it would shield him from the shitstorm about to come his way.

"What are you doing here, Kai? I thought you were coming to the office later today," he asked after a minute of me not saying anything, just staring at him.

It was an intimidation technique, often in uncomfortable situations, a person can find they have a need to fill the silence, and Victor, he played perfectly into my hands.

"I'd had enough of waiting, I gave you enough time to get me what I wanted, and clearly my threats of exposing your sordid activities weren't enough to convince you to provide me with the list of cops I asked for weeks ago."

He nervously ran a hand over his bald head, and his eyes darted around the room, not able to meet mine. The fucker was hiding something, I was sure of it.

"It's just taking a bit of time, there are a lot of cops in this state, it's not as easy as you think," he blathered on but he was full of shit.

"Cut the bullshit, Victor, what are you hiding?"

The hand holding the gun was shaking, but he wasn't pointing at me, it hung loosely in his grip. I wasn't concerned he may try and shoot me, I had reflexes like a cat, and I knew full fucking well he'd find a bullet in between his eyes before he even had the chance to take the safety off.

"I'm not hiding anything, Kai, it's just taking time, honest." He still couldn't meet my eye, and I decided it was time for a different tactic, the constant lying was beginning to get on my nerves.

I could have opted for the angry approach, I had a reputation for being a ruthless bastard when I was angry after all, but with Victor, I had to hit him where it would hurt.

I leaned back in his chair, acting casually as if we were two old friends catching up.

"I saw Helen leave earlier, she looked lovely all dressed up for Church."

His eyes widened in horror. Bingo, I'd hit my mark.

"I hear she does amazing work down at St Mary's Church. Volunteers for Sunday school, right? And helps out in the soup kitchen in East Bay?" I added conversationally.

"Kai, leave my wife out of this, please. She has nothing to do with this," he pleaded weakly.

It wouldn't be long until he cracked, I just needed to push a little harder.

"I dunno, Vic, East Bay is a rough place, robberies go wrong all the time, it would be a shame if something happened to her." I had no intention of hurting his wife, there was more than one way to skin a cat. Didn't mean I wouldn't use the *threat* of hurting her to get what I needed though.

"You don't understand! My family is at risk whatever I do," Victor blurted before slapping his hands over his mouth when he realized he had said too much.

I was done with his shit. "Start talking. Now."

Victor dropped the gun on the desk before leaning forward and placing his head in his hand, muttering a muffled prayer.

God couldn't help this man now.

"You have to understand, Kai, he threatened Heather, I had no choice!" he wailed like a fucking baby, his breathing beginning to quicken.

My patience was wearing thin, and that was very dangerous for him.

Leaning forward, I reached across the desk and knocked his arm away so he would look at me. "Here's how this is going to go. You are going to start from the beginning and tell me everything, and if I get even the slightest feeling you aren't being truthful with me, once I am done mutilating you, I will find Helen and Heather and do the same to them. Do not fuck with me, Victor," I growled, the venom in my tone made it crystal clear he should take my threat *very* seriously.

Victor sighed and his shoulders slumped, he had no choice but to spill the beans. He ran his hand over his balding head again.

"About a week before Theo was killed, a man came to my office at the station. He flashed a police badge, it showed he was a detective, but he wouldn't say what department he worked in," Victor started, his voice shaking as he spoke, and looking like his world was crashing in around him. I kept my face stoic, not giving anything away. "He had pictures of Heather, she was at her university, she had no idea he had been following her around and taking photos of her. He...he had one of her asleep in her bed, for fuck's sake, Kai."

I think Riley was making me soft because I suddenly felt the tiniest twinge of sorrow for the poor bastard.

"What was his name?" I asked, although I didn't really need to know, I knew the name that would come out of Victor's mouth.

"Anderson. Detective Anderson."

Well, there was a shocker. *Not.*

"What did he want?" I kept my voice low, deadly. I'd know if Victor lied again, and he knew it was in his best interest to tell me the whole damn truth. No matter what.

Tears welled in his eyes, and he took a deep calming breath before he continued.

"He wanted information about you and Theo, he threatened to slit Heather's throat in her sleep if I didn't tell him what he wanted to know," Victor implored, giving me fucking puppy dog eyes. He was making the mistake of trying to appeal to my humanity but he should have known, I didn't fucking have any.

"What did you tell him?" My jaw clenched as anger reared to life in my bones. If he had been responsible for giving information that ultimately led to Theo's death, there was no way I'd be leaving this house while he still had air in his lungs. My hands gripped the arms of the chair until my knuckles turned white in anticipation of what he was about to say.

"I kept it bland, Kai, I told him stuff that was common knowledge, you know, you owned Sapphire, you lived in a penthouse that was impenetrable." He trailed off as nerves got the better but he was holding back on something.

Something important.

"What else, Victor?"

"Kai, please, I didn't know what to do."

The tears that had been building in his eyes finally slid down his cheeks as he tried to hold back a sob.

"What. Else?" I said, this time through gritted teeth. My own hands were beginning to shake with the need to reach over and smash his fucking face in until he told me the truth.

"Kai, please. I just wanted to keep my family safe," he whimpered pathetically.

The tenuous grasp I had over my control snapped, and quick as a flash, I launched myself over the desk, knocking Victor onto the floor and gripping his throat hard.

"What did you do, Victor," I snarled, baring my teeth.

Victor's face turned white, and his eyes widened in fear. He had never been on the end of my wrath before, heard the rumors, yes, but never experienced it firsthand.

He finally let out a long sigh as the tears continued to slide down his face. Nodding once, resignation set in. I loosened my grip on his throat so he could talk.

"After the Detective came to my office, I didn't hear from him again so I didn't think anything of it. It wouldn't be the first time the Feds have taken an interest in you, Kai. I was going to tell you but I never had the opportunity." He wasn't looking at me when he spoke, just staring off at a space over my shoulder. Squeezing his eyes shut, he continued. "On the day Theo died, Anderson came to my house and told me to call Theo. He threatened to harm Helen if I didn't do it."

"What did he want you to say to Theo?"

Victor opened his eyes and looked directly at me. His whole body vibrated underneath me with fear.

"He wanted me to tell Theo to meet me at the docks, that I had some important information to share with him, and not to tell you until we had discussed it."

My blood froze in my veins.

Victor hadn't just colluded behind my back, but he'd been the one to lure Theo to his death. I'd always wondered why Theo had gone to the docks that night, and now I knew. Someone we thought we could trust had enticed him there.

"Kai, I didn't know he was going to kill Theo, you have to believe me," Victor cried.

Numbness swept through me.

Theo would have arrived at the dock expecting to meet Victor only to meet his fate. He would have had no reason to believe Victor had set him up, Victor had been in our pockets for years, hell, he'd been in my father's pockets long before he worked for us, and he'd never, *not once*, given any indication that he would betray us.

I stood, leaving Victor crumpled on the floor, sobbing quietly. My hands shook with the need to end his life, and it took all my effort to calm my raging thoughts of how to inflict as much pain on him as possible. Whether he knew Theo was going to die or not didn't matter. He had been the one to lead Theo to his death, and in my eyes, that was as bad as wielding the knife himself.

I couldn't look at Victor for a second longer, his pathetic form whimpering on the floor was doing nothing to calm my temper. I didn't want to end him just yet, I still needed information from him.

Turning, I paced up and down his office for a few minutes, the only sound echoing around the office was the occasional sniff from the piece of shit on the floor.

After a few minutes, Victor found some courage to move. Slowly, he sat up from the chair he had been lying in before getting to his feet and standing the chair back up to its original position. The gun that had been in his hand when he first came in lay untouched on the desk, but he would know better than to try and grab it. There was nothing he could do to protect himself now.

"Kai, I'm sorry," he started, dejection heavy in his voice. "I didn't know he was setting Theo up. I just wanted to protect my family."

"You should have come to me, Victor. You knew I could have arranged for Heather and Helen to be protected." For fuck sake, one of my legitimate business contact specialized in personal protection, it would have been piss easy to have his family protected around the clock.

"I know, Kai, I'm sorry. I didn't know what to do. He said if I told you then he wouldn't just kill Heather, he'd...he'd rape her first. I couldn't risk that."

The rational part of my mind knew Victor had been stuck between a rock and a hard place. But he should have come to me regardless. Instead, his actions to save his family resulted in the death of my brother.

That wouldn't go unpunished.

"I want the list," I ordered, making it clear he had no choice but to give me the list of officers I had requested weeks ago. The cunt had it, he'd just been avoiding me because he knew I'd see the lies written all over his ugly face.

Eager to redeem himself, Victor walked around the desk and opened the top drawer before pulling out a USB stick.

"It's all here," he said reassuringly, hope in his voice that he might walk away from this meeting unscathed.

I didn't trust the corrupt fucker much to start with, but I trusted him even less now.

"Show me." I nodded to his computer, and he quickly set about logging in and loading up the memory stick.

Sure enough, the screen displayed a long list of names for all the different police departments across the state. There were fucking hundreds. When I nodded my approval, Victor removed the stick and handed it to me with shaky hands.

"You know I can't let you go unpunished," I said as I pocketed the stick.

His shoulders slumped in resignation, and he dropped his head to the floor as he accepted his fate.

"I know, Kai, but please, don't hurt my family."

He didn't have time to react to me whipping my blade from its sheath tucked under my jacket and plunging it straight into his gut. I purposely angled the knife upward so it would puncture a lung. Blood spurted out and covered my hand as I held the knife in his stomach. Victor gasped and blood spilled from his lips, but he didn't try to pull away or get the knife out.

"I won't hurt your family," I promised him.

His thin lips formed into a grimace, but he gave me a small nod of understanding. I could have easily killed his family in revenge for the death of my brother, but Victor's death would be enough.

Besides, his family would be destroyed in another way. When pictures of Victor in compromising positions with young male escorts, and the leaking of his hard-core porn addiction I had tasked Miles to find, his family would have no choice but to leave their lives in Hollows Bay.

It didn't take long before his eyes started to close as his life drained away. I pulled my knife out, blood spurting everywhere and pouring to the floor. I lowered him down to the ground as he took his last breaths, not giving a fuck that I was now soaked in his blood.

I wouldn't feel guilt for killing him, nor would I regret it. But I'll admit I did feel something close to sadness that it had come to this. Victor was another victim in my life that Detective Anderson had targeted, and although Victor had died at my hands, I was all the more determined to find the fucker and bring him down.

Once Victor was on the floor, it took less than a minute before he let out one last choked gasp and his eyes closed forever. I wiped my knife on his ugly dressing gown before I re-sheathed it.

Giving my pocket a pat to make sure the memory stick was there, I opened the envelope and threw the contents over his body, my lips curling in disgust at the images of Victor fucking a young man who was tied up, gagged, and blindfolded.

I headed out of Victor's office, through his house, and straight out the front door with what I hoped would be the clue to finding Theo's murderer tucked safely in my pocket.

Chapter 23

Riley

I finally had the best night's sleep in weeks. Actually, it was probably months if I really thought about it, maybe even years.

Had someone said to me when I arrived here that I would be lying in Kai Wolfe's bed grinning from ear to ear, I would have laughed at them and told them to get fucked, but here we were.

I rolled over and stretched out, his scent wrapping around me as I laid my head on his pillow. I'd felt him get out of bed earlier, but I was still half asleep and not in the slightest bit ready to wake up. I figured he'd be going to have a workout like he did most mornings, and there was no way I was dragging my ass out of this comfy bed to hit the gym with him.

A devilish smile curled on my lips when I thought of a different type of workout we could have done though.

Last night had been un-freaking-believable.

I didn't have much to compare it to but that was undoubtedly the best sex of my life, and I couldn't wait for a repeat.

I sat my ass up in the ginormous bed and looked around. Kai's room was bigger than mine, and there was a sliding door that led out onto a balcony that overlooked the city. His bed dominated the space, it was so big, it practically consumed one half of the room.

Aside from the bed, he had minimal furniture, a chest of drawers, and two bedside tables but that was it. I supposed other than sleeping, he didn't spend much time in his room so didn't need much in here anyway.

Like Angel's room, he had two doors leading off the main room which I guessed was a closet and an ensuite. Not bothering with the only scrap of clothing I had, my robe, I hopped out of bed intending to look for the bathroom.

Reaching the first door, I paused momentarily at the sound of running water coming from behind it. Slowly, I opened the door and peeked in when curiosity got the better of me. Steam hit me in the face, and my eyes were instantly drawn to the walk-in shower where Kai was, in all his naked glory, showering under the powerful jets.

His back was to me, showcasing his impressive wolf tattoo, and one hand was leaning against the wall. He was facing down allowing the running water to pour down over his neck and back. Kai hadn't heard me come in and it gave me time to admire him for a minute.

Even from behind, he was hot as sin.

Through the steam and the water, my fingers twitched with the urge to reach out and trace every muscle underneath his bronzed skin. The hand that wasn't pressed against the wall moved up to his neck where he started massaging the muscles. My feet moved on autopilot to get closer to him, I wanted to be the one to rub his aches away.

As I got halfway across the bathroom, my bare toes touched material. Dragging my attention away from the adonis, I looked down, to find a pile of clothes on the floor, soaked in blood. Panic crept up my throat fearing it was Kai's blood, and I launched myself the rest of the way across the bathroom, slamming open the shower door.

"Kai, are you hurt?" I cried as Kai turned around to see what the commotion was all about.

As he turned, I scanned his body, checking for any obvious injuries, and feeling pretty darn relieved when I didn't see any.

Kai looked from my panicked face to the pile of clothes on the floor and then back to me.

"No, baby. That's not my blood."

Without warning he reached out and grabbed my hand, and pulled me into the shower with him. Almost falling against his slippery body, he held me close against his chest with both hands on my lower back, just above my ass. His back was to the water, stopping it from spraying directly in my face.

"Who's blood is it?" I asked worriedly as I looked up at him. Although, I wasn't sure I wanted to know the answer.

"I had some business to take care of this morning. It's nothing to worry about."

His expression said otherwise. His brows pinched together in worry as he ran his hands over my curves before they came up to my face. Cupping both cheeks tenderly, he tipped my head back, his eyes assessing my face. For what, I didn't know. Perhaps to see if there was any regret from the night before?

I let him look, he would find no regret from me.

"I missed you," he finally said, and then his lips came down on mine, pressing against them in a soft kiss.

I sighed, and as I did, my mouth parted. He took the opportunity to slide his tongue in and gently stroked mine. It was completely opposite to the way he had kissed me last night, then it had been raw and needy. Now, it was gentle and caressing, most unlike Kai. Something had rattled him.

My hands crept up his chest and roamed over his toned muscles. Kai stepped closer to me, pressing his hardening length against my stomach.

"How do you feel today?" he asked when our kiss broke apart. Tipping my head back further, he cast his eyes over my throat. I hadn't actually thought about my injuries, they didn't hurt and my head had been so consumed with what had happened between Kai and me that I had almost forgotten about the attack by Anderson.

"I'm fine, Kai. It doesn't hurt." It was a little lie, the bruise on my cheek was tender but I didn't want to tell him that because I didn't want him taking his hands off my face.

The frown he'd been wearing since I stepped in the shower deepened, and I hated seeing him worried. He usually looked so confident, so strong. I reached one hand up to stroke his cheek and he nestled against my touch.

"Tell me what's wrong, Kai. What happened this morning?" I pleaded. I didn't know what, but between the bloodied clothes and Kai's somber mood, something bad had happened. Kai had been worried last night but this was something more, like an additional burden to his growing list.

He took his hands off my cheek and grabbed the wrist that was stroking his face. Turning his head, he kissed my wrist which seemed to have a direct line to my pussy because when he kissed my pulse, tingles shot straight to my core.

"Baby, I'll tell you all about it," he kissed his way down my arm, to my shoulder, and then to my neck. "But, right now I need to be inside your sweet pussy again."

One hand grabbed a handful of my ass and pulled my hips against his hard cock as his mouth continued to kiss a path down to my breasts. My thighs clenched together in anticipation of Kai burying himself deep in me again. My pussy was getting wetter and wetter as Kai's mouth latched onto a nipple, and he sucked it hard into his mouth.

I wanted nothing more than to feel him pounding into me again, but before that could happen, I wanted to do something to distract him from whatever had got him so worried. Stepping back, his mouth popped off my breast, a snarl forming on his lips. But before he had a chance to get too angry at what he thought was me denying him, I dropped to my knees, grinning up at him with a salacious grin on my face.

"Relax, Kai, let me help you forget about whatever has happened this morning."

I wrapped my hand firmly around his shaft and stroked it several times. The anger reflecting in his eyes vanished, replaced with a dark look filled with want.

The tiles were hard on my knees, but I didn't care. Although his broad back was stopping most of the water, the jets sprayed over me, warming my tingling body. I slid my hand to the base of his shaft and leaned forward. My tongue darted from my mouth and licked the tip of his cock, before I wrapped my mouth around the head.

"Fuck, Star," Kai hissed.

I looked up at him to find him staring down at me with hooded eyes, and Christ, did it turn me the hell on. My needy pussy clamped down, wanting to be filled with Kai.

Not wasting another minute, I took him fully in my mouth, sucking him in as far as I could take him. Kai thrust forward, shoving his cock further down my throat and hitting my gag reflex like he had the previous night, almost making me choke, but you know what?

I fucking *loved* it.

Sliding my mouth back, I circled his tip again with my tongue before once again taking him in my mouth, but this time I sucked harder. Kai groaned and wrapped a hand around the back of my head, his fingers grabbed a chunk of my hair and he pulled hard making me moan as my pussy flooded with my own need.

"You have no fucking idea how perfect you look, Riley. On your knees with my cock in your mouth."

He could barely get his words out as he thrust into my mouth, and I took him as deep as I could. Within seconds, I found a rhythm with my lips, tongue, and my hand on his shaft. I peeked up at him through my lashes and saw his head was tipped back and his mouth was open. He looked like he was in ecstasy, and damn, did that spur me on.

I licked and sucked his length as he fucked my mouth hard, his balls slapping against my chin. I reached up to grip them in my other hand and massaged them as he continued to fuck the back of my throat.

"I want to come down your throat so badly, Riley, but not yet. I want to feel that tight little pussy come for me first," Kai growled as he pulled his dick from my swollen lips.

I'd be lying if I said I wasn't disappointed, I wanted to swallow down his release, but I also wasn't going to argue with feeling him in my cunt again.

Kai tugged me to my feet by my hair before pulling me into a bruising kiss, twisting us so the powerful water from the multiple showerheads were now hitting us both. The pressure from the jets made my already sensitive skin vibrate with need. My jaw ached from his rough fucking, but his kiss made the ache worth it. Kai's hand slid between my legs where he cupped my pussy, his finger sliding between my folds and dipping into my entrance finding me wet and wanting.

"I'm glad to see you are ready for me, baby." And that was all the warning I had before Kai spun me around, slammed me against the wall, and held me in place with an arm wrapped around my waist so I didn't fall. With his foot, he kicked my legs wider, and pushed me forward so my ass was against his groin, and my hands were pressed up against the tiles. With one thrust, he was inside me, and I screamed out his name as he buried his cock deep in my cunt.

There was nothing gentle about sex with Kai.

He pulled out and slammed back in again and again, and with every thrust, I cried his name. He felt so damn good, and from this angle, he kept hitting the sweet spot inside that made my knees want to buckle.

"You're mine, Riley. This pussy is mine, your ass is mine, and your mouth is mine. Do you hear me?" He groaned.

He grabbed my hair, wrapping it around his hand, and pulling me so my back was against his chest as he growled his words in my ear.

"I'm all fucking yours. Please," I begged, my orgasm was just out of reach, needing that little bit more to get it.

"Please what?" he moaned deviously against the crook of my neck before biting down and leaving yet another bruise, marking his territory.

"Please, Kai, make me come," I cried, wrapping an arm around his neck and holding his face in the crook so he could carry on biting me and leaving his mark.

Kai's thrusting was relentless, and if it hadn't been for his arm around my waist holding me up, I would have collapsed on the floor. He reached around me to where one of the shower jets protruded from the wall and twisted it so it sprayed up, right against my clit.

"Oh, fuck!"

My knees almost buckled from the intensity of the water jet hitting my swollen nub, and Kai pounding into my pussy which kept clamping around him. Within seconds of the water hitting my clit, my orgasm hit like a bolt of lightning, and I screamed for Kai as I came harder than I had ever come before.

But Kai didn't stop, he held me against the jet and carried on pounding me, taking me immediately into a second orgasm which was so intense, I swear, I blacked out for a few seconds. Thankfully, Kai took pity on me and twisted the jet back to its original position, but his cock was still nestled deep inside of me. I barely had time to recover from my double orgasm before Kai pulled out of me and spun me around to face him again.

Holding his long length in one hand, he used his other hand to push my shoulder down, shoving me back to my knees on the hard floor. As soon as I hit the deck, his hand moved from my shoulder to the back of my head where he once again held me in place as he pumped his cock with his other hand.

"Open your mouth, Star," he demanded, and I didn't dare disobey.

He moved close so the tip of his cock tapped against my lip, and he pumped three times more. Kai roared as he found his release, white ropes of come shot from his tip and covered my lips, tongue, and chin. I'd never swallowed before, and I didn't think I would like it, but staring up at Kai with his come dripping from my mouth, yeah I liked it.

I *really* fucking liked it.

"How do I taste?" he asked as he released my hair and stared down at me with nothing but pride and awe in his dark eyes.

I sucked in my bottom lip, tasting more of his release, and then I used my finger to wipe the rest of my mouth before sucking it into my mouth.

"Delicious," I whispered, my voice husky.

Kai reached down and grabbed my arms, helping me to my feet, and once again, his lips were on me, tasting himself. Only this time, his kiss was slow and sensual.

"You amaze me more and more, every single fucking day," he said between kisses as he slowly moved me back under the water so he could clean me, only to dirty me up all over again.

Chapter 24

Kai

Things moved pretty quickly after I left Riley napping in my room having fucked her twice in the shower.

I hadn't realized how badly my hands had been shaking with the need to shed more blood until my girl was back in my arms and distracting me with her beautiful mouth around my dick.

All of that faded as I stepped out of my room, intending to get her some lunch when Miles came hurrying down the corridor to tell me he thought he had had a breakthrough.

A *big* fucking breakthrough.

As soon as I'd arrived back after my visit to Victor, I had given Miles the USB stick and left him to do whatever it was he needed to do to get me a name. Less than two hours later, he had done exactly that. He had excitedly told me there were seven Detective Anderson's across the whole of the state, and after some quick background checks, he was confident he had found the one we were looking for.

Detective John Anderson was an officer of Huntsville City Police Department, stationed at their 6th Street Precinct. Huntsville was smaller than my city, and on the other side of the state from Hollows Bay. I had some connections to the city, mainly through legitimate business means, and as a result, I had a little knowledge of the criminal world there.

As cities go, Huntsville was neither the best place to live nor the worst. Sure, there'd been the odd murder but most were domestic related, or because some crazy bastard had gotten carried away during a road rage incident, but that kind of shit happened everywhere.

The main problem Huntsville had was from the gang, known as The Stags, who peddled drugs but had little control over the market because of their greed. The leader of The Stags was an arrogant prick named Carlos Rigby, who had made his way up the ranks from a young boy. Carlos had visions of grandeur, but instead of taking control and building his gang and criminal enterprise, he'd run it into the ground resulting in mutiny and subordination throughout the ranks, to the point where the gang nearly ceased to exist.

That had been a few years ago, rumors over the last year were that the gang had been taken over by a silent partner whose identity wasn't even known by Carlos himself, but since then, The Stags functioned as a profitable gang and managed to keep under the radar of law enforcement.

Victor had been good enough to include photos of all the police officers in his list. Against my want to let her sleep, I reluctantly woke Riley up and asked her to come to my office to show her the photo of the man we believed to be Anderson. Sure enough, she confirmed he was the man who had turned up at Club Sin all those months ago, and was indeed the fucker who had strangled her at the charity ball.

Once we had a full name and place of work, it didn't take long for Miles to work his magic and find out what he could about Anderson. It transpired he'd been a cop for the past seventeen years, he had started as a patrol officer and worked his way to becoming a detective, now working on the drug squad. From his personnel file Miles found from hacking into the police department's records, he discovered Anderson lived alone in the suburbs of Huntsville. The other interesting thing Miles found out was

Anderson's medical records were chequered with concerns regarding his mental health, and when he was a young patrol officer, he'd taken three months off work due to a breakdown.

The intel was a start, but it didn't even begin to explain why Anderson had it in for me and Theo, or even a connection to Hollows Bay. It was going to take a lot more digging into his past and Miles didn't have the time for that, so I'd passed the details to Isaac to start finding out what he could.

As soon as I had his home address in my hand, I formulated a plan with Hendrix, Danny, and Miles.

I'd been hesitant to bring them in on my plan, and I fucking hated that there was a little niggle of doubt one of them might have betrayed me. But if it was one of them who had turned tail, I needed to act as if I didn't have a clue, and that meant carrying on as if nothing had changed.

I thought long and hard about it on the drive back from Victor's. Someone had told Anderson about my deal with Riley, did that mean they were working with him? No, not exactly.

Neither Hendrix, Miles, or Danny stood to gain from Theo's death, and they had all been just as cut up as I was when Theo's body had been found. No, it was more likely that someone who was aware of the deal had loose lips and had told someone they shouldn't have, who had then told someone else, who had then probably told Anderson. If you wanted something to remain secret in Hollows Bay, you were better off keeping your mouth shut and taking the secret to the grave with you.

In my heart of hearts, I didn't believe any of my three closest associates would have betrayed me, but it didn't hurt to keep a closer eye on them.

I did, however, accept there was something going on with Hendrix, why else would he tell Riley about my nights at Sapphire? But the more I thought about it, the more I came to see that Hendrix was jealous.

I'd seen the way he looked at Riley, it was with longing in his eyes, probably the same way I looked at her. I couldn't blame him, but Riley was mine, and while I was sure he wouldn't make a move, once I had taken care of my brother's murderer, I'd be having a little chat with Hendrix and reminding him where his place was and who Riley belonged to.

With a plan formulated, I called in two of my top surveillance teams who worked as part of my personal protection company, and with the assistance of some trusted members of my enforcement team, we loaded up the vans with surveillance kits and weapons, and headed off on the five hour drive to Huntsville City.

Before we left, I said my goodbyes to a sulking Riley who had wanted to come with us, but it was too dangerous, and I would never intentionally put her in harm's way. She soon cheered up when I said she could spend as much time as she wanted with Angel while I was away. She even seemed happy when I told her Danny would be staying behind to make sure she was safe.

More suspiciously, *Danny* was okay with staying behind, and the lingering question as to if he had been the one to betray me sprung to mind, but when Riley had teased him about getting to spend more time with Angel's tutor, Jane, and Danny had walked off cursing under his breath, the answer became apparent.

I was still a little reluctant to leave Danny, if he was colluding with an enemy behind my back then I'd be leaving him behind with the one thing Anderson wanted, and the one thing that meant anything to me. But I only had to watch their interactions, and the way he spoke so fondly of both Riley and Angel, I knew without a doubt he was not the one to betray me.

He doted on the two girls like they were his sisters, and the fact that Danny had no family when he was growing up, family meant something to him now.

I said goodbye to Riley in the foyer as Miles and Hendrix joined us with their bags. To make it *crystal clear* just who Riley belonged to, I pulled her into my arms and gave her the deepest, heated kiss I'd ever experienced. When I let her pull away, her cheeks were flushed, and lust filled her gorgeous eyes, and if I hadn't been so focused on the job ahead of me, I would have taken her back to my room and spent the evening buried in her perfect cunt.

But that had to wait.

I'd given her another quick kiss on the lips for good measure and then walked into the waiting elevator, smirking at the flash of jealousy on Hendrix's face as I strolled past him. It looked like I'd be having that conversation with him sooner rather than later.

When we reached the parking level, we bundled into the SUV with Hendrix driving, and we headed off to Huntsville City, confident that in a few hour's time, we'd be returning home with Anderson, who would find himself hanging from his thumbs in my basement, begging for mercy.

That had been a full fucking 48 hours earlier, and we were no closer to tracking him down.

As soon as we arrived in the city, one surveillance team positioned themselves near his home address, and the other team near the police station. They were to watch both locations until Anderson made an appearance. The plan was to make sure Anderson was at his home, tucked up safe and sound in bed, and then we'd attack. But Anderson hadn't been near or by his fucking house, and on day two when I was starting to lose my patience, Miles managed to hack the restricted files of the police department to find out that Anderson had gone awol a week prior to the charity ball, and his senior officers were concerned about his mental stability, so much so they were treating him as a missing person.

But even with them doing their own investigation to find him, he had managed to disappear off the face of the planet.

It was like we had taken one step forward and two huge fucking steps back.

On the second night of being away from Riley, I found myself in my hotel room waiting to hear from Miles and Hendrix. Miles and two of my enforcers, Vince and Steve were going to break into Anderson's house to see if he had left any clues as to where in the fucking world he might be. Huntsville PD had allegedly been in there once and searched it, but most cops were incompetent, and I wanted to be satisfied that every corner of his house had been searched.

Hendrix was at the local nightclub following up on a lead. Isaac had managed to track down Anderson's ex-girlfriend who worked at the club, and Hendrix was going to use his charm to see what intel he could get from her. I had no doubt that his charm would involve scaring the bitch into telling him what he wanted to know.

And so, I found myself alone and craving to see my Star. Two days away from her was two days too long, and I wondered if she was feeling the same way.

I'd checked in regularly with Danny to make sure everything was running smoothly back in Hollows Bay, and to make sure Riley was behaving herself, but I hadn't spoken to her. I needed to remain focused, and as much as she would have been a welcomed distraction, I needed to keep my head in the game when we were *this* close to finding someone who would lead me to the person who killed Theo.

The problem was, I was fucking addicted to that girl, and without anything else to distract me, I couldn't stop thinking about getting my next hit of Riley.

I loaded up my Ipad and used the virtual private network that Miles had set up for me, it meant I could freely use the internet without anyone being able to track my location. Miles had once explained to me how VPNs work when he insisted we all used encrypted phones to ensure we couldn't be hacked, it was something to do with all your data traffic being routed through an encrypted virtual tunnel that disguised your IP address and meant your location was invisible to anyone. Miles had been telling me about it like he was a little kid who had just received a gold star on a project he was working on. I, on the other hand, hadn't given a shit about how it all worked, so long as it did what Miles was saying it did.

I fired a quick text to Danny, telling him to load the secure camera app on my office desktop back at the apartment. His reply was instant, and within minutes, he answered my call.

"Bossman, you good?" he said as he answered. His scarred face filled my screen, and his tone filled with humor.

"What's got you so fucking happy?" I grumbled, not used to seeing Danny with a smile on his face unless he was standing over a body with his knife in hand.

"Sorry, Boss, just that kid man, for someone who is deaf, she's filled with so much fucking sass. She's given Riley some right shit the last two days," he laughed and I couldn't help but smile.

It seemed the Bennett sisters had managed to work their way into the hearts of the city's scariest bastards. A little pang of worry flashed through me when it occurred to me that in just over five months, if Riley decided not to stay, both she and her sister would not be just out of my life, but *all* of our lives.

"She gets it from her sister," I replied, dismissing the thought. It didn't matter if Riley wanted to leave after the agreed time was up, she wasn't going anywhere. Which meant neither was Angel.

"You're telling me. Riles has given me nothing but attitude these last two days. I even told her if she carries on giving me shit, I'd tell you, and you would put her across your knee, but that seemed to encourage her." He smirked as I let out a laugh but then my thoughts turned fucking dark at the mental image of Riley across my knee, her perfectly round ass up in the air getting redder with every spank of my hand.

Fuck. Me.

There was a brief pause on the line as I tried to clear the image from my head.

"Anyway, what's happening, Boss? Any more intel as to where Detective Dick might be?" Danny said, thankfully changing the subject and distracting me from my wicked thoughts of all the things I'd like to do to Riley and her ass.

I filled him in on what Miles had found about Anderson's medical records, he sighed when I told him we weren't the only ones looking for him.

"Shit, where the fuck is he?"

"Fuck knows. He'll pop up somewhere but who knows when. Just make sure security is tighter than a nun's cunt at the apartment, and Riley is not to leave until I'm back."

I'd told him before we left that she wasn't to go anywhere but a little reminder couldn't hurt. I also knew my apartment block was near impossible to breach if you weren't welcome there, but with the knowledge that Anderson had managed to get to Victor with threats of violence against his family, there was no way of knowing if he'd managed to get to anyone else.

Call me paranoid, but I thought I had every right to be given what had happened. I hated knowing Riley was so far away, and if there were any trouble, I'd be too late to get to her.

"Course not. Although she is getting a little frustrated at being stuck indoors, she understands the need."

Danny also understood it, he knew how fucking seriously I was taking her safety, and I knew that if it came to it, Danny would lay down his life to protect Riley.

"Good. Can you get her for me? I'd like to speak to her."

"Sure thing. Keep me posted." And with that, the big man disappeared from my screen. I heard him leaving the office and faint voices in the distance as he went to get my girl. I took the opportunity to move from the table I'd been sitting at and made myself comfortable on the king-size bed that was in my room. As cheap hotels went, this wasn't bad. I wouldn't usually stay in anything less than four stars, but I didn't want to draw attention to our presence in the city, and even though we were all using fake IDs, I wanted to lay as low as possible, so slumming it was the only way.

"Hey."

Riley's beautiful face appeared, and her tone was bright. She looked fucking radiant, and if I could have reached through the screen to touch her, I would have. For the first time in two days, my black heart beat wildly against my chest.

"Hi, Star," I replied, trying my fucking hardest to sound cool, to not show that just her appearance on a fucking computer screen did crazy things to my body.

"Are you okay? I was worried," she said after a few seconds of neither one of us speaking. My lips twitched into a faint smile at the mention of her worrying about me. How times had changed.

"I'm fine, things are just taking a bit longer than what I wanted."

"You haven't found him then?" She frowned and disappointment laced her tone.

"Not yet, it looks like he went to ground a week before the ball. The cops are trying to find him as well but it's like he's just vanished."

I settled back against the pillows in the bed, taking a moment to absorb everything about my girl.

She wore her chestnut hair down around her shoulders, and her cheeks were rosy where she'd been laughing. Only her top half was visible and it looked like she was wearing some kind of vest top. A wave of jealousy rolled through me, not liking the thought that she was wearing her pajamas around Danny.

"Maybe he's dead," she said hopefully, bringing my attention back to her and not the irrational image of me murdering Danny.

"I don't think our luck is that good."

In fairness to her, it was something I had considered, maybe something had happened to him after the ball, but unless I was standing over his cold corpse, I wouldn't believe it.

"Tell me what you have been doing these last couple of days, Star," I said, wanting to change the subject to something other than Anderson.

Riley launched into a long speech, barely stopping to take a breath.

She told me all about her time with Angel, about how well she was doing with her schoolwork, how Angel was like a different kid, and how much Angel liked Danny. I knew Danny had been spending time with Angel, I had assigned him as her personal protection whenever they left the apartment, and he would often rave about how smart she was. I even caught him practicing sign language in front of a mirror one day.

Fuck, we *all* had it bad for the Bennett girls.

The two of us laughed when she regaled an incident where Danny had thrown a tantrum because Angel had beaten him in a shooting game on her computer. He'd thrown the controller down in anger before stomping off.

I was yet to meet Angel, I had purposely kept away not wanting to scare the kid, but the more I heard about her, the more I wanted to meet her.

I laid back on the bed listening to Riley talk, and fuck, did it make my cold heart swell with something. She was so animated and passionate when she spoke, and I was finally beginning to see the real Riley, the Riley who should be enjoying life and not carrying the burden of caring for her younger sister.

She said Angel was a different kid but I didn't think Riley was aware of how much she had changed too. But I was. I saw everything when it came to her, and this side of her? I was so fucking glad I was the one who had given her the chance to discover it and show her what life could offer her.

"When are you coming home, Kai?" she said with a sigh. My lips twitched into a small smile at the fact she'd just referred to the penthouse as home. She was right though, before her, it was somewhere I lived, but with her there, yeah it felt like home.

"Soon, baby. You missing me?" I said it half-jokingly but I was curious as to what she would say.

"Yes," she whispered. I'll be man enough to admit that a small wave of relief rushed through me.

"I miss you too." Neither one of us said anything for a minute and I took the opportunity to just look at her.

She was sitting in my office chair, my city stretched out behind her. It was a glorious fucking sight. When Riley yawned and reached her arms up to stretch them above her head, her pert tits hidden underneath her vest came into view. Her nipples were hard against the material of the top, letting me know she wasn't wearing a bra, and the sight made my dick twitch in my sweatpants.

"Hey, Star, what are you wearing?" I said, mischief heavy in my voice. She threw her head back and laughed, the bruises on her neck were beginning to fade, and right then, I would have given anything to kiss her delicate skin.

"That's a bit cliché isn't it, Mr. Wolfe?" she replied, her voice sultry and full of desire. And hearing her call me Mr. Wolfe, fuck, that went straight to my hardening cock.

"Humor me," I said dryly.

"My pajama vest and shorts." She leaned forward so her face was closer to the camera before she said, "That's all."

A sly smile spread across her lips at her admission of her being naked under her pajamas.

The teasing little minx.

"Take them off, Riley, I want to see you."

She hesitated, eyes widening as she looked at the office door and then back at the screen.

"Go and lock the door and then come back and take your pajamas off," I told her in no uncertain terms.

I knew Danny wouldn't have come back but if it made her more comfortable to lock the door then I would wait. She quirked a brow, and I thought she was going to disobey me, but then she got out of the chair and disappeared off the screen. The lock on the door clicked and then she reappeared, sitting back in my chair, this time her cheeks rosy for a whole other reason.

But she didn't move again, and I could see the internal debate raging in her head.

"I won't tell you again, Star," I growled. My dick was getting uncomfortable with how hard it was, but I refused to touch myself until my girl was naked and touching herself.

Without breaking eye contact, she pulled her vest over her head and dropped it on the floor beside her. She was slightly too short in my chair so I could only make out the top of her luscious tits.

Memories of the first time I fucked her in my office flooded my brain, of how her nipples felt in my mouth and how soft her luscious tits were.

I needed more.

"Take your shorts off, Riley, and lean back in the chair, legs on the table, either side of the computer," I instructed.

She would be fully exposed to me that way, and I couldn't fucking wait to get an eyeful of her beautiful pussy. This time, without hesitation she did as I'd asked.

She looked fucking incredible, sitting back in my chair, full tits and glistening cunt on display, I was beginning to regret starting this because all I wanted to do now was slam into her and fuck her into oblivion. I desperately needed to find Anderson so I could get the fuck back to her.

"Touch yourself, Riley, I want to see you make yourself come."

Without tearing my eyes away from the screen, I finally pulled my rock hard cock out of my pants and gripped it tightly in my hand. I'd imagined fucking Riley time and time again, but now I'd had a taste, and with the visual image of her spread open on display in front of me, it was easy to imagine my hand was really her tight pussy.

She moved one hand over her tit and used a finger and her thumb to play with her nipple. The other hand trailed down her belly until it reached her slit, and she found her clit and started rubbing it in lazy circles with two fingers. Her cunt was soaking wet, and like the addict I was, I imagined licking every drop of her sweetness. Her hips started moving in time with her fingers as they dipped inside of her, her breaths turning to pants as I started moving my hand up and down my shaft.

"Kai, I want to see you." Her voice was husky, wanton.

Who was I to deny my girl?

I yanked my sweat pants down my legs and repositioned the Ipad between my legs so she had a view of me lying on the bed, cock in hand. Her lust-filled eyes widened at the sight, and fuck, that encouraged me to move my hand faster.

"Riley, left-hand top drawer," I grunted as my balls tightened. She moved the hand from her tit and leaned forward to open the drawer, and I heard her gasp. She relaxed back in the chair with a mischievous grin on her face.

"Kai Wolfe, you're a deviant," she said with a grin as she examined the small toy.

Danny had given it to me as a joke months ago when a whore I had fucked one night caused a commotion at Sapphire because I wouldn't fuck her again. She'd drunkenly announced that she had come harder with a vibrator than on my dick. It was a lie of course, otherwise, she wouldn't have been begging for a second round, but I didn't point that out to her when I had her escorted from the club and put on the barred list. But Danny found it hilarious, and gave me the vibrating toy in case I needed backup in the future.

Joke was on him now.

"I hope you haven't used this with anyone else?" Riley gave me a pointed look, a hint of jealousy in her voice.

"No, baby, it's a story for another day, but I promise it's never been used. Use it now, Star, make yourself come for me, imagine it's my cock inside of you, fucking your tight hole."

She pressed the button on the bottom of the toy, and it came to life as it pulsed and buzzed. I watched with wicked fascination as she carried on rubbing her clit with one hand, and used the other to insert the toy into her pussy.

"Holy shit," she gasped when it was buzzing away inside of her. She held onto it with her delicate fingers, and started to pump the toy in and out of herself, all the while rubbing her little nub.

"Fuck, Kai, I wish this was you," she panted as her hips bucked. I started moving my hand up and down my cock faster and harder, in time with her pumping the vibrator in and out of her, imagining it was my cock inside of her.

"Soon, baby, I'm going to make you come so fucking hard when I get home to you. The things I'm going to do to you, every time you move, you'll be reminded of me being inside of you."

Her only reply was a moan as she lost herself to the pleasure. Her eyelids fluttered closed as she continued to fuck herself, and I knew she was so close to reaching her climax. I was close too, trying fucking hard to hold it off so I could watch her come first.

"Open your eyes, Riley, I want them on me when you come."

Her eyes flew open and fixed on me as she continued thrusting the toy and rubbing her clit. We watched each other for a few more seconds before she found her release.

"Fuck, Kai!" she cried as her whole body tensed and shuddered, her eyes momentarily rolling up and into the back of her head.

"Show me your fingers, baby. I want to see your come all over them," I said when she had regained some composure and removed the toy.

Slowly, Riley lifted her hand to the screen, her index finger and middle finger shimmered with her juice and the image almost made me spill.

"Now suck your fingers and taste yourself, Riley," I ordered.

With glazed eyes and red cheeks, Riley lifted her fingers and sucked them into her mouth. Her eyes squeezed close, and she hummed in delight at the taste of herself.

It was all I needed to push me over the edge, one more pump and I came all over my hand with a grunt, it was fucking amazing.

"I think you are going to be a bad influence on me," she whispered seductively as she grabbed the toy and licked her come off the shaft. My dick twitched at the sight, ready to go again.

"Oh, Star, you have no fucking idea."

She gave me a grin that was full of promise, and it took all of my self-control not to abandon my mission and drive all night so I could wake her up in the morning with my cock sliding in and out of her.

"Put your clothes back on and go to bed," I ordered before I gave into that insane thought.

"Yes, Sir," she replied and saluted, making me chuckle.

I fucking loved her sass, she was the only person in my life who dared to give it to me, and I never wanted that to change.

I cleaned my hand up and pulled my sweatpants back on, watching her as she re-dressed. When she was suitably clothed, she leaned forward in the chair again so I could only see her face and shoulders once more.

"Goodnight, Mr. Wolfe, I can't wait for you to come home." Her voice was full of sleepiness and her eyelids drooped.

"Goodnight, Star, dream of me," I whispered back to her, wishing she was falling asleep in my arms.

"I always do."

And with that, I disconnected the call. I laid back on the bed with a grin on my face, not giving a fuck that Riley was turning me into a soppy cunt.

About ten minutes later, my phone rang, Miles' name flashing on the screen.

"What have you got, Miles?" I said upon answering.

"Not much, Boss, house has been cleaned completely out," he said, sounding as disappointed as I felt.

"Fuck."

"Yeah. There was something though, it's a bit of a long shot so I don't want to get your hopes up."

"What," I snapped, my impatience taking hold.

"I found a phone in the backyard, it was under a pile of clothes that had been set fire to. I reckon whoever set the fire left thinking the phone would burn with the clothes, but I'm guessing the fire went out before it could do too much damage."

Excitement spiked through me even though Miles had told me not to get my hopes up, this was sounding promising.

"It's busted too, looks like it's been dropped from a height or stomped on, it's just the shell of a phone. I've given it a once over to make sure it's not a detonator for a device or something but it's all clear. It's definitely a burner phone, and I'm pretty sure I have the kit back home to break into it. If I can, it may give us a clue as to where Anderson is."

Miles was a fucking genius.

For the first time in *months*, we finally fucking had something.

Chapter 25

Riley

"You are not going out in that. Get fucking changed!" Danny growled at me as he stood in the doorway, taking in my outfit.

"Nope," I replied, not in the least bit worried about giving him attitude. Danny was a pussy cat, he may have looked like a scary fucker but he was as soft as shit. Granted, I wouldn't want to meet him down a dark alley, but I knew full well he was harmless to me, and therefore I had no problem sassing him, if anything it kept him on his toes.

"If I've got to go to that place, then I'm going to look my damned finest." I finished adding the last coat of lip gloss and smacked my lips together. Stepping back from the mirror I couldn't help but smile at the reflection staring back at me.

I felt like me again.

When Danny had announced he was taking me to Sapphire, I had been *very* reluctant to go. I didn't want to spend the evening surrounded by beautiful women and constantly wondering which of them Kai had fucked, not for me, thank you very much. But the alternative was spending another evening in Kai's apartment, and quite frankly, I was bored out of my mind.

Kai still wasn't back from his adventures of hunting down Detective Anderson, and I had no clue when he was coming home. As much as

I'd kept myself busy by spending time with Angel, working out in Kai's gym, and playing snooker with Danny, I wasn't used to spending this amount of time inside and I was climbing the walls.

"Come on, Riles, Kai will kill me if he knows you're going out like that." Danny's mouth pressed into a thin line as he once again eyed my outfit.

I understood why he was frustrated, the dress was a *tad* bit on the risqué side. It was a tight-fitting short black dress, so short that my ass cheeks almost peeked out the bottom. The material clung to my skin showing off my curves, and the material at the waistline split into two, each bit coming up and covering a breast, but leaving a gaping hole between them before coming to tie up behind my neck.

I'd opted for skyscraper black heels which made my toned legs look longer than what they were. My makeup was perfect, with smokey eyeshadow, thick eyeliner, and red glossy lips. I'd pulled my hair back into a high ponytail to complete my look.

"Yeah well, Kai isn't here so...." I said, shrugging a shoulder. "Besides, if he didn't want me to wear outfits like this, then why'd he buy it? It was in my closet after all."

Danny huffed and cursed under his breath. He checked the watch on his wrist before huffing again.

"Fine. But you are not to leave my side tonight, you hear?"

I grabbed my clutch purse and made my way over to him, a smug little smile playing on my lips and enjoying the horror on his face as I swayed my hips.

Danny and I had grown closer over the last couple of days, and we had established a relationship where he was like an overprotective big brother and I was his annoying sister, and *oh* how I enjoyed annoying him. He scowled as I got closer and rolled his eyes but didn't comment on my dress anymore. Instead, he turned to walk out of my room and I followed.

"Did Kai say when he would be back?" I asked as my heels clicked against the marble floor.

"No," Danny said, sounding a little softer. We reached the elevator, and he used his thumb to open the door.

"I just don't understand why Kai is letting you take me out when he clearly doesn't want me to leave the apartment." I gave Danny a confused look because I genuinely couldn't understand it. I'd given him an earache with my constant whining about going out these last few days and it had always been met with a resounding *no*, so color me curious.

"I told you earlier, I was fed up with your bitching, and Kai took pity on me. With all the security at Sapphire, you won't be at any more risk than what you are here, so he agreed I could take you there to give my ears a rest." There was humor in his voice, and I wondered if he'd secretly enjoyed these last couple of days of babysitting me.

I knew he'd also enjoyed the extra time getting to know Jane, I had caught him sneaking out of her room one night, much to my amusement.

I didn't say anything as the elevator came to a stop, and Danny ushered me out to the waiting SUV where four armed men, all of whom were wearing suits, waited for us. I guessed they were extra security for my little trip out. I can't say I was particularly looking forward to going to Sapphire of all places. I'd also been hoping all day that Kai would be home tonight and we could spend the night making up for lost time, but it was looking like he'd be away for at least another night.

Danny cursed under his breath as we approached the waiting men, and I realized it was because the four of them were all gawking at me with their mouths open, a look of longing etched on every one of their faces. A little part of me thought I should go back upstairs and put something a little less slutty on, knowing full well Kai wouldn't approve of my outfit choice.

But fuck him. He wasn't here, and I'd actually found something I was comfortable in. I was also feeling a little rebellious knowing there wasn't a damn thing Kai could do to stop me, maybe he shouldn't have locked me up for the last three days.

Frank greeted me as I climbed into the rear of the SUV, although he kept his eyes averted which I was grateful for, I thought I had flashed a little of my barely there panties as I got in.

Danny swiftly followed, and the four other men got in two other waiting vehicles. Within seconds all three cars headed out, maneuvering into some kind of formation so one of the cars the guards were in was at the front of the convoy, the SUV I was in was in the middle, and the last car behind us, as we made out way through the streets towards the club and my own personal version of hell.

Danny and Frank chatted the entire way, talking about a new car Kai was buying. I'd lost interest pretty quickly, having never driven a car in my life and not being able to afford the luxury of getting a cab to and from work, so I knew a big fat zero about makes and models of cars. All I heard was that an insane amount of money was being spent on this car, making me roll my eyes.

I stared out the window, mainly thinking about Kai, and before I knew it, we were pulling up outside Sapphire, the growing sense of trepidation in my belly deepening. Especially when the first thing I saw at the front of the club was two stunning women, dressed in *tiny* gold bikinis, and welcoming in the customers.

I seriously debated feigning a headache to get Danny to take me home, or if I should go with period pains, men always freaked out when women talked about that, but before I had the chance to get my words out, Frank was opening my door and helping me to my feet.

The entrance to the club was lit up in dazzling bright lights. There was a queue of people lined up waiting to get in, the line stretching far back and around the block, and every person had spent hours getting glammed up, making me very freaking glad I had stuck to my guns about the dress I was wearing.

At the front entrance was a red carpet that led up to two black marble steps and into the club itself, and aside from the two bikini-clad babes at the entrance, there were four doormen searching everyone and checking their membership cards.

One of the men leaned forward to shake Danny's hand and as he did, I saw the handle of his gun discreetly tucked inside his jacket. It probably should have worried me that there were armed men at the door, but given what had happened at the charity ball, I was kind of glad they were armed. I knew Danny would be too, he'd previously mentioned that none of them went anywhere without at least one gun strapped to them. The doorman unclipped the rope barrier that was preventing anyone from queue jumping, not that I imagined anyone would be brave enough to chance it in front of these four monster-sized men, and he stepped aside to let us in.

Taking my hand, Danny led me through the foyer and off to a door that had a VIP sign above it, the four armed men following behind.

Twinkling lights lined the dark stairwell Danny led me up, and the music from the club echoed around us, the bass was so loud I could feel it thumping in my chest. Lining the wall was artwork, each framed picture was of the silhouette of a woman pole dancing. I stared at each picture, falling in love with every single one, they were just so classy and elegant which summed up Sapphire.

The club had a reputation for being the best club in the whole of Hollows Bay. Some of the girls at Club Sin had aspirations of working their way up to Sapphire, but it was a place I never imagined myself stepping foot into.

How times had changed.

When we reached the top, another doorman opened the door, and once again shook Danny's hand before nodding his head in a greeting to me.

"Welcome to Sapphire, Riles," Danny announced as he led me through into the main VIP bar.

My mouth dropped open at the surroundings. The area was a level above the club but a long window allowed patrons to see what was going on down below. It also blocked out the heavy music playing in the main atrium of the club, instead, seductive jazz music played throughout. Three huge crystal chandeliers hung from the ceiling giving off a subtle glow, and low brown leather sofas and tables were scattered around the place, each table held a little lamp which also cast a soft glow. The place had a vibe of a very exclusive speak-easy.

A bar ran along the back wall, and a quick glance told me the alcohol here was none of the cheap shit Club Sin stocked, it was all top-end labels, and the bartenders were moving up and down behind the bar, mixing cocktails and working their asses off to serve their guests quickly.

The whole place exuded money, and it would have been a great place to spend a few hours had it not been for the sickeningly beautiful women wearing practically nothing, walking around and flirting with the men. Oh, and swinging themselves around poles. Did I mention the three circular platforms with individual poles dotted throughout the area, each with a gorgeous woman dancing seductively around them?

Instantly, my evil little mind started questioning which of the girls Kai had fucked, and my mood soured, not helped by the tiny blonde girl who came sidling up to Danny and rubbed herself against his arm.

"Hi, Danny, haven't seen you in a while," she purred, not even in the slightest bit bothered he was holding my hand. Not that it bothered me, but come on girl, have some respect for a fellow sister.

"Yeah, been busy," Danny replied dismissively and pried her fingers from where they had curled around his bicep.

"Get your ass back to work, Monica, let the man at least get through the door," another woman said, scowling at the blonde.

She was a little older than Monica, her hair was as black as the night sky, and she had gorgeous light blue eyes. She gave me a beaming friendly smile as if she knew me, which was a bit weird seeing as I had never set foot in this place before.

The blonde, Monica, huffed at the other woman before scurrying away as quickly as she had arrived.

"Sorry about her, she's like a bitch in heat sometimes," the black haired woman said to Monica's retreating form. Danny threw his head back and let out a knowing snort and I smiled too, reminded of what Blaze used to be like around men with a little bit of money or power.

She looked back at me and again gave me a look like she knew me. "Why don't I take Riley to the bar and get her a drink while you go do Whatever it is you do? I'm Kimmy by the way."

How the fuck she knew my name, I did not know but she didn't give Danny the chance to answer as she took my hand and pulled me towards the bar. Danny let me go willingly so I assumed he knew no harm could come to me here. There were about fifty or so other patrons in the VIP section but none of them had bothered to look away from their conversations, or the dancing girls so I figured there was nothing to be worried about.

"How did you know my name?" I finally asked Kimmy when she sat me on a stool at the bar before disappearing behind it to start making me a drink. She grabbed a tall glass and some bottles of spirits from the side and I guessed from the ingredients she was making me a Long Island iced tea, one of my favorites.

"Because the only girl Danny would dare to bring in here is Kai Wolfe's new girlfriend," she said with a wink.

Girlfriend?!

Fucking hell, she'd got that wrong.

"Uh, I'm not Kai's girlfriend," I said, correcting her. She never responded, just carried on pouring shots into the cocktail shaker. "And that never really answered my question either."

"Kai phoned earlier, he wanted me to make sure his girl was looked after tonight, he's got it bad for you."

There was no teasing or jealousy in her tone, on the contrary, she genuinely looked pleased. And if Kai had told her personally about me then he must have trusted her enough, and that helped me to relax.

She shook the cocktail mixer, and I looked around to see where Danny was, he was engrossed in conversation with an old, balding guy who I could have sworn was at the charity ball.

"How long have you worked here?" I asked Kimmy as I turned back to her.

"Since it opened two years ago. I was working in another bar when Kai realized I was wasted there and offered me the managerial job here."

She poured the drink into the tall glass and garnished it with a wedge of lime and a fancy straw before sliding it over the bar to me. I took a slip and relished the sharp taste on my tongue, it was a perfect mix of all the ingredients. I didn't drink often, but if I ever stayed behind after Club Sin closed, this was my go-to drink.

"That's good, thank you."

Kimmy smiled at me as she returned the bottles to their shelves and then came to sit next to me. She was a little bit more covered up than the other girls working in the club, her 'uniform' consisted of a tight black skirt and light blue shirt that hugged her boobs.

"So, you've known Kai a while then?" I said after another few swigs of my drink. I knew I should have let it go, but I couldn't stop the thoughts churning in my head about who Kai had been with, and yeah, I was aware I was beginning to sound like a crazy stalker.

"I've not slept with him if that's what you're asking," Kimmy said with a chuckle. "Look, I won't lie to you, and I'm sure you know Kai isn't exactly a virgin, besides me, there aren't many other girls he hasn't been with." She paused when I snorted into my drink, making her laugh. "But, he hasn't been with anyone for weeks, Riley. There were rumors he'd met someone, but I don't think anyone believed it until you walked through that door a few minutes ago. And now, all the girls know those rumors are true because Danny, Hendrix, and Miles would never dream of bringing one of their fuck buddies here."

I looked around as she was talking and became increasingly aware that pretty much all of the girls here were casting subtle looks in my direction. Some were a bit more obvious and looked at me like I had three heads, some gave me nervous smiles before looking away, and there were others that looked almost as though they wanted to rip my head off.

"Huh."

Kimmy laughed again, and as the warmth of the alcohol started flowing through me, I couldn't help but laugh with her. She was kind and funny, and I found myself liking her and relaxing even more. It felt good to be out of that damn penthouse.

Kimmy and I spent the next two hours talking about all sorts of shit, it didn't seem to bother her that I was dominating all of her time and keeping her from work. The only time she went behind the bar was to make me more Long Island cocktails, and before I knew it, she was sliding my fourth across the bar to me, and I had a nice buzz going on.

Kimmy told me all the gossip about the girls who worked here, how they were all desperate to be in my position with one of Kai's golden boys, AKA Hendrix, Miles, and Danny. She pointed out the girls I should avoid, in particular the petite blonde girl who had greeted Danny when we came in, Monica. Apparently, she had it *really* bad for Kai, and any time I looked over at her, she was glaring daggers at me. As the alcohol started giving me a confidence booster, I found myself waving at her just to piss her off which Kimmy found hilarious.

Just as I was about to start sipping on my drink, Danny and a smartly dressed man joined us at the bar.

"I'm sorry to interrupt you ladies but I'm afraid I need to borrow Kimmy," the man said. He wore an earpiece so I figured he worked at the club.

"Duty calls, babe. Catch you later." Kimmy winked at me before slipping off her stool and walking away with the man.

"For someone who didn't want to come, you look like you're enjoying yourself, Riles," Danny teased.

I'd caught him a number of times looking over to make sure I was where he expected me to be, and I had no doubt that had someone other than Kimmy tried talking to me, he would have been over in a heartbeat. He was holding a bottle of water, and now that I thought about it, it occurred to me that I hadn't seen him drinking anything but water. Being on Riley duty sucked.

"It's not so bad." I shrugged, my words coming out a little bit more slurred than I'd hoped. Enough for Danny to notice too.

"I think that ought to be your last drink, Riles, Kai will have my balls if you get trollied."

"Yeah well, like I said before, Kai isn't here so, tough shit." I stared at him as I sucked more of my drink through my straw, grinning and daring him to stop me. He didn't of course, but his eyes narrowed in anger.

Oh well.

Catcalls drew my attention to behind Danny, and I watched as Monica climbed onto one of the podiums and started gyrating around the pole as a group of men watched on in fascination.

Call me a judgmental bitch, but Monica was a bad dancer. She was sloppy, clinging to the pole as if her life depended on it. She was unnatural and uncomfortable as she pulled herself up into the butterfly position, accidentally slipping down an inch or two before she managed to grip the pole between her thighs. To the untrained eye, no one would have noticed, but to someone who had danced practically every night for the last few years and had grown up with a love for dance, I noticed.

And I was overwhelmed with the sudden urge to show Monica just how it was done right.

Especially, as when she finished her dance and slid down the pole back onto her feet, she looked over at me and smirked, laying down a silent challenge.

I didn't tend to get drawn into bitchiness, in fact, I actively avoided it. Even when Blaze had been downright nasty, it had taken a long time to push me over the edge.

But with the alcohol swimming through my veins, and the smug smirk on Monica's face that got under my skin, I was more than happy to accept the bitch's challenge.

I downed the rest of my drink, eyes fixed solely on the pole, and now I had it in my vision, it was like the rest of the room had faded away and I was being called home. It sounded stupid, but dancing was my life, and I hadn't realized until now how much I was missing it.

I slammed my glass down on the counter and stood up, swaying slightly on my heels. As I took a step forward fully intending to get my ass up on the podium and wipe that smug look off Monica's face, a strong hand wrapped around my arm, stopping me from going anywhere.

"Don't even think about it," Danny, my fucking shadow, grumbled. I tore my eyes away from the pole and the smirking bitch, and looked at him. He was wearing his menacing look, trying his best to intimidate me.

Well, fuck that.

"One dance," I told him in my most authoritative voice I could find, however with four cocktails in me, even to my ears it didn't sound very authoritative.

"No."

"Oh come on, that little bitch was shit on the pole, just let me show her how to do it properly," I whined and tried to yank my arm away, but Danny was having none of it.

"Not a fucking chance, Riley, if Kai knew you were gyrating around a pole, he'd kill us both, and I don't know about you, but I quite like my life."

Danny pulled me away from the bar but not before I caught Monica's smug grin turn into a beaming smile which made me want to stomp over and wipe it off her face.

Drunk Riley could be a feisty little cow sometimes.

"I won't tell him if you don't." I winked at Danny, or at least I tried, I may have just looked like I was having a fit or something. Those iced teas really were quite strong.

"Jesus Christ, you're going to be the death of me," he replied, swiping his hand down his face in frustration. "I'll make a deal with you, no pole dancing but in exchange, I'll give you a tour of the club."

Now that seemed like an intriguing idea.

Sapphire was *the* place to be and attracted the rich and famous from all over, so yeah, having a look around definitely piqued my interest.

"Fine," I deadpanned, letting Danny think he had won when secretly I was quite pleased to be going for a look around. But Danny saw right through me. He shook his head and laughed.

"Come on, you little troublemaker. But don't leave my side, understood?"

"Yes, Sir!" I saluted him, earning me an eye roll.

He let go of my arm and instead took my hand, leading me to a door at the other end of the club from where we had come through earlier. I hadn't noticed until now but the four security guards who had escorted us here were all standing by the door, and as Danny approached, they all stood to attention.

"You two with me," he said pointing to two of them who immediately nodded. "You two," he pointed to the other two, "I want eyes on us at all times."

They mumbled their, '*Yes Sirs,*' before Danny pushed the door open and led me through with the two goons falling behind us.

"Bit of an overkill isn't it?" I giggled. Now I was on my feet, the alcohol was swimming nicely around my body making me feel somewhat lightheaded and a little bit giddy.

Not that I would have said it out loud, but maybe it was a good idea I didn't swing around a pole after drinking as much as I had.

"It'll never be an overkill when it comes to your safety," Danny replied seriously as he typed something into his phone and then put it away.

Fucking hell, he was beginning to sound like Kai now.

Danny led me down a set of stairs, and as we got closer to the bottom, the music grew louder, and the thumping of the bass settled once again in my chest. He opened a door and walked straight out into the heart of the club. Immediately, we were surrounded by hundreds of partiers, all dancing, drinking, and shouting to be heard over the thumping music. The atmosphere was pumping, and the live DJ was riling the crowds up, preparing them for a famous R 'n' B group that would soon be on stage. The two goons who Danny had brought down with us stayed behind us, and Danny's grip on my hand tightened.

"Well as you can see, this is the main club," he shouted to me. I could just about hear him over the noise.

My eyes darted everywhere, taking in the club. Other than Club Sin, I'd never set foot in a nightclub before, I'd never had the money to spare, and after dancing six nights a week, the last thing I wanted to do was go to a nightclub.

But this, this was incredible. The whole atmosphere was different from Club Sin, there were no seedy little men sitting in dark corners nutting one out over the naked girls. Groups of friends danced together, couples gyrated against each other, and bottles of champagne were passed around as if they only cost the price of a bottle of water. Huge cages hung from the ceiling with men and women inside dancing in scantily clad outfits. The room lit up when one of the dancers inside a cage twirled a baton that had flames on either side. I *loved* the place, and it was already in the back of my mind to ask Kai if we could come back again. It was easy to see why this place was as popular as it was.

"Come on, I'll show you the champagne bar," Danny yelled and started tugging me towards a tunnel that led out of this part of the club.

"Champagne bar," I repeated stupidly but with a grin on my face. Since having sampled some of the finest champagne money could buy, I had acquired a taste for it, and now Danny had mentioned a bar dedicated to champagne, yep I was up for a visit to that bar.

The tunnel Danny led me down was dark, but the strobe lighting from the main club cast some light into it, and with the mirrors on either side reflecting it, it was bright enough to make out the faces of people passing through the tunnel.

As we walked through, a man walking towards me knocked into my arm as he side-stepped a couple who were grinding against each other. I turned around to apologize, not because I had knocked into him, but you know, that was the polite thing to do, and as I turned, so did he.

"Sorry," the man said, and recognition instantly dawned on me.

"Toby?" I gasped, not believing my eyes.

The man looked at me for a second, not recognizing who I was before the penny dropped.

"Riley, is that you, babe?" he said curiously, and before I knew it, I had tugged my hand out of Danny's and had run into Toby's arms, a huge grin on my face at seeing my old friend. His arms snaked around my lower back, and he pulled me firmly against his chest.

The boy who had taken Angel and me under his wing when we first lived in Hollows Bay looked so different from the last time I had seen him. Then, he had been a scrawny kid in need of a good meal. But now, well he had obviously been putting in some *serious* time in the gym given how much he had bulked up and how solid he felt under my arms.

His once long afro hair was now shaved, and his dark skin was covered in a variety of tattoos, too many for me to get a look at. He looked good, and whatever he had been doing since leaving Hollows Bay had done wonders for him.

He'd left the city about a month after Angel and I went to live with Joe, and I'd been sad to say goodbye to the only friend I had. Every so often he popped into my head, and I had always wondered where he was and what he was doing.

Clearly jumping into his arms was the wrong thing to do because the second his arms curled around me, I heard the clicking of three sets of guns being cocked. I spun around in Toby's arms to find Danny and the two goons with their guns pointing at Toby.

Thankfully, they couldn't shoot. Mainly because we were surrounded by shocked partygoers who had come to a standstill to watch the drama unfold, and for another, I stood directly in front of Toby, preventing any of them from taking a clean shot at my old friend.

"Wow," Toby said behind me as he raised his hands above his head. I rolled my eyes.

"Fuck sake, put the guns down. He's a friend of mine," I huffed at Danny. He glared at me for a minute, and when I put my hands on my hips and raised an eyebrow as if to say, *'It's not like you can shoot with me standing here'*, he finally lowered his gun, followed by the other two macho morons.

"Say goodbye to your friend, Riley, it's time to go," Danny growled, his beady eyes fixed on Toby. But if he thought I was going to walk away from someone who I hadn't seen in *years*, he had another thing coming.

"Yeah, yeah, in a minute." I waved my hand dismissively and turned back to Toby.

Danny cussed behind me as Toby nervously lowered his hands. "What are you doing here, Toby? You look great." I beamed up at him, he was taller than what I remembered. Maybe it was because he had beefed up, but he seemed to tower over me. He had a hard edge to his face like he'd dealt with a lot of shit over the years, but his eyes were the same. Kind and warm, and filled with a fondness towards me like they had been the very first time he'd laid eyes on me.

Toby had helped me so much when I first arrived in the city. Okay, so he had taught me to shoplift, but if he hadn't, Angel and I would have starved.

I owed him a lot and he became a good friend, perhaps that's why I'd given him my virginity one chilly evening after he '*borrowed*' a car and had driven the two of us out to a secluded wooded area with a bottle of cheap wine.

"I could say the same about you, girl, you look incredible." His eyes roamed up and down my body, but it didn't feel like he was doing it in a sleazy way, more like making sure I was okay. "What are you doing here?"

"It's a long story," I laughed, and waved my hand casually. "I thought you'd moved from Hollows Bay?"

"I did, but I'm back visiting family," he said.

A little voice in the back of my head reminded me that Toby didn't have a family, he'd been a kid in the system years before I was because his parents were killed in a car crash, and there was no one else he could stay with. Before I could ask how he'd found family, he spoke again.

"I've got a kid now, a little girl named Jess."

"Oh, Toby, that's great," I grinned at him, distracting me from asking about his family. Good for Toby, he deserved to be happy.

"So how come you're here in this club?" I asked, briefly wondering why Toby would be in West Bay when he had previously lived in East Bay.

"What I would like to know is," a deep voice rumbled from behind me, one I'd recognize in my sleep. A strong arm wrapped around my belly and pulled me back against a solid chest, and the scent of Kai wrapped around me, sending goosebumps across my skin. "Why the fuck you had your hands on my girl."

Oh fuck.

Chapter 26

Kai

The image of Riley throwing her arms around the cunt was burned into my mind as I stormed from my office and headed towards the tunnel she was currently in.

I'd only stopped into my office to check the cameras to see where Riley and Danny were after he texted me to say he was showing her around the club. It would have been bad enough if it was just some random prick, but imagine my surprise when I zoomed in on the footage and saw the stag tattoo on his neck.

What were the chances of a random gang member from the city where I had just spent the last four days suddenly appearing in my club? A club where I knew and approved *every* fucking member.

Thoughts raced through my head, barely noticing Hendrix and Miles were right behind me as I thundered along the corridor heading towards the door that would take me into the champagne bar.

I'd been back in Hollows Bay for less than ten goddamn minutes only to come back to this shit. I was already agitated, needing to get my hands on Riley, and the entire journey had been fucking torture.

We'd wasted another day in Huntsville trying to get information out of Anderson's ex-girlfriend, but it was pointless. The only thing she was able to tell us was Anderson was clinically unstable, something of which

I was already well fucking aware of. She hadn't been able to give us any indication of his current whereabouts, nor why he would be involved in the murder of Theo, as far as she could remember Anderson had never mentioned the city of Hollows Bay.

Pinning my hopes that Miles would be able to get somewhere with the phone he had found, we set off on the journey home.

The whole way, I'd been thinking about my Star. I'd let Danny take her to Sapphire knowing my little minx wasn't doing so well being cooped up in the penthouse. Someone like Riley wasn't designed to be locked up in a cage, even if it was a golden one. Sapphire was the only other safe place she could be, I had eyes and ears everywhere, and I knew Kimmy would take care of Riley until I got there.

I wanted to surprise her, the entire way home I'd been imagining her reaction when I walked into the champagne bar where I'd told Danny to bring her, she'd see me, come running over, and throw herself into my arms. I'd give her a deep, bruising kiss, letting every fucker in the place know Riley belonged to me.

Yeah, pussy whipped, I know.

I hadn't been expecting to watch her on the security camera throwing herself into the arms of another fucking man. My agitation instantly turned into murderous intent, my sight set on The Stag.

He was a dead man.

The 'staff only' door slammed open as I barged through and into the champagne bar, classic piano music played as people sat around talking, relaxing from the buzz of the main club. All eyes fell on me as I stormed through the club heading towards the dark tunnel. They would have been people I knew, but at that very minute, I couldn't have identified one person, my vision blinkered by my sole focus of getting to Riley as soon as fucking possible.

As I neared, the loud music from the club grew stronger but I blocked it out as my eyes fell on her.

My Star.

She had her back to me, talking to the prick who was going to be meeting his fate in a few minutes. Danny was standing behind her, running a frustrated hand through his hair. He was pissed, his whole body tense, and it looked as though he was about ten seconds away from grabbing hold of Riley's arm and dragging her away. The only thing that would have stopped him was the worry I would hurt him for touching what belonged to me.

Arthur and Jacob, two of my senior men were standing on either side of the dude Riley was talking to, both looked just as unhappy as I felt. Arthur noticed me storming towards them and gave a subtle nod to Danny who turned to look at me, he winced at the rage I was no doubt displaying across my face.

"So how come you're here in the club?" I heard her say, completely oblivious that I was now behind her.

The need to touch her overwhelmed me, my fingers itched to feel her soft skin. Even from behind she looked beautiful. The dress she had on was far too fucking short for my liking though, she had too much skin of her delectable body on display.

As I stepped in closer behind her, her scent of strawberries and sunscreen washed over me, calming me just the tiniest bit.

"What I would like to know is, why the fuck you had your hands on my girl?" I said through gritted teeth as I wrapped an arm around her waist and pulled her back to my chest, back to where she belonged.

"Kai-" she immediately started to protest, but I held her tighter and interrupted her before she could carry on.

"I'd also like to know exactly how the fuck a *Stag* got into my club."

Hendrix and Miles didn't need me to say anymore, the second comprehension dawned on who the fuck was standing in front of us, the pair of them pulled their guns out and aimed them directly at the prick. Following their lead, Danny, Arthur, and Jacob followed suit. Riley's whole body tensed in my arms.

"W-what, I didn't do anything man, I swear," The Stag stuttered, and raised his hands in the air like a little pussy.

"Kai, what the fuck?" Riley hissed and managed to spin around in my arms to face me.

She was mad, and she'd clearly been drinking if the stench of alcohol on her breath was anything to go by, and the fact her words were slurred. She tried to wriggle out of my grasp but there was no way I was letting her go. I tightened my arms around her, silently letting her know she wasn't going anywhere.

"But you did do something, you put your hands on my girl." I ignored her, and instead addressed The Stag, keeping my voice low and deadly. I'd never seen him before which posed the question, just how the fuck did he get into my club.

"Oh, enough of the jealous bullshit, Kai," Riley shrieked, and once again tried to pull out of my grasp. I didn't let her go. "Toby is a friend, nothing more, nothing less. And for your information, I was the one who hugged him, not the other way around."

Her tone was full of rage, no doubt fuelled by the alcohol she'd had. I'd have to speak to Kimmy about not letting Riley drink so much next time.

I dropped one hand from around her waist and grabbed her chin roughly, holding her face to look at me. My whole body was shaking with anger. Anger at seeing another man putting his hands on her, or the fact that he was a Stag, I didn't know, but it didn't really matter. He'd get the full force of my wrath either way.

"I saw that, Riley, and I assure you, I will deal with you. But only after The Stag has been taken care of."

Her eyes narrowed at my words, and her beautiful mouth dropped into an O. If she wasn't happy with my actions before, she was fucking pissed now.

"You'll deal with me? Fuck. You," she hissed, yanking her chin out of my grasp and shoving me in the chest. Something I did not fucking appreciate in the slightest.

While it wasn't a strong push, her actions caught me off guard, and I dropped the other hand that had been holding her waist. Now my hands weren't on her, she spun on her heel and marched her fine ass over to The Stag. When she stopped in front of him, she crossed her arms over her chest and glared back at me, raising an eyebrow and offering a silent challenge.

To say I was fucking *livid* would be an understatement.

Red mist blurred my vision, my pulse thumped in my ears, and my hands clenched into fists.

I'd never felt the rage that was rampaging through me now. Riley was *mine*, she belonged to *me*. Not this punk ass-bitch standing with his arms in the air.

"Put The Stag in the basement," I growled, low and deadly to my men, my eyes never leaving Riley's. They moved as one as they were trained to do, the five of them descending on him. At the same time they moved, I took two long strides toward Riley, watching as fear took hold of her.

"Kai, wait-" she started, and raised her hands in defense. But before she could continue, I grabbed her around her thighs and hoisted her up over my shoulder.

I'd deal with The Stag later, right now I needed to remind my Star who she belonged to.

She squealed and tried to kick her legs, her tiny fists pounded my back. It was a moment reminiscent of when I'd taken her from the alley a few weeks ago. Her efforts earned her a hard spank on her perfect ass, and even with the bass of the music, I heard her cry out.

I marched through the club, people jumping to one side to let me through, and not one person dared to step forward to help the girl slung over my shoulder. Wise move on their part. She pleaded for me to put her down, but there was no fucking chance of that. Not yet at least.

I made my way through the champagne bar and back through the 'staff only' door. Stomping down the corridor, my footsteps and her curses echoed until I reached my office door, kicked it open, and went inside. Using my foot to kick the door closed behind me, I threw Riley down on the leather sofa ungracefully. She bounced as she landed making her dress ride up and giving me a peek of the black lacy thong she had on underneath, which did nothing to quell the rising anger.

What the fuck was she thinking coming out dressed like that?

She cursed, but I paid her little attention as I marched over to my desk.

My office here was bigger than the one at home but it had no windows. The only light was from the bright ceiling light, and the furniture was minimal. Besides the leather sofa, I had my desk and my chair, but that was it. I rarely used this office, therefore I didn't need a ton of shit in here.

My arms were rigid as I leaned over my desk and tried to take some calming breaths, otherwise, I would end up hurting her, and as much as I was angry now, and as much as I did want to hurt someone, I didn't want to hurt *her*.

I couldn't look at her for a second, I needed to get a grip on the out-of-control feelings I had. She brought something out of me, something I didn't like. I wasn't impulsive, yet she made me react without thinking. I wasn't jealous, yet I couldn't bear someone else touching her.

I was in control of every one of my actions, yet I wasn't when she was the only thing I could think about.

It was fucking with my head and I hated the way she made me feel.

And yet, I *craved* this feeling.

"Who is he?" My jaw clenched when I finally felt like I could speak without the tiny thread of my restraint snapping. I didn't bother to turn back to look at her because that might have been the thing that pushed me over the edge.

"An old friend," she huffed like a stroppy child.

An old friend.

Right.

I'd seen the way he was looking at her, there was more to it than that. And if that was the case, then why the fuck was Riley friends with a Stag?

I was going to ask her that very question, how did she know The Stag, only something else slipped from my mouth, once again proving I wasn't in control of my actions when it came to her.

"Have you fucked him?"

I wasn't sure I really wanted to know the answer, I couldn't bear the thought of someone else having her, but once it was out, I couldn't take it back.

"Not recently," she retorted, a hint of amusement in her voice. I spun around, catching the smirk on her face.

It was enough to push me over the precarious edge I had been standing on. I pushed off my desk, launching myself across the room before she even had a chance to comprehend what was happening. Wrapping a hand around her delicate throat, I pushed her down on the sofa so she was laying on her back and I was above her, my snarling face mere inches away from hers.

"You don't want to push my buttons right now, Riley. I'm *this* fucking close to snapping and it won't end well for your *friend* if that happens," I growled menacingly.

Blind fury coursed through me, and it was taking a hell of a lot of restraint not to squeeze her throat harder.

I glared down at her, she was staring back at me with her own anger burning in her eyes, but to my utter surprise, there was something else mixed in with her rage.

Lust.

My beautiful Star liked me being rough with her.

Despite the anger she was radiating toward me, she couldn't help her eyes drifting to my mouth before she licked her lips, the action sending blood straight to my dick which twitched to life, hardening against her stomach.

"Then don't fucking ask a question you don't want to hear the answer to, Kai," she bit out as she managed to get a hand up between us and jabbed me in the chest with a finger.

It was a good job I was stir fucking crazy about this girl otherwise she'd be finding herself in a shallow grave before the evening was out.

"Toby is a friend. He was the only person who helped Angel and me when we first arrived in Hollows Bay. I owe him my fucking life for helping us out. Yes I did fuck him, not that it's any of your business, but I haven't seen him in close to five fucking years, so quit being a jealous bitch," she sneered.

I was momentarily stunned she had the audacity to call me a bitch, no one in their right fucking mind would ever dare, but then she poked me again in the chest and I snapped out of my stupor.

Releasing her throat and climbing off her tiny frame, I grabbed her by her arms and hauled her up to her feet. She stumbled in her ridiculous heels as I pulled her over to my desk and pushed her face down, pinning both her hands behind her back with one of my hands.

Her dress was so fucking short that as she bent over, her delectable ass peeked out from underneath. She gasped but it wasn't a gasp of pain, it was one of *want*, and at no point did she ask me to let her go.

My filthy Star fucking wanted this.

"You bet your fucking ass I'm a jealous bitch, Riley, I'll kill any cunt that puts his hands on you," I growled as I kicked her legs apart and then stood to the side of her. "Maybe I need to remind you who you belong to, remind you that every inch of you belongs to me."

I didn't give her any time to prepare as I brought my hand down and smacked her hard on her ass cheek. The creamy white skin instantly heated with the mark of my handprint, and she cried out, but she didn't try to pull away, her hands were still pinned behind her back and she made no attempt to break free of my grasp.

"You gave yourself to me, Riley, you told me you belonged to me but you ran into the arms of another man. That can't go unpunished."

The second slap echoed around the room as her other ass cheek reddened, matching the mark I'd already given her.

"Kai, please," she begged, although it wasn't a plea for me to stop, far from it, and I knew full damn well that if I slid a finger into her cunt, it would be dripping for me.

The knowledge that she was getting off on me spanking her hit me straight in my groin, my cock hardening to the point it hurt, and if I didn't let it out, I was likely to come in my pants like some pathetic teenage boy.

"Do you know what it did to me to see you run into the arms of another man?"

I didn't give her time to respond, instead, I brought my hand down again, cracking against the skin that was already burning bright red.

"I....I'm sorry," she panted.

And yet, she still wasn't telling me to stop.

"It took all of my strength not to put a bullet in that cunts head for daring to lay a finger on what's mine."

Smack.

She moaned, her whole body shaking against my desk and if I didn't know better, I would have said she was close to coming. My cock ached, and the urge to take her was all-consuming, but I wasn't finished yet. I needed her to know that her actions would have consequences.

"Who do you belong to, Riley?" I growled.

My hand tanned her ass again, branding her with my palm print and making sure that whenever she sat down over the next few days, she'd be reminded of who she belonged to.

"You, Kai, I belong to you, only you," she choked out on a cry, and her words lodged deep in my chest. My resolve at holding back broke.

I *had* to have her.

"You"

Smack.

"Belong"

Smack.

"To"

Smack.

"Me."

The seconds the word left my lips, I let go of her tiny hands and dropped to my knees. Her thong didn't stand a chance as I ripped it off with one hand and then shoved my face into her pussy, my tongue immediately swiping up her juices.

She was fucking soaked.

She cried out at the first touch but within seconds, her cries turned to pants as she rode my face. She tasted delicious, and I couldn't get enough. Four fucking days without her sweet pussy had seemed like a fucking lifetime. I licked her slit from front to back, right up to her asshole, and back again, and when I reached her clit, I took the little nub in between my lips and sucked hard making her legs almost buckle from underneath her.

"Kai, fuck.....please," she hissed and clawed at my desk. I chuckled as I continued to lick, nibble, and suck her clit as three of my fingers plunged into her tight pussy. She was so close to finding her release, her legs were beginning to tense, and as much as I wanted her to come on my face and drown me in her juices, I wasn't finished punishing her, she didn't deserve to come just yet.

Just before she reached her crescendo, I pulled my fingers out and stood back up, picking her shredded thong up and stuffing it in my pants pocket. Riley groaned in frustration at the sudden loss of contact, but when she tried to stand up, I put one hand on the back of her neck and held her down. Using my other hand, I undid my pants and pulled them and my boxer briefs down, releasing my aching cock.

"Who do you belong to, Riley?" I asked again, needing to hear her say it once more.

"You, Kai. I'm all yours," she said without a hint of doubt, her voice husky and filled with need.

And with that, I thrust straight into her tight cunt, not giving her any chance to get accustomed to my size.

She cried out at the sudden intrusion, her nails digging into my desk, and her moans were music to my fucking ears. This girl, I wanted everything from her, her pleasure, her pain, her fucking heart.

It all belonged to me.

I didn't show her any mercy as I fucked her, I held her head down with one hand and her hip so tightly with the other that I knew she'd have my fingerprints bruised into her skin for days to come.

I slammed into her over and over, her cries of pleasure spurring me on. Her perfect little cunt tightened around me, and once again, I knew she was close.

I wouldn't deprive her of her orgasm this time, but I wanted to come with her. I grunted in time with my thrusts and every time I hit her sweet spot, she cried out and begged for more, begged for it harder. The ache in my balls grew, and it wasn't going to be long until I came.

Releasing her neck, I moved my hand underneath her and found her clit with my thumb. With a couple of strokes, her whole body tensed as she cried out, and her pussy clamped down with an ironclad grip around my cock as she reached her peak.

It was all I needed to finish. I thrust into her once more before I spilled my seed deep inside of her.

Riley's legs trembled, and if it wasn't for the desk she was still bent over, she would have been a puddle on the floor. I held onto her, still buried inside of her as we both fought to find our breaths, and the tremors of our climaxes ceased. The only sound in the room was the echoes of our pants.

Before pulling out of her, I stroked my hand softly down her back and to her beautifully reddened ass, watching as a shudder ran down her spine. As I slipped out of her, our combined juices trailing down her thigh, I pulled her up off the desk, holding her back to my chest. She leaned back against me as her head came to rest against my shoulder, and her face tipped up to look at me.

Her beautiful eyes were filled with heat and desire, and as she gave me a lazy smile, I wrapped my hand gently around her delicate neck and leaned down to kiss her, pouring all of my emotions into it.

"You drive me fucking wild, Star," I whispered against her lips. Grabbing her thighs, I lifted her into my arms and carried her over to the sofa, she wrapped her arms around my neck and snuggled into my chest, and I held her there for a few minutes, enjoying the feeling of her being back in my arms where she belonged.

"Did you know he was a Stag?" I finally asked when we had both recovered our breath.

"I don't even know what that's supposed to mean, Kai," She replied, her voice wary. I didn't want to argue with her again but I couldn't ignore the elephant in the room, aside from the fact he had touched my girl, he was also a fucking rival gang member.

I sighed and stroked her arm. "He's a gang member. The Stags run Huntsville City. I don't believe it's a coincidence that I've spent the last four days in Huntsville looking for Anderson, and then I find a Stag in my club. Not when I vet and approve every single member of this club."

Her eyes widened and her shoulders slumped. Not that I had any doubt in my mind, but it was clear from her expression she had no idea that Toby, as she had called him, was now running for a gang.

"Are you sure?" she asked, a tiny hint of hope in her voice that I was wrong. But she should know me better than that by now.

"I'm sure, baby." I kissed her hair, hopefully showing her I wasn't mad anymore, at least, not at her. I just wanted to figure out what the fuck was going on. "I saw the video footage of you hugging him and when I zoomed in, there on his neck was the tattoo all of The Stags have. Believe me, Riley, it's no coincidence."

It was her turn to sigh this time, and I gave her a little squeeze, enjoying the feel of her body against mine. She still had her dress on and it felt like there were far too many layers between us. She was silent, staring at nothing but I could see the cogs turning.

"Did he tell you why he was here?"

"No, he said he was back visiting family. I thought it was a bit weird, his parents died when he was about four or five, he didn't have any family, and as far as I could remember he had no links to West Bay." She turned her chocolate eyes on me and gave me a pleading look. "I honestly didn't know he was part of that gang."

"I believe you, Riley, but he was here for a reason. As I've said, it's too much of a coincidence that he turned up when I've been in Huntsville for the last four days."

"I agree, it does seem strange. But there might be a reason, Kai, can't you talk to him and find out what he has to say?"

That was exactly what I planned to do. Only my version of talking to him meant him being strung up in my basement and tortured while I got the truth from him. Not to mention making him pay for touching my girl.

"Yeah, I will. But tomorrow, I'm not spending another night away from you." I tipped her head back and kissed her softly, hoping it would distract her from dwelling on what my little chat with The Stag might actually turn out like.

"Okay. Does that mean we can go home now?" she said when I dragged my mouth away from her. She looked and sounded exhausted, a combination of the alcohol and the adrenaline from the turn of events in the last hour.

"Yeah, baby, let's go."

Reluctantly, I released her from my arms. She slowly stood and looked around the room before she turned back to look at me, a vision of beauty with her just fucked hair and her tired eyes.

"Can I have my panties back?" she asked.

I gave her a wicked grin and her brows raised in question. "No. I want you bare."

She huffed in exasperation, and I silently dared her to challenge me. "Fine, I need a minute to clean myself up."

I grabbed her hips again and pulled her to me, using a finger to tilt her chin up so she had no choice but to look at me.

"No, you don't. I want you to walk through that club holding my hand, my come dripping between your thighs. I want everyone to see who you belong to," I whispered in her ear.

Her eyes widened in surprise and her cheeks flushed red with embarrassment but she didn't refuse.

As we walked through the club hand in hand, I had a moment of worry knowing I was being reckless by putting Riley on display, letting the world see that she belonged to me. But I dismissed the thought, I had zero fucks to give.

Riley was mine and I would protect her with everything I had.

Chapter 27

Riley

The following morning, I woke up to find Kai lifting my leg and draping it over his body as he lay behind me. He plunged his thick cock inside me and fucked me from behind slowly.

The man was insatiable, not that I was complaining.

It was sweet, blissful torture as he took his time to draw out my orgasm. Afterwards, we lay in his huge bed wrapped up in each other's arms, his hand softly running up and down my back as my fingers danced lightly over his chest. I ached all over but in a good way. My ass was tender from where he spanked me, and I had love bites and bruises covering my neck, chest, and thighs from where he had marked me as his again and again after we arrived home from Sapphire.

I sighed in contentment, happy and satisfied for the first time in as long as I could remember.

Of course, it was never going to last.

"I need to go and deal with The Stag," Kai eventually said, sounding resigned at the fact he was going to have to drag himself away from our little bubble. He dropped his arms and gently rolled me off his chest before pulling himself out of bed. I took the opportunity to admire his gorgeous body, every single one of his muscles were sculpted to perfection, his skin a light golden brown, and with that wolf tattoo on his back, fuck, he really was something else. I could have spent hours staring at his body, or running my hands over it, or better yet, my tongue…

"If you keep looking at me like that, Riley, the only thing that will get done is you," he growled, his eyes hooded as he raked them over my naked body.

"You make that sound like it's a bad thing," I replied, giving him my best seductive smile, and running my hands over my breasts, hoping like hell he would change his mind and jump back into bed again.

I should have known better though. Kai grabbed my arms and pulled me to my knees, my naked body pressed firmly against his solid torso. The way he handled me was possessive and demanding, and I couldn't get enough of it.

He wound his hand into the back of my hair and held me in place while he gave me a rough kiss, his tongue invading my mouth and battling with mine. He groaned but pulled away from me, much to my dismay.

"I'd love nothing more than to spend the day fucking you in every hole until you can't walk." Holy hell, did his wicked words make my entire body clench with need. "But I need to get to the bottom of why that prick was in my club and deal with him."

The venom in his voice when he spoke of Toby doused the fire burning within me, and the reality of last night hit me like a ton of bricks.

I'd put the whole thing with Toby to the back of my mind, distracted by all the orgasms Kai had given me, but now the cold reality hit me. He was going to hurt Toby, or probably kill him.

And I couldn't allow that.

For whatever reason Toby was in the club, he'd still been the one to help me all those years ago, and I wouldn't stand back and let Kai do what he clearly intended on doing, especially knowing Toby now had a little girl to take care of.

Perhaps I was being a bit naïve, but maybe Toby had an innocent reason for being in the club, maybe him being there really was a coincidence.

It was pointless to try and talk Kai out of his plans though, he could be a stubborn bastard when he wanted to be. But I had to try, and hadn't I persuaded him to let me help out with the situation at the warehouse with Luis? If I could at least get him to let *me* talk to Toby first, and find out why he was there, maybe I could convince Kai that Toby had nothing to hide and let him go.

It was unlikely he would, but I had to try something.

"I want to come with you," I said, mustering up as much confidence as I could find. His eyes narrowed at me before he dropped his hand from behind my head and stomped over to where his clothes were in a pile on the floor.

"No."

Fuck sake.

"Come on, Kai, I know Toby. There will be an innocent explanation as to why he was there, you'll just go in all guns blazing and won't believe a word he has to say." I jumped out of bed, wrapping the sheet around me.

Stupid really, it wasn't like Kai hadn't seen me naked.

"No, Riley. It's not fucking happening," he hissed and the relaxed, lust-filled haze that had fogged my brain moments earlier rapidly changed to anger. All the rage I had felt last night when Kai was being a possessive asshat swirled to the surface once more.

I didn't want to come across as a sulking little girl, but honestly, Kai Wolfe was possibly one of the most frustrating human beings on this fucking planet.

"Why? Because you think I'll fall madly in love with him and decide to run off with him?" I marched across the room and stood in front of him, planting a hand on my hip. "Get over yourself, Kai. I just want to talk to him."

He smirked. That arrogant smirk that equally drove me mad and turned me on.

Gah!

He pulled his pants up and grabbed a fresh shirt from his closet before returning to stand back in front of me and tugging at the bed sheet wrapped around me, pulling me close against him. He gripped my chin between his thumb and forefinger and tilted my head up, holding me in place.

It fucking annoyed me when he did that.

"I'm not worried about you running off with him, Star, he isn't going anywhere. And even if you did run, I would hunt you down and drag your ass back here and remind you once again who you belong to."

He ran a thumb down my cheek eliciting a shiver down my spine. He spoke so softly, enough that you could be mistaken for thinking he was being charming, *romantic* even. But the menacing look in his eyes betrayed his words, and though I wanted Kai more than anyone I had ever wanted before, I couldn't help but feel a little bit terrified of him and how far he was willing to go to make sure that I knew I belonged to him.

He tenderly tucked a strand of hair behind my ear, kissed me on the forehead, and went to leave the room.

But I wasn't giving up easily, I just had to try a different angle.

"Wait, Kai."

He huffed but he stopped by the door and turned back to face me, an expectant look on his face.

"You wanted me to be your assistant, right? That was the deal we made when I first came here."

"So?" he replied, but his eyes narrowed on me, and I could tell he was curious as to what my point was.

"Well, if you want me to work for you, if you want me to be by your side like you claim you do, then you need to let me be by your side for things like this. Even if it turns a little....messy."

I was silently praying things with Toby wouldn't get as far as being messy, but right then, all I could focus on was getting Kai to let me into the room as a starting point, I'd figure the next step out once I was there. He stared at me as he rubbed the fresh smatterings of stubble on his chin considering my words, and as intimidating as his glare could be, I held my nerve. After what seemed like an eternity, he spoke.

"You're right, Riley, I do want you by my side. Get dressed," he ordered.

Hmm.

Okay, that was far too easy. An unsettling feeling washed over me but I ignored it, at least I would have an opportunity to speak with Toby, that was a starting point.

I went to walk out the door but before I could open it, Kai grabbed my arm and pushed me up against it, putting his hands next to my head and caging me in with his body.

"But I warn you now, Riley, my mind won't be changed. The Stag was in my club for a reason, and I will do *whatever* it takes to get the information out of him. And if you insist on coming, then you will stay in that room with me no matter what."

His voice dripped with malice, and I swallowed nervously, dread knotting my stomach. I tried to keep myself composed, to not show any weakness, but it turns out that is a fucking difficult thing to do when you are staring in the face of the devil himself. But no matter what Kai said, I wouldn't leave Toby to face his wrath alone.

"Okay," I managed to say in a shaky voice. Kai held my gaze for another beat before he nodded once and then stepped back, allowing me to go to my room. I quickly ran down the hallway draped in his bed sheet, worrying I had bitten off far more than I could chew.

Less than five minutes later, I emerged from my room dressed in jeans and a vest to find Kai waiting for me. He didn't say anything, didn't rake his eyes down my curves like he usually did. He turned on his heel and started down the hallway to the elevator.

"You sure you want to do this?" Kai finally said once we were in the elevator and plummeting to the basement. His intense stare was burning into me like it always did, but I couldn't look at him, my mind was running away with the anticipation of what the hell was about to happen, and my stomach lurched with nerves. Instead, I kept my eyes glued to the doors when I gave my reply.

"Yes."

Kai's phone pinged in his pocket right then, cutting off any retort he may have had to my feeble response. From the corner of my eye, I saw him take out his phone and read a message. His lips twitched into the smallest hint of a smile before he wiped it from his face and returned to his stern look before putting his phone away.

The elevator came to a smooth stop and the doors slid open to reveal a small hallway I had never seen before. Danny had told me about the basement when he had given me the tour of the apartment, and I'd thought at the time that I would never want to find myself down here. My heart pounded furiously in my chest as anxiety kicked in.

At the end of the hallway, a man I'd never seen before stood in front of a closed door, his arms folded across his broad chest.

It must have been in the job description that to work for Kai, you had to be the size of a house and have the strength to squeeze the life out of a person with your bare hands. All of Kai's security guards were built with walls of solid muscles, and the man guarding the door was no exception. He looked like a mean motherfucker with dark and brooding features, and arms the size of tree trunks.

"Boss." The man bobbed his head at Kai and then placed his fingerprint on the pad by the door before standing aside to let us through.

I'd bet any money there was another fingerprint pad on the other side of the door to give an extra layer of security. If anyone managed to escape from Kai's basement of doom, they'd not only have to get through this door, pass the big scary bastard standing guard, and then access the elevator before someone realized they had escaped. No easy task, especially with the glaringly obvious camera aimed directly at the door.

I trailed into the room behind Kai feeling like a little lost sheep and seriously regretting my decision, but the second I saw Toby strung up by his arms, hanging by his wrists from a hook in the ceiling, his feet barely touching the floor, and dried blood on his face from a wound to his eye, my fear turned to outright rage.

"What the fuck, Kai?" I barged passed him and stomped over to Toby, refusing to acknowledge Hendrix, Danny, and one of the goons from the club last night, who were all standing in the room. I'm pretty sure one of them snorted a laugh when I reached Toby and saw that not only did he have a cut to his eyebrow, but he also had two black eyes and a swollen lip.

Fucking animals.

Gently, I reached out and touched Toby's chin, his closed eyes fluttered open, and despite the situation he was in, he gave me a soft smile. The growl from behind me echoed around the room and made me instantly drop Toby's chin. I'd just unintentionally pissed Kai off even more.

Shit.

I turned back to face him, catching Hendrix leaning against the wall with his arms folded and that fucking irritating smug smirk on his face. Danny stood next to him, he at least had the good graces to look slightly ashamed of his actions. Only slightly though.

The other goon stood by the door, standing as if he was ready to pounce on Toby if he managed to break free from his restraints and make a beeline for the door. Which was highly fucking unlikely.

"I'm only going to tell you this once, Riley. Do not lay another fucking finger on him ever again," Kai hissed, his face twisted into a scowl, and fire raged behind his black eyes.

Jeez, he was one hell of a possessive asshole.

"Did they really need to rough him up?" I asked, raising a brow. I withered under the heated stare from Kai, he looked like he was ten seconds away from snapping Toby's neck.

Followed by mine, probably.

"He wouldn't come quietly," Hendrix shrugged before Kai could respond, leaving his place against the wall to come and stand by Kai's side like a good little pet.

God, I hated him.

"That's bullshit and you know it," Toby winced, his voice scratchy. Hendrix opened his mouth to reply, but Kai held up a hand.

"Enough."

There was an air of finality to Kai's tone, and both Hendrix and Toby must have heard it too as they fell quiet.

Kai faced me, and a shudder ran down my spine at the coldness in his eyes. Gone was the man who less than half an hour ago was affectionate and caring. This was his work mode, and fucking hell, was it scary.

"You wanted to be here for this, Riley. Just remember you were the one who insisted on witnessing this," he reminded me, his tone was cruel and unkind, and the feelings I had for him when I first met him, the ones of pure hatred, stirred in my belly.

This was not the man I had spent the last couple of weeks with, the man I was falling for. How had I allowed myself to forget that deep down, under all the pretend bullshit, Kai was a cold-hearted murderer? I narrowed my eyes at him but kept my mouth shut. It would do Toby no good if I antagonized Kai intentionally or unintentionally, and the purpose of me coming down to the basement was to help Toby out of this mess, not make it worse for him. When this was over, I'd have to pick through the confused emotions I was feeling, but right then, I had to focus on getting Toby out of there.

I gave Kai a nod and then walked my ass over to the wall behind where Kai stood, ignoring the urge to ask him to let Toby down from his ceiling restraints.

He must have been in utter agony hanging all night, but I resisted asking, accepting I needed to pick my battles, and I had one hell of a battle coming up if I wanted Toby to walk out of here alive. He'd have to cope with the pain for now, surely that would be worth doing if it meant he still had a life to live.

The position I chose in the room gave me the best view of Toby, and I hoped that maybe I could silently communicate with him, letting him know he would be okay.

At least, I hoped he would be.

"I'll tell you anything you want to know, man, please don't hurt me," Toby begged.

Kai's lips curled up into a cruel smile, making the unease in my gut churn more. "I'm glad to hear that, Stag. Let's start with an easy one. How the fuck did you get into my club?"

Toby licked his lips, and his eyes flashed to me. He was terrified, and my heart broke for him.

"I was let in through the back," Toby said.

"By whom?"

Again, Toby's eyes flashed to mine, almost like he was asking for permission for some bizarre reason. I gave him a subtle nod and he grimaced.

"By one of the bartenders, Terry Robson. He…he owed money to The Stags. Carlos agreed to wipe his debt if he let one of us into the club when we needed to get in."

Kai was silent for a minute, his eyes fixed on Toby, determining if he was telling the truth. After a minute, he looked at Hendrix.

"Deal with Terry. Take Jacob with you," Kai ordered.

"Yes, Boss," Hendrix replied and both he and the goon, Jacob, walked out of the room without saying another word, not needing to clarify how Kai wanted Terry to be dealt with. From the look of guilt etched across Toby's face, he knew he had just signed Terry's death warrant, the price to be paid for betraying Kai.

Nausea swam in my belly. I didn't know who this Terry person was, yet I couldn't help but feel sorry for him. But if Toby was giving Kai information that helped weed out rats in Kai's organization, that had to go in his favor, right?

"Was last night the first time you came into my club?" Kai returned to his interrogation after the door had closed behind Hendrix and Jacob, Danny had taken guard at the door.

Toby closed his eyes and when he reopened them, there was a steely resolve in them. "Yes."

"And what was the reason for your visit to my club?" Kai's tone was deadly calm and controlled, making him seem all the more intimidating.

This time, Toby didn't look over at me, but I saw him swallow nervously.

"I....I was there to see if Riley was there," he stuttered, still not meeting my eye.

My heart dropped into my gut and a feeling of betrayal crept over me.

What the actual fuck was he talking about?

The muscle in Kai's jaw ticked and his whole body tensed. This wasn't good.

"I...I'm sorry. I came to warn her, honestly," Toby cried loudly, his voice laced with desperation.

As quick as a flash, Kai leaped forward and wrapped his big hand around Toby's throat. I didn't need to see Toby's eyes widen in fear to know how hard Kai was squeezing, and as he did so, a memory sprung to life of the time Detective Anderson had his hands around my throat, squeezing the life out of me.

It's funny, Kai had wrapped his hand around my throat the evening before when we were in the club, and he'd been angry, but I hadn't felt scared. Quite the opposite in fact, it had turned me on. But with the menacing way Kai was gripping Toby, the only thing I could feel was fear.

Without realizing it, my hand lifted to my own throat, and I rubbed the area where the last of the bruises were fading, and a soft sob ripped from my throat. It was loud enough for Kai to hear, he looked over his shoulder, and a momentary flash of guilt crossed his face before he hardened again, but he at least let go of Toby who gulped in a huge breath.

"You better start fucking explaining yourself, Stag, or I swear to all that is holy, I will break every single bone in your body before skinning you alive," Kai growled.

Toby finally met my eyes, shame, sorrow, and regret marred his face. Now I could see him properly in the harsh lighting of this cold room,

I could see how exhausted he was. Dark bags lay underneath his eyes, and he looked like he had the weight of the world on his shoulders.

I wanted to reach out and comfort him, just like he'd done when he found me five years ago, but I was pinned to the wall by fear that Toby was about to reveal something that was going to shatter me.

"Don't you dare look at her." Kai grabbed Toby's chin and yanked his face away so that he had to look at Kai, his body swayed from the movement. "I'm going to give you ten fucking seconds to start talking, Stag."

He didn't need to say, 'or else', the threat was crystal clear.

"I... I don't know everything, I'm not high up enough in the chain to be fully clued in on everything," Toby started, and Kai dropped his hand from Toby's chin before taking a step back and folding his arms across his chest, waiting expectantly for Toby to talk. He didn't take his eyes off Toby the entire time he spoke.

"About a week ago, I was at a warehouse that belongs to The Stags. I was only there to pick up some more gear, but I overheard Markus, he's the leader of our quarter. He was talking to his second-in-command about the big boss rallying everyone to take over another gang in another city. I didn't pay too much attention, you know how it is, man, gangs always try to take over turf."

He paused as if waiting for Kai to respond but Kai continued glaring, a neutral expression settled on his face. Toby sighed before taking a deep breath to continue.

"They carried on talking, and I didn't pay any attention until I heard Markus say the name, Riley Bennett. I didn't know they were looking for her, I swear, man."

"What happened?" I found myself saying quietly and taking a tiny step forward, desperate to know what happened next and why the hell my name was being bandied around by a gang I'd never heard of, in a city I'd never been to.

Toby risked the wrath of Kai and looked over at me, meeting my gaze with a shamed expression on his bruised face. "I stupidly said I knew you from old, and then before I knew it, I was in front of the leader of The Stags, Carlos, and he was telling me the big boss wanted Riley, and that I was going to help get her."

I stared back at my old friend, a million thoughts rushing through my head as his words churned around.

Was Kai right?

Had Toby lied to me?

"What does he want with Riley?" Kai asked through gritted teeth, asking the question that was on the tip of my tongue. Kai was calm, but I could tell it was taking a hell of a lot of self-control to keep himself from snapping Toby's neck.

"I don't know, honestly I don't. They knew a lot about her though, that she was living with you, and supposedly working for you. Carlos said Riley was going to be the key to bringing the wolf down, I didn't know what he meant at the time, it was only afterwards that Markus told me who you were and it was your organization the boss wanted to bring down."

Silence filled the room for a minute, and all eyes were on Toby. I glanced out the corner of my eye at Danny to see his brows had narrowed and his jawline was tense. He was processing everything Toby had said as I imagined Kai was.

If this Carlos person knew stuff about me, how was he getting his information? Kai hadn't wanted to believe that one of his closest associates had betrayed him, but *someone* was feeding information to this gang.

"What were you to do with Riley?" Kai asked, breaking the silence and asking the question I wasn't sure I wanted to hear the answer to.

I wanted Toby to look at me, for me to see that he never intended to hurt me, but he didn't dare. He closed his eyes briefly, and when he next spoke, his voice was full of pain.

"They wanted me to find her and act like it was an innocent meeting and then get her to meet me the following day."

My gullible, naïve heart sank further, and tears pricked the back of my eyes. It was stupid, I hadn't seen Toby in years, he didn't owe me anything, and yet the betrayal I felt now was like a knife to my gut.

"How did you know she was in the club?" Danny spoke when Kai remained silent. I wondered if he was feeling guilty, it was him after all who had taken me to the club last night.

"Markus. He knew Mr. Wolfe was out of town and I'd been sent to wait in Hollows Bay for an opportunity to arise to approach her. He texted me last night to say he had it on good authority Riley was at the club," Toby replied, stabbing the knife and twisting it into my wounded soul.

There had been so many people in the club, any one of them could have informed this Markus person I was there. I tried to cast my mind back to anyone who had been acting strange but with the alcohol I had consumed and the events of what happened after Kai had arrived, I couldn't think straight.

"And what was going to happen when you met with her the following day?" Kai asked flatly, breaking me out of my thoughts as to who could be letting information out. I wanted to get the hell out of this room, but my feet were rooted to the spot.

Despite Kai's warning, Toby dared another glance at me, his mouth pressed into a thin line of disappointment.

Disappointment in himself.

"They were going to kidnap her," he muttered.

Kai's response was not something I expected.

He laughed.

But there was no humor to it, and that sent chills down my spine.

"Did Markus really think I would be dumb enough to let Riley go and meet you the next day unprotected? Give me a break," Kai said. He had a point, after what happened with Anderson at the charity ball, I wasn't even allowed to go for a piss on my own.

"Markus knew that," Toby replied, and then he kept his eyes downcast when he said, "but he was hoping I'd be able to talk her into sneaking out, he thought I could use our old connection to convince her to meet me. He could tell that even after this time had passed, I still cared for her."

A lone tear slid down my cheek at his words. The sad thing was, he was probably right. I never would have given it a second thought that Toby would hurt me, I would have gone with him willingly like a lamb to the slaughter.

When Kai didn't say anything, Toby spoke again. "I swear to you, Mr. Wolfe, I wasn't going to let anything happen to her, I was going to warn her, you've got to believe me!"

Once again, Kai leaped forward and grabbed Toby around the throat. His shoulders hunched up with rage, and even Danny looked like he wanted an ounce of Toby's flesh.

"Believe you? Why the fuck would I believe you?" Kai sneered into Toby's face.

This time, at the sight of seeing Toby being strangled, I didn't react. My whole body was stunned into numbness from his admission, and a little part of me wanted Toby to feel fear, the same fear I had when Detective Anderson had grabbed me at the ball, the fear of not knowing if I was going to live or die.

"I'm...telling...the truth," Toby managed to wheeze out, his lips beginning to turn purple the longer Kai held onto him.

"Who is he? Who the fuck is the big boss?" Kai dropped his hand, allowing Toby to answer unrestricted.

"I don't know, I never met him. He stays hidden, no one knows who he is, not even Carlos. He puts out his order through his generals. I told you man, I'm not high up enough to know the details."

Toby swayed by his wrists from the motion of being let go by Kai and looked at me. Not just braving a glance at me this time, no, he stared at me, letting me see the raw emotion written all over his face, and that he was telling the truth.

"Riley, girl, I'm so sorry. I'd never hurt you, you know I would never do anything to hurt you." His voice was shaky and sounded rougher than what he had at the start of this joyful discussion.

I tried to swallow past the thick lump lodged in my throat and pushed down the little part of me that wanted Toby to hurt the way I was hurting now.

Did I believe him?

The boy who helped me survive when I was so alone, who taught me how to look after myself, and was so gentle with me when I gave him my innocence? The boy who spent many nights cuddled up to me so I could stay warm, or who held me when I cried over my guilt for dragging Angel away from a better life.

I stared at the man he had become, and underneath the muscle and the tattoos, I could see the little boy he once was, the one who was trying to make it through life as best he could, and I knew deep down, he would never have done anything to hurt me.

"I believe you," I whispered, stepping forward.

Kai twisted to face me, his face was contorted into a menacing snarl.

"You can't be fucking serious," he roared at me, making me flinch. "He's just fucking admitted to being involved in an attempt to kidnap you, and you believe he was going to warn you? Don't be so fucking naive, Riley."

Urgh, how I was going to get this man to see reason, I did not know, he was wild with rage.

His words pissed me off. Yeah, sometimes I could be naive, and I didn't care how much time had passed since I last saw Toby, I still knew deep down he wasn't capable of hurting me.

"I am being serious. Toby wouldn't hurt me, he's not lying." I held my nerve, not letting the fear or anger I was feeling underneath show. Both Kai and Danny glared at me like they couldn't believe what I was saying.

"Riley, you haven't seen this fucker for five years," Kai replied, disbelief in his voice. "You don't know him, you don't know what he's capable of. You don't know what kind of shit people like him will do to get ahead in their gangs."

"You'd know all about that wouldn't you, Kai," I hit back, resentment thick in my tone.

It was a weak argument, of course he was capable of all kinds of shit, how else would he be in the position he was in now, but my head was spinning, and I didn't know what else I could say at this point.

Kai ran a hand down his shirt, a habit he did regularly even though his shirts were always pristine, not even a tiny crease could be seen.

"Exactly. I know *exactly* what people do to manipulate others to get what they want," he sneered at me, raking his eyes up and down my body and making his point that he had manipulated me into thinking he was some kind of saint instead of the devil he really was. He even had the audacity to look proud of himself.

Low fucking blow.

The absolute asshole.

"He's not lying," I gritted out, desperately trying to hold my tongue and not lose my temper at Kai. There would be one heck of a fallout from his comment when this shit was done and dusted, but for now, I focused on my sole mission of getting Toby out of here.

"Don't be so fucking naive, Star," Kai growled at me, and I wanted to punch him in the gut for daring to use my nickname. "What did he tell you when you 'bumped' into him last night?" He used his fingers to quote 'bumped,' highlighting the point that my reacquaintance with Toby was not accidental.

I didn't say anything, just glared back at Kai, the pair of us facing off against the other.

"Didn't he tell you he was back in the area seeing family? He could have told you the second he bumped into you the real reason he was in the club, but he didn't. He lied to you like he is doing now."

Fuck.

My eye twitched as the truth of that statement settled in. As much as I didn't want to accept what Kai had said, he had a point. Toby had lied to me, so how could I be so sure he was telling the truth now? Could I be so sure my trust wasn't misplaced?

"I only did that because I didn't want to scare you, Riley. I promise I was going to tell you," Toby pleaded, drawing my attention away from Kai and on to him.

My throat clogged with thick emotion, and another tear slid down my cheek. My head was swirling, and I needed a minute or two to think things through. I wanted to believe Toby so badly, and as I stood staring at him, I was reminded of the first time I had seen him five years ago when he had given me a boyish grin and told me everything would be okay. I had believed him then, and I believed him now.

Besides, he was telling Kai the truth now, why would he do that if he genuinely didn't want to help?

"Why are you helping us now, Toby? Why are you telling us all of this?" My voice shook as I spoke and I held my breath, waiting for his answer.

"Because I couldn't bear the thought of something happening to you, Riley," he replied softly. The tension in the air was so thick I could hardly breathe. "Even if I was going to do what they wanted me to do, the second I saw you last night, I knew I'd never be able to go through with it. You're my girl, Riley."

Smack.

I jumped back in surprise when Kai's fist connected with Toby's face, his head snapping to one side, and for a second, I thought he'd been knocked out.

Kai grabbed Toby's jaw and yanked his face up, fresh blood poured from his nose. Based on the crack that echoed around the room, I think it was fair to say Toby's nose was broken.

"She is not *your* girl, you hear me, you little cunt. She will *never* be your girl," Kai hissed, his voice low and deadly. Toby's eyes watered, and for a moment, he seemed dazed, but he managed to mumble his agreement.

"Kai, please don't," I whispered. I needed to get out of this room, away from what was happening right now. Mixed emotions had wrapped around me so tight I was choking on them, and I couldn't bear to see Toby hurting any longer.

"We're done here now anyway," Kai said, dropping Toby's face, his head lolled forward almost as if it weighed too much to hold up.

Kai turned to Danny and held out a hand, and Danny obliged by taking a gun from the waistband of his trousers and handing it over to Kai. My eyes widened at the sight as panic spread through me at the gun in Kai's hand.

"Kai, wait." I reached over to touch his arm, hoping to placate him. "Please don't kill him, he's told you everything he knows, please let him go."

"Riley, he was going to lure you into a fucking trap so they could kidnap you. You might be foolish enough to believe he was going to help you, but I'm not. He was going to hurt you and I won't stand for that."

Kai didn't take his eyes off Toby's limp body, the air of finality was back in his voice. I was fighting a losing battle.

So, I did something that seemed to be becoming a stupid habit.

A really fucking stupid habit.

I stepped in front of Toby, earning me a murderous look from Kai. Danny cursed under his breath and glared at me. But I held my ground.

"I may be a fool, but I know Toby. He helped me before and I believe he was going to help me again. Regardless, he's got a daughter, Kai, you can't take her dad away from her."

It was my final shot at getting Kai to stop this madness, if anything would get him to change his mind, it would be the mention of family. If I had learned anything about Kai Wolfe over these past weeks it was that he was fiercely loyal when it came to family. He may have been a cold-hearted murderer, but family was at the top of his priority, and this was the last thing I was sure I could use to get him to let Toby go.

But when his lips turned into a cruel smile, I knew I had lost.

"Do you know where his daughter is now, Riley? I bet he didn't tell you that, did he?"

Toby groaned from behind me, and my brows furrowed in confusion.

What in the ever-loving fuck was Kai talking about now? When I didn't say anything, Kai continued.

"The message I received when we were in the elevator earlier was from Miles. I had him do some background checks on your friend here. I bet he didn't tell you he hasn't seen his kid in over two years, did he? Or that he hasn't paid a penny in child support? Or did he tell you he doesn't even know where his kid is? He couldn't give two shits about his precious daughter, it was just another means of drawing you in so you'd agree to meet him."

Embarrassment, betrayal, and rage all mixed together and churned in my belly.

Kai was right.

I was foolish.

Foolish for believing Toby. Foolish for believing I could try to help him.

Foolish for letting myself get involved with someone as brutal as Kai fucking Wolfe.

My heart wasn't just hurting, it had been cut out and stomped all over, not just at Toby's betrayal but at the way Kai had taken glee in telling me. The way he was proud of himself for manipulating me into thinking he wasn't the devil.

I needed to get out of this room. I needed air so I could breathe again.

And yet, when all was said and done, I still couldn't let him hurt Toby.

"I don't care," I whispered, battling against the tears threatening to fall. "If you kill him, then he'll never have the chance to make things right with his daughter. Please, Kai, I'll do anything."

"There's nothing you can do, Riley. It was over for The Stag the second he agreed to set you up."

"If you kill him, I'll never forgive you." Tears streaked my cheek, but I held my gaze firm on Kai, letting him know how damn serious I was being.

"That's a consequence I'm willing to accept, Star." There was no emotion to Kai when he spoke, he was the stone-cold killer that had one objective in mind. He nodded his head at Danny. "Get her out of here."

I was about to protest when Danny grabbed me and flung me over his shoulder.

I was beginning to get a bit fucking sick of people doing that.

Danny marched out of the room, the door slamming closed behind him. As he walked towards the elevator, a gunshot echoed from the room we had just left.

And then my heart completely shattered.

Chapter 28

Kai

Riley refused to speak to me for the next three days. She locked herself in her bedroom and refused to come out, barricading the door with a chest of drawers to stop me from coming in, and only moving them when Jacqueline brought her food.

She didn't even want to see Angel.

I didn't push her. I knew some of the things I had said to her in the basement had been cruel, particularly the bit about manipulating her. It wasn't fucking true, I had been nothing but open and honest with Riley. I had shown her every part of me. The murderous, controlling asshole side, but also the different person I was when I was around her. She made me softer, more caring. She brought out a side of me where my heart wasn't quite so black. So I don't know why I had implied that the only reason she had fallen for me was because I had manipulated her when it couldn't have been farther from the truth. I had a long way to go to make it up to her when she finally stopped sulking.

She needed time to understand why I killed The Stag. I couldn't let him go back, he'd earned his death sentence when he agreed to set Riley up. No one would get away with hurting my girl, and she was still my girl despite the fact she hated me right now.

Besides, if it wasn't my bullet that killed Toby, Carlos would have done the deed himself. If I had sent him on his merry way, Carlos would have tortured Toby in order to get him to spill all the things he had told me. Frankly, I had done Toby a favor by making his death quick, and *that*, I did for her. I could have drawn out his death, skinned him alive like I had intended to, but putting a bullet through his brain and making it quick was a death he did not deserve, but it was the least I could do for her.

Despite wanting to force Riley out of her room and back to my side where she belonged, I let her stew.

The first night, she didn't sleep a wink. I watched her on camera crying into her pillow, and fuck, did it kill me not to go and comfort her. By the second evening, I instructed Jacqueline to sprinkle some crushed-up sleeping pills into Riley's water, which she did against her better judgment.

Riley fell into a deep sleep, and once I was sure she was asleep, I snuck into her room using the secret doorway between my room and hers. She hadn't discovered it yet, and I had almost told her about it when we were laying in bed together the morning before I killed The Stag, but I was fucking glad I had kept that bit of information to myself.

The secret door in her room was in the alcove next to her dressing table, to the naked eye it looked like just a bare alcove, when really the wall slid across, revealing a small passageway that led to another door hidden at the back of my closet. Even if Riley had discovered it, she wouldn't have been able to open it, it could only be opened from my room.

I'd climbed onto the bed next to her and pulled her into my arms, holding her against me and breathing in her scent like the fucking addict I was. Although she was fast asleep, she rolled willingly into my arms and settled her head in the crook of my arm, and stayed there all night, cuddling into me as if her subconscious knew I was there.

It was only when the sun started to rise that I moved her back to her side of the bed and snuck out. From the camera feed, I watched her wake up with confusion etched across her pretty features as she reached out to touch the bed sheets where I had lay. But the confusion quickly turned to anger, and she stormed off to her bathroom.

It didn't stop me from repeating my actions the following night.

If getting to touch her meant I had to drug her and sneak in at night, then so be it.

I hated Riley being angry at me but in my defense, I had warned her.

She should have known there was no way I'd spare The Stag's life, especially with what he confessed. She was lucky I let Danny take her out of the room before I blew his brains out. It was a good job I didn't have a gun on me when I went into the basement, otherwise, the cunt would have met his fate minutes earlier when he called Riley *his* girl.

Fucker.

One good thing came out of Riley not talking to me, it gave me time to focus on the problem at hand, finding out just what the fuck The Stags thought they were playing at.

It was too much of a coincidence that Anderson was a cop in the city where a gang was plotting my alleged downfall, Anderson had to be working for The Stags, or vice versa. Either way, I needed to get my hands on Anderson as soon as fucking possible.

"Give me some good fucking news, Jimmy," I said into the speaker-phone on my desk in my office.

Jimmy was the head of my surveillance team who had assisted in Huntsville when we were trying to track down Anderson. After the information from Toby, I sent Jimmy and his team back to Huntsville with one objective: find out who the fucking boss of The Stags was. It was a near impossible task, but there was no way this anonymous prick could stay hidden forever. Carlos, or *someone* in the gang must have some idea who he was, we just had to find the weak link.

"Sorry, Boss, we've followed Carlos and staked his home out for the last three days but nothing." Jimmy's deep voice came from the speakerphone. "We've got photos of every person he's met with which I've sent to Miles but they are all lower level gang members."

"Yeah, they are," Miles nodded, confirming he had received the images. "They're all Stags, street level or one rank above, but no one of importance. I'm doing background checks on them to see if any of them have links to Anderson but so far I've drawn a blank."

I nodded and ran my hand through my hair in frustration at the lack of progress. It didn't help that Huntsville was not my city to control. I only had links through legitimate businesses, I had no one under my control within the police department otherwise we would have been making a lot more progress.

"What else can you tell me, Jimmy?" I said, returning my attention back to the phone.

"He tends to coordinate his business from his home, we really need to get a bug planted inside so we can see and hear what's going on but there is always someone in the house, and the security is tight. I'm going to need a few more days, we'll need to come up with a distraction plan to draw everyone away from the house so I can get one of the team inside without being caught."

"What do you need to make that happen?" I asked, willing to throw whatever resources and money I had to get this fucking problem sorted.

"I'll need another surveillance team, my team have been on the clock twenty-four-seven and it's starting to catch up. I'll also need an armed backup team if things go to shit when we manage to get someone inside the house," Jimmy said in a no-nonsense tone.

Jimmy was ex-police. He'd been kicked out of Hollows Bay Police Department after getting a bit heavy handed with a kid who had been a complete shithead and smacked off his face on crack. He'd fought Jimmy when Jimmy had tried to arrest him, and it had resulted in Jimmy breaking the kid's arm, but because the boy was only fifteen, HBPD had taken his word over Jimmy's and had kicked him off the force and paid the kid a hefty sum in compensation.

It was HBPD's loss. Jimmy was an asset, and luckily for me, he saw a good deal when I offered him one. He mainly worked on the right side of the law, but he also wasn't afraid to get his hands dirty if what I asked him to do broke a few laws. He was good at what he did, and if he needed more men, more equipment, and more weapons, he'd get it.

"Consider it done. Hendrix will be in touch to coordinate with you." I looked at Hendrix who bobbed his head in acknowledgment.

"Thank you, Sir," Jimmy replied, professional as ever.

"Keep me posted, I want to know straight away if there are any developments, no matter what the time of day or night is."

"Of course," he replied and hung up the phone.

I flopped back in my chair and rubbed my hand over my jaw while Hendrix sighed, Danny cursed under his breath, and Miles rolled his eyes.

I'd called them into my office so I could get updates on various businesses I was still trying to run while sorting out this shitshow with Detective fucking Anderson and now The Stags.

Danny had been present when Toby disclosed that The Stags knew things about Riley that would only be known by a select few people, and when he'd questioned me on it, I told him my concerns that someone had been leaking information. Miles and Hendrix had walked in half way through that conversation so I filled them in with my suspicions too. The three of them had been furious at me for even thinking one of them could have been responsible, pledging their allegiance to me and vowing to find the cunt who was responsible.

I felt fucking foolish for considering that one of them could have betrayed my trust, they were loyal through and through.

"What about their communications?" I asked Miles who was standing across the room in his usual corner, pressed up against a wall and staring down the tablet he held as if it had personally offended him.

"Can't tap their lines, they use encrypted phones like we do. I've got some software running on a computer linked to Carlos' home address and from the amount of usage, I'd hazard a guess and say he uses the dark web to communicate with whoever the silent partner is," Miles explained, never once taking his eyes off his tablet.

"Surely you can tell who he is talking to on the dark web," Danny said, earning him a scowl from Miles.

"It doesn't work like that, dickhead. If it was easy to trace who you were talking to, no one would use the dark web," Miles snapped back.

Danny's knuckles clenched on his lap, no doubt at being called a dickhead. We were all getting frustrated with the lack of progress but the last thing we needed was to start turning on each other.

"Enough. We're all doing what we can to get somewhere," I growled, silently cursing Victor as I had done many times for not alerting me to the fact Anderson had visited him all those months ago. If he'd had fucking said something, Theo would have known the meeting at the docks was a setup and he'd still be alive and breathing today.

As much as I hated to admit it, that thought tasted like acid in my mouth. If Theo hadn't been killed I wouldn't have had any reason to venture to East Bay, or more specifically, Club Sin, and then I would never have met the stubborn little minx who was consuming the majority of my thoughts.

"What about the rest of the gang?" I directed my question to Hendrix who had spent the last few days trying to find people in Huntsville to give him information. He'd only arrived back to Hollows Bay this morning and he looked as exhausted as I felt.

"Nothing of interest, Kai. There is talk about Toby on the street, The Stags believe you killed him, but doesn't seem like they give a fuck, there's no talk of retribution for his death," Hendrix replied with a yawn.

Right then, my phone buzzed with a message. I pulled it out of my pocket and looked at the screen, seeing a message from Isaac. I tapped in my pin and pulled up the messaging app.

I have some information. Are you free to come to the office today?

Isaac never asked for me to go to the office, usually, we arranged a neutral place to meet up at a time suitable for both of us. If he wanted me to go to him today, it must have been for something urgent. I quickly replied, telling him I'd be there in twenty minutes.

I stood abruptly from my chair, the three men looked at me with questioning brows. "Isaac's got some information. Hendrix, you're with me. Miles, keep trying to crack that fucking phone, it could be our key to something useful."

"Sure thing, I've just downloaded some software that should help, I'm hoping the phone will be cracked by the end of today," Miles said, stepping away from the wall and out the door to head back to his apartment where he had been working night and day to try and break into the damned phone. I was grateful to him, even if I was fucking frustrated at the lack of progress.

"Want me to come too, Boss?" Danny asked as he stood from his seat.

"No. I want you to stay here. I don't want Riley unprotected." If the stubborn minx was talking to me, I'd take her with me so I could keep an eye on her myself, but Danny wouldn't let anything happen to her, I trusted him implicitly to keep my girl safe.

"Understood," he grumbled. Danny had been sullen since the shit with Toby, and I knew he partially blamed himself for coming up with the idea of taking her to the club. I'd heard him outside her room the day before trying to talk to her, she did at least speak to him, but it was along the lines of, 'Fuck off', 'Go to hell' and, 'Kiss my ass'. The usual curses from her when she was angry.

I clapped him on the back as I walked out of the office with Hendrix following. "Maybe you can try to talk some sense into her again," I smirked.

Danny winced. "Not fucking likely, sticking pins under my fingernails would be more fun than trying to talk to that girl."

Both Hendrix and I chuckled all the way to the car.

I decided to drive rather than asking Frank to take us, or Hendrix driving me. I was feeling the need to be in control of something seeing as everything around me felt like it was falling to shit.

During the drive, Hendrix and I discussed what little we knew about The Stags, trying to come up with a reason as to why they would be wanting to take over my organization, and why now. The obvious reason was because I had a good business model and excellent control over my city. I didn't allow rival gangs into my territory, I controlled the contraband on the street and it worked, it worked for me as it had worked for my father and my grandfather.

But if I was honest, I didn't believe that was the reason The Stags wanted to overthrow me. No, this had something to do with Anderson, I was sure of it.

We had been treating Anderson and the silent partner of The Stags as two different people, but maybe Anderson *was* the silent partner of The Stags, secretly pulling all the strings. I hoped Isaac was about to shed some light.

"Maybe you should move Riley to one of our safe houses," Hendrix suggested as we turned into the street where Isaac's office was.

"No fucking chance. I want her where I can protect her," I said firmly, not even entertaining the suggestion.

It made sense, I supposed. Move her out of harm's way until this shit was sorted but that could take weeks, months even, and I wasn't prepared for her to be away from me for that length of time. Fuck, these last few days of her not talking to me were slowly killing me. It was only the fact I could sneak into her room and touch her that kept me from going completely insane.

Besides, there were only three people I could count on to protect Riley besides me, and I needed them to help me resolve this, I couldn't afford to lose any of my closest assets.

"Come on, Kai, it's the safest option. We move her to one of the houses outside of the state, put around the clock protection on her, and then we can concentrate on tracking down this Detective prick and dealing with The Stags without constantly worrying about her."

My lips thinned into a line, and my hands tightened on the steering wheel. I didn't like the way he'd just implied he was concerned about her, she wasn't his to worry about. I still hadn't spoken to him about why he told her about the girls from my club and his feelings towards her, but quite frankly, I didn't care anymore. All he needed to know was that Riley was mine, mine to protect, mine to do with as I so wished. The only time he was to have any interest in her safety was if I instructed him to protect her.

I pulled the car into a space outside Isaac's office block and cut the engine but made no move to get out. Instead, I turned to face him.

"Riley isn't going anywhere. I appreciate your concern, but it's misplaced, she's not yours to worry about. She stays where I can protect her, and the only time you need to concern yourself with her is when I tell you to protect her with your fucking life. Understood?" My tone was full of threat, the kind I reserved for those who were about to die.

Hendrix swallowed nervously and held his hands up in defense. "Yeah, of course, Boss. I'm sorry, I didn't mean to overstep, I just know you care about her. We all do, she's become part of the family."

A twinge of guilt flashed through me. I was being a jealous prick and I knew it. I couldn't help myself when it came to my Star, and Hendrix was only thinking about her safety.

I gave him a nod and stepped out of the car. He followed behind me and as we were about to step into the office building, his phone rang. I paused to wait for him to answer it, he pulled it out and grimaced before looking at me.

"I got to take this, Boss, it's Anderson's ex-girlfriend. I told her to call me if she remembered anything useful."

"Come up when you're done."

I turned to leave him to it, no wonder he'd grimaced when he saw who was calling, apparently she had taken a bit of a shine to Hendrix when he grilled her in Huntsville, and had now taken to texting him several times a day.

Isaac was waiting for me when the elevator opened on his floor, he bobbed his head in acknowledgment and indicated for me to follow to his office.

"Thanks for coming, Mr. Wolfe," he said as he took his seat behind his desk and held out his hand for me to sit in the chair opposite.

"I'm hoping this will be worth my while, Isaac." I gave him a faint smile and he suddenly looked nervous, the Adam's apple in his throat bobbing.

"I, uh...I managed to find some information on the Detective, John Anderson. It's taken me longer than I'd hoped but the information was difficult to come by," Isaac stuttered.

I relaxed back in my chair, hoping it would ease him. Isaac was an ally, and one I intended to keep so I didn't want to scare him.

Unless I really had to, of course.

"How so?" I asked. Isaac opened his mouth to speak but was interrupted by a knock on the door before Hendrix walked in without waiting for an invitation. He greeted Isaac who again bobbed his head in reply and then sat in the chair next to me.

"Anything?" I asked Hendrix, referring to the phone call he had just had. He smirked but shook his head.

"Silly cunt wanted to know when I would be back in Huntsville so I could take her on a date." He waved his hand, dismissing the whole thing and I turned my attention back to Isaac.

"Why was the information difficult to come by?"

"Perhaps I should start from the beginning." Isaac adjusted his dark-rimmed glasses and sat up straight in his chair. He was an odd looking fella, with mousy features and floppy blonde hair. There wasn't anything remarkable about him, but that's what made him good at his job, he had a face you would instantly forget.

"Anderson's mother died when he was three years old, it seems no one knew who his father was, so he went into the foster system. He spent the next six years bouncing around foster homes. He was a difficult child, constantly sick, and was slow developing."

"Fuck me, Isaac," Hendrix interrupted. "When you said you were going to start from the beginning, I didn't think we'd be getting a blow by blow account of the bastard's life," he chuckled, earning himself a scathing look from me.

"It's relevant," Isaac hissed back, his cheeks turning red.

"Go on," I said, giving Hendrix a look that said, *'Shut the fuck up.'* Isaac glared at Hendrix for another beat before sucking in a breath and continuing.

"He was eventually taken in by a family, the Brown family who lived in Jacksonville, and he was moved across the country to live with them. The couple fostered a whole bunch of kids over the years, and it seemed Anderson stayed with them from the age of nine until he enrolled in the police academy in Florida aged nineteen." Isaac paused and readjusted his glasses, almost like it was a nervous tick.

I leaned forward in my seat, ready to hurry this the fuck along. "Struggling to see where the difficulty in getting the information is, Isaac."

"Well, that's the thing. I said *it seems* Anderson stayed with the family until he was nineteen, but there are no records to confirm that. Between the ages of nine and nineteen, there are no records of Anderson. No school reports, no medical reports. Nothing for the entire ten years. And as for the records before he turned nine, some exist, for example, a few of the foster homes he lived in. But a lot no longer exists, including things like his birth certificate, and where he lived for the first three years of his life." He sat back in his chair, looking pleased with himself.

"How is that even possible?" I asked, my brows narrowed in confusion as I tried to comprehend what Isaac was trying to tell me. Someone didn't just disappear for ten years of their lives, especially not at the age of nine. There would have been some public record of his existence. And what about the records from when he was born? It didn't make sense.

"It's not possible unless someone hacked into government databases and wiped his records for periods of his life. That could only be done by a really good hacker or someone official and high ranking who would have access."

Well. Didn't this make things a whole lot more interesting?

I looked at Hendrix who was looking equally confused, and when he saw me staring, he gave a shrug of his shoulders.

"That's not all," Isaac continued. "I thought I'd look into the records of the Brown family, see if I could identify any foster siblings, but all of those records have been erased too. There is literally zero information available as to who Anderson was living with besides Carol and Anthony Brown."

"What about the foster parents? Surely they can shed some light, where are they?" I asked, already plotting a journey across the country to visit them if they were still living in Florida.

"They're dead."

Fuck sake.

Of course they were.

Every fucking turn resulted in a dead end. I rolled my eyes and swiped my hand down over my face in frustration.

"When?" I gritted out. Not that it would make a difference, the dead didn't speak, I knew that all too fucking well.

"One month after Anderson popped back up at the Police Academy. They died in a house fire along with another foster child, a young man named Michael Tucker. He was a year younger than Anderson but again, all of his records had been erased so there is no way of knowing how long he was living with the Browns before he died. It was three months after they died that Anderson had his first documented breakdown, it was only for the fact that he was already in the Academy and doing exceptionally well that he was allowed to continue."

"Fucking hell," I cursed under my breath. My hands were beginning to tremble with anger. Not at Isaac, but at this whole goddamn situation.

Just who the fuck was John Anderson?

"So, for Anderson to have been able to join the Police Academy, he would have had to have records, right?" Hendrix said, sitting forward.

"Yes, of course he would have. But the records held by the academy have been tampered with which is why your friend Miles could only get certain information. Whoever has tampered with the files only wants certain information to be available. It's almost as if they are giving you little clues to follow.

"Why else would the records have provided Anderson's current home address but not where he grew up? Or giving you snippets of his current medical record but nothing about his medical history during his teenage years? And all the details about the foster kids have been erased with the exception of Micheal Tucker. It doesn't make sense, Mr. Wolfe. To me, it seems like someone is leaving you little breadcrumbs to follow."

He made some good fucking points. Some fucker was playing games with me, games I had no choice but to play if I wanted to find out just what the hell was going on.

"Is there anything else you can tell us about Anderson during his time in the police service?" Hendrix asked the question that had been on my lips.

"The next seventeen years are all documented, including the subsequent mental health episodes, but I believe you already have access to those?"

Isaac raised a brow and I nodded at the reference to the material Miles had identified when he had first looked into Anderson's background.

"I assume you haven't found anything to identify his current whereabouts?" I asked, already knowing the answer.

If he had known, Isaac would have started this whole conversation with that. He wasn't one for dramatics and wouldn't have dragged it out, it was one of the reasons I liked him. He gave me an apologetic smile but shook his head.

"Very well. Send me the files on what you have been able to find. I want the old family address he lived in even if it was seventeen years ago that he lived there, and anything else you have, no matter how irrelevant you think it is. There's got to be something we're missing," I said the last part more to myself, but Isaac murmured his agreement and went about tapping at the laptop on his desk.

"It's a big file, it may take a few moments to land in your inbox," Isaac said. I took that as my cue to leave and stood from my chair, buttoning up my suit jacket before holding out my hand to Isaac. He too stood and reached out to shake my hand. "I will of course keep looking, Mr. Wolfe."

"Thank you, Isaac. I'll be in touch." Hendrix stood and also shook Isaac's hand, and we both turned, ready to walk out.

"Mr. Wolfe. One more thing before you go," Isaac said and I heard the hint of nervousness in his voice. I turned back to face him, the look on his face confirming he was worried about the next thing he was going to tell me.

"I....I thought you ought to know," he sounded apologetic and lifted a shoulder in a shrug. "I dip into the dark web from time to time to keep an eye on what jobs are being advertised. Last night, there was an advert from an anonymous source advertising the capture of the young girl you had me follow, Ms. Bennett. The reward offered to capture her was just shy of one million dollars and there were a lot of people interested.

"The advert was for her to be captured by any means possible, and erm, the...the source said once they had finished with her she would be given back to the person who captured her to, er well...to do whatever they wanted with her."

My whole body tensed and my hands curled into fists by my side. No wonder Isaac had been nervous to tell me, he would have known exactly how I would react.

Red blurred my vision, and even though I knew Isaac was only passing on the information, it didn't stop me from wanting to reach across the desk and squeeze the life out of him.

Taking a deep breath and making a real effort to uncurl my fists, I straightened my suit jacket and gave Isaac a nod.

"Is there any way of finding out who the person that posted the request is?" I gritted out, clenching my teeth so hard I feared they were about to crack.

Whoever had posted it was a dead man.

"I'm afraid not, that's the beauty and frustration of the dark web. I guess one could reply to the advert and see if contact could be established that way, but I suspect, like most people who use the dark web, their tracks will well and truly be covered," Isaac said apologetically.

"Thank you for telling me." The words tasted like acid in my mouth as I tried to get them out. And with that, I turned and walked out of the office.

As we descended in the lift, I made a mental note to speak to Miles about the advert when I got home in hopes he could reach out and establish communication with the cunt who had posted it. It was a long shot, but it was a starting point.

Hendrix was silent as I drove us home, for which I was thankful. I knew Riley was at risk, I wasn't fucking naïve enough to think the threat would go away after I had killed Toby. But now every man and his dog had been made aware of the price on her ass, she would be fair game, and the risk had increased significantly.

Maybe the idea of moving her to a safe house wasn't such a bad idea.

If only I could convince my stubborn pride it was the right thing to do.

Chapter 29

Riley

The previous three days were an emotional roller coaster ride, leaving me feeling exhausted and all out of tears. One minute I would sob my heart out over the cold-blooded murder of Toby, and then the tears would turn to furious anger at Kai for being the one to pull the trigger.

It was like I had a devil and an angel sitting on my shoulder, whispering things into each ear and confusing the hell out of me.

One side said Kai was deserving of my anger, he had unnecessarily killed Toby because he was a jealous asshole, and was punishing me for hugging Toby. The other side, the devil, whispered Toby deserved what was coming, he had lied to me and betrayed me, and if he hadn't been caught, bad things would have happened to me.

I would have moments where I listened more to the devil than the angel, and then times when I would listen more to the angel than the devil, resulting in my head being completely and utterly confused.

In between the moments of grieving for Toby or being angry at the world, the comment Kai made about manipulating me popped into my head. It was almost as though my brain had found a way of causing me more pain when I was already suffering.

Once again the angel and devil would whisper their conflicting comments, and I didn't know who to believe. The angel told me Kai *had* manipulated me, that he was only interested in me because I was a trophy he could show off as a result of winning a deal, that he was all about image and reputation.

The devil, who I *really* wanted to listen to, told me Kai had said something nasty in the heat of the moment, and that his feelings for me were genuine. But self-doubt overruled heart and head, and I was back to thinking Kai saw me as nothing more than a hole to fuck for the next six months.

Or five months,

I wasn't quite sure how long was left in our agreement.

It didn't help that Kai had somehow been sneaking into my room when I slept at night. I didn't know how he had been getting in as each night I barricaded the door with the chest of drawers, but each morning when I woke to find his scent lingering on the pillows, I knew without a shadow of a doubt he had slept next to me. I had zero memories of him actually being there with me though which led me to one conclusion, he'd been drugging me so that I slept. I didn't know whether to be mad at him for that, but then with just how exhausted I was, I was quite grateful for the dreamless sleep, and as much as I hated to admit it, I found comfort in waking up surrounded by his scent.

I would need some serious therapy when this shit was all over.

By day four, I decided it was time to pull myself together and face up to reality. The hard truth of it was Toby *had* lied to me, *had* deceived me.

The more I thought about it, the more I came to the realization that Toby had intended to trick me, otherwise, why wouldn't he have warned me the second he met me in the club instead of making out like he accidentally bumped into me and feeding me the line about his daughter? Whether he would have warned me about the threat at some point, who knew. Maybe he was genuine when he said as soon as he saw me, he couldn't go through with it, but I'd never be able to talk to him again so there was no way I'd ever know, and torturing myself over it was only sending me cuckoo.

As for Kai, we needed to have a long hard talk.

Deep down, I didn't think he had manipulated me, he never once tried to hide the psycho-killer part of him. I just allowed myself to forget that part of him when he was treating me to spa days, showering me with attention, and giving me orgasm after orgasm. But I didn't like the way he hurt me with his comment. Ironically, I could stomach him killing people, but I wouldn't stand for him taking his anger out on me.

I blamed my fucked up teenage years for my weird morals.

Aside from creeping into my room when I was passed out, Kai had made no attempt to talk to me. He'd kept his distance these last few days so maybe he wasn't interested in sorting things out with me after all....

Arghhhhhh!

Why did this have to be so hard?

I was lying on the bed, staring up at the ceiling and replaying everything over again in my head, and trying to summon up the courage to leave my room to find Kai, when a knock on the door drew me from my thoughts. A little pang of hope shot through me, hope that it might have been Kai coming to make amends, but hope was quickly followed by disappointment when Danny's gruff voice called out.

"Riles, I need to talk to you."

Danny had tried once before to talk to me but I wasn't ready to talk to anyone. I'd heard him mutter an apology outside my door when I had told him to fuck off before he stomped away, and that was the last anyone tried to talk to me. Even Jacqueline had barely squeaked at me when she brought me food on a daily basis. I really had been a grumpy bitch.

Biting the bullet, I slid the chest of drawers away from the door which I had placed to stop Kai from barging in unannounced, and pulled the door open to find a confused look on Danny's face, probably because I'd actually opened the door this time. He shook the look from his face and gave me a half smile.

"You okay?" he asked, which in my opinion was a stupid fucking question.

"Wonderful," I replied dryly. He looked tired like he hadn't had much sleep these last few nights, and I couldn't help feeling a pang of guilt for him.

"Riles, I'm sorry, but I need you to pack a bag," he said, grimacing.

I raised an eyebrow, wondering what the hell he was talking about. Why would I need to pack a bag? Unless Kai had officially had enough of my sulking and was kicking me out. That notion sat heavy in my gut.

When I didn't ask or make a move to jump at his command, he sighed and rubbed a hand down his jaw. "It's an order that has come from Kai. He wants to move you and Angel to a safe house. It's too risky keeping you in the city," he explained.

"And Kai couldn't tell me this himself?" I huffed, pissed that the man hadn't made any effort to talk to me these last few days and was now ordering me to go fuck knows where.

"He's out doing some stuff, but he wants to get you moved as soon as possible. He'll come and see you in a few days."

"Fuck that, I'm not going anywhere without speaking to him!" I made to slam the door, but Danny stopped it with his giant hand, reminding me how strong he was. A frustrated look crossed his face as he took a deep breath.

"Look, I don't like it either. But Kai is doing this to keep your ass safe, you know that man fucking cares about you, so stop being a stubborn little cow and let him protect you," he snapped, surprising me. I'd never heard Danny be anything but funny and kind toward me, and it caught me off guard. I glared at him, sending daggers in his direction. "I'm sorry, I'm worried about you, okay. Some cunt is out there making it clear you're their number one target, and I don't think I could live with myself if we failed to protect you. You're a good person, Riles," he said, softer this time.

For fuck sake.

How could I protest when the pain was so clear in Danny's voice? He was genuinely worried and I didn't want to worry him anymore.

At least Angel would be coming, that was one positive. I'd barely thought about her over these last few days thanks to all the shit that was hogging my brain space, so maybe some time with my sister, and away from the penthouse and Kai was exactly what I needed. I huffed loudly but didn't argue anymore.

A short time later, after being hurried along to pack my bag by Danny, I found myself in Angel's room, explaining to her we were going to stay in a different house for a few days as I shoved her clothes into another bag. I didn't tell Angel the reason we were being moved, she'd only worry when there was no need, in fact, this whole 'moving to a safe house' thing felt a bit overkill to me, and the first opportunity I'd get, I'd tell Kai what I thought about his ridiculous plan.

The only question Angel asked was if she'd be able to take her games console with us. I rolled my eyes and told her we'd get it delivered in a few days, hoping Kai would come good for her like he did the last time the little brat wanted her games.

We were soon ushered into the elevator by Danny who had both of our bags slung over his shoulder as we made our way down to the parking level.

"Isn't Jane coming?" I asked Danny when I realized she was nowhere to be seen.

"She went to visit her mom, she'll meet you at the safe house later," Danny answered.

It briefly crossed my mind whether Jane needed a guard with her when she went out but I didn't voice the question, from the minute Danny had knocked on my door, he had been tense, and there was no sign of that easing up. His whole demeanor was making me feel downright anxious with his hunched up shoulders and his eyes constantly darting around as if a threat was going to jump out on us at any moment.

I took Angel's hand, feeling the need to have some comfort but trying my hardest to disguise my growing anxiety. I didn't like the idea that Kai was sending me away without coming to explain it personally. But the perceptive little bugger knew something was wrong if the reassuring squeeze to my hand was anything to go by.

We reached the parking level and I followed Danny towards the row of cars, towing Angel behind me. Frank appeared out of an office I had never seen before, normally he was always waiting by the car, but he looked like he'd been caught off guard, not expecting to chauffeur us anywhere.

"Everything okay?" he asked Danny with a hint of suspicion in his voice.

"All good, Franky boy, we're headed out," Danny replied with a hint of tension in his voice. He put his hand into his pocket and pulled out a car key, aiming it at a black Audi I'd never been in before. He pressed a button and the car bleeped as the doors unlocked.

"Where are you going?" Frank said looking between the bags Danny was dropping into the trunk of the car, and me clutching Angel's hand. He wore a strange look on his face, one of….concern, maybe?

"Riley's being moved to a safe house. Kai's orders."

I was glad Danny had his back to Angel, I didn't want her lip reading and realizing we were going to a safe house rather than just a different house.

"Kai said that?" Frank continued.

Danny opened the rear door of the car and waved his hand for Angel and me to get in, she ducked in first, and as I was about to get in next to her, Danny answered Frank.

"Yeah, man, what's the problem? I got a call from Hendrix like twenty minutes ago saying Kai wanted Riley moved to the safe house pronto. Give him a call if you don't fucking believe me," he snapped. And with that, Danny got in the car and slammed the door, muttering under his breath about Frank being a nosy cunt.

It occurred to me that it was strange Frank hadn't been told where we were going, but then Kai still hadn't figured out if one of his staff had been spilling his secrets, so maybe he was just being cautious about sharing information with the wider team.

Danny pulled out of the underground car park and into the light traffic. The sun beamed down on the car, instantly warming it up. I spun around in my seat to look out of the rear window to find there were no vehicles following us from the apartment block. It was strange, whenever I'd been out with Kai previously, we'd always been followed by at least one vehicle which had men armed to the nines.

An uneasy feeling spread through me, and my stomach started churning with worry. If Kai was so worried about my safety, surely he would have had more than just Danny taking me to wherever we were going. Or, was it another way to keep my location as secret as possible?

I twisted back in my seat, looking at Danny through the rear-view mirror. His eyes were fixed firmly on the road ahead and appeared unfazed by this whole situation.

Angel, who was sitting in the seat behind Danny, was staring out of the window, engrossed in the scenery passing us by, her little nose pressed against the window and completely oblivious to the anxiety coursing through my body. I tried to relax, but I couldn't switch off the feeling that something felt off.

Very, very off.

As the car made its way through the city, and Danny turned off the main street, his phone started ringing. He clicked a button on the steering wheel, connecting his phone to the in-car speaker system.

"What's up, Miles?" Danny said cheerily as soon as the phone had connected. There was a brief pause before Miles spoke.

"How could you, Danny?" Miles' serious voice echoed around the car, emotion thick in his tone. "How could you fucking do it to Kai? And Theo for that matter!" he yelled angrily.

"What the fuck are you talking about?" Danny growled. His eyes flashed to mine, and the uneasy feeling in the pit of my stomach grew heavier.

"Don't you dare play fucking innocent. I trusted you. *Kai* fucking trusted you," Miles snarled down the line.

Danny smacked his hand against the steering wheel, rage pouring from his tense body. "You better fucking start talking, Miles, I don't have time for this shit."

He tugged hard on the steering wheel, turning the car onto another road. The quick jerk caused Angel to look over at me with a concerned look, and I grabbed her hand and gave her a soft smile, trying my hardest to not let the panic I was feeling show on my face.

"Kai was right," Miles chuckled, but there was no humor to it, he sounded almost resigned. "There is a traitor, and Kai is going to kill you when I tell him it's *you*."

Despair, betrayal, and fear seeped into my bones as I stared at the back of Danny's head. He was silent, not denying the claims Miles had made and not looking away from the road ahead of him.

And then he threw his head back and let out a chilling humorless laugh which sent a shiver of terror down my spine.

"You're a fucking moron, Miles. I haven't betrayed anyone," Danny said stoically.

"Liar!" Miles roared, making me flinch. Angel gaped at me with a worried expression on her face. I squeezed her hand to reassure her, which was pretty fucking hard to do when I had no clue what was going on.

"Miles, I swear to fucking god-" Danny started, but Miles interrupted.

"I finally got into the burner phone we found at Anderson's, there was only one person he was in contact with, but you would know that wouldn't you, Danny, seeing as that person was *you*," Miles sneered.

My brain was struggling to keep up, trying to put the pieces together, but failing even though the answer was obvious.

Danny was the one who had betrayed Kai, I just didn't want to believe it.

"I'll ask again, what the fuck are you talking about?" Danny growled, only to be interrupted by Miles again.

"Tell me, is your bitch, Jane, involved in this as well?"

Ho-ly shit.

This whole time I thought Hendrix was the one to be wary of, I never even considered it could be Danny, the gentle giant who played freaking computer games with my little sister.

And Jane?

"Miles-" Danny started, but he never had a chance to finish whatever he was about to say.

Time seemed to speed up in the next few minutes, and everything felt like it happened all at once.

The squeal of tires dragged my attention away from Danny, and I looked in the direction it came from which happened to be on my side of the car. I barely had time to acknowledge the van hurtling towards us. On instinct,

I threw my hands up to protect my head before the van smashed into my door causing an *almighty* bang. Pain lanced through my whole body at the impact, and glass shattered all over me.

At first, I thought my head was playing tricks on me but I quickly realized the car was flipping onto its side, and then onto the roof where we'd been hit so hard. Despite the agony coursing through my body, I tried to dive onto Angel to cover her, but my damn seatbelt held me in place.

The car came to a stop on its roof, and it took me a few seconds to get my bearings. My head was spinning, and I was in so much pain, everywhere hurt so much. I was hanging upside down by the darn seatbelt holding me tightly across my waist. I tried to move my arm, but it wouldn't listen to my brain, it had taken the full force of the hit, and I was sure without a shadow of a doubt it was broken. Blood trickled down my face and my vision blurred as my head continued spinning in nauseating circles. Screams and shouts echoed from outside, and I prayed someone was calling for help.

I looked over to Angel and breathed a huge sigh of relief to find her looking back at me, frightened to fuck, but conscious, and on the face of it, fairly uninjured besides the odd cut from the glass. I couldn't move my hand to sign to her, so I mouthed, *'Are you okay?'*

She nodded, her eyes wide with fear as they raked over my injuries. I wanted nothing more than to reach out and hold her, but my body was working against my fuzzy brain, holding me still.

Movement from the front of the car drew my attention to where Danny was. Only he wasn't in the driver's seat anymore, he'd managed to pull himself out of the car, and I gasped when I saw the gun in his hand hanging down by his side.

The next thing I knew, Danny had flung open the back door to where Angel was and crouched down enough for me to see his face. A huge bump had already formed on his forehead, his eyes were bloodshot, and splashes of bright red blood covered his white shirt.

"Riles, I'm sorry," he wheezed as if talking was taking a lot of effort to speak.

"Why?" Tears rolled down my cheeks, my voice barely audible because even talking hurt so damn much.

I froze when Danny reached over and unclipped Angel from her seatbelt, catching her in his arms so she didn't fall and hurt herself. I screamed at him not to touch her, or at least I tried, my pounding head hurt so much that the words wouldn't form properly.

Danny started fiddling with Angel's seatbelt. His mouth was moving but I could only make out some of his words thanks to the pounding in my head. "Stay still…..I'm going to get Angel out….. I'll come back for you," he panted, his hands moving fast to release her.

"Don't fucking touch her," I tried to yell and make my stupid broken arm move to stop him, but pain shot through me to the point I was going to vomit.

Helplessness settled deep in my bones. There was nothing I could do but scream as Danny unstrapped Angel and dragged her out. He yanked her out of the car and onto her feet, her sobs breaking my heart. Her little feet tried to kick at Danny, but as I twisted in my seat, pain once again ripped through me, stopping me from turning to see what the fuck was happening.

Danny shouted something, but my screams of frustration prevented me from hearing what he said. Noises echoed all around the upturned car, but I had no idea what was going on.

It was only when I heard the sound of retreating footsteps and the sounds of Angel's cries getting weaker that I registered Danny was gone.

And he'd taken Angel with him.

My sluggish brain was struggling to comprehend what had happened as my heart crumbled into tiny pieces. The pain throughout my entire body was beginning to take hold, dragging me into terrifying darkness. I needed to get out of the car, I was a sitting duck but I wasn't sure I'd be able to.

The thought of Kai coming to my rescue flashed through my head and I so badly wanted to believe he would, that any second now I'd feel his strong arms wrap around me, and his comforting words telling me everything would be okay.

But the truth was, Kai probably didn't even know I was gone from the apartment. Danny had planned this, he'd betrayed Kai, betrayed me, and now I was waiting for him or someone else to come and take me next.

Well fuck that.

I may have been injured but I sure as fuck wasn't going to sit there and wait for whoever had caused us to crash to come and get me.

Determination rolled through me, and with my good arm, I unclipped my seatbelt, cursing like a motherfucker when I fell against the roof of the car and making the pain in my shoulder feel like I had been burned by a white-hot poker. It was a silly move, the pain became too much to cope with and the fuzziness in my head doubled, the blackness inching closer and closer. I tried to fight it, I really did, but it was useless.

My body started to relax, my eyes closed, and as I succumbed to the darkness, I felt hands reach in and grab my body.

And they weren't the hands of the man I was falling for.

Chapter 30

Kai

The drive home from Isaac's office had been a silent one, neither Hendrix nor I speaking, while we both digested the new information.

The silence had given me time to think about what to do with Riley, and I had come to the decision that she wasn't going anywhere.

If I had to chain her to my side so I could keep an eye on her every minute of the day and night, so be it. I was done with letting her sulk, the second I got back I was going straight to her room and not leaving until she spoke to me. Shit was getting too fucking dangerous for her to be in a mood with me.

I pulled the SUV into the underground garage, noticing Danny's Audi was nowhere to be seen. My eyes narrowed on the empty space and fury spiked through my blood, Danny knew better than to leave Riley alone.

Where the fuck was he?

My attention snapped to Frank who was at the end of the garage, pacing with his phone to his ear. As soon as he heard the rumble of the engine he pulled the phone away and started running through the garage toward me. I stopped the car next to him and wound down the window.

"Sir, I've been trying to call you," he panted, his tone was accusatory and ordinarily, I wouldn't stand for someone talking to me like that, but the panic-stricken look on his face told me there was something wrong.

"What the fuck is going on? My phone hasn't rung," I took my phone out of my pocket and checked the screen, confirming that I had no missed calls from anyone.

"I don't understand, it's been ringing from my end. Anyway, it doesn't matter. It's Danny, he's the one that's been betraying you, and he's....he's taken Riley and Angel," Frank choked out as my entire body turned to ice, his words ringing in my ears.

Danny's the one that's been betraying you.

He's taken Riley.

"What the fuck are you talking about?" Hendrix leaned over and huffed at Frank through the open window, confusion etched on his face which mirrored my own.

"You need to speak to Miles, he cracked the burner phone, and the only person Anderson has been communicating with is Danny," Frank rushed to explain. His mouth was moving and words were coming out, but I couldn't make sense of what he was saying.

He's taken Riley.

"He's tracking them now, but Danny left here about five minutes ago with Riley and her sister, he said you'd instructed him to take them to a safe house."

"Get in the fucking car," I ordered Frank as my brain finally processed what he was saying.

Before he had time to shut the back door, I spun the car around, the tires squealing on the concrete, and slammed my foot down on the gas, heading for the exit ramp.

"Get Miles on the phone," I ordered Hendrix. He took out his phone, and as I started weaving through the traffic, he started pressing buttons to dial Miles.

"Engaged. Fuck!" Hendrix punched the dash in frustration as the engaged tone echoed around the car.

"Track the Audi," I instructed him instead, trying to keep my head clear and not imagining all the dreaded things my brain was trying to throw up.

If anything happened to Riley.....

"They're heading down West Street," Hendrix said once he loaded up the app.

We all had the tracking apps on our phones, and every single one of my cars had a tracking device so we all knew where we were at any given time. Miles had insisted on it after Theo's death, and right now I was so fucking glad I had listened to him.

I pushed the gas to the floor and the SUV responded, lurching all of us forward. Thankfully the traffic was light as I weaved in and out of cars, heading in the direction Hendrix had indicated. I knew the city like the back of my hand so took the most direct route to catch up to their location. They weren't too far away.

"Did Miles say anything else?" Hendrix asked Frank as he fumbled in the glove compartment and pulled out two handguns.

"No, just that he had been trying to phone Kai but the phone kept ringing out," Frank replied. He took one of the handguns from Hendrix along with the box of bullets Hendrix also passed over and started loading bullets into the gun. There were also a few weapons in the lock box between the back seats should we need them.

I didn't know what the fuck we were going to find when we caught up to Danny, and we all had enough experience to know that being over armed was better than being under prepared.

"Danny doesn't die. Understood?" My voice was low and deadly, ensuring my men knew how fucking serious I was.

Danny *would* die, but not for a long time.

Not until I had pulled every last scream from him, until he begged for death, and even then, he would suffer until I deemed it was time for him to die.

He would pay for taking Riley from me.

His betrayal had earned him a death sentence, but the fact he had tried to take my girl away, that earned him a fucking slow and painful death. And if he hurt one single strand of hair on her head, he wouldn't suffer a painful death. He would suffer *months* of excruciating torture before I finally ended him.

Mutters of acknowledgment echoed around the car from the rest of my men.

"They've just turned onto Queens Avenue," Hendrix said and I yanked the steering wheel, taking a sharp right turn so we could catch up to them the quickest way possible.

"Try Miles again, Frank," I said as I maneuvered the car down a tiny side street, nearly knocking off one of my mirrors when a car door opened.

Frank fumbled with his phone, and thankfully, *thankfully*, the fucking thing rang this time instead of signaling the engaged tone.

"Frank!" Miles barked out through the speakerphone Frank was holding in his palm so we could all hear.

"What the fuck is going on, Miles?" I growled down the phone as I floored it passed a slow-moving vehicle being driven by a fucking old woman.

"Kai, thank fuck. I've been trying to call you," Miles replied, relief in his tone.

"Clearly there is a fucking problem with my phone. Tell me what the fuck is going on." This time I shouted in frustration at not getting any fucking answers anywhere near damn quick enough.

"Danny. He's been talking to Anderson. The burner phone was full of text and calls between the two of them."

My hand gripped the steering wheel tightly and my knuckles turned white at hearing Miles confirm what I had already been told.

Danny was a traitorous bastard.

"They're on Bridge Street, I think they've stopped," Hendrix chimed in, and I turned the wheel again to head in that direction. Bridge Street wasn't far, maybe a little over a minute away.

"I'm tracking him too. I don't know where the fuck he is going," Miles replied.

"He's got Riley," I said, saying out loud the words that had been plaguing me since Frank had first uttered them.

Stunned silence filled the car before there was a loud thud that sounded very much like Miles had just punched his wheel.

"Fuck!" he hissed. "Fuck, Kai. I didn't know. I….fuck, I've just spoken to him."

I maneuvered the car onto the other side of the road to overtake a lorry, cars heading towards us honking at me to get the fuck out of the way.

"Explain," I snapped, losing my composure. I never fell apart in situations like this, I always kept a cool head. But that was before I had something precious to lose.

"I tried to phone you, but you didn't answer. I was so angry with him, I didn't even know I was ringing him until he answered. I swear, Kai, I didn't know he had Riley with him."

"What did he say?" I said through gritted teeth. My hand ached from gripping the wheel so tight and I itched to shed blood. Danny's blood in particular.

"He denied it. Said he didn't know what the hell I was on about and then the line went dead."

"Not like he'd say anything else," Hendrix added unhelpfully. "They've stopped, the tracker isn't moving. They're at the top of Bridge Street, junction with York Road."

"I'm turning onto Bridge Street now," Miles confirmed. "Kai, I think....I think something might have happened, there was a loud bang before the line went dead. It didn't sound good."

My heart stopped in my chest, fear suffocating me. I floored the gas, needing to get to where they were stationary on the map Hendrix was showing me. My whole body shook with a mix of rage and trepidation. If Riley was hurt, I wasn't sure I'd be able to stop myself from killing Danny on the spot.

"Oh, shit," Miles' voice came through in almost a whisper, and my gut lurched out of my throat.

Whatever he was seeing wasn't going to be good.

I didn't need to ask what was happening. I spun the car onto Bridge Street to come face to face with the devastation.

Up ahead, Danny's Audi was on the roof, and an abandoned van with a smashed up front end was stopped nearby, smoke coming from the engine. From the van, at least ten men, all armed with guns and wearing balaclavas were creeping up on the wreckage of the Audi.

People were running on the street, looks of horror on their faces as they watched the scene unfold and tried to find somewhere to take cover. I slammed on the brakes next to Miles' car, he had already got out with his own weapon in hand.

Hendrix chucked a gun at me which I grabbed with one hand, despite having two strapped to me, and I launched myself out of the car with Hendrix and Frank behind me.

Thanks to the positioning of the van and the screams and chaos surrounding us with the people on the street, we were able to fire off a few rounds and take down two of the balaclava men before they even noticed we were there, but at the sound of our weapons firing, the remaining men turned and started firing towards us.

The four of us broke apart, ducking for cover behind parked cars. Shots were fired in all directions, and the screams around us got louder as people rushed to take cover inside restaurants and shops. I fired off a couple of shots, hitting two of the cunts directly in the head who were firing back at me, and watching with sick pleasure as they fell to the floor.

My attention caught on one of the cunts who was crouching down by the side of the Audi, arms stretched out to reach inside. I glanced over at Frank, Hendrix, and Miles, the three of them popping off rounds, engaged in a battle with the masked men.

My vision became tunneled, focusing only on the Audi where I hoped Riley was. Deciding the three of them had it in hand, I ran towards the Audi, firing a bullet straight into the heart of one of the men who turned his gun on me as I darted between parked vehicles to get to the overturned car.

The bastard who was crouched down hadn't heard me coming, too fixated on pulling a lifeless Riley from the car. Fury like I'd never felt before burned through me, I had never been this enraged, not even when I was told the news about Theo.

Riley's eyes were closed, and her body was limp, her shoulder poking out at a funny angle, and blood pouring from a gash in her head. I wasn't a religious man, far from it. But at that moment, I offered up a prayer, asking for her not to be dead. I didn't deserve to be given anything, but Riley had her whole life ahead of her and she was such a good, pure soul. She didn't deserve this life I had dragged her into.

The masked man tugged her the rest of the way out of the car, oblivious to the gunfight going on around him or the fact he was about to die. I grabbed his head from behind and slammed my fist into his jaw. He immediately dropped Riley, and I winced at seeing her limp body crumple to the ground. But in my rage, all I could think about was ending the life of the prick who dared to put his hands on my girl.

He tried to stand up, but my punch had dazed him, and I took the opportunity to pounce on him. I grabbed his head once again, only this time, instead of using my fists to do the damage, I smashed his head against the concrete again and again and again, letting him feel the full force of my wrath until there was nothing left other than a bloody mess.

His face was unrecognizable, and as he choked on his own blood and took his last breath, I dragged his dead body away so I could get to Riley. I reached out and touched her delicate throat with two fingers, almost crying aloud with relief when I felt a pulse. As gently as possible, I lifted her into my arms. Her eyes fluttered but they looked empty like she wasn't really seeing me.

"Danny.....took...Angel," she stuttered before her eyes closed again.

Not really comprehending what she meant, I ducked down to look in the rear of the car. Only when I saw there was no one else with her, did understanding dawn.

Motherfucker!

I'd kill him, I would kill him with my bare hands for breaking Riley's heart, and then I'd find a way to bring him back to life and inflict the pain on him all over again.

Ducking down behind the Audi, I sat down and held her against my chest, trying my fucking hardest not to squeeze her but needing to feel her skin against mine, needing to know she would be okay. I shuffled us so I was sitting with my back against the car with her in my lap, and I held her there, thanking whichever greater power was out there for letting my girl live.

The gunshots around me eventually died down until the only sounds left were the screams of people who had witnessed the gunfight, and the distant sound of sirens. Two sets of footsteps pounded the ground before Hendrix and Miles' faces appeared at the trunk of the Audi.

"Cops will be here soon, Kai," Hendrix panted. His clothes were splattered with blood, but he seemed uninjured.

"I don't give a fuck," I said quietly, resting my head against Riley's. My number one priority was getting her medical attention. Besides, the majority of the police department were on my payroll, they'd clear the mess up without asking any questions once they knew I was involved.

"Check the rest of the car," I instructed even though it was pointless, Danny was long gone, and he would know better than to leave any clues as to where he was headed.

Still, Hendrix disappeared, doing as he was told.

"Want me to get the Doc on standby?" Miles asked, nodding at Riley. He hadn't quite gotten out of the fight unscathed, blood trickled down his arm but he wasn't bothered by it so it couldn't be bad.

"Yeah."

As delicately as I could, I stood holding Riley in my arms, intent on getting her into the back of my car and getting her to Harris' place so he could assess her. Hendrix reappeared, confirming the car was indeed empty.

The first of the ambulances arrived, EMTs hopping out and straight over to a body. Ignoring their calls to bring Riley to them, Hendrix, Miles, and I headed over to our abandoned cars which, unsurprisingly, were covered in bullet holes.

"Where's Frank?" I asked. Not that I needed them to tell me what I already knew.

He was nowhere to be seen.

"He didn't make it," Miles replied.

Shame, Frank was a good man, a loyal one, he'd be missed. Such was the risk in our lives though, and Frank knew that, and as cruel as it sounded, I'd rather it be Frank than Riley.

Refusing to let Miles or Hendrix take Riley from me, I managed to get into the back of the SUV with her remaining in my arms, not once did she regain consciousness. Needing to feel that she was still with me, my fingers found her pulse in her wrist as Hendrix got behind the wheel and started to maneuver the car away from the crime scene. Miles followed in the car he had arrived in.

As we pulled away, I surveyed the carnage. Bodies lay dead in the road, guns strewn across the pavement, and innocent bystanders stared, traumatized by what they had witnessed. Cop cars started pulling up with their sirens blaring and lights flashing, followed by several more EMTs.

The whole scene was fucking surreal.

Shit like this did not happen in Hollows Bay.

In my city.

In the rearview mirror, I could see Hendrix taking in the scene like I was. He was white. His eyes flicked to the mirror and met my gaze.

"We find Danny, and we find the fucker behind this. And when we do, we will make them pay for every fucking hit they've taken at us, for every one of our men they've killed. We take back what they owe us, and then we fucking end them," I growled venomously.

"Damn straight," he whispered.

Hendrix hit the gas as soon as we were clear of the street, and as he headed towards the private hospital Dr. Harris owned, I stared down at my gorgeous girl who was caked in blood and dirt and held her close against my chest.

Silently, I vowed to protect her with everything I had.

Even if it meant I would die as a result.

To be continued.....

Bonus Chapter

Want to read a bonus chapter from Kai's POV of the night he and Riley hooked up?
Then read on...

Bonus Chapter

Kai

I stared out the window, watching over my city, my thoughts spiraling into madness as rage pumped through my body. I should have been focusing on who the fuck was out to get me, yet all I could think about was her.

My Star.

I needed to let her go. Tonight could have gone a whole lot differently if the waiter hadn't seen her being dragged away by Anderson, and then what would have happened to her?

My hand tightened around the glass of whiskey I was holding, squeezing it so damn tight it was a miracle the glass didn't shatter. Knocking back the remainder of my drink, I slammed the tumbler down on my desk and deliberated about pouring myself another. But I was in for a long night. I wasn't going to rest until I had news, and if there wasn't a fucking breakthrough, then heads were going to roll.

A few more minutes passed as I continued to stare at my city below, wondering if Anderson was out there somewhere watching, waiting for his next opportunity to strike.

A soft knock at my door dragged me from my thoughts. Assuming it was either Hendrix, Danny, or Miles with news, I didn't bother turning as I called out, telling them to come in.

Instead of one of my men striding into the room, a tiny figure tentatively stepped in. Meeting her reflection in the glass, a mix of emotions rushed through me. Annoyance because she wasn't asleep. Anger for what the fucker did to her. And calmness.

The only time I ever felt calm was when she was near, and for the first time since I'd discovered Anderson had snatched her, the chaotic noises in my head quietened.

"You should be getting some rest," I said, trying to keep the anger out of my voice.

"I couldn't sleep," Riley replied, igniting the rage simmering underneath my skin. She hadn't even *tried* to sleep.

"That's why the doctor gave you pills," I barked, unable to keep my temper in check.

Ordinarily, when I was this consumed with rage, I'd either fuck or fight it out of my system. Right then, my preference would have been to fuck a woman so damn hard in every hole, so that every time she moved tomorrow, she'd feel me.

But there was only one woman I wanted to fuck, the one standing behind me, looking irresistible in her vest and shorts, and I knew if I laid one finger on her with the mood I was in, I'd break her and undo all the fucking progress we'd made.

"I didn't want to sleep alone," she admitted, vulnerability evident in her voice and knocking the anger in my blood down a notch or two. I hated that she was scared, it was up to me to protect her, but I'd failed her, and even though I knew she was safe in my apartment, it was understandable that she was frightened to sleep alone.

After all, she should have been safe under my protection at the ball, but she wasn't.

Finally, I turned to her, allowing my gaze to roam over every inch of bare skin. Christ, she was so damn beautiful. But when my eyes landed on the angry marks on her neck, the fury that had started to diminish roared to life again. Every part of me wanted to storm out of the room to hit the streets, raiding as many fucking places as necessary to find Detective Cunt.

"It doesn't hurt, Kai," Riley said softly, crossing my office and coming to stand only inches away from me.

Like a moth drawn to a flame, I couldn't resist touching her. I reached out and gently stroked my thumb over the bruise forming on her cheek.

Riley was the only person I'd ever been gentle with in my life, the thought of marking her in any other way than to show her how much she fucking meant to me made my blood boil, and the fact that someone had dared hurt her made me see red.

It made me *murderous*.

"You could have died tonight, Riley, and it would have been my fault," I whispered, needing her to know how fucking terrified I was of the thought of losing her.

"It wasn't your fault, Kai, Anderson did this. Not you. And he wasn't going to kill me, he said as much. He said he was under instructions not to kill me, but he would hurt me if he needed to."

Her words hit me like a sledgehammer, and I had to turn away so the snarl curling on my lips wasn't aimed at her.

I knew when I brought Riley into my life there was a chance she could be used as bait to lure me in by my enemies, but my own fucking arrogance thought I'd be able to keep her safe. All I'd done was put her in the spotlight.

"You should never have got mixed up in this shit, Riley. I never should have brought you into my life." Yet as I said the words, I knew how untrue they were. I was too stubborn not to have her, no matter the consequences.

Hurt flashed across her face, making me feel like a cunt. The one thing I didn't want to do was hurt her, yet I'd done exactly that.

Fuck, I didn't deserve her. If she had any fucking sense, she'd run a mile in the opposite direction and never look back.

"You don't mean that," she said, almost choking on her words.

Why the fuck wasn't she listening to me? I needed to make her see that being in my life was only putting her in danger. Why did she have to be so damn stubborn?

"Riley, you got hurt because of me," I said, failing to stop my temper from rising with every spoken word. "I'll never forgive myself for that. And all this means now is that you've got a target painted on your back because of me, because Anderson knows you're my weakness."

Needing to expel the rage charging through my body, I threw my fist against the window. The window wouldn't break, it was reinforced glass, but pain shot through my knuckles in an instant, making me feel infinitesimally better.

Hoping she would realize she might bear the brunt of my rage if she didn't leave, I refused to look back at Riley. But when she tentatively reached out and grabbed my hand, tugging it toward her, I couldn't stop myself from turning to her, my brows raised in question.

What was she doing?

As if to answer my unspoken question, Riley reached up on tiptoes before brushing her lips against mine, and taking me by surprise.

I didn't trust myself to react knowing I wouldn't be able to hold back from devouring her, but when she reached her arms up and wrapped them around my neck, and pressed her mouth harder against mine, I snapped.

I was a weak man for Riley, unable to resist the temptation of getting my next fix of her like a fucking addict, and she was an addiction that I had no plans to quit.

She opened her mouth, and my tongue instantly sought hers as I wrapped an arm around her to pull her closer to me, needing to feel her soft body against mine. My other hand went to her hair, and I grabbed a chunk to pull her head back so I could hold her right where she was as I ate her whole.

My cock stiffened, and the need to drive into her pussy consumed me, the only thing preventing me from doing exactly that was the damn robe she had wrapped around her. My hands acted on their own, untying the belt and shoving her robe off her shoulders, letting it pool to the floor, and revealing Riley's gorgeous pajama clad body.

Why the fuck were there so many layers preventing me from claiming what was mine?

I needed to be inside her.

Right. Fucking. Now.

The anger rampaging through me began to spill over from frustration. I grabbed Riley's ass and lifted her on the desk, fully intent on fucking her right here, right now, until she begged me to stop. I wasn't thinking straight, all rational thoughts had left my mind, leaving behind a raw need for the one thing that would satiate my anger.

Riley groaned, but the softness in her voice made reality crash down around me. I usually didn't have any issues fucking a woman roughly, but this was Riley. I didn't want to hurt her, and I had too much fucking anger pumping through me to take things slow.

I knew I'd fucking kick myself for not seizing this moment, but I knew I'd regret it if I was too rough with her, and caused her even more pain.

Breaking our kiss, I rested my head against her forehead and squeezed my eyes closed, not wanting to see the disappointment in her beautiful eyes when I told her this needed to stop.

"Riley, I can't," I said, the words tasting like acid as they left my mouth.

Her body tensed under my hands, and deciding I needed to stop being a coward and look her in the face, I pulled my head away from hers, finding hurt and rejection in her beautiful chocolate orbs, and Christ, did that make me feel like even more of a cunt.

"I can't be gentle with you, I've got too much fucking anger pumping through my body. I don't want to hurt you," I tried to explain, but I couldn't stop my gaze from dropping to her perfect tits, her nipples straining against the thin material of her vest.

Despite me telling her this couldn't happen, I made no attempt to move from her, regret already consuming me.

What a fucking time to grow a conscience.

I half expected Riley to jump off the desk and run from embarrassment of my rejection, but Riley always had a way of surprising me. She reached up and gently cupped my cheek, her soft palm warm against my skin.

"I don't need you to be gentle, Kai," she said, her voice full of want, making my cock harder than it already was. "I need you. All of you."

Fuck.

Her eyes dropped to my lips, which I was sure were swollen from our kiss, just like hers were. A battle raged in my head, the anger forgotten for now as the raw need for her warred with doing the right thing for once in my fucking life.

But the decision was taken out of my hands when Riley lifted her vest, revealing her luscious tits to me for the first time. Any sense of doing the right thing was long gone when my gaze landed on her rosy pink nipples, taut and begging to be sucked.

Unable to fight any longer, I slammed my mouth back down on hers, giving in to the need. I couldn't promise I wouldn't be rough with her, but I'd make damn sure to make her feel fucking incredible along the way.

My hands gripped her hips and I pulled her forward, my cock pressing against her cunt, and her bare breasts brushing against my shirt. I pulled my mouth away and immediately latched on to a nipple, sucking it in before flicking the bud with my tongue and grazing it with my teeth.

Riley thrust her chest forward, her other tit demanding attention, and I suddenly had a vision of her breasts being covered in my bite marks, so anyone who dared look knew she belonged to me. Not that anyone would dare look at what belonged to me.

Cupping her tits together, I set about marking her, her groans of pleasure encouraging me to carry on, and my hand dropping to squeeze her thigh until the need for more became too much to resist.

Pulling my mouth away from her tits, pleased with the bruising already beginning to form, I pulled the material of her sleep shorts to one side, revealing her glistening pussy just begging to be fucked.

I swiped a finger down her slit until I reached her hole, and without giving her any warning, I shoved three fingers into her warm cunt. Her head tipped back, and a silent scream left her mouth as her pussy gripped my fingers.

"Fuck, you're soaked, Star," I said as I pulled my fingers out, marveling at how her juices covered each digit, before I pushed them back in, stretching her tight channel.

I couldn't fucking wait to bury my cock in her.

But before my cock went anywhere near her cunt, I fully intended on feasting on her first. I'd waited too long wondering what RIley tasted like, and now I was about to find out.

Claiming her mouth, I continued to fuck her with my fingers, her hips grinding with every thrust, and her pussy growing wetter and wetter.

"So goddamn tight," I whispered in her ear as her groans grew louder.

She was going to come, but I was a selfish bastard, and I always got what I wanted.

And I wanted my Star to come on my face.

Pulling my fingers out, I stifled a laugh at the displeasure furrowing her brows before a scowl twisted on her face.

"Kai," she panted, pleading for me, and who was I to tell my girl no?

"Lay back, Riley, I want to taste you. I want to be eating your delicious cunt when you come," I demanded, making it clear she had no choice in the matter.

She hesitated for only a second, and I almost thought she was going to deny me, but for once, Riley did as she was told and slowly laid back on the desk, her legs dangling off the edge.

Grabbing her sleep shorts, I tugged them down her legs and threw them to the floor with her vest before pushing her thighs wide open.

My breath caught in my throat as I drank in the sight of her pretty little cunt. Images flashed through my mind of all the things I wanted to do to her, all the positions I fully intended to fuck her in, and all the toys I intended to use on her until she lost her voice from screaming.

"You have no fucking idea how many times I've imagined this," I said, before grabbing her ankles and pulling her ass towards the end of the desk, stopping just before I pulled her off completely.

Dropping to my knees, I draped her legs over my shoulders and buried my face in her pussy, inhaling her intoxicating scent before taking my first taste of Riley.

Fucking delicious.

I brushed my tongue over her clit a few times, eliciting soft groans from my girl, but she wasn't loud enough, I wanted her to be bellowing my name from the top of her lungs.

Wrapping my lips around her throbbing clit, I sucked, making her groan a little louder, but still not loud enough. I eased off, letting her think I was giving her a reprieve before I sucked her clit again, this time harder, making her hips buck off the table, and my name leaving her mouth on a scream.

That was more like it.

"Fuck, I could eat this pussy every day for the rest of my life, and it would never be enough," I muttered to myself, knowing that if I got to feast on her for the rest of my life, I'd die a very happy man.

Riley's needy groans spurred me on as I ate her cunt like I was a starved man. When her legs began to tense, I thrust two fingers inside her, curling them around to hit her internal walls.

She screamed again, her cries growing more and more desperate, and I couldn't help but chuckle when her hand reached out and her fingers grabbed my hair as she held my face against her pussy, making sure I wasn't going anywhere until she had reached her climax.

I could have spent all night with my face between her legs, but by now, my cock was unbearably hard, and now I knew what it was like to taste her, I wanted to find out what her cunt felt like to be wrapped around my cock.

Adding a third finger to the two thrusting in and out of Riley, and sucking on her clit a final time, Riley came, her juices gushing all over my face.

"Fuck, Kai!" she cried as her thighs tightened around my face to the point she could have suffocated me, and what a fucking way it would have been to meet my fate.

After a few seconds, her thighs unclenched before I could meet my fate in the most heavenly way, and she took in deep breaths to try and calm her panting. Wiping her excess juices on her thigh, I stood and dropped her legs as she sat herself up. Her hair was mussed from where she'd been writhing on the desk, and her cheeks were flushed.

"You taste like fucking heaven, Riley. I always knew once I got a taste of your sweet cunt, I would be more obsessed with you than I already was."

Before she had a chance to reply, I took her mouth, letting her taste her release on my tongue. She groaned into my mouth, her hands gripping my shirt as I tugged her hair back, making her look at me.

"Tell me, Star. Do you want me to fuck you hard and fast over this desk? Does your needy little cunt want my cock to pound it into oblivion?" Fuck, I hoped she didn't tell me she wanted our first time together to be sweet and gentle, there was no fucking way I had the patience for that.

"Yes, Kai. Fuck me hard," she whispered, and there was nothing but honesty and desperation written on her face. She wanted whatever it was I was going to give her.

"Take my shirt off," I commanded, desperate to feel her hands on me.

Slowly her hands crept up my chest, and she started toying with the buttons, taking her sweet time to undo them with a little flirtatious grin playing on her lips.

I knew what she was doing, she thought she could tease me, drive me wild until I begged her to hurry. She should have already known that I was wild for her, and teasing a hungry wolf would only end up with her being my victim.

I knocked her hand away and ripped the rest of my shirt open, not giving a fuck about the buttons scattering everywhere.

"Don't play games with me, little girl, you won't like it when you lose," I growled, grabbing her chin. I intended for it to be a warning, but when it was met with a smirk, my temper snapped.

Riley wanted me as I was? Then she was going to get it.

Tugging her roughly off the desk, I shoved her to her knees, unbuckling my belt at the same time and pulling out my achingly hard cock. When Riley's mouth dropped open at seeing my size, I didn't give her any chance to brace as I thrust into her mouth, making sure to drive deep into her throat.

She tried to splutter, but I wrapped my hand around the back of her head and held her in place. Her hands came up to rest on my thighs as she tried her best to take my length as far as she could without choking on me.

I thrust several times, her warm mouth feeling like fucking heaven, and it would have been so damn easy to carry on fucking her mouth like this until I blew my load and made her swallow, but I wasn't going to miss this opportunity to claim her sweet cunt.

Pulling out, I grabbed her arms and yanked her to her feet, spinning her around so her back was to my chest before she had a chance to do or say anything. My hands gripped her hips as I leaned down to whisper into her ear.

"You have no idea how much I want to come down the back of your throat, Riley. But right now, I need to claim your pussy."

Riley's response was to lean forward, bending over my desk and offering herself to me on a platter. Her ass cheeks parted the further forward she leaned, and I stroked a hand down her spine, wanting to feel every inch of her soft skin.

When I reached her ass, I pressed a finger against her hole, wondering if anyone had claimed her ass before.

I fucking hoped not.

"One day, I will fuck you here, Riley, and you will fucking love it." I paused as a rare moment of uncertainty filled me. I suddenly needed to hear her tell me she was mine, because I knew, after I'd fucked her, I'd never be able to let her go. "But right now, I need to hear you tell me that you belong to me."

"I'm yours, Kai." There wasn't even a second of hesitation before she replied softly.

My name had barely left her lips before I thrust into her dripping pussy. She cried out at the intrusion, and it took all of my willpower not to roar with her, she felt *that* fucking good.

"Fuck, Riley," I said through gritted teeth, pulling out almost all of the way before thrusting deeper into her. My gaze dropped to where we were connected, and I couldn't help but admire the sight as I drove in and out of her, it would be a sight that I would remember for the rest of my life.

I wanted to drive in deeper into her, I wanted us to be joined like this forever. I grabbed her hair and pulled her back, making her back arch.

"Kai, please," she whimpered, as my cock hit the spot deep inside of her that would push her towards another orgasm, her toes curling into the carpet.

"So fucking tight, Star. You feel so fucking good, I'm going to love every second of claiming this pussy as mine," I said, breathless from how hard I was fucking her.

I pulled her back even further so her back was almost to my chest, and my teeth clamped down on her shoulder, leaving yet another mark. I wanted to erase every single mark Detective Dick had left on my girl, and replace them with mine.

Needing to erase him from my thoughts, I focused on pounding into Riley again, and again, and again, her moans turning more desperate as she neared her climax.

But this time, I wanted to see what she looked like when she came. I pulled out of her, and spun her around, her cheeks flushed and her eyes burning with lust.

"I want to see your pretty face when you come on my cock, Riley," I said as I grabbed her thighs and lifted her into my arms. She wrapped her legs around me, and I walked us to my sofa. As I sat, Riley impaled herself on my cock, the two of us groaning in sync.

It didn't take long until she was bouncing up and down on my shaft, our eyes burning into each other, and in that moment I knew Riley was it for me. For the rest of my life, she was the only one I ever wanted.

"You're so fucking beautiful, Riley, the way you are milking my cock. I can't fucking wait to fill you up with my come," I hissed as my balls began to tighten. Riley wasn't the only one barreling straight toward finding her release.

Her tits jiggled in front of me, her movements grew faster, her nipples erect. Wrapping my lips around one, I sucked and nibbled like I'd done earlier, earning a desperate groan from her as she threw her head back.

But in doing so, she exposed the angry red marks on her throat, and the familiar feeling of anger started to rear its head.

Only, with my cock buried deep in Riley, the calmness she brought quickly extinguished the anger, and instead of wrapping my hands around her throat like I would have done if she was any other woman, I gently ran a hand over the marks, wishing I could take them away.

Her groans turned more needy, and I was almost at the point where I couldn't hold on any longer. Seeking out her clit, I moved a hand between us and started rubbing the bud, and when I flicked her nipple with my tongue one last time, her whole body tensed and her pussy clamped down around my cock.

She cried out my name, loud enough to wake everyone in the fucking city, but I didn't care, I wanted everyone to know she was mine.

With her cunt still holding my cock in a vise-like grip, I was all the more desperate to come. I flipped her onto her back, and pounded into her a few more times before, finally, I erupted, shooting my come deep inside her.

As my heart pounded fiercely, and my breathing slowly recovered, I stared down at my beautiful Star, and right then, for the first time in my entire life, I felt genuine happiness.

I felt like my life had finally started.

Acknowledgements

Well, what a journey it has been to get to the point of publishing my first novel. I was actually midway through another story when Riley & Kai popped into my head, and they just wouldn't go away!

I have loved every minute of writing their story, and for those that hate cliffhangers, book two (Implode), and book three (Explode) are out now, so go grab them to find out what happens next!

Reaching the point of publishing this book has been a huge learning experience, and there were times when I was totally overwhelmed and wanted to chuck it all in, but there have been some amazing people supporting me through this journey, so I would like to take this opportunity to thank them.

Firstly, to my alpha reader, Sandra, who is forever nagging me to get more chapters written so she can find out what happens next. Thank you for keeping me going when my motivation ran out and for being honest when you didn't feel the chapters flowed right.

To my beta readers, April, Whitney, and Senga. Thank you all for your kind words and feedback which gave me the courage to push on and have a little faith in myself that maybe, *just maybe*, I'm not so bad at this writing gig!

To my mum, who always believes in me, no matter what crazy ideas I come up with, and who doesn't blush or blink an eye when she reads my smut...Thank you for not slut shaming me!

To my husband, Tom. Thank you doesn't seem to cover the enormous gratitude I have for you, your encouragement and support has kept me going, and even though you still load the dishwasher wrong, I love you with all of my heart. Thank you for being my biggest supporter and for putting up with me when I bored you with incessant details about this book, I couldn't have done it without you.

And finally, to every reader who picked up Collide and gave me a chance, Thank you. I can't tell you how much it means to me that you have given your time to read this story. It has taken me nearly two years to get the Hollows Bay Trilogy to a point where I am ready to share it with the world, and I can tell you the self-doubt and imposter syndrome has been unreal. So for every person who picked this book up and read it, from the bottom of my heart, thank you.

My focus for the last few months has been firmly in Hollows Bay, but I have already started plotting several standalone's which I am hoping will come after Hollows Bay, including a step-brother romance, and an enemies-to-lovers duet, but in all honesty, sometimes ideas just pop into my head and I have to go with them, so who knows what will come after Hollows Bay! If you'd like to be kept updated with new releases and teasers for upcoming books, please join my social media groups:

Facebook: Hunter's Pack

Instagram: e.k.hunterauthor

If you have any questions, please get in touch with me via my website: www.ekhunterauthor.com

If you enjoyed Collide, I would be very grateful if you could leave a review on whatever platform you use, and if you have any comments or feedback, then I'd love to hear from you.

About the Author

Elizabeth-Kate lives in Oxfordshire with her Husband and two Sprocker Spaniels. She spends a lot of time with her nose in a book, usually the kind with morally gray characters and feisty female leads! When she isn't reading, you'll find her in her writing cave dreaming up new ideas for plots and characters.

Elizabeth-Kate likes to take her Spaniels, known as the Smelly Weasels, on long walks. She can't start the day without coffee otherwise she turns into a monster, and her party trick is devouring a pack of cookies in one sitting!

Also By

Hollows Bay Trilogy
Collide

Implode

Explode

Printed in Great Britain
by Amazon